Choose your Lane to love!

Readers love the Fish Out of Water series by AMY LANE

Fish Out of Water

"*Fish Out of Water* delivers an intense plot as well as a sizzling relationship between Ellery and Jackson."

—Gay Book Reviews

"…I will promise you this, you WILL be left with one hell of a book hangover."

—Rainbow Gold Book Reviews

"*Fish Out of Water*… really captured my attention and kept it. This book is gritty and urban. It's suspenseful and I found myself gasping more than a few times."

—Diverse Reader

Red Fish, Dead Fish

"Packed full of action, suspense, and of course steamy goodness, *Red Fish, Dead Fish* is the sequel we have all been anxiously waiting for."

—Love Bytes

"The suspense is done so well, and the relationship between Ellery and Jackson is really engaging."

—Joyfully Jay

"I hope she has more plans for the Fish Out of Water series; I'm hooked!"

—The Novel Approach

By AMY LANE

Published by DREAMSPINNER PRESS
www.dreamspinnerpress.com

By AMY LANE (CONT.)

KEEPING PROMISE ROCK
Keeping Promise Rock
Making Promises
Living Promises
Forever Promised

TALKER
Talker • Talker's Redemption
Talker's Graduation
The Talker Collection Anthology

JOHNNIES
Chase in Shadow • Dex in Blue
Ethan in Gold • Black John
Bobby Green
Super Sock Man

WINTER BALL
Winter Ball • Summer Lessons

GRANBY KNITTING
The Winter Courtship Rituals of
Fur-Bearing Critters
How to Raise an Honest Rabbit
Knitter in His Natural Habitat
Blackbird Knitting in a Bunny's Lair
The Granby Knitting Menagerie
Anthology

Published by Harmony Ink Press
BITTER MOON SAGA
Triane's Son Rising
Triane's Son Learning
Triane's Son Fighting
Triane's Son Reigning

Published by DREAMSPINNER PRESS
www.dreamspinnerpress.com

A FEW GOOD FISH

Amy Lane

Published by

DREAMSPINNER PRESS

5032 Capital Circle SW, Suite 2, PMB# 279, Tallahassee, FL 32305-7886 USA
www.dreamspinnerpress.com

A Few Good Fish
© 2018 Amy Lane.

Cover Art
© 2018 Reese Dante.
http://www.reesedante.com
Cover content is for illustrative purposes only and any person depicted on the cover is a model.

Trade Paperback ISBN: 978-1-64080-817-1
Digital ISBN: 978-1-64080-816-4
Library of Congress Control Number: 2018940580
Trade Paperback published August 2018
v. 1.0

Printed in the United States of America
∞
This paper meets the requirements of
ANSI/NISO Z39.48-1992 (Permanence of Paper).

Mate. Kids. Mary. Karen.
And my FB group who has never let these guys down.
You are my few good fish—and I love you all.

Acknowledgments

TO ANYONE who has answered a random question about the military or fighting or guns or planes or trains or automobiles. These are things I know very little about and you have thrown me a rope when I've been in deep waters. Thank you.

Author's Note

IT SHOULD go without saying, but all of this is fictional. ALL OF THIS IS FICTIONAL. Reading this particular set of books for actual data on the military or lawyers or PIs is like watching *Hawaii Five-0* for its accuracy on crime statistics and police procedure. Watch it for the shit going boom. Watch it for the cute guys making entertaining snark. Don't watch it for factual accuracy—trust me, it will only disappoint.

Burt and Ernie and the Fish in the Desert

ERNIE JAMES Caulfield looked around the little nontown of Victoriana with a feeling of intense joy. The place was mostly a gas station with a fast-food place on one side of the highway and a tiny garage with a house for the owners on the other. Desert surrounded it, and even in the encroaching fall the landscape was flat and unexciting, with saguaro and creosote bushes for miles.

But for Ernie, this was the best place on earth.

"Really?" He turned toward Burton, body practically thrumming with excitement. "I'm staying here?"

Lee Burton, the assassin who'd been sent to kill Ernie and who had rescued him instead, arched a suspicious eyebrow in his sculpted bronze-toned face and said nothing.

"It is, right? I mean, that house—it's got an add-on to it. Like, new. Even the siding is new. That's your place, right?"

Burton frowned. "How would you know that?"

Ernie grinned, unrepentant. "I heard you talking to Ace. He's nice. Your voice said so."

Burton's frown intensified. "You were supposed to be asleep."

Ernie bit his lip shyly. He had been, until he'd heard Burton talking next to him. He didn't need the gift to reckon Lee was uncomfortable with where their relationship had gone mere hours after he'd bailed Ernie's ass out of the fire.

Well, not that Ernie wasn't slutty as hell on any given day, but the thing that had bloomed between him and Lee was based solely on the fact that when they looked at each other and touched, the world stopped spinning, and that included Ernie's ever-questing, witchy trouble-magnet of a brain.

Ernie didn't need to be slutty anymore. He'd found the safety he'd been looking for his entire life.

"Safety" just didn't know it yet.

"I was mostly asleep," Ernie soothed. "You like Ace."

Burton let out a sigh. "Yeah. Ace is good people. Not educated, mind you, so—"

"He's smart, though," Ernie said sunnily. Yeah, he'd read that much from the voice on the other end of the phone. That and the fact that Burton was scary smart, and he'd never be able to tolerate someone not scary smart like he was. But he was also—whether he knew it or not—intuitive, in the same way Ernie was intuitive, but not nearly as powerful.

Burton could see through what people were supposed to be and right into what they were. He'd watched Ernie for days when he should have just done his job and shot. Ernie was still walking around converting oxygen because Burton had seen there was more to Ernie than a brainless party boy who liked to make donuts.

"Yeah, he's smart." Burton let out a sigh. "Look, kid—"

"You know my name." Ernie knew all the tricks to making somebody not important. Calling him "kid" was just one.

"Ernie…." And it came out like a plea, just like it had in the hotel room they'd shared—in the *bed* they'd shared not hours ago.

"Yeah?" he said sweetly.

"I need to go away—you understand—"

"Under cover." Ernie wasn't stupid either. "The guy who put the hit out on me, he's bad news—"

"And he's legit. Like, a real guy in the real military, and he wanted you dead. I need to find a way to work for him so I know why. This isn't…. The hit out on you should never have happened—"

"You're not just saving me," Ernie said. "You're saving anybody who carried out orders in good faith."

Burton started to grimace, but it came out a look of complete tenderness. "You're so… so very wise." Like he couldn't help himself, he reached out and cupped Ernie's cheek. "God… so pretty." For a moment his muscles tensed and he was going to pull his hand back, but Ernie licked his lips on purpose, knowing it would make him look soft and vulnerable, and wanting Burton to kiss him at least one more time before he fled.

Burton didn't disappoint him. He leaned forward, claiming Ernie's mouth with his own, and Ernie opened for him, as soft and as giving as he knew how to be.

He knew a lot. He was a sexual genius, mostly, and it took Burton a whole thirty seconds before he was groaning into Ernie's mouth and trying to haul him across the center island of the SUV they were sitting in.

Ernie would have gone. Ernie would have shucked his jeans and sat on Burton's cock if that's what it would take to get Burton to commit, but the damned SUV was too small, and Burton smacked his elbow on the steering wheel in mid-Ernie-maul maneuver.

"Ouch!" He jerked back, letting Ernie go and looking damned embarrassed. "Dammit. Why can't I…. It's *weird* what you do to me, kid."

"Ernie," Ernie whispered throatily. "Don't go. Stay here. We can have all the sex you want until it doesn't seem so strange anymore that you want me. You can quit being an assassin super-black-ops guy and be my guy. Nobody will even know our names."

He pulled in a quick breath, surprised at himself. That's not what he'd intended to come out of his mouth at all, even a little.

Burton was looking as torn as a man could get. "Ernie… I… even if I come back, I might not be the guy for—"

Ernie pulled away and opened his door. "Let's go meet Ace and Sonny," he said, not wanting to hear it. At least when Burton was talking to his friend, Ernie wouldn't have to hear him lie, not to himself and not to Ernie. "Will you at least be able to come visit over holidays?" he asked after he'd slid out.

Burton stopped and grabbed the duffel of clothes they'd bought Ernie on their way from Albuquerque. They'd had to leave Ernie's little apartment, with his cats and everything, without stopping to get clothes. Burton had called the super and made arrangements for the cats—mostly strays that would just show up unbidden—and Ernie didn't want to know what a colossal pain in the ass tying up that loose end had been.

But Burton had done it for him. It wasn't even part of his job, just like being Ernie's savior wasn't part of his job, and Ernie didn't want to think of the prices Lee Burton had paid for stepping out of himself in order to successfully not kill Ernie James Caulfield's scrawny psychic ass.

But he had. And he seemed to be willing to pay any price needed to keep Ernie as happy as possible, considering he was a target or a dead man or worse.

Ernie was going to just keep on hoping the man would recognize that what they shared in the hotel room on the way here didn't happen every time two men met, fell into each other's eyes, and touched each other's bare skin.

"No," Burton said, sighing. "No, I won't see you for Thanksgiving. Do you have the phone I bought you?"

Ernie nodded. "Yeah." Clean, untraceable. It had been preloaded with Ace's number, Sonny's number, and Burton's number.

The end.

"I'll text you when I can."

Ernie brightened. "I'll text you when you can't."

Lee Burton gave out a groan and clapped his hands over his eyes. "Kid—"

"Ernie."

"Ernie—"

"Don't worry. Once you start thinking about me, I'll fill in the gaps in the conversation just fine." That wasn't really how the gift worked, except Ernie was pretty sure he'd be just as connected to Burton from however far away as he was now.

"That, uh, actually makes me a little itchy…," Burton said, slamming his door in a fit of what was probably pique.

Ernie smiled, so relieved he couldn't let Burton piss on his parade. "It shouldn't. You just have to tell the truth. To yourself. Especially to yourself."

Burton's low moan reassured Ernie to no end. It meant the man believed him. Took him seriously. Would work hard to be as truthful as possible.

Ernie already knew what Burton felt for him. He could wait until Burton figured it out in his own head.

ACE WAS exactly what Ernie expected, except way better looking. Sonny was not.

For one thing, Burton had figured Sonny to be spelled with a *u* and Sonny to be a she, which just went to show that sometimes the gift was a reliable way to get information and sometimes it was a big fat nuisance that overloaded Ernie's synapses and made him absolute garbage at dealing with the rest of the human race like a sane person.

Ace was a solid guy with a chest like a brick wall and arms built like pistons. He had hazel-brown eyes and a mouth that could be cruel, Ernie supposed, but when he shook Ace's hand, all he felt was a decent guy trying to live a decent life.

There was a current of darkness, but everybody had that. This guy had just negotiated his current and decided how it flowed, was all.

Sonny was much smaller, muscular too, but in the whip-thin way of someone who was all activity and nerves and not so much effort. He had blond hair, almost pretty, and a fox-pointed but narrow face.

His darkness was like a box, and Sonny would rabbit into his box and bound out even as they were talking. The three-billionth time Sonny rabbited into the dark box in his soul, Ernie let out a rough sigh and grabbed his arm over his shirt.

"I'm not here to take him away from you," Ernie said, exasperated. "As if anybody could. Now calm down. You're making Burton jumpy."

Sonny gave a long, slow blink with his enormous blue-gray eyes and some of the rabbit jumped out of him. "Yeah. Sure." He retreated behind Ace, touching him at the shoulder, then scooped up the tiny dog yapping at his feet. The dog shut up, and Ernie had a chance to look around their little house.

And it was little. The little kitchen opened up into a little dining room with a small table, which in turn opened up into a little living room. There were four doors. The bathroom—obviously, since Ernie could see it, and a laundry room next to it—a bedroom, probably Sonny and Ace's-- and a newly painted porthole to what was obviously Burton's personal space.

"Thank you, Ace and Sonny, for letting me stay here," Ernie said with a yawn. He wasn't usually awake in the day. "I'll get up and you can show me how to earn my keep, okay? But I have to nap and say goodbye to Burton."

With that he grabbed Burton's hand and dragged him away from their surprised hosts and through the door to Burton's space.

Ernie looked around carefully once they were there, biting his lip.

"He made this for you," he said, awe apparent. "Like… like he loves you. Like a friend, 'cause he's romantically attached to Sonny, which must be hard because Sonny's not easy, but look."

Burton looked around, saw what Ernie did. The simplicity of the room and the small serviceable attached bathroom, the nice queen-sized bed with the good mattress and a practical, high-quality quilt in a warm tan that matched the curtains, the wood paneling that matched the dresser. Ernie moved toward it and picked up a piece of driftwood sanded into a ball until it gleamed. There were a couple of other doodads there—a glass boat from San Diego, a snow globe from Tahoe, a small picture at the Chandelier Tree.

"Ace and Sonny," Burton said quietly. "They go on vacations now and then, and they bring back things. Something for Alba, their receptionist at the garage, something for Jai, their employee, something for Kat, a girl Ace sort of adopted who's living with Ace's parents, and something for me. Every time."

"It makes them really happy to bring stuff home for you guys," Ernie said easily. "It's… nice. You brought me to a nice place. This is your…." He looked around, feeling a sort of peace here.

"Haven," Burton said softly.

"Church," Ernie said, naming it for what it was. "When you go out and do the things you have to, you're thinking about Ace and Sonny and protecting them."

Burton shrugged. "Somebody's got to."

Ernie nodded. "So now you're protecting me here too."

"Somebody's got to," Burton rasped, and Ernie heard the need.

He turned and rushed into Burton's arms, held him tight. "Be careful," he begged softly. "Come back. Become a part of this, of these people you love. They're here for you."

"I'm a—"

"A man." Ernie tilted his face up and took Burton's kiss like it was a given. Ernie knew it wasn't. But he'd lost himself already. Burton was going to do dangerous things to try to bring the people behind Ernie's contract to justice, but afterward, Ernie was going to hope for Burton by his side.

Burton ripped away from the kiss like he was gulping air.

"Kid—"

"Ernie."

"Ernie...." His voice ached with tenderness. "You and me, we're not over."

Ernie smiled. "At last, he sees."

Burton laughed gruffly. "Okay, I've got to—"

And then, dammit, the goddamned shining hit Ernie right in the gut. "You've got to protect them too," he said, his voice remote.

"Ace and Sonny?"

"They're far away, and they're tied into this and...." Ernie sighed. "Broken. One of them is broken. Tiny little pieces, a shattered fish in a bowl of refracted light. A shark who loves him. And they're coming. You'll know them. You'll protect them. They'll need you."

Burton blinked. "I, uh...."

Oh, goddammit. Ernie liked these people, the tough, battered one and the slick one in the suit. He couldn't see their faces, but he could feel their decency, even through the shining. He rose to his tiptoes and kissed Burton's cheek. "Come back to me," he said simply.

Because that's what you did when you loved a force of nature. You let him go be a force for good.

Burton left, and Ernie fell onto the bed dispiritedly. He was crying, because his heart was on his sleeve, would always be on his sleeve, had never not been on his sleeve.

He knew the door opened, and the small dog bounded on the bed and licked his face, but it wasn't until he felt the tentative hand in his hair that he realized he might have, for once, truly landed someplace that would feel like home.

"Don't mind Duke," Sonny Daye said, voice matter-of-fact. "He knows you're sad. I'm just gonna leave him here to keep you company while me and Ace go open the garage. You feel free to eat what you wanna—we'll go shopping for you later, and Ace says that's fine if you help with paperwork and stuff and—"

Ernie rolled over and grabbed Sonny's hand. "Sonny Daye?"

"Yessir?"

"We're friends already. Don't worry about making me happy. Burton wouldn't have brought me here if it wasn't a good place. I'm comfortable. I get up around six or seven. Want me to make dinner?"

Sonny smiled a little. "That would be kind."

"Okay, then. Don't worry. I'll get along here just fine."

Sonny stood and left, and Ernie yawned and sank back down into the bed. In his pocket, his phone buzzed.

Was damned hard leaving you, kid. Be good until I get back.

Yeah. Until the fish and the shark got here, it was gonna be okay.

Temple Fish

ELLERY'S PHONE alarm went off and Jackson lunged for it, crawling over Ellery's body to kill the alarm before Ellery could even wake up.

As. If.

"Jackson, what the… mmm…."

Jackson started by kissing his neck.

They were warm, they were in bed, they'd showered the night before. All that was sweet and soft and warm about two men in bed on a cold January Saturday, that's what they were right now. And while Jackson was a man on a mission, he had a very clear goal in mind, and he knew he could not accomplish what he wanted to if he rushed things.

Besides. The faint salt tang of Ellery's skin tingled on his tongue, and while he'd started out with an Ellery-centric goal in mind, he was remembering reasons this was good for both of them.

"Really?" Ellery mumbled as Jackson made his way down Ellery's chest, rucking his shirt up so he could latch on to Ellery's nipple. He pulled gently at first, then teased with his tongue, and Ellery grunted, knotting his fingers in Jackson's hair and tugging rhythmically.

Jackson didn't answer his question; he figured it was rhetorical anyway. He just kept his mouth busy, busy, busy… sucking, arching his own hips against the bed, reaching down to slide his hand under Ellery's sleep pants to find him more than halfway erect. He pulled away long enough to shove at Ellery's pants, then his own sweats and shirt, but as soon as he was done, he went back to what he wanted to do—skin on skin.

He kept sucking and started squeezing gently, his own arousal growing more intense as he thrust against the bed. Damn, this was better than he'd planned—he'd been so focused on his intent he'd forgotten that this wasn't a chore, had never been a chore, should *never, ever* be anything but a pleasure.

Ellery's groan vibrated in the pit of his groin. Jackson let go of the stiffened, wet nipple reluctantly, but it was time to move down to little-head-quarters, as it were.

As he squeezed Ellery's erection, stroking up to the mushroom head, he found himself relaxing.

It used to be, when he was pleasing a lover, he'd treat this part of sex like the hardest part of the obstacle course—the wall. He *had* to do well here. He had to bring his lover, male or female, off here, in the most spectacular way possible, before they moved on to actual penetration.

He owed them. They were sleeping in his bed to save him from the terrible silences in his head, in his heart, and he needed to pay them up front, in the best currency he had.

Ellery wouldn't let him do that.

Ellery had started to recognize "power blow job" and protest against it. Nothing killed a mood—or made Jackson feel more inadequate—than "Jackson, stay with me!"

Jackson still had a goal here, but he needed to enjoy this, needed to move with it. Ellery had made it crystal clear that all Jackson owed him in bed was his own enjoyment.

Jackson did so enjoy pulling Ellery's cock into his mouth. Slow, slow, slow, slow... he allowed the head to stretch his throat. He'd had lots of practice doing this, but none of those lovers were as important to him as Ellery Cramer.

Ellery hit bottom and Jackson swallowed, allowing his tongue and palate to caress Ellery's bell and his lips to squeeze the shaft at the base. Ellery groaned, so loudly, so uninhibited, that Jackson's cat, who had been asleep on the other half of Jackson's pillow, jumped off the bed with an affronted hiss.

They both ignored Billy Bob, and Ellery beat at the bed with his fist as he bucked and arched into Jackson's mouth.

Oh yeah. Jackson had him right where he wanted him.

With a satisfied slurp, Jackson pulled off Ellery's cock, spread open his cheeks, and spat on his hole a couple of times. This act—wanton, filthy in its way—was new to the two of them, and it seemed to send Ellery whimpering out of sheer eroticism.

This time was no exception, and Ellery was starting to make little pretend words interspersed with gasps. Jackson ignored him and instead sucked his thumb into his mouth, getting it nice and slick, and then thrust in, just the end, while he engulfed Ellery's prick again.

Ellery screamed into his bitten palm and then, pushy bastard, made a demand.

"Fuck me, goddammit! Stop screwing around and fuck me!"

Jackson went back to his original plan—mouth working, thumb opening Ellery up, his own body amped to the point of torture, and then Ellery pulled out the big guns.

"C'mon, Jackson. You know you want it. Want my ass. The only way to shut me up is to kiss me, right? I'll talk you into orgasm if you don't get up here and fuck me. Bet your cock's aching, needs touch. Can't grab it yourself, right? Too busy blowing... ah.... God, come on, baby—come here and fuck me!"

Jackson had every intention of staying strong. He did, but something about the endearment. The begging. The emotional security of someone who, spread out, at Jackson's mercy, could beg for Jackson to make him *more* vulnerable—it awed Jackson.

He was sliding up Ellery's body, his cock leaving a streak of precome on Ellery's thigh, before he was aware of making the decision. Ellery cupped his neck when he got there, pulling him down into a kiss, undulating his hips, grinding them both together.

Jackson lost himself, forgot why he'd started this, caught up in their bodies twining against one another and the pressure mounting in his groin.

Oh *damn*, but he wanted to possess Ellery too. Ellery fumbled under his pillow and pulled out the lubricant. He didn't hand off to Jackson, though. Instead, he snicked the top of the bottle open and *handled* Jackson, reaching down between them and oiling Jackson's cock, squeezing him, running his thumb over Jackson's head until Jackson buried his face in the hollow of Ellery's neck.

"You're gonna make me co-ome...," he sang softly.

"Then fuck me," Ellery demanded.

"Fine." Ah... he found Ellery's entrance, positioned himself, and drove in.

Ellery arched his back and sighed, like Jackson was the missing puzzle piece of his body, the one that made him complete, and then relaxed into the sort of dreamy acceptance he employed sometimes to let Jackson inside.

Jackson pushed up to start a rhythm and—*damn*. His arm almost gave. Fuck. Fuck fuck fuck. He'd destroyed that shoulder—twice—the second time not more than two months ago, and he forgot sometimes how far he had to go to heal.

With a growl he pulled back so more of his weight was on his knees and hauled Ellery's legs up so his knees were bent over Jackson's shoulders. It was blatant, it was porny, but God, Jackson could really get some traction as he drove himself into Ellery's ass.

Ellery was making sounds again, begging, gasping, pleading sounds, and Jackson was so damned grateful he could put out, answer those noises with a savage thrusting, an insatiable physical howl of desire.

Jackson felt his climax building, fast and hard, surprised into action in the same way Jackson had been surprised into fucking, and damn if he didn't need Ellery to come first.

"You ready?" he panted, not letting up.

"Nungh!"

"C'mon, Ellery—you wanted fucking, you got it. Now give me your climax!"

"Augh! God! Don't stop!"

"Come, dammit, come!"

"Yes!"

Yesssss.... Ellery's body convulsed, practically seizing as Jackson kept rutting away inside him, trapped by the way he clamped down on Jackson's cock as he climaxed. He started to shudder, orgasm sweeping away his control as his blood boiled and his breath stopped.

He pumped inside Ellery's body, vision going black, and then fell forward, supporting his weight on his good arm as he tried to pull himself together before he'd even finished coming.

"All of you, Jackson!" Ellery demanded.

Jackson's good arm buckled and he fell on top of Ellery, still rutting, still pumping come into the haven of his lover's body, breathing so hard he saw spots.

"Sh...." Ellery slicked his hair back from his face and whispered to him as he collapsed limply, Ellery's long limbs sheltering him from the cold outside their little bed.

"Sorry," Jackson said, blinking hard, irritated at himself for losing sight of his plan. He was supposed to keep control, dammit. He was supposed to blow Ellery's mind, not get swept away in the sexual tide himself!

"For what?" Ellery asked tenderly.

"Was trying to make it holy," Jackson told him, lost enough to tell the truth.

Ellery struggled out from under him, pushing Jackson to his side while Ellery rolled over to face him. "Tell me this wasn't!" he demanded.

Jackson grimaced. "Do you have to?" he asked. "I mean, if our sex is holy and shit, doesn't that mean you don't have to go?"

"Nobody is holding a gun to my head! God*dammit*, Jackson, do you not get why I have to do this?"

"Aren't you too late to go this week?" Jackson asked hopefully.

Ellery laughed, grim satisfaction in every syllable. "I set the alarm early so we could have breakfast." He glanced over his shoulder. "And you know what? We still can."

Jackson grimaced. Dammit. "But...."

Ellery's expression softened, and he reached out to brush Jackson's cheekbone with his fingertips. "Baby, why does this bother you so much?"

Jackson scowled. "Because if you're thanking God for me, God's going to show you what a mistake that is, and I like it here."

With a groan and a heave, Ellery rolled off the bed. "There is no talking to you about this! Now get in the shower, and I'll make pancakes. And no! You can't wear jeans!"

"But you said I didn't have to get out of the car!" Jackson hollered, finding a clean set of boxers in the dresser Ellery had set aside for him.

"I lied! You at least have to visit the outside, dammit!" Ellery grabbed his sleep pants and his sweatshirt from the folds of the covers and started dragging them on.

"But won't I burst into fire?" Jackson asked, only partially kidding. His past... oh God. His past wasn't *checkered*, it was chicken-pocked! "I mean, won't you get kicked out and excommunicated if you show up with me next to you?"

"No, Jackson, they've got a big ol' reformed-slut alarm that sounds as soon as you step foot on the ground, and then a force field shoots up, separating us and catapulting you to purgatory for the length of the service. After your first six visits, they give you the option of walking there on your own while a sorcerer whispers arcane words and tries to set me up with a doctor, because that's just how Jews roll."

Jackson stared at him, cheeks flushed with color, fine brown eyes sparkling with righteous anger, and like it usually did, the thing in his chest melted into a gooey little puddle.

"I can see your sarcasm is functioning well this morning. Isn't that going to taint the pancakes?"

Ellery struggled to keep his mouth firm. "I can make *my* pancakes both strawberry *and* sarcastic. But if you want whipped cream, you're going to have to shut up, get dressed, and let me have this. Understand?"

Jackson let out a sigh. "If I see anybody there in jeans, I'm not wearing slacks next time."

"That, too, is understood."

"And if anybody gives you shit about the gay—"

"We shall find a temple that has no shits to give. Also understood."

"If you find someone there who's better than me...." He scowled and stared at the picture of them Ellery had put up on the end table, Jackson looking uncomfortable in his best dinnerwear and Ellery smiling charmingly for his father, who was perhaps the dearest man Jackson had ever met. The picture had been taken outside Ellery's parents' house in Boston over Thanksgiving, and while Jackson could say for certain it had been a good time, every single memory he had seemed to be tempered with the stomach-churning anxiety he was dealing with now.

An Ellery Cramer and a Jackson Rivers did not make sense in any way, shape, or form. The longer they were together, the more Jackson looked for the chapped, palsied hand of fate to try to rip them apart. And every time Ellery said he was being ridiculous, Jackson had to walk away, because the fact was, he had almost died—twice—since the two of them had gotten together in the summer.

If that wasn't God trying to tell Jackson the facts of life, Jackson didn't know what was.

So Ellery going to temple out of some sort of weird deal he'd made with the big guy—on the one hand, it never hurt to suck up to the person in charge.

On the other hand, Jackson was a fan of the old Irish saying "May you be in heaven half an hour before the devil knows you're dead."

In this case, he would just as soon nobody, God or devil, even knew he was on the planet. He'd had forces bigger than he was meddle in his life, and he had the layers of scar tissue to show he'd barely survived.

"If I find somebody who's better than you," Ellery snapped, bringing him to the present, "*I'm* not the one he'll be hitting on."

Jackson scowled at him. "You're being stupid."

Ellery's thin lips curled up into a smile. "So are you."

"Fine. Fine, I'll go. I'll even be a grown-up. But Ellery, those had better be some damned good pancakes."

Ellery rolled his eyes and grabbed his robe, swanning out for his exit, singing "My pancakes bring all the boys to the yard…" as he went.

After he left the room, Jackson allowed himself a fond smile. God, he really was being ridiculous. Who over the age of twelve pitched this big a fit over church, or temple, or whatever?

But as he jumped in the shower and started to wash, he just couldn't shake the unease that knotted in his stomach.

For much of his life, things like food, shelter, basic safety—things Ellery had taken for granted every day of his life—had been dreams to Jackson Rivers. Now, living with Ellery in his posh American River Drive house with cavernous rooms and real wood floors, Jackson had food and shelter and, God help him, emotional safety on a daily basis.

He was just waiting for God to *stop* helping him and rip it all away.

But Ellery seemed to think Jackson was worth keeping. Jackson wasn't going to dissuade him, because frankly, that hadn't worked at the beginning of their relationship, and after what had gone down before Thanksgiving, it certainly wasn't going to happen now.

THE PANCAKES were wonderful, and Jackson dressed in his courtroom suit and tried not to be a bigger pain in Ellery's ass than he had been that morning, when Ellery had been *begging* him to be a pain in his ass.

They'd already planned their day—the visit to the synagogue wasn't the only thing they were doing Saturday. Ellery, who worked as a defense attorney at the firm where Jackson worked as an investigator, had a client who had been released on bail for vehicular manslaughter the day before but would need to be deposed before her arraignment on Monday. Ellery and Jackson had gotten lots of time off after Jackson had been injured. Ellery had gone back for the month of December, while Jackson had tried, again, to get to the point where he could run five miles without hauling wind like a trucker hauled ass.

He was feeling pretty fit as he and Ellery parked Ellery's beloved Lexus in the small side lot next to the impressively modern brick-and-glass building set on the small lawn.

"Hunh," he said as Ellery locked the car and they looked for people heading toward some sort of entrance for the service.

"Hunh what?" Ellery asked, caution in his voice. He seemed to think that was a scary word coming from Jackson. Jackson had no idea why.

"It's all new and shit. I mean… that shitty architecture of twenty years ago but, you know… not…." He made gestures indicating pointy things and bulbous roofs and something you'd see in a Russian fairy tale.

"It's a Reformed synagogue," Ellery said dryly. "That means a modern belief system and a modern building. Not an ancient mosque. Wrong religion, cowboy."

"Oh." Jackson's face washed with heat. Way to showcase his ignorance. "Sorry."

Ellery grimaced and walked around the car to take his hand. In public. Which they never did. "I can't blame you. In my neighborhood we had maybe twenty synagogues in a five-mile radius—Reformed, Reconstructionist, Orthodox, Reformed Orthodox, you name your flavor, you had three to choose from. I checked. *You* have maybe ten synagogues in fifty miles. It's not a thing you've grown up with all your life, Jackson. Nobody is expecting you to know." He crimped his mouth. "I've told you repeatedly to stay home."

"It's important to you," Jackson muttered, finally admitting why he was here, even if he was being a big baby about it.

Ellery dropped his chin to his tie and rubbed the back of his neck. "So. Are. You."

"Which is why I'm here. Now go. There's sort of an entrance hall and shit. Go introduce yourself. Do what you do…."

"Mark my Torah for the reading, use the program to mark the hymnal so I can find the songs when it's time, and…." Ellery grimaced, then reached into his pocket and pulled out a small, plain, disc-shaped skullcap. "Remember to put on my goddamned yarmulke."

"How does that thing stay on?" Jackson asked, squinting.

"Honestly? I usually use pins. That's why I'm going to put it on after I go in and sit down." His face softened as they approached the front door. The place had big windows in the front, and there seemed to be a sort of reception anteroom in front of the sanctuary. People were filtering through there, taking programs from ushers standing on either side of the inside doors. "There's a bench here. You can come in or wait for me here." He rummaged in his pockets and pulled out his keys. "Or, if you get cold, go wait in the car."

Jackson looked around the neighborhood, which seemed primarily residential. He took the keys and asked, "Can I go get coffee?"

"Sure. But text me so I know where you are."

For a moment Jackson was going to retort, "Sure, Mom," and then, like it always did, memories of November smacked him in the face. He didn't get to be a smartass about Ellery worrying. He just fucking didn't.

"Yeah. Promise. I'll probably just sit out here and do work on my phone." Jackson had started plowing through his emails from home after Ellery had gone back to work, and he'd even taken one or two low-level computer search cases from the firm, things that didn't involve a lot of physical work.

But now he was back full-time and he had to keep his house in order. It was a relief, finally, to be useful again.

"You could always play games," Ellery said, dimpling. They'd started playing silly games on their phones while on the plane to Ellery's family's house over Thanksgiving—and hadn't stopped. Words with Friends, Word Cookies, Plants vs. Zombies, Angry Birds—name a dumb phone game, they'd held a pitched battle with each other while using it.

It was such a small way of communicating, but Jackson had come to cherish seeing a challenge from Ellery on his phone every morning.

Just one more way to reassure Jackson that the words they'd said in November weren't going away.

"Fine," Jackson said, sighing. "Now go. You're going to be late, and then you're going to blame me, and we'll have to go for another year because I made you late."

Ellery shook his head. "Your view of religion is really warped. Seriously." But he walked inside anyway, putting his yarmulke on as he went.

Jackson felt a little bit of relief as the door closed behind him. He sank down onto the bench in the front, pulling his coat a little tighter around his shoulders and checking the sky to see if he needed the hood.

No rain, not yet, so he pulled out his phone, gave his surroundings a brief, practiced once-over for any occupational hazards—strangers, guns, suspicious activity—and hit the button to play Words with Friends. He and Ellery had seven or eight games going, and it was Jackson's turn.

He smelled tobacco and heard the footsteps before he saw the guy, and he was grateful for it too. He didn't startle when a midsized man in his forties, with a few silver hairs in his beard and peeking out from under his rainbow-colored yarmulke, emerged from a little strip of nothing that existed between the synagogue and the bushes on the side.

Jackson eyed the guy with amusement. He was wearing jeans and a sport coat and looked as surprised to see Jackson as Jackson had been to hear him.

"You're not going in?" the man said.

"Waiting for my boyfriend," Jackson told him. The guy didn't bat an eyelash, so Jackson figured Ellery was safe in there, but he had a lot to answer for in the clothing department, because Jackson could *too* have worn jeans.

"It's warm in there," the man said, smiling winningly. "There's cookies at the end, I guarantee it."

Jackson inclined his head in appreciation. "That's nice of you, but I think I can guilt Ellery into Starbucks afterward. We're good."

"Hm…." Jackson's companion tilted his head, regarding Jackson steadily. "Why wouldn't you eat free cookies? I'm curious."

Oh Lord. Quite literally. Jackson swallowed. "There's no such thing as free cookies," he said, keeping his voice mild.

"Who taught you that?" The man's voice was nothing but kind.

A memory swamped him so quickly he barely had time to brace for it. Back when he was a kid, before he'd become friends with Jade and Kaden

Cameron and their mother had stepped in, taking over his raising. When Celia had spent their check on drugs—per usual—and they'd had no heat and no food. She'd dragged him to a shelter, and for a whole minute, he'd gotten food and a place to curl up and get warm, and he'd been grateful.

Then he'd had to sit in a room while a guy with a loud voice and furrows on his forehead had told him and a bunch of other people dressed in rags that they needed to repent and earn their cookies.

Those probably hadn't been his exact words, but Jackson remembered that moment—when all his gratitude had flown into the winter rain and he'd been left with a big stinking pile of resentment instead.

"General lesson," he said with a shrug. "You're going to be late, aren't you?"

"The first ten minutes are silent reflection anyway." The man shrugged back. "I'm not missing much."

"A good time to sneak a smoke," Jackson noted drily.

His companion's laugh was deep and unapologetic. "Busted! Don't tell?"

"Nobody to tell." Jackson gestured around them. "See? Secret's safe."

"Fair enough. You're a mensch. Do you know what that means?"

Jackson had seen enough movies to figure it out. "A buddy or a pal—a good guy." He shrugged. "I do what I can."

"But you don't go into the synagogue?"

"Sir, I'm not Jewish. I'm not even Christian. I just told my boyfriend I'd come to support him, but I don't belong there."

"Why did your boyfriend come?" Damn, this guy was not going to let this go. "And scoot over. I can sit with you for a moment."

Jackson made room. "He… well, he felt like he sort of owed God. See, I got… I had a really bad day or two. And I almost died. And he… I guess he made a deal, in his head, you know? If I got through that, he'd go to temple. And I told him…." Oh, how embarrassing. But this nice middle-aged guy with the laugh lines at the corners of his brown eyes invited confidence.

"What?"

"Well, I'm not a fan of God, mostly. But… with him…." He couldn't say this out loud. Not to a stranger.

"You see God in your lover's eyes," the man said, but gently, so it didn't sound corny.

"Yeah." Jackson looked away. "Anyway, he still felt like he had a debt. And I get that. I mean, there's shit I can't pay back either. So if he's here, I'm here. I just… I don't belong in there with those nice people, you know?"

"No. What makes you not belong there? And don't say you're not Jewish, because anybody is welcome here. I'm curious."

Jackson shrugged, not wanting to think about his mother, or how he seemed to miss her less after her murder than he'd missed her when she'd been alive. Or the things he'd done—and had done to him—the day he'd seen her corpse on the slab. He didn't want to think about his time as a cop and the betrayal that ended the career. All the willing bodies in the dark.

"God really doesn't give a crap about me," Jackson said after a moment. "But… but he seems to watch out for Ellery okay. I don't want to fu… screw that up. So I'm here."

"What do you do for a living, young man?"

Jackson let a skeptical eyebrow arch. "You're not that much older than I am," he said and was glad to see the guy dimple under his beard.

"Occupational hazard. What do you do for a living?"

"I'm a PI for a legal defense firm." Ellery was their young up-and-comer. They'd managed to avoid each other for years before they'd been forced to work together—and Ellery had staked his claim.

"So you defend the innocent?"

Jackson shrugged. "We try to. You know, make sure they don't get hammered too bad, even if they're a little guilty. Everyone should get a second chance." Jackson couldn't keep looking at this nice man—it was embarrassing. He started scanning the road in front of them. The parking lot. The little white-bricked store with bars on the windows across the street.

But his companion was still engaged in the conversation. "That's pretty noble, isn't it?"

Another shrug. "Seriously—aren't you going to be late?"

"Humor me."

"Sometimes we defend scumbags," Jackson told him bluntly, narrowing his eyes at the kid coming out of the store. He was ducking his head and looking both ways as he ran through the crosswalk, toward the parking lot for the synagogue. "And I dig up dirt on their accusers, same as I do with the innocent ones. But yeah. We try to make it noble. Don't know if we succeed, but we try."

"That's the best a man can do. You know, there's a saying—it's part of our faith, actually. That he who saves one soul saves the world. Have you heard that?"

Jackson thought about it, angling his body a little. He could see some of the cars still in the line of sight past the building. "No. But I like it." He stood up, still watching to see where the boy had gone while he talked to his new shadow.

"Me too. Maybe, you know, next time you come with your boyfriend, you remember the last time you tried to save the world and you'll feel more like coming in."

Jackson watched the kid pause at Ellery's horribly ostentatious silver Lexus—his many-times-repaired baby, which he insisted on driving everywhere. Jackson was still without a car after his had been destroyed in November, and Ellery insisted on driving. He was crap at it too, and Jackson felt like he was eating in somebody's guest room whenever they stopped for takeout.

"*You're* not in there," Jackson said absently. "If it's so awesome inside, why are you still out here with me?" And the kid was looking at his hand and looking at Ellery's license plate.

"Holy wow," the guy on the bench said. "I mean seriously. Oy gevalt. You are not getting this."

"What is that kid doing?" Jackson mumbled to himself. He remembered he was having a conversation and looked behind him. "Which is probably why I'm better off on the bench. Could you excuse me a sec? This does not look kosher."

He took a few steps toward the parking lot, his dress shoes ringing on the concrete walkway, and the kid—scruffy, wearing Army surplus, with dirty brown hair and pale, grubby skin—popped up from his half crouch by the driver's side door and looked around like a meerkat.

"Oh no you don't, you little vandal," Jackson muttered, taking off on a capture mission before the kid could do something irrevocable to the paint job. He was halfway to the vehicle before he realized just how wrong it was to leave a conversation this way. No wonder he didn't belong at the synagogue—seriously!

Losing Balance

ELLERY OPENED the door just in time to see Jackson disappear around the corner and the congregation's missing rabbi stand up in surprise.

"Rabbi Watson?"

"Mr. Cramer! So nice to see you again!" Ellery had visited before deciding to attend. He was a lawyer—research was his specialty.

"Everybody's, uh, waiting for—where'd Jackson go?"

"Your young man?"

Rabbi Watson was in his midforties, but maybe it helped to be a confidant and community leader if you assumed more age than you actually had. "Yes, sir, he was waiting for me and—"

From around the corner, they could both hear Jackson's breathless voice raised in triumph. "Ha! You little bastard—I gotcha! What were you doing to our car?"

"Nothing! I swear! Not a damned thing! I was just—give that back!"

Rabbi Watson's eyes got huge, and Ellery's heart expanded to his stomach. "I don't even believe this," he muttered, walking past the rabbi so he could look around the corner.

Where Jackson stood, his slacks and coat looking scuffed at the knees and elbows, holding a young man with one arm behind his back.

"Jackson?"

Jackson had that boyish look of triumph he wore when he'd brought in a particularly tough informant. "Someone was trying to break into your car," he said, eyes sparkling.

"I was not!"

"You were too! I saw you!"

"I wasn't supposed to break into it!" the boy said, honestly indignant. "I was trying to put that thing on it! They said they'd pay me if I put the thing on the bottom—that's all I was doin', I swear!"

Jackson scowled and looked around, catching Ellery's eye. "Ellery— c'mere and look at this thing. It's damned hinky."

"I'm sorry, Rabbi. I should really see what that's—"

"Not a problem." Rabbi Watson waved his hand airily. "I'll see you next week, Ellery?"

"Yes, sir—"

"Good. Maybe next week we'll get your young man to come inside." Rabbi Watson waved bemusedly at Jackson. "You have fun doing—" His hand made a few passes. "—whatever it is you do. I'll see you both later."

Ellery was already hustling over to where Jackson stood, one hand still pinning the boy in place, the other holding out a small plastic bag and shaking it imperiously. "Yeah—sorry, Rabbi—"

But the leader of the congregation was already inside, and Ellery was left with Jackson and his squirming charge.

"What is that?" he asked without preamble, taking the small plastic package from his hand. Jackson used the freedom to secure the boy's wrists again.

"I don't know. Kid, what is that?"

"*I don't know!*" the kid complained. "I have no idea. But that guy—the one in the liquor store—he gave it to me and told me to put it under your car. Showed me a twenty, said I could have it if I just… popped it on." The kid suddenly went limp. "Should have known it was too good to be—hey!"

Jackson dropped him like a hot rock and snapped, "Ellery, you get him!" before taking off for the liquor store.

Ellery and the boy stared at each other for a long minute.

Curly dark blond hair, dirty white face, maybe twelve years old, with sort of a delicate beauty in the cheekbones and bright blue eyes with thick lashes around them.

For a moment—the barest second—Ellery thought about Jackson as a child, and the kid's eyes widened like he spotted an opportunity.

Shit. Ellery wasn't going to wrestle this urchin like Jackson had, and Jackson would *kill* him if he let the kid go.

"I'll pay you," he blurted.

The kid recoiled, and he looked appalled. "I'm not a fuckin' whore!"

Oh hell no. "Not for *that*. Just to stay put until he gets back. Seriously—he wants to ask you some questions."

"Oh." Little shit didn't look embarrassed in the least. "How much?"

"Am I going to pay you?" Well, geez—what was the going rate for not looking like a schmuck in front of your action-hero boyfriend?

"Yeah. The guy over there said he'd give me a twenty if I put the thing on your car. How much you gonna pay me for not doing it?"

Ellery shrugged. "Forty, I guess."

A wily look of triumph crossed the kid's pointed features, and he practically danced on his toes. "Ha! I woulda took twenty-five!"

Fucking hell. "Lucky you. You get forty. What're you gonna spend it on?"

"Hunh." Oh Jesus—it was Jackson's word, right down to that weird intonation Ellery hated because it hinted at so much more than just the one syllable. "I never had that much money before. I don't know. Maybe...." The kid bit his lip, showing a vulnerability that tugged at Ellery's heart. "Maybe some clothes?" He looked down at himself, and Ellery took in the battered sneakers with bare feet showing through, the jeans that were too short, and the Army surplus jacket that was too big and threadbare. "I'm fuckin' cold."

Ellery winced. "Kid? I'll give you fifty if you pretend you're not a grown-up and don't swear in front of us. I know you know those words, probably knew them in the cradle, but just, for me, pretend like you live in a world where you didn't hear those words unless they were in the movies, okay?"

The kid rolled his eyes. "Easiest fu... oh, fifty dollars I ever earned. Stand still and shut up. I'm gold." The kid looked at Ellery for a moment and fidgeted. "Fu... uh, da... uh.... Geez, mister, what's taking the other guy so long?"

A quick glance up to the liquor store revealed nothing, but as they watched, Jackson came out, the grim set of his shoulders unmistakable. He was on the phone, talking even as he crossed the street.

"Yeah, Kryzynski, I'm not shitting around. We'll be across from the synagogue on El Camino. Yeah, Ellery too. At the liquor store—but don't come in guns blazing, sirens on overdrive. Because it'll put the kid in more danger, that's why. No, I got no idea why him. No, I don't know how they knew we were here either. No, I don't know who's behind it. I know that me catching the little shit was probably the luckiest thing to happen to him in his entire life. Now get your asses over here and try not to interrupt the service. Because the rabbi's a nice guy, that's why. I'm not, but Ellery is. Spare me. Are you fucking coming or fucking not?" Jackson looked up and rolled his eyes at Ellery, letting Ellery know fully what he thought of the young, newly promoted police detective who had hitched his wagon to Jackson and Ellery's star more than once in the past year and gotten a boost up the ranks when things panned out.

"What's up?" Ellery asked, concerned. Jackson didn't like help, and he didn't like cops—but he knew their usefulness and the consequences when he didn't call them when they were needed legally. For him to call Kryzynski in, things were pretty dire.

Jackson gave him a "not yet" nod and turned to the kid.

"Kid, you got a name?"

"Anthony Cooper," the kid replied promptly.

"Good name."

"I like it. Why do you need to know?"

"You got folks, Anthony? Mom, Dad, whatever?"

Anthony looked uncomfortable. "Got a foster family."

"They okay?" Jackson was good with this kid—matter-of-fact, not full of pity. But then, he would have been *lucky* to have a foster family at this kid's age, so maybe he should work with *all* the juvenile delinquents.

"They're all right." He shrugged. "Three meals, they give a crap when I get home. Try to keep me clean."

Jackson gave the kid a skeptical once-over.

"Didn't say it *worked*," the kid snapped. "I'm like their service to God. God can service me on his own time."

Jackson's snort probably echoed in the synagogue. "I'm sure he's all for that, kid." Then he sobered. "Look—this is really important. The guy who asked you to put the thing on the car—tell me how that went down."

Anthony looked at him strangely—and so did Ellery. Jackson's jaw was clenched, and his green eyes were snapping bright and tense. And the police were coming.

"Well, I was…." He grimaced. "I wanted a candy bar, and… and Smitty usually lets me have one if I pick up around the back. He's a good guy. This time he said he'd give me food instead and a candy bar later, and I got sort of shitty with him and he told me I looked like hell and I said…." The kid swallowed. "I said some shit I shouldnta, and I need to tell him sorry. Anyway, a guy was in the back by the beer cooler, scoping the Jewish place out through the window. I went to go do the boxes, and the guy says, 'Hey—you wanna earn your own money? That fat bastard can't tell you what to buy.' I was like, 'You talk nice about Smitty,' 'cause, you know. Food is good and Smitty gives me some. And he offered me money. So I told Smitty I'd be back to break down the boxes and…." The kid shrugged. "You got me dead to rights, but I don't know what I was doing wrong."

Ellery wanted to smile, but the expression on Jackson's face was… sorrowful.

"Tampering with someone else's stuff, on the whole," he said, voice mild, "just not a good idea. Kid, can you give a description of this guy? Like to draw?"

"Well, sure." The kid shrugged. "Big white guy. Built like Jason Momoa. Mean little piggy eyes. Walked like he had a stick up his ass. But ask Smitty—he knows everybody in the store."

Jackson swallowed, and Ellery saw the flicker of lights from a half mile away, and that's when he knew things were really, really wrong.

"Kid, uh...." Jackson took a deep breath and looked away, and then swallowed and looked back. "I'm afraid your friend... your friend Smitty isn't going to be around anymore. I'm... I'm thinking me catching you wasn't the worst thing in the world."

The kid bit his lip. "What... what... I don't understand?" And all his swagger fell away, his streetwise *I-got-this*. Suddenly he was just a kid who'd been mean to his friend, mostly because he was a kid, and kids didn't know how quick life could change. He was a kid who felt bad, and who didn't want grief to strip away what innocence he had quite so brutally.

Jackson saw the lights too. He looked over his shoulder and shook his head, like he was shaking off the temptation to just bail on this moment right here.

Ellery wouldn't have blamed him if he did.

"Whoever paid you to bug our car shot your friend in the liquor store. Kid, I'm sorry—Smitty's dead, and it looks like the person who killed him tried to get him to spill about you." Jackson made an indeterminate, hostile noise. "We... we need to keep you under wraps. Safe."

Three police cars pulled up in front of the liquor store, and one unmarked vehicle.

Ellery watched them come to a halt and watched Sean Kryzynski come out of the tan unmarked, another detective at his side.

"Think they believe us about stuff now?" he asked idly, and Jackson nodded in bemusement.

"Seriously—where was all this fu... er, frickin' backup three months ago?"

Ellery looked at the frightened boy and thought about how much work it usually took to get someone into protective custody.

"Don't count on that much help this time around," he said quietly. "We may want a plan B for young Anthony here."

This kid's eyes—limpid and blue—went even wider. "Plan B?"

"Don't worry," Jackson said quietly. "Here. You and me, we're gonna talk some more—you okay with that?"

Anthony nodded weakly and used his newly freed arm to wipe his eyes. "Smitty... is... I mean, I was gonna go back and do the boxes, right?"

"Yeah, kid. Don't worry. I think he forgave you for being snotty to him. He was a good guy?"

Another nod. "The best," he whispered.

"Good guys, they know what's inside you isn't always what you say. I think you were probably square."

Another nod and a big, long, suspicious breath. Jackson tilted his head back and rolled his eyes to heaven—and then looked at the kid and held out his arms tentatively.

Anthony, the urchin who'd tried to plant a bug on their car, ran into a complete stranger's arms and cried like his heart was breaking.

TWENTY MINUTES later Ellery had to hold Jackson back to keep him from assaulting an officer.

"What do you *mean* you can't protect him?" Jackson snarled, lunging for Kryzynski, their on-again, off-again contact in SPD.

Kryzynski was young—it was his tentative friendship with Ellery that had helped promote him up the food chain—and he fidgeted, pulling his fingers through his slick blond hair as he tried to explain why he was so excited about kissing up to the department now.

"Look, Rivers—I called the DA, and they say it's not enough. Do we even know what that thing is?"

"Can we maybe, I don't know, find out?" Jackson asked acidly, the tension in his shoulders unmistakable. "Could we, I don't know, at least move the kid's foster placement just in case—"

"What? The guy who knocked over the liquor store comes back to grab a twelve-year-old vandalizing a car?"

"*It's bigger than that!*" Jackson roared. "He was putting a bug on the car—did you check it out? It's got a little magnet on it—all the kid was supposed to do was put it underneath. Bug, tracking device—whatever. They wanted to know our movements."

"And who is 'they'?" Kryzynski gazed levelly at him, and Jackson broke free from Ellery with a grunt.

"Who do you think?" he asked in disgust. "We told you the Owens thing wasn't over. Didn't we? I'm pretty sure we did."

"Because why?" And for the first time, Ellery heard compassion in Kryzynski's voice. "Because Ellery met a guy from the military who pissed him off? Because Owens was a psychopath who apparently picked up his mass-murdering skills from basic training? I got news for you, Rivers— everybody pisses Ellery off, and psychos train in all sorts of places. It's just not enough to put the kid into custody, you understand?"

"Can we take him?" Jackson asked suddenly.

"What the what?" Oh Jesus—Ellery was so surprised his brain hurt. "Jackson, I hate to tell you this, but he's not a lot safer with us than he is on his own!"

Jackson shot him a disgusted look. "I've got an idea," he said quietly. "And a favor to call in. I just need permission to have custody of the kid."

Kryzynski looked at Ellery for permission, his blue eyes skeptical, and Ellery shrugged. Seriously, like he'd been able to stop Jackson from doing anything he set his mind to up to this point?

"I'll get the paperwork in order," Kryzynski said, pulling out his phone. "Let me make a few calls."

"Uh, Sean?" Ellery asked, pained. "Is there any way we can keep the units away from the front of the synagogue? I'm uh...." Oh Lord. He was trying to make a good impression, as embarrassing as that was.

Kryzynski tilted his head at Ellery. "You were *attending* the services?" he asked, bemused.

"Well, I was, but then the rabbi didn't show because he was talking to Jackson and Jackson was chasing the kid and—"

Kryzynski's dry chuckle was all Ellery needed at that point. "You ever think maybe, you want to go to church or temple or whatever, you shouldn't take you-know-who?"

Jackson looked at Ellery and nodded, although Ellery had the feeling he and Rabbi Watson had been having a pretty decent conversation.

"No," Ellery told him, hating him almost as much as Jackson did. "No, I don't think I should leave him home. I think if I left him home, it would get hit by a meteor or infested by snakes or something. The only way to keep him safe is to drag him by the ear and put him somewhere near a house of God."

"Unbelievable," Jackson muttered, and Kryzynski burst into guffaws.

But he also asked the units to move to the other side of the liquor store.

Before he did, Jackson walked up to where Anthony was working with a policeman to describe the man who'd offered him twenty dollars to put a tracker on Ellery's car. Ellery dogged after him, curious again to see him interact with the boy.

"I don't know," the kid whined. "He was... he was that guy's height."

Anthony pointed to Jackson, who said promptly, "Six one." The officer nodded and wrote it down. "Hair color?" Jackson prompted.

"I dunno. Tan? Not like yours, like, blond but brown underneath. Just not a lot of... brown. Or blond. Or...."

"Sandy brown," Jackson filled in for the cop. "Eyes?"

"Uh… wore sunglasses. The kind that get dark in the sun, right? And there's big windows at Smitty's…." His voice dropped. "Even if they're the kind with the bars."

"Was there anything interesting about his face?" Jackson asked. "Big nose? Crooked jaw? Bad skin?"

The kid frowned. "Like you—like you had zits when you were a kid, but they got better."

Jackson gave Ellery a quick glance then, almost embarrassed. "Old acne scars," he said to the officer, his voice not betraying that small burst of insecurity in the least. "Nose? Chin? Lips?"

"Like a Superman jaw," Anthony said promptly. "But his nose was crooked. Like yours. Like it had been broken in fights before. And…." The kid wrinkled his lip. "His forehead was really big. Like, so big you could put another face on it. Just saying."

Jackson half laughed and looked at the officer. "This enough?"

The officer shook his head and took Anthony through his paces, Jackson translating, giving him a human connection to the scary world of police procedure. By the time they finished, people were trickling out of the synagogue, and Jackson and Ellery got the signal from Kryzynski that they were free to go.

They loaded up into the Lexus, Anthony in back with the seat belt done, and Ellery said, "I give. Where to?"

"First off, through the drive-thru," Jackson muttered. "Someplace we can get something sweet." He raised his voice. "Food and dessert, Anthony?"

"Yeah? Please?"

"Then what?" Ellery was seriously at a loss. They couldn't care for a twelve-year-old kid—not at this juncture in their lives, and especially not if they were under surveillance and someone was trying to bug their car. Speaking of which— "And how did they know we'd be there?"

"You went there before," Jackson said, almost accusingly. "You seemed to know the rabbi."

Oh, he'd caught that. "I called them up," he confessed. "To make sure they were American Reform or Reconstructionist—you know. So they'd be cool with the…." Ellery's eyes darted to the back seat, where Anthony was listening, his brown eyes enormous. "The thing," Ellery finished, holding on to his dignity.

"The gay?" the kid asked—and again, Jackson's exact phrasing. "What's the big deal? Seriously?"

"There is none," Jackson said dryly. "But sometimes churches and temples and shit get hung up on it."

"Oh. You could still adopt me. I don't mind."

Jackson's eyes went comically wide. "Wow, kid—moving in a little fast. For all you know, that was the American Reform Cannibal Association and you're what's for dinner!"

The kid cackled, and then his voice dropped. "Was just a joke," he mumbled.

"Look, Anthony?" Jackson turned in the seat, and once again, Ellery was rendered a fly on the wall. "You're a great kid. Your foster parents are right—you could use a bath, but you and Smitty, you were friends. And he must have thought something good about you, because… just because. Anyway, me and him, we get shot at a lot. I mean, this summer my cat almost died because of what we do for a living. You're such a great kid, I don't want you to get shot."

"Was your cat okay?" the kid asked.

"Lost his back leg. And some asshole asked the vet to cut off his balls—"

"Not. Apologizing." Ellery scowled. God, how long could Jackson hold a grudge about that, anyway?

"But he's okay?" the kid asked again, suddenly concerned for a cat he'd never met.

"He's fine. He's sitting on the table as we speak, his face in the trough. Anyway, the cat barely got out with his life. We want something better for you."

"Where exactly is better for me?" Anthony asked, the vulnerability giving him an edge. "This is my third foster home—and the first one that didn't suck. You got a line on movie people who want me or something?"

"Like, people in the movies?"

"Yeah. Real people don't want grown-ups."

Jackson rolled his eyes. "You're going to be so disappointed when you realize how not grown up you are. But no. No movie people. I just have an idea. One that will keep you safe and out of the way until we get to the bottom of this, okay?"

"And the idea is…." Ellery looked at him sideways. It wasn't like Jackson to be evasive.

"Waiting for me to get a burner phone to initiate," Jackson told him. "Where were you when you called the rabbi?"

Ellery frowned. "Work, why?"

"Because. Somebody found out where we were going to be today and tried to use that opportunity to plant a bug on the car. Did you use your own phone?"

Oh. Oh Lord. "No. I used the one at work."

"So hopefully they don't have a tap on our cells, but who knows. So yes. Let me get a burner phone, give me a couple of hours to get this kid safe, and you and me have a plane ticket to SoCal to buy."

"And a client!" Ellery muttered. Shit. He'd almost forgotten!

"Well, I figured you'd be doing that while I was getting the kid safe."

Ugh. "Look," Ellery muttered. "Let's bring the kid to the office, see the client together, and then go do all the other stuff—"

"You don't trust me on my own?" Jackson demanded, stung.

"No, but that's not the point. The point is, the client actually needs you. In fact...." Ellery frowned. "In fact, I was going to book tickets to Southern California because of her case alone. This guy in the liquor store just makes me think I'm right. Did the hit look professional?"

"Yeah," Jackson said quietly. "It did."

Ellery grunted and they were silent as they came to a stop at the eternal light at Howe and Fair Oaks. For a moment Ellery was sorely tempted to go straight, because American River Drive and their home was that way, and even if it meant setting the urchin up in the spare room and buying him clothes, home was safe.

Home was *not* bugs on their car or dead liquor store owners or scared kids on the run or trips to Southern California to investigate a psychotic military officer who preyed on the vulnerable and unstable to create serial killers.

Which is where this kid—and Ellery's case back at the firm—were leading them.

Ellery could remember, clear as day, being in the back of an ambulance with Jackson, his body burning with fever, his newly restarted heart pumping threadily. He'd said, "Peace. We deserve some peace."

Two months of peace was not enough. Maybe for Jackson's heart, but not for Ellery's. A kid in their house—what could be more domestic than that? How easy would it be to just back off? Take the kid home, peace out of the investigation, stop being the people expected at a hinky crime scene or who got called when a defendant was not just innocent, but framed by forces beyond his or her control?

"You didn't tell me about her," Jackson said at last, as Ellery consciously went right and hoped the cat would forgive them.

"I told you I wanted you to hear her story."

"Well, yeah. I thought you were humoring me."

Ellery stopped a little short at the traffic on the bridge. "I'm sorry?"

Jackson threw a look over his shoulder at the kid, and Ellery couldn't see what his expression was, but Jackson didn't seem reassured. "You've been making a big deal about recovery," Jackson mumbled, not able to look at him. "Just... I don't know. Wasn't sure you were going to let me in on anything real."

Ellery's heart grew chilly. "Peace," he rasped. "You promised me peace."

"You think I don't want peace?" His voice sank—Ellery could hardly hear it, much less the urchin behind them. "But I get no peace if you think I'm weak."

For a whole half second, Ellery tried to hold on to his temper, because there was another human being in the car and he didn't want to parade his dirty laundry in front of a stranger, child or not.

Then his mother shut up in his head and the person he'd become since Jackson entered his life sat up and roared.

"*You are not weak!*"

Jackson stared at him, obviously stunned. "Ellery!" he hissed. "This is not—"

"You're not weak. You almost died. There's a difference. I need you to... to know that's not what's going on here." Ellery's stomach kicked up a notch, and he remembered Jackson's seduction that morning.

His shoulder had given out.

He'd hidden the shoulder, had pushed himself until he could run five miles, and hid how tired he was at the end of the day. Didn't talk about the nightmares—oh God, the fucking nightmares that had gone from one, maybe two a week when they'd met to a nightly, sweat-drenching terrifying occurrence.

He conceded to the little things—the time off work, the visit to temple, eating what Ellery put in front of him no matter how much he didn't want food—but the hard things, those were the elephant that could destroy the room.

"Whatever," Jackson said sourly. "Look, there's a McD's. Let's get Anthony anything the hell he wants plus cookies and a shake and then drop us off at the mall. I'll get a couple of burner phones."

Ellery negotiated with traffic, and Anthony spoke up behind them. "You almost died?" he asked, awe in his voice. "I thought it was the cat."

Jackson shrugged. "See, kid? We need to get you someplace… good. You're easy to take care of—I'm a frickin' nightmare."

Anthony laughed like he was supposed to, and Ellery wished fervently they were back at the synagogue. Which reminded him….

"What did Rabbi Watson say to you?"

"I don't know, never met him."

"You did too—you were talking to him right before you caught Anthony."

The blank silence on Jackson's side of the car was not reassuring. "That was the rabbi?"

"Yeah."

"He was sneaking a cigarette. Isn't that… I don't know. Unholy or something?"

"Only in California. What did he say?"

"Come to the Jewish side, they have cookies."

Anthony chortled, and Ellery tried not to smirk. "Seriously."

"No! I *am* being serious. He said I should come in and sit with you because there were cookies afterwards."

Ellery let out a frustrated breath and rolled down the window. "What am I ordering again?"

Anthony apparently wanted two of everything, including a giant shake, and Jackson wanted a cheeseburger. The end.

Ellery ordered him a double-cheese. And cookies.

And a salad for himself, because not even McDonald's could make lettuce fattening, right?

He dropped them off at the K Street Mall with a bag full of takeout trash and some reservations, but Jackson assured him they could walk to the firm on their own.

"I'm leaving the bug with you, okay?" Jackson tucked it in Ellery's coat pocket as it rested over the seat. "Make sure you bring it to Crystal. If she can't magic it, somebody she knows can."

"Yeah, got it." Ellery grabbed his hand as he was climbing out of the car. What the hell—the kid was apparently more enlightened than the rest of the world. "Look—you're not weak. I'll take care of the niceties, but I need you with this case. I'm not running the bad guys down alone."

A corner of Jackson's plush mouth lifted. "You're slow," he admitted.

"Yeah. I'll see you at the office."

Jackson squeezed his hand and winked and then opened the door for Anthony so they could load onto the sidewalk.

"Put the phones on my card," Ellery called, but he wasn't surprised when Jackson said "Fuck no!" and slammed the door.

A Little Wobbly

"YOU SAID a bad word!" Anthony's outrage seemed to completely overlook all the bad words either of them had employed since the moment Jackson spotted him on his hands and knees, trying to find a place to put the little electronic tracker or whatever on Ellery's car.

"I did." Jackson kept his eyes open in all directions as he started for the mall entrance, making sure Anthony was tight on his heels.

"But that guy's your boyfriend!"

Well, couldn't deny it. "He is."

"But he was trying to pay for your stuff!"

Jackson slowed his pace, more for Anthony than for himself. Hopefully. "I can pay for my own damned stuff!"

"But if that was his car, he's loaded! Jesus, mister—"

"Call me Jackson."

"Whatever. If you're too stupid to take something like that for free, I'm gonna call you dumbass."

Jackson turned around and lowered his shoulders so he and junior here could see eye to eye. "Look, kid—did I or did I not *bust you* for taking money from a guy for something that might have gotten you killed? Think this through. Guy offers you money, you go do his thing. You get *caught*. Guy goes to your friend and says, 'Tell me about this kid,' and your friend says, 'I didn't see no kid,' 'cause he's got your back. And what happens next?"

Anthony's face crumpled, and Jackson felt like shit. "He's dead."

"Yeah." Jackson's voice dropped, and he tried not to be too much of a dick. "Nothing's for free, Anthony. And Ellery knows how I feel about shit being for free, so he was… was reminding me of something."

"What?" His lower lip was wobbling, and he wasn't giving up. Jackson had to hand it to him—he was sort of a trouper.

"He was reminding me that he was there for me. Money I got, but someone to have my back is something I'm getting used to. He was reminding me he had my back. And I was reminding him that I could take care of myself."

"Why didn't you guys just say that? That was stupid."

"You ever gonna take money from someone for free again?" Jackson asked, and Anthony bit his lip and shook his head.

"No."

"Ellery's offering me something I've never had in my life. And I know he means it, and I know he can make it stick, but it's hard for me to take it. You get that?"

"Yeah." Anthony looked away. "I don't want to see another foster family if they aren't gonna want me."

"Yeah. How attached were you to this one?"

Anthony shrugged. "They were okay. But…."

Jackson let out a sigh. "You had a thing for the mom and the dad, the ones who would love you and take care of you and want you to come back more than they were glad you were leaving."

"Yeah." Anthony looked away. "Pipe dream, huh?"

"No." Jackson's chest suddenly ached for this kid. "Look. I got strings. I know people all over the city. I can't make promises because if I break this one it would really suck, but I can promise I'll try. When this all shakes out, I'll try to make sure you're in a place you love. And in the meantime, I'm going to set you up with someone out of this fucking city. Someone who knows how to love kids and how to take care of them. You'll only be there temporary, like, but it'll be like—"

"Like Disneyland," the kid said, a sad smile on his mouth. "Like… kids told me. They went. And it was perfect. And it was all made up, but for a little while they got to see what it would look like if the world was perfect."

"Yeah," Jackson said, heart hurting a little more. Part of him was sneering—it was more than he'd ever had as a child. But most of him was wishing this kid could live in Disneyland for his whole life. "Come on. I'm going to get us three phones and call my own personal cavalry. You ready?"

Anthony nodded, and Jackson went in to wrangle with the store guy about burner phones.

WHEN THEY came out, Ellery's new phone in his pocket, Anthony clutching his brightly colored phone case like it was pure gold, Jackson couldn't help but smile. The kid had put up a good front, but Jackson knew it was probably the most expensive thing he'd ever owned.

"This isn't for free," he'd cautioned. "I know it seems like it, but you're going to owe me some shit when I buy this for you. You understand?"

Anthony had looked at the phone with pure covetousness. "What's the price?" he'd rasped.

"I'm tracking it. I will know where you are. So when my friend comes here to get you, you're not really leaving my sight. And if my brother or his wife, Rhonda, or his two kids tell me you are being a royal pain in the ass, I shut off everything but 911 and my number, you hear me? Right now you've got a pay-by-the-month data plan, so you can play games and shit. One *whiff* of you being an asshole, that becomes a radioactive paperweight. Understand?"

He'd actually stroked the bright, clean glass with a grimy finger. "I understand."

"And one more thing."

Oh, that kid's eyes were big limpid pools of pure greed. "What?"

"You need to bathe as often as they tell you. Got it?"

He'd smiled, showing all his gunky teeth.

"And brush your teeth."

The kid nodded, and Jackson thought that was as good as it was going to get.

They left the mall, and Jackson pointed the kid toward Eighth and L Street and dialed his brother's number by heart.

"K, it's me."

"Jackson? You're okay?" Well, lots of times Jackson hadn't been.

Jackson grimaced. "Yeah, K—fine. No worries. I just need a favor."

Kaden's resonant "Hunh" practically vibrated the phone. "A favor?"

Well, yeah. Kaden was not, in the strictest sense, Jackson's brother. But his mother had taken Jackson in when Jackson had been a surly teenager—like Anthony, but without the kid's charm. Jackson, Kaden, Kaden's sweetheart, Rhonda, and Kaden's sister, Jade, had kept themselves safe in one of the shittiest neighborhoods in the city by sticking together. The day Kaden and Jade's mom, Toni, had passed away had been one of the darkest days of Jackson's life—and that included the three times he'd almost died since then.

But Kaden had known Jackson since the sixth grade. Everything Jackson had learned about not taking shit for free, he'd learned before he and Kaden had even spoken.

Jackson had once pilfered candy bars every day for a month, to pay Jade and Kaden back for being his friends. They'd made him stop before they told their mother, but through all the years after that, through his on-again, off-again with Jade, through Kaden and Rhonda's two kids and all the shit in between, Jackson had never asked for a damned thing.

Until now.

Jackson spilled the story as he and Anthony made their way down toward the courthouse on L and the law offices of Pfeist, Langdon, Harrelson, and Cooper, where Ellery practiced law and Jackson ran his ass off.

Well, they each had their strengths.

"Wait," Kaden commanded. "Go back."

"To which part?" Jackson kept his hand on Anthony's shoulder, and while it should have been oppressive, he was getting the vibe from Anthony that having someone rein him in like that was mostly a luxury.

"The part where you sat outside a church—"

"A synagogue."

"A place of God, you asshole. And you didn't go in. What? You're too good for God now? You moved into a fancy house with some rich lawyer and you're too goddamned good for God?"

Jackson gave a sudden tug on Anthony's shoulder, earning him an indignant glare. "Sorry, Anthony, my brother's being an asshole. No, Kaden, I'm not too goddamned good for God. And you're missing the point. The point is—"

"The point is, you thinking you're not good enough for God or the fancy rich lawyer, and the point is, you can kiss my wide black ass!"

"Your ass ain't wide," Jackson said staunchly. "And the point is, a kid tried to plant a bug on my car, and then his friend got shot. The kid's in trouble, Kaden—police won't help—"

"Because why?"

"Because they're not freaked-out and paranoid like we are." Kaden had been unjustly accused of killing a policeman that summer—the wounds were raw and wide. "But I'm calling you from a burner phone, because I think they got a spy or a bug at Ellery's office."

"You want me to take the kid?" Kaden sounded genuinely surprised.

"Could you?" Jackson asked, pained. "I was going to call AJ and have him run the boy up to you. He's been… restless." AJ was recovering from drug addiction—and a horrific experience that he and Jackson had shared in a way. Jackson had opened up half his old duplex as sort of a halfway recovery home for those who had been addicted or imprisoned, and AJ was one of the residents. Sad, fragile, and at loose ends in his life, Jackson had been able to get AJ a job waiting tables near the duplex, but he'd been keeping a weather eye out for the boy as well. A trip up to the hills of the Sierra Nevada would give him focus—he'd told Jackson his days off were the worst.

"I'll take him," Kaden said, lowering his voice kindly. "That room we've been saving for you will sleep him *and* AJ. I've got some work up here they can do."

Kaden had taken a shine to AJ that Christmas, and AJ, still smarting from being kicked out of the house when he'd come out, had talked wistfully of Kaden's family as well.

Jackson grunted. "Fine. That's fine. That'll work. It's not permanent—"

"You mad because they're taking your room?" Kaden wheedled, and Jackson had to take a deep breath.

"I've got a room. A half a room, but I got a room." Dammit. He'd given up the duplex to move in with Ellery, and that had been fine—more than fine. Waking up next to Ellery for the past months had been the safest he'd ever felt in his life.

But it was like the trip to the synagogue. It was a beautiful dream, being with this one person who loved him. He could warm himself by that dream and wake up in its bed every day and every night—but he wasn't sure if he could ever really inhabit that dream.

The spare room at Kaden's place had been his theoretical escape hatch. Not that he'd need one. But he had one. The light in front of them changed, and Jackson looked both ways before nudging Anthony to proceed. The kid went trustingly—Jackson had somehow become somebody who would look out for him, and Jackson had seen... he'd seen....

He closed his eyes against how the kid's friend had been killed and effectively tortured. So many awful things behind his eyes—he didn't need that as a prod.

"So it's okay if we give up your room and you can admit you're in a relationship like a grown man," Kaden prompted.

"Of course it is. I didn't really expect you to keep a real room for me in the first place," Jackson retorted. No. He hadn't. But he'd been almost tearful that Kaden had made sure he'd have one after Kaden and his family moved from Sacramento to the foothills.

"Jackson—you know we're always your family, right?"

Absurd question for a grown-assed man. "Course, K. I appreciate this. You're doing me a solid. I'll call AJ. I need to be off the phone before we get to the law firm. Expect them sometime this afternoon—and I owe you."

K grunted. "Jackson?"

"Yeah?"

"You want to pay me back?"

"Anything." K's family was Jackson's heart. Without K and Jade, he wouldn't have enough heart in him to even try to love Ellery.

"Next time that nice lawyer man takes you to church—"

"A synagogue—"

"I don't care if it's a mosque, a monastery, or a motherfucking cathedral. The next time that man wants to take you to a holy place and thank a higher power for you, *go with him*. And thank God personally, from me, that you have somebody who loves you like you deserve."

Augh! That nice man who'd been sneaking a cigarette—the *rabbi*—had tried to tell him something like this too. And Jackson had responded by setting up four units, complete with whirling lights, across the street.

"Couldn't I just help you clear your property?" Jackson asked plaintively.

"I'm gonna say no." Jackson recognized that tone—Kaden could be surprisingly stubborn.

"Fine. Yes. Whatever. I'll go to church."

He spotted a Starbucks as they were walking, empty because it was Saturday after ten, and he tugged on the kid again. No, he wasn't hungry, but he *did* need more coffee. He also needed another ten minutes because he didn't want to end up at the firm while he was still talking to Kaden.

"Good," Kaden said. "The more you talk to God on this side of the fence, the less likely you'll have to hop over to finish your business."

Jackson grunted. "You and Ellery worry too much."

"I'm fucking serious, Jackson. If I have to walk into that hospital one more goddamned time to see you looking like death, I swear to God it will kill me."

Jackson took a deep breath. Yeah. Fine. Good reason. "Look—all the more reason to get the kid away from us until we figure this out."

"I hear you. I'll tell Rhonda to be ready for him. Does he have clothes?"

"Hold on." Jackson caught Anthony's eyes—the kid was looking at the big buildings in the legal district like he'd never seen anything like it. Apparently he'd spent most of his life in the suburbs. "Anthony, you got anything at your foster home you really need?"

Anthony bit his lip, stricken, and shook his head. "I got...." He grimaced. "I got a Lego set for Christmas last year. I got to bring it to this foster home—but I don't need it." Shrug. "I mean, it's one toy, right?"

Jackson's heart cracked a little. The first Christmas he'd known Kaden, Kaden had gotten two toy action figures. He and Kaden had played with those things for hours, and every time he had to go back to his own shitty apartment with whomever or whatever his mother had dragged in for the night, he'd set those little guys on Kaden's shelf with a reverence other people saved for church. For Christmas the next year, Kaden had humbly presented him with one of the guys, carefully wrapped, and his mom had given Jackson a second one, brand-new. Jackson still kept them, in his underwear drawer. Not even Ellery knew about them.

"We'll make sure you have some stuff of your own," Jackson promised. "Hold still—let me see your tag." He made note of the T-shirt size, which was about two sizes too big, and of the pants size, which was the same number too small. "Okay."

"Jackson, do I need to be on the phone for this? I have to go tell Rhonda we've got guests coming and to watch out for strangers."

"You know AJ—if you call him a stranger, you'll break his heart."

Kaden grunted. "If I could get that kid to move up here, I would. Send him up. Bring another one. I don't care. It's not like I get more than ten minutes in the john as it is."

"Thanks, K."

"Go to church, asshole."

"Whatever."

Jackson hung up and looked at Anthony while shaking his head. "Kid, you'd better grow up to be a stellar human being, you know that?"

Anthony batted thick-lashed eyes at him. "I'll be lucky if I'm not dead on the streets at eighteen and a half. You know *that*, right?"

Damn. Grim statistics—but most foster kids knew their own odds. "You know if you live through the next week those odds just went up considerably," he said truthfully. "I'm not sure where you'll end up or how you'll end up, but if there's one thing I've got faith in, it's the people you're about to meet. Now let's go in and get warm. I've got one more phone call to make."

AJ showed up fifteen minutes later, driving a crappy loaner-mobile that Jackson's old neighbor, Mike, had refurbished for the people living in the other half of the duplex. Right now AJ was living there with four other kids his age—those kids fresh out of jail. They could use the car to get jobs, to go to the store as long as it was for the household, and to pick each other up if they worked too late for public transportation.

Or if Jackson called in a rare favor, because every kid living in that house owed Jackson big in one way or another, and mostly Jackson's one caveat had been simply that they took the free rent and got their shit together.

AJ pulled up next to the meter in front of the Starbucks and waved to Jackson and Anthony through the window. In his early twenties, with a slight build, skin cool tawny-brown, and reddish-brown hair he twisted into tight corkscrews around his head, AJ had the look of someone who could fade easily into a sunset or a cold dawn. He'd been coming down from a weeklong heroin high when Jackson met him, and after enduring detox, he'd been making rehab stick for the last three months.

But it hadn't been easy, and keeping him busy during his days off had become a group project. Mike and Kaden's sister, who lived in the other half of the duplex, made it a point to enlist him in gardening or home repair or even just walking their German shepherd, Albert. Ellery often had him run errands for the firm.

Jackson—recovering physically himself—mostly just asked him if he wanted to come over and play video games and get out of the house.

AJ had three-quarters of a college education and a quiet understanding of politics and literature that his housemates, ex-drug dealers, simply lacked.

And AJ was gay—his housemates knew about it and didn't judge but Jackson knew that sometimes the quiet, painfully shy AJ came over just so he could talk freely about TV crushes and movies he watched on his phone, in his room, where the other guys couldn't see and give him shit.

Right now he hit the horn, stood partially out of the door, and waved. Jackson made sure Anthony was done with his hot chocolate and pulled him outside.

"Hop in, kid. Now remember—you made promises. Do what you're told. Be respectful of the adults around you. I swear to you, these guys will treat you right, you understand?"

Anthony shrugged, looking like he probably needed a nap.

"And don't sleep yet. AJ has to take you shopping on the way up the hill, okay?"

Anthony's eyes brightened. "Can I get shoes?" he asked plaintively, showing tennis shoes that were blown out at the toes. "It's not the foster folks' fault—my feet grew two sizes in, like, a month."

Jackson tousled his hair. "Kids do that. Don't worry—stick with AJ. He'll treat you right."

Anthony got into the front and belted up, smiling shyly at AJ as Jackson called him around to the sidewalk.

AJ waved, a small smile on his face. "Sweet kid. What's the story?"

"The story is, someone paid him to do something mildly illegal to Ellery's car and then killed his friend when he got busted."

AJ recoiled. "Sweet kid with a price on his head," he deduced. "I hear you. What's the plan?"

"The plan is, you take him to Kaden and Rhonda's, with a stop in Rocklin for clothes at Target or Walmart, and…." Jackson bit his lip. "Toys. Legos. Maybe even something else he likes. Here." Jackson pulled out his wallet and dished out three large. He'd gotten the money at the mall kiosk, and he hated having that much cash on him, but he didn't want AJ easy to track either. "Don't spend it all on him at once—keep some back for food and expenses, especially if you think you're being followed. Contact me on the burner number when you get there, and have K do the same. We good?"

AJ nodded, eyes big. "I'll take good care of him, Jackson. Don't worry."

"Well, take care of you too, okay? We're watching out for both of you here."

And there—right there—was the reason AJ got the car and the special place at dinner and Jackson's whole family worried about him.

He smiled, the glow of it a cool and soothing balm on the painful friction of every damned thing in the world. "Will do. Thanks, Jackson. I'll call you when I get there. Deal?"

Jackson shook his hand and brought him in for the chest bump. "Deal."

He swallowed, hoping this plan would work, and waved them on their way. As they pulled out, his phone rang in his pocket—his actual phone, the one that flashed a picture of Ellery sleeping as it rang.

"On my way," he said tersely, making his way back into the coffee shop. He had a to-go order waiting. As he spoke he winked at the barista and added an extra tip to the jar. "I'll tell you about it later."

"Good—because our client is starting to freak out. She seems to think I'm scary."

Jackson laughed maliciously. "Your patented charm not working?" He emerged from the coffee shop and, balancing the tray in one hand, began his stride through the streets like he could knock obstacles away with his shoulders alone.

"Fuck off. Get your ass in here, I need you."

"It's not usually my ass you need, Counselor. But the other way is good too."

"It's a good thing you're cute," Ellery growled, and Jackson grinned. "Do you still have An—"

"Not on this phone," Jackson insisted. "And not at the office either."

"Can we talk in bed?" Ellery asked sweetly. "Is the house bugged too?"

Jackson's blood ran a little cold.

And then it ran a lot hot.

"If the house is bugged, you and me are going to have so much sex you won't be able to walk for a month. We're having sex until the floor collapses. We're having sex until the neighbors call the cops, and then we're having sex in *front* of the cops. I swear to Christ, if these assholes bugged our fucking home, I am going to make them regret it to the depths of their fucking *balls*."

"Our home?" Ellery said, of course picking up on the one thing Jackson hadn't meant to say. "It's our home now, right? Not just my house?"

"I swear to God, Ellery—"

"Just get here," Ellery said crisply, like he hadn't completely mooned over Jackson's slip of the tongue.

"Gimme five. I'm gonna talk to Crystal before I get to your office."

"Understood."

Ellery hung up, and Jackson had a moment to adjust to that thing Ellery was mooning over. *Our home.* Okay. So, fine. Jackson's duplex had gotten shot up in August and Ellery had just moved him in—and then kept him. Jackson had harbored delusions that he'd move back to his duplex in November, but then.

November.

November hadn't just been a physical and emotional train wreck. It had been the physical and emotional train wreck Jackson had been putting off his entire life.

And Ellery had been there to witness it.

And had been there to pick up the pieces.

Jackson had never, in his entire life, known a person like that existed for him. Kaden and Jade had been there—no doubt. But he'd never let them see him raw. They still didn't know all the things November had been to him.

But Ellery did.

It had to be *their* home. Because Jackson literally had no place else to go, either in his person or in his heart.

Scary Monsters, Running Fish

JACKSON ARRIVED none too soon. Ellery really thought Janie Isaacson was going to bolt if she had to wait one more minute.

"Sorry I'm late," Jackson apologized. He held a tray of travel cups in one hand. "Here, Janie?"

The young woman—twenty-five—who had been nervously shredding her tissue as she waited in their shared office nodded. "Yessir. Are you the PI?"

Jackson smiled, tiny dimples in the corners of his mouth appearing, and Ellery tried to tell his traitorous libido to tone it down a little. They were at work, and this poor kid didn't need Ellery's adolescent fawning.

"I am. So sorry I'm late. But I did bring drinks." He set a Venti chai tea in front of Ellery without looking and carried a cup the same size to the client. "Hot chocolate," he said, inclining his head. "I had a meet with someone at the coffee place, and I got a flat of them."

"Thank you," she said quietly, taking a tentative sip. As soon as it hit her tongue, though, Ellery watched her shoulders relax.

Yeah, Jackson earned his keep as PI by just talking to people sometimes.

"Not a problem. Now Mr. Cramer here says you've got a very interesting story to tell. I'm the one who's going to be digging up the evidence to back up the story, so you need to tell me everything, okay?"

Janie nodded and cradled the chocolate in hands covered with bright red fingerless gloves. The girl wore her hair in a shiny blonde bob with mulberry streaks along the top of it, and her clothes were quirky—a plain black skirt with a retro crocheted tabard over it. This girl dressed and carried herself as though most days she was fearless.

But not today.

"Okay," she rasped, taking another sip. "It's… it's so strange. I mean… one minute my day was pretty normal, right? I'm… I *was* a nanny for this nice couple who live in the forties—you know, the Fabulous Forties?"

They both nodded. The Fabulous Forties was a ten-block stretch of downtown that housed the most affluent of the city dwellers, and the houses were pretty impressive.

"Anyway, so I drop the kids off at a little private school on H Street—"

"I know the one," Jackson said, not surprising Ellery in the least. "Has the little rainbow board on the front? It's by a church—"

"But not affiliated with it," the girl hastened to explain. "It's... you know. Independent." She flushed and sipped her chocolate. "Just... Jasmine and Forrest—those are the kids I nanny for. Their parents are really... not religious. So when I got hired, they, you know. Wanted to make sure I wasn't, like, a nutjob or anything." She smiled briefly. "They're just super nice." Her face fell. "It's just... it's important to know that they're super nice. So you know why I did what I did."

Ellery swallowed, because here was the hard part.

"What did you do?" Jackson asked kindly.

"Well, see, I didn't do anything. Really. I dropped Jasmine and Forrest off at preschool, and they kissed me and hugged me and ran inside and I waved—like I do. Then I pulled out of the school and turned right—I guess west, down J, and I was slowing to a stop at the sign. There was a woman and her two kids crossing the street, so I'm, like, way careful, right? Anyway, this...."

She shook her head, gesturing madly, her red hands a blur.

"This big blue fuckin', I mean frickin', government car comes out of frickin' nowhere. It whips around me and...." Her voice started to break. "And *hits* the mom. He was going so fast, you know? He probably didn't realize that's why I slowed down. She threw the kids in front of her, but she's down, and I screech to a halt and put the car in park, and I'm on the phone with the cops and running to check on her and keep the kids out of the road—" She paused and nodded, like this was really important. "I had to keep the kids out of the road. You get it, right, Mr. Rivers? I'm a nanny. It's like... like having kids in the middle of the road just fuckin' terrifies me."

"We get it," Jackson said gently, touching her hand. "You're a good person. You can't just let bad things happen to people when you're a good person."

She shook her head, and her eyes spilled over, but she kept telling her story.

"So I'm in the middle of the road, and this woman looks... broken. Like... like not doing too good, and the kids are freaking out and I'm on the phone, and this guy gets out of this car. He's wearing a uniform, right? I got no idea what the stuff means on it—I'm sorry. But he gets out of the car and tells me... well, he tells me she's dead and to stop bawling. And then... then he squats down and looks me in the eyes. And says, 'You know, you're a reckless driver. It would be a shame if your little ones got hurt because somebody drove into them like you drove into this woman.'"

Jackson gasped, just like Ellery had, and poor Janie nodded.

"I didn't hit her," she moaned. "I swear I didn't. But while I was squatting there, he walked up to the minivan—you know, I got the minivan 'cause I'm driving the kids? And he kicked in the bumper. And I'm still on the phone, mind you, but me and the kids—we just scream. And we're still screaming when he walks back by us and gets in his big blue car and drives away."

She closed her eyes and wrung her hands, her pretty half gloves stretching out. "I… the cops got there and the woman was taken away in an ambulance and somebody got her kids and they asked me what happened…." She took a big gulp of air. "And I said I did it. And they arrested me. And I lost my job and the kids' parents are suing me for damage to their car and my mom had to hire this guy to get me out on bail… and it's worth it. I'd totally do my time if the kids would just be okay, but he… he just drove away. And he's out there. And he must have seen me with Forrest and Jasmine, and I can't let him… I can't let him…."

The girl broke into sobs, and Jackson rubbed her back, letting her cry.

"Forensics," he said after she'd calmed down. "Ellery, we need a crash specialist to look at the car."

Ellery nodded. "I emailed yesterday, but I didn't get a response." Well, they were frequently backed up.

"Witnesses. Janie, who was there to take the kids to their classes? Somebody must have seen you drive away."

Janie paused for breath and mumbled a name. Ellery shoved a yellow pad of paper at her, and Jackson took it from him and pushed it more gently. "Here, sweetheart. We need the spelling here. Evidence. We're looking for evidence."

"But what if he threatens them too?" she asked, gulping for air.

Jackson met Ellery's eyes and frowned. "Okay—here's the thing. People think the bad guys know it all, right?"

She nodded miserably, and he patted her hand.

"Sometimes they do—I had a bad guy get my phone, and bad shit happened."

She recoiled, and Ellery fought the temptation to smack him on the back of the head.

"But sometimes they don't. In this case I don't think he did. He probably saw you coming out of the preschool, so he knows you dropped kids off. But if he really knew you, he'd know they weren't yours. If he *really* knew you and wanted to scare you, he would have used their names. Now, maybe he got the minivan license plate number—that's a concern. So we're going to have a talk with your employers—maybe, if they know you didn't do it, they won't be so quick to throw you under the bus, but that's not the point. The point is, they can up security, maybe get out of town for a little while, because what happened, that's so not right. Now we can subpoena medical records and see what her injuries would be—and I've got a connection at the highway patrol. See, the thing is, he must have been going pretty fast if he just zoomed past the preschool and whipped around you—and you *couldn't* have been going that fast, and we know this because there's no room to accelerate. So all your witness has to do is say you *weren't* driving like a bat out of hell, and we've already got reasonable doubt, and keeping you out of jail is key."

Ellery had thought of this already—in fact, he'd written some of it down. But Jackson had two or three things on his checklist that Ellery didn't, and that was impressive. But even more important, Jackson had managed to calm down the client, to instill some faith so she trusted them. If she trusted them, she'd tell them things she might have forgotten she knew.

"So I know you're afraid of this guy," Jackson continued. "And you should be. But the quicker we find out who he is and prove you didn't do it, the quicker he'll have more to worry about than harassing you or following through on that threat, you understand?"

Janie nodded, tears flowing, but she wasn't sobbing yet. Ellery had noted rather clinically that sometimes women cried when they were scared but that it seldom incapacitated them. One of his guiltiest clients once wiped out an entire box of Kleenex while telling the story of how she'd killed her crime-boss husband because he'd threatened to molest her daughter. The murder had been perfectly executed, and Ellery had actually gotten the woman off, and she'd been allowed to keep her husband's inheritance as well. Smart, tough, fearless—tears were a sign of nothing but an emotional trigger system that didn't mesh well with mascara.

"Do you remember anything about him—anything at all? You said he had a military uniform on—was it formal or informal?"

"It was... I think it was formal," she said. "It wasn't camouflage or anything. It was all dark blue."

"Navy," Jackson said with a faint smile. "That's great—that helps immediately. So, he was wearing a jacket with bright stuff on his sleeves, right? Stripes? How many? One? Two?"

"Three, at least three," Janie said, running her own fingertip around her wrist as though she was imagining things. "And silver—he had silver spangly things on his shoulders."

Ellery made a sound. He recognized the uniform—he even recognized the rank.

And he knew somebody with that rank. Somebody who had a very specific interest in Jackson and Ellery. It was the reason he'd needed Jackson here in the first place.

"Was he really tall?" Ellery asked thoughtfully, and she must have grown used to him because she didn't startle.

Janie bit her lip. "Yeah. He had like… like that silver hair—the kind that looks like spray paint."

Jackson glanced at him sharply. "You know this guy?"

Ellery nodded but didn't say anything. Jackson gave him a level look and then turned his attention back to Janie. "Okay. This gives him a few more resources—but none that he can tap without setting off alarms. When's your arraignment?"

"Wednesday," she said hesitantly. "I got out on bail this morning." She pulled another Kleenex. "This is gonna fucking kill my mom, you guys. She was so proud of me. I mean, I was going to get my degree this year, and the Evanders would have made good references. Now I'm just so damned scared for *everybody*."

Jackson nodded, biting his lip in thought. "We're going to do our best," he said quietly. "We want two things. One is to prove you're innocent, and the other is to make the guy who did it concentrate on something else besides you. So I'm going to start collecting evidence right now. Who's got your car?"

"The Evanders," she said, voice dipping sadly. "I managed to call them while we were waiting for the ambulance. They were there when the police arrested me." This time her voice *did* break. "The damned disappointment on Susie Evander's face…."

Jackson patted her back for a moment. "Okay, Janie. Do you want to go to the ladies' washroom and clean up?"

Janie shook her head, miserable, and Jackson grimaced. "Well then, how about you give Mr. Cramer and me a chance to talk about you where you can't hear."

She startled and let a small smile escape. "I'd love to go to the ladies' room and clean up," she said dutifully.

"Awesome." Jackson stood as she did. "Now there's coffee and vastly inferior hot chocolate in the little station by the hallway, and I think there's cookies in the cupboard underneath if you're interested. Ellery and I need about ten minutes, okay?"

Janie nodded and made her exit, and Jackson turned to Ellery so fast Ellery had to take a step back.

"What gives?" Jackson asked, all business.

"Do you remember when I told you we met with a Navy douchebag stationed out by Las Vegas in November?"

Jackson had been missing when Ellery and Jade had held that meeting. Ellery would never know how he held himself together during his confrontation with Commander Karl Lacey, the man in charge of personnel departments that Ellery had never heard of, with names like Personnel Behavior Modification.

Somehow Ellery and Jade had done it, and the man had flown back to his hole in the desert pissed off enough to pull some of Ellery's mother's corporate contracts. Ellery's mother had shaken off the inconvenience while hardly ruffling her coif, but she *had* warned Ellery to make sure Jackson was good and healthy before they went fishing in Lacey's pond.

Apparently Lacey was in town to do some fishing of his own.

"I remember," Jackson said, nodding. "He trained Owens, and possibly a few other scumbags—and possibly on purpose." He swallowed, his eyes going flat and grim. "We've been waiting for this."

Ellery nodded. "Yeah. I mean, if it was just Janie's story, I'd go looking into Navy personnel. But what are the odds this guy is in town the same weekend someone tries to slip a bug on our car—"

"And kills a witness."

Oh yeah. Couldn't forget that. "And kills a witness."

Jackson scrubbed his face with his hands for a moment, squeezing his eyes shut. "This is bad. So bad. I mean, it's *great* for you and me and the investigation, but it's really not so great for…." He trailed off, and Ellery shuddered. They couldn't even say the boy's name.

"No," Ellery agreed. "And it's also not so wonderful for…." They both looked at the vacant spot at the cheap Formica table where Janie had sat.

The office itself was comfortable, modern, and pretty posh. Ellery had thrown a dark blue throw rug over the cream carpeting to add some gravitas to the pale walls, and his own desk was solid darkly stained oak.

There was a comfortable client chair in front of it—he'd been prepared to make Janie Isaacson as at ease in his presence as possible.

Janie had taken two steps into the room and settled down at Jackson's Formica table, which told Ellery a lot, actually.

It told him that her mother had probably cashed in her retirement to get Janie out of jail. It told him that Janie was uncomfortable in luxury and didn't like to take advantage of things.

And it told him that Janie was honest—the kind of honest that's used to getting the short end of the stick because it didn't complain a whole lot.

Ellery's first meeting with the girl had been the day before, when he'd posted her bail. Watching her make herself comfortable in Jackson's part of the room made him fiercely protective of her as well.

"Shit," Jackson muttered. "Okay, first things first. We get her off on general evidence. If I can get pictures and get Mac to take a look at the minivan before it's fixed—"

"I can't believe the police didn't impound it," Ellery muttered.

"Why would they?" Jackson asked bitterly. "She confessed. But that's first on my list. Second is going to interview the people at the preschool. You need to get me that list while I'm in transit. Third is interviewing the first responders—you get me those names too. I want so much evidence that points anywhere but her that nobody asks who actually did it until she's off."

Ellery nodded. "And then?"

"Then we nail him to the wall."

They paused for a moment, eyeball to eyeball. "You know," Ellery said into the tense silence that followed. "You know where this is going to have to go."

They both shuddered, remembering a tidy little garage with a bunch of very dangerous people living in a protective nest.

Jackson had liked those people—had, in fact, intuited more about them than Ellery could ever prove. But the odds were good that one of those people had been affected by the things Karl Lacey was doing in his little forbidden branch of the government, and Jackson and Ellery were going to have to ask him about that.

Or maybe Jackson would.

Because they didn't seem to like Ellery all that much.

"We'll reserve those plane tickets when we get there," Jackson said, nodding. Then he gave a little lopsided smile and took a step back. "Wish me luck, Counselor—"

Ellery wasn't letting him get away with that. He took a step forward and put his hands on Jackson's shoulders, whirling him around until *he* was the one with his back against the wall.

"I want a fucking kiss goodbye," Ellery murmured throatily. "There's no running out of this office with a little wave—not after this fall."

A corner of Jackson's mouth twitched up, and Ellery took that as yes. He pushed up against Jackson until their bodies pressed together, making the kiss as intimate in their office as he would at home.

He was making a point.

Jackson gasped, mouth open, and Ellery took advantage and pushed in some more, until Jackson groaned, wrapped his arms around Ellery's shoulders, and plundered back. He finished, and Ellery sighed and rested his forehead against Jackson's.

"Contact me," he said, remembering the last time they'd done this in November, when Jackson had taken off on a tail and had just... just kept going. Had followed a lead down a rabbit hole and practically disappeared, both in body and soul. "Promise."

"Sure—I do tha—"

"The last time you didn't." The throbbing in Ellery's voice told them both how loath he was to let Jackson go.

Jackson sighed. "I know. I promise. I'll text as I go."

"Take the Lexus—"

"Crap!"

He hadn't gotten a car yet. Neither of them had said anything, but Jackson had been home on sick leave and Ellery had been happy like that. Jackson had gone through three cars in a matter of months. Ellery's family could absorb the expense—his mother had asked him three times in the last month what kind of car Jackson wanted to replace the old one—but Ellery just needed some time to absorb the shock.

"We can get a car tomorrow," Jackson said firmly.

Ellery just shook his head. "Take the Lexus. I'll Lyft home. I don't give a crap about the car. And I know this is your job and you've done it for years. Just... just don't go anywhere dangerous alone."

He expected a pained grimace, an insistence on being able to take care of himself—any of the things that had colored these exchanges before November.

What he got was a grin and a wink. "Counselor, who says your bed isn't dangerous?"

Great. This. "Yeah, but you're never fucking alone."

Jackson chortled and slid away. "I'd better not be." He pecked Ellery quickly on the cheek and opened the door. "Keys?"

"Yeah." Ellery handed them over without a qualm. He loved that car—babied it, cherished it, got it a wax job and an oil change every 3,000 miles. Had even replaced the engine in August when it got shot through—along with Jackson.

But it was sturdy and it performed, and better the car than Jackson, even though Jackson left little rolled-up receipts and fast-food wrappers in the back—an obsessive habit Ellery hadn't had the heart to break.

He'd had so few things that were his in his life. That habit, the duplex he'd been living in when they met, a battered car, and a battered three-legged tomcat.

And Ellery.

The car had been destroyed in their first week and his half of the duplex shot up and then donated to young people getting their life back together. The tomcat was currently living in their house and had adopted Ellery, making Jackson not sole owner anymore.

Jackson had his strange, obsessive habit and Ellery, and Ellery couldn't be with him when he went out on a run.

"See you tonight, at seven—"

"But what if something—"

"Tonight. At seven." Ellery's voice hardened. "It's our day off."

Jackson grimaced. "I'll see what I can do."

Which wasn't a promise, but Ellery had to take it as he disappeared out the door. By the time Janie got back, munching dispiritedly on a cookie, Ellery had already contacted a dealership online and was well on the way to finishing the paperwork for an Infiniti QX. He contemplated getting Jackson another CR-V, but something about that car spelled bad luck—Jackson had already gone through two of them.

No, the thought of asking Jackson had never even entered his mind. If Jackson still had his way, he'd be riding around in his old Toyota, bullet holes and all.

"Did Mr. Rivers go already?"

Ellery nodded. "First he's going to try to get the minivan from your employers—a man's shoe leaves a very different impact than hitting a person—that's the first thing. Then, if you don't mind, I'm going to take down those names—the teachers who were there when you pulled away."

"You're sure they'll be okay?" she asked, sounding horrified.

Ellery wished Jackson were there; he could tell the truth and not sound like a dick. "Look, even if the suspect tries to warn them off—they'll at least get a warning, and it's up to them. Right now we just need to ask if they're willing to do the right thing."

Janie nodded, and for a moment he thought she was going to cry again. But he'd been right in his first assessment of her—tougher than she looked. "Okay. You're right. This guy—he's official. He just can't swoop around killing people left and right. It makes sense that he'd try to warn them off if he was really worried. Thank you, Mr. Cramer."

She went to work, pulling contacts out of her phone and writing them down, and Crystal stuck her head in the door.

"Ellery?"

Her voice wobbled a little, but then Crystal was frequently off center. The firm's technology guru, she was a genius with pretty much any computer system and, in Jackson's words, witchy as hell.

She looked perfectly normal—brown hair, shoulder length, wispy and flyaway, and a rather piquant little face with eyes hidden behind glasses. She wore long-sleeved shirts year-round to hide the old track marks that Ellery increasingly believed were what happened when someone who was not quite of this world was forced to live in some of its ugliest parts.

"Hey, Crystal. Jackson said he was stopping by your office. I still feel bad that you're here on a Saturday."

She shrugged. "Extra work, extra hours. I need an assistant. But Jackson gave me the thing—" She shot an anxious look at Janie, and Ellery stood up so he could have a word with Crystal outside his office.

"Yeah?" he asked when the door had shut behind them and they were in the cream-carpeted, white-walled open space that made up the offices of Pfeist, Langdon, Harrelson, and Cooper.

"Oh, it was definitely a bug," she said, not even pretending like it had been a challenge. "Not even a tracker—wired for sound. In fact, I think it's military issue. I called up a couple of friends, and they sent me specs on some of the more recent techware. This isn't it, by the way. I'd say about five years out-of-date, which means that somebody's fighting for funding, which sounds even more like military issue if you ask me."

Ellery could feel his eyebrows doing the jumping thing that tended to frighten people.

"Uh, Army or Navy?" he asked, wondering if there'd be little insignia impressed on what had been a really tiny surface.

Crystal rolled her eyes. "Like I would know! It's military intelligence issue, but other than that, I've got no idea."

Ellery swallowed, remembering his and Jackson's kiss—and how somebody would know they would be at a synagogue on their day off. "Is there… do you have any way to see if there's one of those in other places? Like… uh, my office? My work phone? Uh, my… our…." He couldn't say it. Jackson had snarled about having all the fucking sex in the house if there was a bug there, but he couldn't even think about it.

The things Jackson had told him, the personal, painful, haunting things that had nothing to do with sex and everything to do with the two of them together echoed under the roof of *their* home, and Ellery shuddered to think of those things belonging to somebody else.

"Your house?" Crystal asked, eyes widening. "I can get something by tomorrow morning. Why would somebody bug your house?"

Ellery shook his head and put his finger to his lips, and Crystal scowled.

"I may never sleep again," she said definitively. "I'll be back tomorrow with a bug detector—can you be here too?"

"Absolutely." After he and Jackson spent the night at a hotel. Or on a plane. Or in a cave. "We can meet here, you show us how to use it, and we'll check out our house." He shuddered. "And I'm not sure what I'll do if there's one in the house."

"Throw up," Crystal said seriously, her eyes big. "I'd definitely throw up." She swallowed and shuddered. "Why is someone bugging you, Ellery? Is this related to the shit that went down in November?"

Ellery was wondering if they could write a song about November. Something dreary and dramatic and frightening. "Possibly." He bit his lip, and then he and Crystal had the same thought at the same time.

"But why now?" she said.

Why would Commander Karl Lacey of whatever bullshit division he'd created out of thin air come to Sacramento now?

"That's an excellent question. I think I should answer that question. I think that might be really goddamned important." Ellery scowled, trying to work himself up for what he had to do next.

"Who can help answer that question?"

Goddammit. "The DA's office." Godfuckingdammit. "And they're still pretty pissed at me and Jackson for November."

Fish vs. the Potted Plant

OOH—JACKSON HAD forgotten how nicely Ellery's car drove. It was like having a two-ton piece of body armor that moved with you when you breathed.

He followed the GPS—which Ellery had programmed as a male's voice with an Australian accent, a thing that tickled Jackson to no end—and found the little house about six blocks from the intersection where Janie had been arrested.

It was cute—a lot of the houses in this section of town were cute. A converted Victorian, it stood a narrow two stories of purple-painted, white-trimmed, turreted charm. The yard was raised—as were many of them—by concrete planters that brought the front walk to the level of the porch. The driveway stayed level with the street, so the raised planters formed a concrete wall about waist high, decorated with big vases filled with bright seasonal flowers.

The guy must have spent a fortune on gardeners, but that's not what Jackson noticed.

A silver Dodge Caravan sat in the driveway, the front bumper buckled downward and falling off the car.

Jackson pulled up behind the Caravan, blocking it in on purpose, and pulled out his phone.

"Mack?"

"Jackson? I've got an insanely hot man next to me, and that hasn't happened since you. Could you maybe give me a break here?"

Jackson chuckled. William McPherson was an old hookup from days gone by. He worked highway patrol, and after Jackson had left the force in a cloud of suspicion and blood, Mack remained one of the few people in law enforcement he could trust.

"You get so much action. I'm not even going to comment on that." Mack wasn't a looker. Early forties, bad childhood nutrition, and the same acne that had haunted Jackson into his early twenties, there was still something decent about Mack. He looked like a real human being, and when he smiled warmly and made one of those little courtly gestures—like a hand in the small of the back or a touch on the shoulder—there was something genuinely appealing about him.

"Then what are you calling for?" He still sounded surly, but judging from the bed creaking and the rustling near the phone, Jackson thought he might be putting on a T-shirt, and that was a start.

"There was a hit-and-run in the Fab Forties yesterday. Did you catch it?"

Mack grunted. "No. That was Spooner. Ty Spooner. Said it was a lock—the girl confessed, he arrested her, all good. Why?"

Jackson got out of the car, closing the door as quietly as he could. Nobody seemed to be stirring. There was plenty of room on the concrete driveway, so he suspected the family was out. He put the phone on speaker and began to take pictures of the front bumper, sending them to Mack as he did.

"What do you think?"

Mack grunted. "I think Ty Spooner is a fucking idiot. That bumper didn't hit anybody."

"That's what I'm fuckin' saying." Jackson felt a surge of relief. "Look—the poor kid was terrified. Said a guy in a uniform got out of the car, threatened the kids she'd just dropped off, and told her to confess."

"Oh Jesus. What kind of uniform?"

"Dress blues. Three stripes. Silver oak leaves at the shoulders."

"Navy? There was a Navy commander in Sacramento? What the fuck?"

Jackson so didn't want to involve Mack in that part. "We have an idea," he said reluctantly. "But mostly we just want to get the girl off. She's a good kid, Mack. If we can make a case saying she didn't do it without involving the actual perp—"

"But Jackson! That guy deserves to have charges brought up! I know you're working for a defense attorney, but usually you think bigger than this!"

Augh! Jackson really treasured Mack's good opinion. Their hookup days were long gone, but he was one of the few people Jackson called a steady friend over the last nine years.

"Can we talk when you get here?" he asked, reluctant to talk on the phone.

"What makes you think I'm coming to check it out?" Mack countered, all suspicion.

"I can hear you getting dressed. I'll send you the address—but hurry. The owners, the people with the kids, are out, and it's just me, standing on these nice people's yard, looking like an asshole."

"That's you pretty much every day, you know that, right?"

"Fuck you." In the background, Jackson heard water running. "ETA?"

"Twenty minutes. Don't let the car go anywhere."

Jackson looked at the placement of the Lexus—cattywampus, directly behind the minivan, in case they tried to sneak by on the one-and-three-quarter-lane driveway.

"Way ahead of you," he said, feeling cocky for the first time in forever. "See you soon."

He continued to take pictures, keeping an eye on his surroundings. Somebody lived here. There was enough room in the driveway for another car, so either the family was coming back from somewhere, or only one parent had left and everybody else was in the house. Jackson wasn't going to risk his biggest piece of evidence disappearing.

He wasn't happy, but he wasn't surprised when, ten minutes after he got off the phone with Mack, a cream-colored Volvo sedan pulled up the driveway, honking impatiently when it became clear Jackson was parked like an asshole.

Jackson nodded to the driver of the car dispassionately and gestured for him to walk over to where Jackson stood, leaning against the Lexus.

"This is my property!"

Jackson eyed the midsized, stocky young father and tried not to judge. He looked pretty successful for someone in his early thirties. This wasn't the sort of area where the newly rich or the dot com people moved.

"This is my property!" the guy repeated.

Yeah. Not scared. Volvo-driver's sand-colored hair was thinning a little over a broad forehead, and Jackson would place his bet on family money and being the very middle of his class in business. Not incompetent, maybe, but the man walked like he was used to being given things—money, cars, houses, enough room to park.

This guy thought those things should be his.

"I know it is," Jackson said, shrugging. "You're Cedric Evander, the guy who let Janie Isaacson throw herself under the bus for your kids."

Cedric gaped at him. "I beg your pardon?"

"Where's your family, Cedric?"

Evander's fair skin blotched fairly easily. "On a trip," he said weakly. "I took them to—"

"Don't tell me," Jackson interrupted. "Don't tell me where they are. Believe it or not, it was a good move, but in the meantime poor Janie is swinging in the breeze while you cover your own ass. How's that fair?"

"She confessed," he said, looking away.

"And the dent on your front bumper says that's bullshit," Jackson shot back. "Any cop could have looked at that and said, 'Oh hey, some asshole kicked that in,' but not one cop on site did, which tells me whoever was in charge of the investigation knows more than you do about who kicked it in."

"Greaves," Cedric mumbled. "Officer Paul Greaves."

"Not Ty Spooner?" Hunh. If the officer on scene had changed, that was interesting. Very, very interesting. Something to tell Mack, at any rate.

"I think he was there, but by the time Marilyn and I got there to pick up the car, Janie was being arrested and Greaves was on scene."

Jackson nodded like this was protocol. "Don't know him, which is too bad, because Greaves and I are about to become real fuckin' personal. Now I don't want to put you on the spot, and I'm not about getting anybody to name names. We got a lock on this asshole for something else. All I'm here about is getting Janie off. Even *you* have to admit that's what's right."

Evander recoiled. "That's not fair!" he said unhappily. "Janie's wonderful. The kids are devastated, and my wife isn't fuckin' speaking to me, okay? But… but—"

Jackson held up a hand. "We're not going to talk about that," he said brutally. "But I'm working for her, so you need to just let me do my thing."

Evander's head drooped on his neck. "Okay, fine. What thing are you doing, anyway?"

"See this bumper here?" Jackson pulled him around to the front. "What do you think caused that bend?"

Evander took a breath "It's not a body," he said after a moment. "I saw someone hit a deer on the highway once. The front of their car—way more damaged than this."

"Exactly. And Janie wasn't going fast enough as she left to do the sort of damage that would kill someone on impact. There's what? Twenty feet to accelerate? I mean, yeah—can still hurt someone, but it would be a lot easier to slow down, to stop, from that distance. The person driving the car that struck down that woman—"

"Mindy Alves." And to his credit, Evander sounded ashamed. "Her name was Mindy Alves, and she had her two children with her. And there's nobody to care for them—we knew Mindy. She was a parent volunteer."

Ugh. This just got worse and worse and worse. "Janie doesn't deserve to go to prison for this," Jackson said softly.

Evander's broad forehead creased, and that air of entitlement disappeared. What was left was a very humble, very frightened husband and father.

"We got a phone call," he whispered, so low Jackson could barely hear him over the leaf blower two blocks down. "Said better Mindy than my own kids, and just to leave things be."

Jackson swallowed. Oh, he so did not want to know this. "Which part of proving her innocent without naming the guilty did you not understand?" he asked a little desperately. "Mr. Evander, we don't know who's listening!"

But Cedric Evander wasn't hearing him. "I love that girl," he said, then grimaced. "Not in the bad way. Like she was my little sister. I mean, she's a sweet kid. And she did what she did for my own children. And I didn't want that to be in vain."

He was sweating in the January chill, and watching his face flush reminded Jackson that he was still wearing his sports coat over his dress clothes and he wasn't that warm either. As he pulled his blue cashmere scarf—a gift from Ellery—closer around his ears and tried to figure how to shut this guy up, he caught a flash of red out of the corner of his eye.

He scowled. "Mr. Evander, I think that's my friend coming, but why he'd run the cherry lights I have no id—" An unmarked Buick pulled haphazardly up behind Evander's car, and just as Jackson identified Mack behind the wheel, he realized the red wasn't an LED light. It was a tiny laser dot, right above Cedric Evander's heart.

"*Gun!*" Jackson shouted, throwing himself on top of Evander. They went down just as a big flower vase exploded right behind Cedric Evander's shoulder.

Evander grunted as they hit the ground, and Jackson was checking to make sure he was okay when something big thunked him on the back of the head and he blacked out.

HE CAME to on a gurney with a bright light in his eyes.

"No," he mumbled, trying to sit up. "Oh hell no. No ambulances. My boyfriend's gonna fuckin' kill me if he has to pick me up from the hospital. No. There's two nurses there that'll finish the job. Let me up—fuckin' *ouch*."

His head. Oh dear Lord, his head was going to blow up on his shoulders, and what would be left would just twitch and drop.

"My head," he moaned. "Jesus fucking head grenades on a goddamned maypole, what in the hell was that?"

"A fifty-pound planter," Mack said dryly next to the gurney. "Or part of it. You fell on top of Evander, and it fell on top of you, bounced off, and smashed his face. It was amazing. I mean, getting shot at with a gun with a scope isn't new to you, but I defy you to say you get your head taken off by a planter every day."

"You are an evil, awful little man, and I can't believe we fucked," Jackson muttered, then remembered Mack really *was* out to everybody and was relieved. "Do I have to go to the hospital?"

"X-rays, Mr. Rivers."

Jackson squinted at the EMT and then grimaced. "Didn't you patch up my shoulder in November?" He looked like a round, jolly fortysomething elf with thinning blond hair and ruddy cheeks, and he was always so enthusiastic about Jackson's ability to just go into the hospital and take care of whatever ailed him.

"I did. And you wouldn't remember this, but I was part of the detail that got you to the hospital about three days later. You are quite the frequent flyer, aren't you?"

Jackson blinked at him and then just shut his eyes. "How's Cedric Evander?" he asked Mack, and his words sounded a little slurred to his own ears.

"In a coma—but alive. You saved him from the gunshot, and seriously—who saw the planter coming? But he's alive. Did you learn anything from him?"

Jackson nodded and opened his eyes, wincing when the light hurt his head. "Closer," he muttered. "We might be bugged."

Mack's surprise was almost comical. Almost.

"Ty Spooner wasn't the officer he dealt with. Paul Greaves was. And they got a phone call to not say anything about Janie—to let her take the fall. He stashed the wife and kids I don't know where, and I think it's better for everyone if we don't look. Did you see where the shot came from?"

"House across the way is vacant," Mack said, nodding toward it. "I saw you two go down, called it in, and waited. Heard a door slam, possibly from the back, but...." He shrugged. "Would rather you not bleed out from a head wound while I'm chasing the bad guy, you feel me, Jackson?"

Jackson let his eyes drift down. "You're a good friend," he said, meaning it. "Now, do you want to call Ellery for me and tell him to come get his car?"

"Augh!" Mack's freckled face scrunched up in frustration. "You're killing me! He'll *kill* me! Do you have any idea how much it sucks to pick someone up from the hospital?"

Jackson grunted. "I do not," he admitted. "I'm usually the one getting picked up."

"Yeah, I know it." Mack ruffled his hair without touching his scalp at all, which took some doing. "Rivers, I'll call your boyfriend, but I hope—I sincerely hope—you never find out what you've been putting us through for all these years. You're a decent guy. I think it'll hit you kind of hard."

"Your head hurt?" the EMT said nicely.

"More now than before this asshole opened his mouth," Jackson told him, sourness in his stomach, his voice, his expression.

"I'm going to give you some IV fluids and some painkillers, and you can have your friend meet you at UCD."

"They've probably got a suite in his name," Mack cracked, and then he sobered and drew close to Jackson again. "I'll text sixty dozen people with your info," he said. "And have them tell sixty dozen more. I know you're used to going it alone, but not this time. Understood?"

Jackson grunted since he couldn't nod. "Ellery'll be happier that way," he mumbled. "Hey, at least the Lexus didn't get shot!"

"I SWEAR to God, Ellery, I was just standing there."

Ellery rolled his eyes, but Jackson could tell by the pallor of his face and the way his knuckles clenched whitely around the chrome of Jackson's hospital gurney that he was not pleased.

"I mean, I didn't get shot, right?" Jackson smiled winningly—because technically it *was* a win, and he saw a corner of Ellery's mouth twist up.

"That's immaterial," Ellery said, and Jackson could see his Adam's apple bob. "Do you have any other evidence you weren't being cavalier with your life?"

Times like this when Ellery reminded Jackson of Lucy Satan, Ellery's mother, were the times Jackson felt most like running for the hills.

"Mack was already there when the shot was fired? I, uh, wasn't alone."

For the first time, Ellery made eye contact. "That was on purpose?" he asked, and Jackson would have nodded, but... *concussion*!

"Yeah. I was taking pictures, and I thought Mack could come and clear up that the car hadn't struck an actual person, like, immediately, and you could get Janie off at the arraignment, and we could, you know, spend our time on Karl Lacey."

Ellery made that hissing noise, like Jackson had said something unseemly, and Jackson remembered that, hey, the guy might be taping their conversation.

"So, you didn't call for backup because of the threat to your life—"

"Which I didn't know was present!" Jackson protested.

"You called for backup to help with the case." Ellery pinned him with a worried glare, and Jackson covered those white knuckles with his own fingers.

"It escalated fast," he said gently. "Baby, I'm used to getting knocked around a bit, but you know. After what I put you through this fall, I'm not gonna do that again if I can help it."

Ellery nodded, and his voice buckled slightly. "I... I want to wrap you in cotton, and then again in bubble wrap and then in packing peanuts and put you in a big shipping container and send it out to sea so nobody can get you."

It was a beautiful bit of hyperbole from a man who dealt almost exclusively in facts.

"And the container would sink and I'd drown or suffocate, and you'd miss me in the meantime," Jackson said, smiling slightly. He bit his lip but kept his gaze even. "And I'd die a little inside from not being free."

"Yeah." Ellery turned his hand palm up and captured Jackson's fingers. "How long you in here for?"

Jackson closed his eyes against the flurry of spots that danced in front of them. "Until I can get out of bed without falling down," he said honestly. "They expect two days."

"Hunh." Ellery let go of his hand so he could drag a chair near the gurney and sit down.

"What does that sound mean?" Jackson asked suspiciously. "I know what it means when *I* make that sound, but what does it mean when *you* make that sound?"

Ellery grabbed his hand again. "It means Crystal will be able to check the house out for bugs tomorrow. I, uh, may just spend the night here until that happens."

"Mm." Jackson closed his eyes again against his swimming vision. He was suddenly tired, which meant the assessment of a pretty serious concussion with the possibility of a subdural hematoma was probably spot-on, and he hadn't fought to get up and go anywhere when it had been made. He might not have argued a year ago—but then, he might *have* argued then, and he might have gone out and chased down a perp when his brain exploded and he died.

He seemed to have more to live for these days.

"Mm what?" Ellery's voice penetrated his fog.

"Mm I'm tired, and the hardest thing I was supposed to do today was go to church. I wouldn't mind some company, Counselor, but I'm afraid I'm not up for conversation."

Ellery gave his hand a squeeze. "Fair enough. You nap. I'm going to talk to Mack and Arizona and see if we can get Janie into protective custody ASAP. I think we're back in the pressure cooker again."

"Augh!" Jackson couldn't even scream to make the sound convincing. "That's excellent. Do you think you could hand me that emesis bowl? And then you might want to leave the room to celebrate."

"Oh, baby...."

He didn't leave the room, which was humiliating enough. But afterward, and after the nurse came in to assist with cleanup, Jackson was lying in the darkened room wishing he was anyone but Jackson Rivers, ex-cop, disposable boy, when Ellery started smoothing his hair back from his forehead.

Such a simple gesture, but Jackson closed his eyes, soothed by Ellery's touch—and by the painkillers currently dripped into his arm via IV.

"Ellery?"

"Yeah?"

"You make being me not such a bad thing."

The kiss on Jackson's temple warmed him, and he fell into a healing sleep.

Sharks in the Water, Fish in the Air

ELLERY WASN'T particularly glad Jackson had gotten hurt again, but he *was* glad he was still in the hospital at this particular moment in time.

"How many of them?" he asked, feeling sick to his stomach. He'd been fine when he'd watched Jackson lose his lunch—this was a whole new level of queasy.

"I found three," Crystal said softly. "Kitchen, living room…." She trailed off apologetically.

"Bedroom," Ellery snarled. "Any way of knowing how long they've been there?"

"No." She shook her head, holding her small feedback machine in one hand and the three offending transmitters in the other. "But you and Jackson took off on vacation during Thanksgiving, right? I'm betting that's when they were installed."

"Don't they need batteries or something?" He'd read that somewhere—couldn't remember where.

"Yeah—I'd check your maid service. That's either who was replacing them or how they got in to replace them. Is it the…."

Ellery groaned. "The same one used by the firm? No. I don't recognize any of the people."

"Then probably they just came in and changed stuff out. It's a good scam—pretend to be a repairman and the maid will let you in. And there's so many people in and out of the offices—"

God. "A good pickpocket could get into the office while the cleaning crew works. I hear you."

Ellery scrubbed at his face with one hand and—incongruously enough—petted Billy Bob as he sat on the table with the other.

Jackson's snaggletoothed, three-legged battered Siamese cat looked like an escapee from a horror movie *about* cats, but boy, had he been glad when Ellery had gotten home that morning to feed him and clean his litter box.

For his part, Ellery was getting more and more used to the creature's way of closing his eyes and purring until he drooled—usually all over Ellery's suits, but Ellery didn't care. He'd never owned a cat before, but this cat certainly decided he owned Ellery as well as Jackson, and that was fine all around.

Where Jackson went, Billy Bob went, and right now the cat wasn't moving from Ellery's house off American River Drive.

"What are you thinking?" Crystal asked quietly.

Ellery let a terrible smile curl up at the corners of his mouth. "I'm thinking we had sex in all of those rooms," he said, channeling Jackson in his soul. "I hope they're homophobic as fuck."

Crystal's pure, chiming laughter sounded nearly cacophonous in the tenseness of that room, but Ellery couldn't hold it against her. She'd found two bugs at the firm—one in Ellery's office and one in the office of Carlyle Langdon, Ellery's immediate superior. They had *not* found any bugs at Jade's workstation, which was both a relief and not a surprise.

Jade Cameron was part of Jackson's de facto family—they'd been lovers for a while, but mostly they were siblings of the heart. Jade worked for Ellery's firm as a paralegal—sharp as a tack, bossy as hell, the firm would collapse without Jade.

But Jade was a woman of color, and Karl Lacey had made it clear at their last meeting that he didn't regard her as a threat.

Not having a bug at her workstation was almost an insult, but it was also a relief. It meant that Jade and her boyfriend, Mike, were off the radar, and hopefully so was Kaden, her twin, who lived with his family up in the mountains somewhere. Ellery had visited with Jackson over Christmas, but he still never had a grasp of the geography north of Sacramento—and now he was glad.

Jackson's family was, for the most part, safe.

Which meant Jackson could, maybe, worry about his own health for a change.

Yeah. Sure. That's what he was going to worry about when Ellery presented him with this news. His health.

"I'm thinking Jackson's gonna be pissed," Crystal said, damned near reading his mind. "I have no idea what you two are into that someone would be bugging you—"

Ellery started waving his hands around to get her to not ask.

"And I'm not going to ask," she conceded. "But whatever it is, you should resolve it quickly. What are you going to do tonight?"

Billy Bob took that moment to meow piteously, because in spite of Ellery's nonstop touch as the cat had been eating, nobody loved him and nobody fed him either.

"I'm going to take Billy Bob somewhere safe," he said, thinking fast. "And I'm going to find a place to sleep tonight."

He didn't elaborate. For one thing, his "place" was in a cot next to Jackson's hospital bed where he'd spent *last* night. For another, he was going to destroy the bugs in Crystal's hands, then come back with her little handheld bug finder the next day and see how fast their opposition worked.

And he was pretty sure he wasn't going to spend another night in his own house until they'd figured out how to stop their enemy cold.

"THREE BUGS?" Jackson asked, looking pale still, but not quite so woozy. "There were three bugs in our house?"

"Yeah." Ellery sighed and leaned his head back against the rest. "And Crystal has your cat."

"Why not Jade?" Jackson tilted his head carefully to catch Ellery's eyes, and Ellery grimaced.

"Because Crystal was already there. If she left with the cat, well, she was already part of the equation. But Jade and Kaden are out of this, apparently. No bugs at Jade's station, and Mike actually had one of those little bug finders in his garage."

"Heh." Jackson's tenant—and best friend—had lived next to Jackson in the duplex for nearly eight years. He'd been part of Jackson's holidays, along with Jade, Kaden, and Rhonda, and he'd worried about Jackson with all of them. He wasn't the most diplomatic of guys, but Ellery was proud of the friendship they'd forged since that August—especially because Mike and Jade were now living together, and passing muster with Jade and Mike meant he could be part of Jackson's family.

Mike had his own weapons cache, his own Kevlar, an air compressor, every tool known to man, and a garage organized within an inch of its life. That there was a bug finder in the back recesses of a drawer somewhere and Mike would know where it was didn't surprise either of them in the least.

But it was pretty amusing.

"They're clear," Jackson breathed, his relief palpable.

"They're not the center of this one," Ellery reassured him. "Once again, it's you and me."

Jackson grunted. "A couple month's peace."

"And it's over."

"They listened to us have sex." He sounded plaintive, and Ellery didn't blame him. Jackson had so little that was his.

"They listened to us have a *lot* of sex," Ellery amended grimly. "Think that was fun for them?"

Jackson chuckled, low and dirty. "I think we should ask them. Do we have a plan?"

Ellery breathed out slowly. "Yeah. And you're going to need to feel good enough to travel. How we doing?"

Jackson thought about it, which was reassuring. New, but reassuring.

"No," he said reluctantly. "Not tomorrow." He shuddered hard, and Ellery watched a sweat pop out on his brow.

"Are you going to throw up again?" he asked, hating to see Jackson hurt like this.

"Could you, please, just this once, for me, leave the goddamned room?" Jackson begged.

No.

WHILE JACKSON lay sleeping in the aftermath, Ellery grabbed his freshly charged burner phone and started making calls.

"Ellery!"

"Dad?" He'd thought he dialed his mother's cell phone.

"Sh… she fell asleep. This isn't your usual phone?"

Ellery took a deep breath. He was used to asking his mother for advice. Not because his father was incapable or incompetent—just the opposite, in fact. But his father was all about nurturing and his mother was all about going out and slitting the throat of the opposition. Ellery had always assumed he needed to be about slitting the throat of the opposition—right up until he'd met Jackson.

Suddenly nurturing skills seemed to be high on his priority list.

"My office and home were bugged," he said, and now that it was out of his little bubble of associates, he realized how dire that sounded. "We caught someone trying to bug my car. We just thought—"

"Oh yes. I can see how this would feel much safer. That's very clever of you, son—well done."

Ellery glanced to where Jackson lay on his side, eyes closed. "Thanks, Dad," he said, needing the praise badly. "But now we have to go get the guys who did it."

"Who do you think did it?"

Wow. This was tough. Saying *military people* sounded paranoid. Saying *Commander Karl Lacey, US Navy, officer in charge of really illegal behavior experiments* sounded way worse.

But this was his father. His father would believe him.

"Dad, remember Tim Owens?"

"The serial killer who almost killed Jackson? Yes, son. I'm not senile."

Ellery grimaced. No. "We… I'm not sure how much Mom told you, but we think he was… trained. Messed with somehow, in the military. Like somebody was supposed to teach him how to shoot a gun, but they taught him to like killing instead."

"This would be the man who tried to put pressure on our finances, right?"

"Yeah, Dad." He'd forced three of his mother's contracts to bail on her firm. His mother—being his mother, actually—had garnered four more in their stead, but even if she hadn't, both his parents were pretty wealthy, independent of their jobs as lawyers.

It was the principle of the thing.

"Well, he's a bad man. He must be stopped. Do you have a plan?"

Ellery stifled a laugh. It was an absurdly simplistic way of looking at the situation. But then, it was exactly the way Jackson would look at it.

"We…." He looked around reflexively. "We have a line on some people who may have some ideas. But first there's a client I need to look after. I got her into protective custody yesterday—"

"Did somebody try to harm her?" Sid Cramer always sounded so worried, even about people who weren't his, strictly speaking.

"No, but they tried to harm the man Jackson was talking to—"

"How's Jackson?"

Ellery grunted. "A concussion—"

"Oi. How's he doing?"

Ellery couldn't stop himself from smoothing Jackson's hair back. "He volunteered to stay for an extra day so he can move without throwing up."

"That's encouraging!"

Well, yeah. Actually.

"He even had backup at the scene," Ellery told him, hoping to reassure.

"Oh, that's wonderful! Ellery—he's starting to trust other people! You should be very proud."

Ellery's dad—the man could spin sunshine out of bird shit. "Mostly he just didn't want to piss me off," Ellery replied, but he couldn't sound sour—that was an improvement too.

"So, what are you going to do about your client?"

Ellery pinched the bridge of his nose, a habit he'd learned from his mother, although it never had helped him think any more clearly. "I think I may have to turn her over to my boss," he said thoughtfully. "I…." He hated to do it. Carlyle Langdon was a damned good attorney, but Ellery couldn't see him running all over town to make sure Janie Isaacson wasn't convicted—or killed—because of what she'd seen. "I don't trust anybody but us," he said after a moment. "But if we don't check out this lead, I don't know if I can…." So much he didn't want to say. He pulled up his father's own words. "Can stop the bad guys," he finished pathetically.

His father's silence had an assessing quality to it. "You *do* plan to send your mother a brief about this, don't you?"

"And the assistant DA and all my bosses and the lawyer I dated back in school and Jackson's old cop buddy from the force and—"

His father chuckled. "Very good, son. I'm impressed." Then he sobered. "But they didn't believe you last time. I think you need to go one step further."

Ellery grunted. He knew what his father was talking about. "Print won't touch it," he said after a moment. "But you're right. Someone not afraid to put it out there in the public."

"Do you follow any bloggers who'd be willing?"

Ellery sighed and tried to rack his brain. "I'll ask around," he said. God. It was Sunday. He and Jackson had entertained wild plans of doing absolutely nothing this day. And Ellery was mortally tired of hospitals.

But if Ellery hated them, Jackson hated them even more—to the point of phobia.

"I'll let you go, son—just keep us posted."

"Course, Dad. You know me."

"Always the good son. Stay safe."

Ellery's father hung up, and Ellery stood, stretching and prowling restlessly around the hospital room.

"You don't have to stay," Jackson said softly.

Ellery startled and whirled and saw that no, his eyes weren't open, but he'd obviously heard.

"You don't like the hospital," Ellery responded automatically.

"Yeah, but you're making me twitchy. What did your father say?"

Ellery moved toward the bed. "He said I should tell the press."

"Smart guy. But put a hold on it—we don't want to spook them."

"Do you know anybody who would do it?" Ellery had been planning to ask Crystal.

"Look in my phone contacts under bloggers—"

"You have your contacts organized?" Ellery asked, aghast. He actually had to run a search for people—he still hadn't figured out how to get them alphabetized by last name only. He had to remind himself not to underestimate Jackson Rivers—he always had a surprise up his sleeve.

"My contacts are my life," Jackson grunted, not even kidding a little. "Find Valerie Palmer—she'll take all your stuff and sit on the story until you're ready. I've used her before to flush out informants."

Ellery's turn to grunt. "I've never even heard you mention her." He felt absurdly hurt. "Ex-lover?" He always had to ask.

"Yup. And now, she's not the only one in my phone," Jackson told him, smiling slightly. "Where's my cat again?"

"Our computer friend's," Ellery said to avoid saying her name.

"Yeah. You told me." Jackson swallowed. "I'm gonna miss him."

"When?" By habit, Ellery checked Jackson's monitors.

"When we go on the road. That's where we're going, right?"

"Yeah."

In September, Ellery had been running down a lead that would clear one of his clients—and he and Jackson had found a little garage in Victoriana instead.

The occupants—Ace Atchison and Sonny Daye—had set off both their alarms, but after a little bit of poking around, Jackson had come to some pretty sound conclusions.

The first was that if nobody bothered Ace and Sonny and their little entourage of fiercely loyal employees, then Ace and Sonny wouldn't bother nobody back.

The second was that if somebody *did* bother Ace and Sonny, Ace would be deadly and Sonny unbalanced. They'd very carefully backed away and let Ellery's client—who was guilty of so very many *other* things besides the one he was accused of—take a plea.

But when Ace and Sonny's name had come up in an investigation of Karl Lacey in November, they'd both known this day was coming.

"Ellery?"

"Yeah?"

"We shouldn't take the Lexus."

Ellery sighed. "I hear you." Reluctantly he began to gather his briefcase and his coat. He left his small overnight bag because he would be coming back, but he had to hurry now or he wouldn't make it.

It was three o'clock on a Sunday afternoon, but most of his paperwork was already filled out, and the local car dealerships wouldn't be closed until five.

"I've planned something big," Ellery said, mostly to warn him. He'd been doing research. "Something with power and a dependability—"

"Not a gas guzzler," Jackson said, sounding like that was a make-or-break item.

"Fine. But sturdy. Like an SUV built like a tank."

"Oh God. Nobody needs that much SUV—ostentation is bad."

Ellery found a chuckle—first one of the day. "Oh, Jackson. Six months together and still so much to learn."

Jackson groaned. "Send me pictures," he said, pointing to his phone by his bedside. "I get veto power."

And Ellery was going to refuse—he was.

Then he saw the helpless mutiny on Jackson's face and remembered how well he'd handled pretty much everything the day before—right up until a planter had fallen on his head.

"Fine," he said gracelessly. "I'll send you pictures."

And then he kissed Jackson's cheek softly and turned to leave.

"I'll call Val," Jackson mumbled. "You and me. Team."

"Sleep first."

"Fine."

But as Ellery turned around and left the room, he had no doubt—none at all—that Jackson would wake up and finish his job.

THE NEXT morning, after running more errands than he could count, he settled Jackson into a smoky gray Infiniti QX30—and tried hard to ignore Jackson's grumbling.

"Are you kidding me? Wait—what did you pack for me?"

"Pink satin thongs," Ellery snapped, throwing his suitcase in the back. "You own three pairs of jeans, Jackson, and you were wearing one when you went into the hospital."

"Four now," Jackson reminded him sourly.

"How could I forget. I packed three pairs of jeans, which means you've got nothing left."

"Underwear?"

"No, because I want you to go commando."

"You know, you are an awfully big smartass for a guy who had to beg me to get this car instead of a Chevy Tahoe."

"Do you know I had to buy you new underwear?" Ellery had stopped by Penney's that morning. "Seriously, I can't believe you got laid so much when you had more holes in your boxer briefs than you do in your body!"

"You left a few pair of the old ones in for luck, right?" Jackson asked, sounding legitimately worried.

"Luck? Is that what the little action figures were for?" Ellery got into the driver's seat and belted himself in. He'd left his Lexus in a long-term parking garage and double-set the alarms on the house that morning as well. Billy Bob was with Crystal—and by all accounts destroying her carpet, which Ellery had promised to reimburse her for.

Jackson blushed, one of those things that always caught Ellery unaware, like his self-consciousness about his old acne scars. "No, they were just… uh…."

Ellery felt stupid—and then stupidly glad he'd brought the little plastic toys, tucking them into a corner of Jackson's duffel. "Mementos," he said, thinking about how much Jackson *hadn't* brought from his old duplex. Granted, much of it had been destroyed, but it was a patent reminder of all the things Jackson had never had but Ellery took for granted.

Jade had called Jackson that morning, pissed because usually *she* watched Jackson's cat, and Crystal had apparently told her about the bugs. Jackson had called her back on the burner phone and explained the situation to her.

She was not pleased.

Ellery hadn't heard her exact words, but Jackson had pulled the phone away from his ear and grimaced until Ellery took it.

"Finish getting dressed," he ordered, ignoring Jackson's rolled eyes. "If you throw up again, we're staying here."

"Swear to fuckin' Christ," Jackson muttered, but he didn't look queasy, so that was a relief.

"You do know he's in the hospital with a concussion, right?" he asked, stalking away from Jackson's bed, where Jackson was struggling with his clothes.

"No, because neither of you assholes told me!" she snapped. "I got the message about the new phone numbers and the kid from my brother, but a concussion? What in the hell did he do?"

"Nothing," Ellery muttered, because every account confirmed this version. "He tackled someone to keep him from getting shot, and a planter fell on his head. Everybody swears it wasn't his fault."

"Hunh."

Unlike with Jackson, where Ellery really hated that sound, Ellery got it with Jade. With Jade, that sound meant "I think you're speaking utter and complete bullshit, but you're not worth the trouble it would take to get a better answer from you."

"And I'm sorry about Billy Bob." He meant that—Jade and Mike were both really attached to the drooling, shedding nuisance, and Ellery wouldn't hurt their feelings over him for the world. "We sent him with someone who, quite frankly, isn't so attached to Jackson and I." He'd taken the phone from Jackson in the room, but now he looked through the glass at Jackson—who was getting dressed—and nodded down the hall. He started toward the main entrance, in a corridor with people and no expectation of privacy—and no place to put bugs.

"Why would you do that?" she asked. "And why are you picking him up and taking him on vacation? That's what you told Langdon, and he passed it on to the office."

"Okay, what part of 'Someone tried to bug our car' did you not get?" he asked sharply. "And that same person bugged our home. And if you look at the file on the Janie Isaacson case, you'll see that her entire family got threatened, and Jackson was hurt during an attempt to make good on that threat. Remember what started in November, Jade? It's back. And since there were no bugs at your station, and we're on a clean phone in a public place now, I'm going to tell you that we think it started and ended down south, and we left the cat somewhere it can't be traced to anybody Jackson cares about."

"What about you?" she asked, voice subdued.

"He's the person I care about on this coast—and my mother and father have a file with everything and contacts they've already shared it with. No, Jackson's the one they've got the most leverage on, so we tried to protect his people."

"And the cat."

Ellery tried not to think about what they'd do to the damned cat. "Crystal is paranoid as hell," he told her, because it was true and Crystal had assured him as he'd been loading Billy Bob into her car. "She's got a zillion different alarms and bug trackers in her own home—and old hacker friends who will avenge her death if anything goes down. If these people aren't legitimately afraid of Crystal's network, they've got computer resources I don't want to know about. But Jackson's people—"

"I hear you," Jade said humbly. "You're protecting us. Just don't protect us out of the loop, understood?"

"I gotcha. I'm sorry I didn't call you. I seriously didn't want you showing up at the hospital so they could get a look at you guys and maybe bug your car. Did Kaden tell you the deal with the kid?"

"Yeah. That's messed up about the guy in the liquor store—what do the cops say?"

Ellery drew a blank. "Uh…." That was usually Jackson's job.

"I would check with your people before you go haring off into the wild blue," she said judiciously. "I mean, maybe it was just a simple case of bad timing."

Ellery snapped out of his blank. "Jackson seemed to feel the guy had been tortured. I don't know how smart the cops are—"

"What about the ones who looked at Janie Isaacson's car?"

God, she was smart *and* relentless. "*Those* cops got switched out," he said. "I need to look at my notes, but the guy who was supposed to do Janie's investigation was *not* the guy Evander talked to—"

"Evander is…?"

"Janie's boss. He's the guy Jackson was tackling when the planter got shot on top of his head."

"Ugh." Jade's sound had the rolling of eyes in it. "Of course he was. So we've got crooked cops again?"

It was Ellery's turn to say, "Hunh."

"You're waffling because…?"

Ellery found a relatively quiet hallway and leaned against the wall. "Because I'm not sure if it's crooked cops or just manipulated cops. If a bigwig from the military calls his buddy and says, 'Hey, a friend of mine is in a pickle, can I have someone in there who knows what he's doing?' then we end up with the guy with the most military-friendly eye."

"So good ol' boy," she said thoughtfully. "That's promising."

"Well, a little," Ellery had to admit. "Because that means they're not really corrupt, just being… twisted."

"So we can twist them back." She sounded relieved, and Ellery didn't blame her. They'd had to fight the police force before, and Jackson had spent the last ten years engaged in that battle. It would be swell if that was someone they didn't have to count as an enemy this time around.

"My thought." Ellery sighed then and rubbed the back of his neck. The cots in the hospital were not comfortable, and more than anything, he longed to be able to take Jackson home.

Home was not an option right now, and that thought was like a kick to the gut. He and Jackson had to resolve this issue *now* if they were to have any expectation of privacy or safety for the rest of their lives.

Ellery shivered, thinking about a hotel room and living on the road, and suddenly wondered if this was how Jackson had felt, his first fifteen years of life, before he'd moved in with Jade and Kaden Cameron and their mother, Toni.

Except Jackson had possessed no options then, no resources—and Ellery did.

And Ellery had Jackson.

Ellery shook off the feeling of helplessness and counted his blessings. Jade was one.

"So we're going in search of the bad guys," Ellery said, avoiding specifics. "But I need you here. I'm going to text you the name of the officer who was assigned and the name of the one who ended up handling the case—"

"I'll send you their records ASAP," she said confidently. "Anything else?"

"Yeah. Get me a computer appointment with the ADA—"

"Arizona?"

Arizona Brooks was Ellery's contact at the ADA, and while she hadn't been exactly receptive in the past, the last time her office had ignored Ellery and Jackson they'd ended up with a house full of ODs and a cop tortured in captivity. He was pretty sure he'd have her ear this time.

"Yeah—but not until tomorrow afternoon, late."

"You planning to sleep in?" Jade drawled, and Ellery let out a sigh.

"Hospital cots suck," he told her, feeling stupid and helpless. To his surprise, his honesty earned her compassion.

"Yeah, and you got a long drive ahead of you. Do me a favor, okay?"

"Sure."

"My brother's been sending me some pictures that might make you and Jackson feel better—show him, okay?"

For a moment Ellery drew a blank. Then it hit him. "Oh! How they doing?"

"They're doing good," she said warmly. "Mike and I went up this weekend. It was… it was a good thing, what Jackson did for that boy. Both those boys. I mean, AJ tries so hard here, but he's floundering. I think Kaden's going to try to get a job up there for him."

Ellery breathed out steadily, reminded once again of why they all worked so hard to keep Jackson alive.

Because without even trying, he could do things like this.

"We'd both like that," Ellery said quietly. "Thank you. Now I need to get going—Jackson and I are taking off from here."

"Text me when you get wherever you're going," she said dryly. She'd been with Ellery when he'd spoken to Karl Lacey—she knew which plane he'd been on and where it had taken off from. But she also apparently knew Ellery was right. The less people knew she was connected to Jackson, the safer she would be.

"Keep us briefed of any suspicious activity," he told her, and she grunted affirmative.

And then he signed off.

That quickly, he and Jackson were detached from their home, from anyone who would expect to see them in Sacramento, and they were on their own.

So now, with Jackson next to him in the new Infiniti, Ellery wasn't in any mood to take any shit about not giving Jackson his way.

"What in the hell would we do with a Chevy Tahoe?" Ellery asked, shaking his head. "We certainly couldn't *drive* it, it costs a zillion dollars! We couldn't camp in it, because I hate forests, I hate trees, and I hate water that's not chlorinated. About the only thing we could do in a Chevy Tahoe is get shot at, and you know what?"

"Been there done that?" Jackson asked dryly. He was playing with the seat while they talked.

"Wasn't as glamorous as it sounds," Ellery retorted. "What are you doing?"

"Lying down flat and covering my head with a sweater. Do you know there's a big yellow ball of light in the fucking sky? It's obscene."

Ellery's eyes widened behind his sunshades. "You said your head was fine." He'd heard Jackson with the doctor that morning.

"I lied. You do it all the time."

"I don't lie—I just give orders."

"You lie. Remember the cough syrup in the tea?"

Ellery grunted. "It's not lying when you just assume the tea tastes vile. In fact, it's negligence on your part for not drinking tea when I've offered to brew it for you because it's better."

Jackson chuckled sleepily. "How you managed to make that my fault is a thing of beauty."

"You lied about your head."

"I did."

"But now you're—"

"Lying in a car with a sweatshirt over my head hoping you'll shut up and listen to music so my painkillers can work."

"But why?" Ellery demanded. "We were safe in the hospital—"

"The quicker we get this done, the better," Jackson muttered harshly. "Your house, Ellery. Not to sound like a big maudlin baby, but I've never felt as safe in my life as I did in your house. I want that safety back. I'd also like to have sex without it being monitored. For all I know, they've got someone at a computer screen going, 'Oh, hey, this guy's doing it all wrong. How does the lawyer guy not know he can't fuck?'"

Ellery snickered. "That's the dumbest thing I've ever heard in my life."

"It is not—"

"No, it totally is. I'd know if you couldn't fuck. You do fine. You do outstanding, in fact. But I'd like to know it's… private again too. So I get your need for hurry. Just…."

Jackson hauled a gray hooded sweatshirt out of the back and wrapped it around his head—part was a pillow and part was a blindfold—and then he yawned.

"Just what?"

"Just take it easy until your head doesn't ache, okay? We've got two weeks. You don't need to bounce your skull around for another ten days. I'm serious."

"I want to be back with my cat before then," Jackson mumbled. "Let's make it five."

"Let's wait until you can face the daystar without whining about bursting into flame," Ellery told him. "Any choice of music?"

"I've got a mix in my phone." Jackson yawned again. "Wake me if you need me to drive."

"Us into a ditch," Ellery muttered, grabbing his phone from the island and pulling up his mixes.

Great. Nirvana, Offspring, Green Day, Linkin Park, Pearl Jam, Foo Fighters, and the Killers.

"You know this is going to give *me* a headache," Ellery muttered, getting ready to push the button.

"There's a cello mix of the same shit for you," Jackson murmured. "Quityerbitchin, Ellery, I got your back."

Ellery spotted it and hit the link, and 2Cellos came up with "Thunderstruck." Ellery's neck, which had been killing him since he woke up on the cot that morning, melted, and the pain drizzled out of his body.

Of course Jackson had an Ellery mix there.

Because Jackson looked out for him too.

Weird how that worked.

Fish on the Run

JACKSON WOKE up with a gasp and a shiver and struggled out of the material swathed around his head so he could orient himself.

His head felt very much better, but "Oh my God, I'm blind?"

"No," Ellery said quietly at the wheel by his side. "You're not blind. It's nighttime. You just slept for a solid seven hours in the front seat of the car."

Jackson grunted and raised the seat, smooth as butter. Wow, Ellery didn't seem to give a crap what kind of car they ended up in, but Jackson was both impressed and intimidated by silver-gray leather upholstery and a ride so quiet it was like you were gliding.

"Seven hours? Is that why I'm starving?" His stomach literally cramped.

"You're hungry?" The surprise in Ellery's voice was like an arrow of guilt. "There's a sandwich in the cooler. Go for it." Ellery nodded toward the island, which had a little cooler built into it. "And I tried to wake you up when I stopped for those, but you said 'Fuck off and let me die,' so I gave it up."

"Sorry about that." Jackson lifted the lid to the console and breathed in the scent of captured roast beef and avo. "Oh wow. Cold soda too. It's like you know me."

He seized the sandwich and set the soda in the cup holder, noting groceries on the floor behind him as he did. "Did you have those when you picked me up, or did I just miss an entire whack of time?"

"No—I had those already. You were asleep, but you weren't dead."

Jackson chuckled and bit into the sandwich, moaning a little because it was real food and the roast beef was sublime. "You're amazing—I was basically converting oxygen, and you got a car and packed and remembered snacks—"

"Groceries."

"Anyway, you did real good, Counselor. I'm sorry I was out of commission."

Ellery sighed and squeezed the bridge of his nose. "Not your fault," he conceded. "In fact, it actually gave us a place they couldn't bug so we could plan—that was nice."

"Sure," Jackson said, nodding. "I'll try being noncritically injured more often."

"Don't be an asshole."

"Whatever."

"You don't sleep in hospitals," Ellery said quietly. "I mean, you haven't slept much in months, but…."

Jackson grunted, embarrassed. It was bad enough that Ellery got to see him waking up in a cold sweat, struggling not to scream. The nurses in the hospital—and not just Dave and Alex, Jackson's personal friends—had taken to touching his shoulder softly and whispering their names and what they were doing in the room, every time they came to check his vitals.

"Hospitals are the suck for sleeping. What's your point?"

"Don't be an asshole," Ellery said again, but this time it came out resignedly, like a sigh.

"Where the hell are we going?" Jackson asked, ignoring the asshole thing because he didn't have a choice.

"Well, I'm thinking a random hotel in San Diego," Ellery mused, and Jackson felt himself light up.

"Can we get one of those nice ones on the waterfront?" he asked wistfully. He and Ellery had stayed in the Marriott on the Marina the last time they'd flown down, and while Jackson tried really hard not to get attached to all of Ellery's creature comforts, something about the way the balcony overlooked the waterfront and most of downtown had made Jackson feel like a smarter, stronger, more blessed human being.

"Sure," Ellery said, and Jackson looked at him to see if he'd be wearing the shy half smile he got when something romantic he'd tried actually worked.

He was.

Score.

"Don't think they'll be anticipating that?"

Ellery shrugged. "Hard to say. They weren't watching us until November. There's a lot of different hotels down there—we'll go to a different one. I think what you said to Janie is pretty true. We assume the bad guys know all the things, but I don't think Karl Lacey can use the full threat of the US military on us. For one thing, it would draw attention. If he starts commandeering computers and throwing trackers on us, the people he has to ask for help are going to hear our investigation. He can only ask a few people. I'm pretty sure we didn't leave much of a trace. I told Langdon we'd be going off the grid. I told Crystal we'd be investigating the bugs.

They may know we're coming down south. If they've got a credit card trace on us, they're going to be shit out of luck, because I went old-school and withdrew cash and bought a shit-ton of prepaid Visas—there's a card in every pair of jeans, now you know. And Crystal and I swapped emergency credit cards, so she's using mine up in Sacramento so I can hold down a hotel deposit down here."

Jackson blinked. "God."

"What?"

"I've seen drug addicts less paranoid than we are."

Ellery grunted. "I've seen guilty mobsters worse at covering their tracks. We've got two weeks, maybe three, to get this shit resolved. We're starting at a nice hotel in San Diego and hoping for the best."

Jackson took a deep breath and talked about the people they'd been avoiding talking about for the last four days.

"I'm going to need to call Ace and Sonny—you know that."

Ellery grunted again. "Yeah. Yeah, I know that. Do you want to call them now?"

Jackson looked out into the winter nightscape of the Tehachapi Mountains. Back in September they'd been vacationing—and part of their vacation was fleshing out an alibi for one of Ellery's clients.

They'd spent half an hour in a tiny gas station where the client had claimed to have tracked the guy he'd been chasing, and had decided to leave the scumbag to hang in the wind.

For starters, he might not have been guilty of the crime he'd been accused of, but his alibi for not committing *that* crime was that he'd been running away from the consequences of another, *worse* crime he'd committed.

In addition, the guys at the garage had been guilty of nothing worse than sheltering a victim of the mob from the guys chasing him. Dragging them into the limelight to testify for someone who wasn't the least bit sorry was not something Jackson wanted to do. And even if Ellery had been so inclined—it had been his vacation, after all—their witnesses all hated Ellery and really only talked to Jackson, so Ellery would have had to convince Jackson, and that wasn't happening.

And the final thing that convinced the two of them to leave Ace and Sonny alone had been the thing neither of them had admitted out loud: together, left to themselves, Ace Atchison and Sonny Daye were invisible. Two combat vets who owned a garage and outfitted cars. They raced illegally sometimes, sure, but given how paranoid Sonny was about Ace's health, Jackson was pretty sure that was only when they were really hard up for cash.

Desert dwellers. Rattlesnakes, perfectly content under their rock.

But if you poked the two guys with a stick, Jackson was pretty sure things would get bloody.

He'd asked Ellery to measure—truly measure—how necessary it would be to poke those guys with a stick, given that in trying to exonerate their client they'd come up with evidence for at least three other crimes, as well as reason to believe prison would be the safest place for the guy. It seemed all his cronies had been wiped out in some sort of violent territory dispute that he and his buddy had narrowly escaped. When Ellery pointed out that defending him in court would bring more attention from people who wanted to kill him, and that he didn't have a thing to offer WitSec, the guy had agreed to plead guilty.

Ace and Sonny never had to know.

But when Sonny's name had come up while investigating the origins of a serial killer in November, Jackson and Ellery had both known that someday they were going to have to go back to Victoriana with a very gentle, very quiet stick.

"Not now," Jackson said, yawning behind his napkin. The one thing he really hated about travel was how tired you got while not doing anything. "Tomorrow—"

"How do you feel?" Ellery asked abruptly.

Shit.

"No more nausea!" Jackson said brightly, tearing into his sandwich again.

"And...."

"My headache is about ten percent what it was," he replied, deflating a little. "But it's still there."

"Then tomorrow we enjoy a pricey hotel room," Ellery told him, voice firm. "And you and I start doing research. I got Crystal a burner phone—we can call her for help. But let's get our snakes in a row before we go poking them with sticks."

Jackson yawned again and took another bite of his sandwich. "You want me to drive?"

Ellery shook his head. "No. There's a Motel Six at the next exit. We can sleep there for a few hours and finish the trip tomorrow."

"And then the good hotel," Jackson confirmed suspiciously.

Ellery actually laughed, the lines around his mouth and forehead easing up. "Yes, you spoiled boy, we can sleep in the pricey hotel tomorrow."

"Good," Jackson said through his last bite of sandwich. He swallowed and started to lick his fingers methodically. "I think we need sex, and the beds in the shitty hotels will fuck up my back."

That did it. Jackson saw his full smile, minus all the worry lines, and he got to feel like he'd done his job. Yeah, he was a fuckup who couldn't seem to do the most basic things without taking a kill shot to the head. But Ellery, who had pretty much orchestrated their disappearance from Sacramento with a cell phone and some serious imagination, thought he was funny.

Jackson might just be worth keeping around.

THE STOP at the shitty hotel was utilitarian and necessary. Jackson offered to sleep in the other queen-sized bed so Ellery could get some real sleep, but Ellery shook his head.

"You're not broken," he mumbled, crawling into the bed in his boxers. "Come sleep with me so I can touch you. You're not the only one who hates hospitals."

Oh.

"Sure."

Jackson gave the blanket on top of the empty bed a jerk and threw it over the one they were using, because he was cold for one, and because Ellery stole covers for another, and this way Ellery could steal all he wanted and Jackson would still have something to sleep under. Then he hit all the lights and the blackout curtains, made sure their phones were plugged in on the bed stand—both the burners and their regular phones—and joined Ellery.

"Look at your phone," Ellery mumbled, spooning him from behind.

"Why?"

"Because Jade sent you pictures while you were getting dressed in the hospital."

"Hunh—"

"No, not hunh. Just nice. Look."

Jackson grabbed his phone and switched it on, squinting from the glare.

Kaden, Anthony, AJ, Kaden's wife, Rhonda, and his children, River and Diamond, were playing in the snow around Kaden's house out near

Truckee. River, at ten, sported an almost swoony smile as Anthony helped her across a frost-crusted bridge, and Diamond and AJ had managed the head—only—of a snowman in Kaden's front yard.

Anthony was wearing new clothes—warm ones—and a stocking cap with the logo of the Sacramento Kings on it. AJ, for once, didn't look distracted, or nervous, or like he should be somewhere else.

"Look at them," Jackson murmured. "They had a good time."

"Yeah. Like family," Ellery said gently. It was true. Kaden and Rhonda's complexions were both teakwood dark, and River and Diamond's as well. AJ's pale bronze and Anthony's chapped pink cheeks in his lemon-sallow face didn't match, but the looks on their faces as they played with Kaden's kids were identical: belonging. They felt like they belonged there.

"I... I hope Anthony can keep the good time inside him." Jackson wasn't sure if he phrased that right. "AJ too. I... I mean, when they have to come back to Sacramento."

"Who says they have to come back?" Ellery asked curiously. "Kaden's mother took you in. Why wouldn't Kaden and Rhonda want to do the same thing?"

Jackson swallowed hard. "Because I want too much for those boys to be happy," he admitted. "I don't even want to hope, because it's not fair to ask them. They have to love them too."

Ellery's soft sigh into his neck seemed to ease the ache in his chest. "Someday it'll be our turn," he said softly. "Just in case you were wondering if you'd ever get to give back."

"You're assuming I'll live that long," Jackson grunted, thinking he was being funny. God, he'd gotten hurt a lot since he'd met Ellery.

"You'd fucking better," Ellery snarled, turning over abruptly. Jackson missed the heat at his back. With a sigh and an excess of drama, he plugged his phone back in, rolled over, pummeling the pillow and settling in like an old dog before wrapping his arm around Ellery's waist and yanking him into Jackson's big spoon.

"Don't be shitty," Jackson muttered into his hair. "I was joking."

"Leave me alone. I'm asleep."

"You are not."

"You're bothering me."

Jackson grunted. "You'll still be alive," he offered, conciliatorily. "You can have the family."

"Jackson, it's been a long, crappy day, after a long, crappy weekend, and we have a long, crappy two weeks ahead of us that, yes, neither of us might survive—"

"You'll be fine," Jackson reassured, cold in his groin at the thought that Ellery wouldn't be.

"So will you."

"I… it's just easier for me to think of a world without me than a world without you."

"God, you suck."

"Not in the last three days," Jackson said with dignity. He'd thought it was one of his better lines, and he'd been sort of hoping for a better response.

"Do you think I don't feel the same way about you?" Ellery asked in exasperation. "Jesus—I know the concussion was not your fault, but can't you at least see that it hurts to imagine a life without you? It's like those pictures on your phone. Sure, those boys are new to Kaden and Rhonda, but do you think they can be happy without the boys in their lives now that they've met?"

Jackson closed his eyes in the darkness and saw the happy smiles again. "No."

"Then why can't you believe I feel that way about you?" His voice ached with injury, and Jackson sighed.

"I've been telling you for months that I'm a bad bet," he said, defeated.

"And I've been telling you for months that there's no such thing as luck." Yeah, Ellery said that, but he punctuated it with a kiss on the back of Jackson's hands.

Jackson's head, which was aching fiercely again, backed off a degree, and he melted into the pillow some more. "I'm lucky," he mumbled. "You love me. Lucky me. Night, Counselor."

"Night, moron."

Jackson chuckled before falling asleep.

ELLERY WOULDN'T let him drive the next day either, but they left at nine o'clock—after morning traffic and not quite in time for lunchtime traffic. They made it to San Diego in two and a half hours, and thank God for that.

Ellery checked them into the hotel, and they both went down to the pool to swim laps.

Something about the cool of the water, the way his muscles responded to the release from gravity, took away the last of the headache. They went back up to shower, Ellery going first so Jackson could look up a small garage in Victoriana.

It took him longer than it should have.

"What's got your dick in a knot?" Ellery asked, wrapped in one of those plushy white hotel bathrobes and toweling his hair as he emerged. He liked to air dry under the bathrobes, and Jackson's funk lightened up marginally.

"Do you have any idea what their business is named?"

Ellery's eyes widened, and his lips parted slightly.

"Yup. I drew a big fat blank too. Wasn't a sign anywhere. I had to call the goddamned chamber of commerce—the one in Barstow, because Victoriana is too damned small to have one of its own. Some poor woman had to look the thing up in an actual file—a paper file—so she could tell me they named the garage Sonny's Place. Holy Jesus. Is that not the stupidest name for a garage ever? It sounds like a goddamned café."

Ellery shook himself, like he was trying to shake off the whole idea of it. "Well, you know. It *is* sweet. I mean, as romantic gestures go, Ace had to be the one filing the paperwork. Maybe it's what got Sonny to like him?"

Jackson just shook his head. "Like Sonny needed any encouragement. I mean, Sonny's Garage? I looked up Sonny's Garage. And Ace's Garage. And Sonny and Ace's Garage. Jesus—how those two guys keep a business alive in what amounts to an intersection in the middle of hell is beyond me."

"But you *did* get a phone number," Ellery said impatiently.

"Yeah. I'll call when I get out of the shower. If I call right now I'll rip someone's face off."

It took ten minutes for the hot water to massage Jackson's irritation away, but by the time he emerged, wearing a towel around his waist after drying his hair with it, he came to a halt as he entered the room.

The room itself had that hallmark of good hotel rooms—a giant white cotton comforter over a king-sized bed. The walls were painted a sage green with cream trim, and with the light coming in from the big sliding glass door to the little patio, the effect was that of airy space—especially because they were on the twenty-fifth floor and all you could see beyond the patio was blue sky.

Ellery was sitting at his computer desk, one leg tucked under his bottom, his robe gaping around his chest *and* around his thighs. He'd combed his hair back but had neglected product, and it hung in his eyes, threatening to curl in the humidity—something Ellery's sister teased him unmercifully about but Jackson had never personally seen.

Jackson was slugged hard in the gut with how innocent Ellery was.

Sure, he was a big bad defense attorney—and most of Sacramento thought he was a shark and an asshole, and he liked it that way.

But Jackson knew—knew Ellery hoped most of his clients were innocent even when he knew the odds against that. Knew Ellery was rooting for Anthony as hard as Jackson was, and probably for AJ too; he just never found words that weren't awkward or dry.

And the skin peeking out from the gaps in the robe was just really, really delicious.

Jackson gave Ellery the warning of a warm hand on his shoulder. Ellery glanced up from the new-looking laptop and frowned. "You don't even comb your hair, do you? Ever."

And that was it. Jackson swiveled the office chair around so the back was to the desk and sank to his knees, parting the bottom of the robe until Ellery's groin was completely exposed.

Ellery's gasp sent shivers dancing down Jackson's spine.

"Real-*y*?" Ellery squeaked, but then Jackson decided to play with him.

"No," he breathed, the puff of wind dusting the fine hairs on the inside of Ellery's thigh.

"No what?"

Jackson opened his mouth and pulled on the soft inside skin, laving with his tongue. He sucked lightly, teasingly, until Ellery's fingers knotted in his unkempt hair and tugged.

"No what?" he insisted breathily. "No you don't comb your hair, or no, we're not real... oh God...."

Jackson pulled back while he was talking and spat on Ellery's gloriously pink, sparkling clean hole, and then went back to his tender inner thigh. Very carefully, he used a single finger to tease Ellery's rim.

Ellery's thighs began to shake. He pulled them up wantonly, resting his feet on Jackson's shoulders, and Jackson continued to torment.

He moved from inner thigh to the join between leg and groin, knowing it would be clean and sweet. Ellery let out a gasp, still shaking, and yanked authoritatively on Jackson's hair.

Jackson ignored him.

"Don't be an asshole," Ellery breathed, and as a reward, Jackson moved his fingertip just enough to push against his pucker—and left it there.

Ellery squirmed, and the chair rocked dangerously. Jackson paused what he was doing and looked Ellery in the eye, waiting.

Ellery's eyes narrowed mutinously. "So help me, Jackson, I will throw you against the wall and fuck you dry," he threatened. "I'll fuck you till you come and then fuck you through it, until you beg, screaming for my jizz in your ass. Dammit...." Jackson stared at him levelly and twitched his finger just enough to tickle. Ellery's cock stuck out stiffly from his body by this time, drooling and shiny, bright red.

Ellery's arms were propped back on the armrests, the better to catch the chair on the desk if he needed to. With a snarl he moved his hand from Jackson's hair to his own cock, and Jackson caught it, midair, and laced fingers.

Jackson knew Ellery was stuck then, legs spread wantonly, Jackson between his thighs. If he moved his other arm, the chair would rock and he'd probably fall. If he didn't, Jackson had full permission to toy with his toy box until Ellery screamed.

"Nungh!" Ellery moved his hand back to Jackson's hair and pushed down. As a reward Jackson licked a fine line right between his balls, digging the tip of his tongue into the base of his cock right when he thrust a teeny bit more with the tip of his finger.

Ellery started issuing more threats. "So help me, Jackson, I will tie you to this fucking bed, and I will fuck your ass with a vibrator while you watch me jerk off. You'll never come, just watch me spill over my hands, watch me lick my fingers dry, and you'll be stuck, shaking, and I'll be unmerci—*ful?*"

Very carefully, Jackson grazed the bell of his cock with gentle teeth while he thrust in to the first knuckle. Then, like a cat, he lapped a circle around the head, using the slightest pressure from one tooth on the frenulum while breathing on his wet cockhead.

Ellery let out a whine. Jackson kept his mouth over Ellery's cock, letting his tongue or his teeth or his lips brush up against it, seemingly at random, while Ellery let go of his head and bit the palm of his free hand, stifling a scream.

He shook all over—but didn't come.

Jackson arched an eyebrow and stared him down.

"You. Inside me," Ellery ordered. "Or me inside you. No power blow jobs this time."

Jackson responded by thrusting his finger in fully and licking long and lazily across Ellery's cockhead. Ellery shook some more, because Jackson's message was clear.

He could do this all day, and he'd definitely enjoy himself doing it.

"Not… gonna… work…," Ellery panted.

Jackson narrowed his eyes, jerking his head back. "Is that a challenge?"

Ellery made to lower his feet, but Jackson shoved forward and took him completely into his mouth, closing over his cock like a cave until he relented. He pulled back and glared at him.

"No seduction," Ellery panted. "All of you. Goddammit, I need all of you."

Jackson lowered his head and added another finger, twisting them hard while he swallowed.

"Ahhh…." Ellery breathed out, hard, body going limp while his cock stayed thick and throbbing. God, he was fighting hard.

"You think we're just going to do this once?" Jackson asked, letting his breath torment the damp end of Ellery's cock. "This is a teaser."

Ellery grabbed his hair again, hauling his head back, thighs still spread, Jackson's fingers in his ass. "The hospital, Jackson. And bugs in our fucking house. If you're not going to fuck me until I scream, I need to do the same to you."

Nungh. The last time they'd done this in a hotel room after Ellery had been scared, he'd dominated Jackson practically through the floorboards. Jackson couldn't pretend it hadn't felt good—or that he hadn't needed to turn his fate over to Ellery's capable hands, just once.

But not this time.

Jackson twisted his fingers hard, nailing Ellery's prostate. "You'll lie facedown on the fucking bed—"

"Face *up!*" His back arched, his cheeks flushed, and he pushed against Jackson's shoulders with his feet like he meant it and, more importantly, like Jackson could take it.

"Ass hanging off the bed," Jackson finished, spreading his fingers and teasing Ellery's banjo string with his tongue.

Ellery spurted precome, sweat popping out on his stomach, his forehead, his thighs with the fight not to come.

"Deal!" he cried. "Lube's in my suitcase."

Jackson pulled his fingers out abruptly, hoping the absence would leave Ellery hollow and aching, like it did when he pulled out of Jackson.

Ellery's suitcase lay on the rack in the closet, and Jackson wiped his hand off on his towel before he rooted through the neatly rolled pairs of boxers and black dress socks. There—a small kit, with lubricant. "And a cock ring and a plug?" Jackson wondered, standing up with the lubricant only.

"Do you think you're the only one with a hotel room kink?" Ellery asked archly.

He lay on the bed, as ordered, propped on his elbows, his feet braced against the edge, the robe falling off his shoulders and draped under his body. He was flushed pretty much from his toes to his nose, his eyes half-hooded and sultry. Ellery had probably never been a club bunny, never seduced guys for fun, but right now he could make a dead man hard.

Jackson was so damned glad he wasn't dead.

"These aren't the toys for a man with a one-night stand," Jackson noted, striding to the bed while slicking up his own aching erection.

Ellery fell back against the mattress, smiling wickedly. "That right there was for my wild nights alone," he said, shivering, in anticipation or recollection, Jackson couldn't tell.

"I'd like to watch you have one of those sometime," Jackson whispered. He didn't thrust in right away, because Ellery's small brown nipples called to him. He settled between Ellery's thighs, bent his head, and teased.

Ellery groaned and bucked up against him. "Hard and real this time," he ordered. "God, Jackson—I need real from you."

Jackson was too aroused to sigh. He grunted and pushed himself up to his knees, hauled at Ellery's thighs until they were draped over his shoulders, and thrust into Ellery without delay or ceremony.

Ellery sobbed hard, his ass contracting, rippling around Jackson almost immediately.

"You wanted this?" Jackson demanded.

"Yes!"

"Wanted me?"

"Needed, asshole. Fucking needed. Hard—*augh! Yes! That!*"

Jackson couldn't hold back—apparently wasn't supposed to. Ellery didn't want finesse, didn't want seduction. Just wanted Jackson, thrusting hard, fast, while Ellery's hand blurred on his own cock.

"God, what you do to me!" Jackson gasped, closing his eyes against the picture Ellery made, debauched, cock spitting pre, eyes closed, biting his lip as his body rocked with pleasure.

"Please," Ellery chanted. "Please, please, please, please...."

"Oh!" Oh no! So fast! His skin tingled—*everywhere*. His swollen groin contracted, his taint, his asshole, his stomach. He roared, trying to stay upright, but Ellery dropped his hips and he slid out.

"Dammit!"

Ellery kept his hips down and spread his thighs. "Down here," he ordered, shoving a pillow under his lower back and ass. "Balance on your good arm. Closer. Kiss me first."

Jackson needed back inside him so bad, he'd follow any order. He lowered his head, their chests brushing, and kissed him hard, their tongues meshing, tangling, the momentum in their bodies building again, harder, until Jackson blindly positioned himself and thrust in one more time.

The lube was running thin, and they both moaned slightly with the friction. Jackson scrabbled on the bed by Ellery's head, looking for the lube. Ellery grabbed his wrist and groaned.

"Hard, fast, dry—fuck me. Now."

Jackson spurted precome, just enough—it was the only way he could thrust his way in. Ellery moaned, head back, eyes closed, while Jackson pistoned his hips, lost to the rhythm, the dance, the overwhelming hunger that swamped him, drove him again and again into his lover's body until Ellery spasmed around him, gasping softly, then crying out, his voice pitching at the end as his cock spat come over his own fingers.

Oh! Jackson felt it, every ripple, every muscle in Ellery's body, clamping around Jackson inside him. Eyes still closed, lips half-parted, Ellery raised his hand to his mouth and licked the white ejaculate from his fingers, and that sent Jackson crashing into orgasm.

He screamed, his body taking over, leaving his will behind, and Ellery arched off the bed, then pulled him down into an embrace while Jackson rutted inside him, spilling hotly into Ellery's clenching ass.

He moaned then and collapsed against Ellery's chest. In the aftermath he could hear the faint whirr of the ceiling fan above him. Stealthily his headache threatened to crawl back up his spine.

"God," he panted, eyes closed because his body was apparently done for the day. "God, you made that hard."

Ellery's throaty laughter told Jackson he took that at pun value. "I hope so."

With a little sigh, Jackson rested his head on Ellery's shoulder while his cock popped out of Ellery's ass. "That's not what I meant."

Ellery dropped a kiss on his hair, the tenderness at odds with the bossy little shit he'd just been. "I know what you mean. You mean you seduce me and give me the mighty gift of your cock, oh endowed one, and you feel like you're out of debt."

Jackson grunted. "That's not—"

"That's *exactly* how you think about it when you do that," Ellery returned. "And sometimes it's okay. Sometimes I like it when you woo me like you owe me hearts and flowers, because I fucking like hearts and flowers."

"But now?" Jackson's eyes closed. Dammit. They really did have stuff to do, but apparently his head thought he got one more day of naps.

"You owe me staying alive," Ellery whispered, like this hurt him. "And you owe me acting like you want to live."

Jackson grunted. "I'm never going to not want this," he said, raw and wanting this resolved before he fell asleep. "Are you saying your ass is something to live for, Counselor?"

"Damned straight." Ellery chuckled. He kissed Jackson's forehead. "C'mon—let's get you under the covers. I'll wake you in a couple of hours and you can make your calls."

It was the promise that Ellery would wake him, wouldn't leave him out of the important stuff, wouldn't sideline him when their lives and home were on the line that let him get up, still dripping with sex, and crawl back into bed.

Ellery joined him until he fell asleep, still tapping on his phone.

"'D I say I love you?" Jackson asked before he completely lost consciousness.

"With every touch," Ellery told him softly. "Love you too."

JACKSON WOKE up about two hours later, surprised by the quality of the sleep. Ellery had ordered room service while he'd been out, but the roast beef sandwich the night before had been an anomaly—relief, perhaps, about being freed from the hospital. Ellery nagged like a bitter fishwife—but for good reason.

Jackson had lost maybe twenty-five pounds since November.

"Eat," Ellery muttered without looking up from his computer.

"No," Jackson said shortly, hauling himself up and blinking into the dimness of the hotel room. The late-afternoon shadows stretched long from the patio, and Jackson tilted his head back for a moment and scented the sea nearby. Ellery—dressed in sweats and a T-shirt, which was probably a good thing because Jackson wanted round two already—looked over his shoulder, dark brows knitted, product-less hair falling forward into his eyes. Jackson loved him best like this, usually curled up on their couch or sitting at the dinner table with a glass of wine Jackson couldn't pronounce. He'd taken to buying pinot grigio because it tasted like fruit juice and that was Jackson's favorite. Jackson would join him in the ritual, wondering why it was at these moments that Ellery looked relaxed and without artifice, but Jackson felt the most vulnerable.

"Please—"

"We can go out for dinner," Jackson said, smiling a little. "You can order wine."

Ellery bit his lip and lifted a shoulder. "Only if you eat a slider," he said. "We can leave in a couple of hours."

"Okay. Yeah. Let me make my phone call first. And then I need to text Crystal and Jade. Too much shit I left alone. Needs to be done."

Ellery nodded like he was just going to let it drop, but he wasn't fooling Jackson in the least. Jackson got out of bed, their sex still on his skin, and walked naked to the bathroom to wash up. When he came back, he put on a brand-new pair of underwear and a clean pair of Ellery's sweats, since his own had apparently not passed muster to pack. The T-shirt was his, though, a gift from Jade. It read "I am currently unsupervised. I know, it freaks me out too, but the possibilities are endless!"

Jackson found the shirt hilarious, but Ellery had just narrowed his eyes and shaken his head. Well, they'd established from the very beginning that Jackson needed a keeper and was too ornery to keep one around.

The room had a small couch, denim-colored, and Jackson grabbed his phone off the charger and shoved back into it and stretched his legs out in front of him before he found the number on his phone. Ace was a prickly sonovabitch, and Jackson silently debated whether he was going to need a sweatshirt or a sports jacket or a pair of cast-iron jockey shorts before he hit that call.

He decided on a hooded sweatshirt, got himself settled again, and hit the number.

"Garage."

Jackson recognized the voice on the other end of the line—nearing college age, Latina, and just as prickly as Ace. The girl had looked like any bored receptionist anywhere, but the way she'd defended her employers at their last meeting told Jackson everything he needed to know about family.

"That's it?" he asked. "You're just going to say 'garage'? Not Sonny's Place—"

"Who in the fuck are you?"

"I need to talk to Ace," he said, glad that the niceties were over.

"And you are…?"

"We met before in September—"

"You're the guy who had to use the bathroom."

Yes, he was—and he'd learned a whole lot talking to people while Ace had stonewalled Ellery in the garage.

"And you're the smart girl studying science. How'd you do in that class, anyway?"

"An A," she said reluctantly. "I got a 3.8 last semester. My mommy cried. It was beautiful. Why do you need to talk to Ace?"

Well, shit. "Because someone who fucked with Sonny back in the military might be the key to a general badass fucker all around. I need to talk to Ace because I'd like to talk to Sonny, and I know one won't happen without the other."

The girl grunted. "He won't let you talk to Sonny."

"Then maybe he'll talk to me. I'm not a cop, sweetheart. He meets me someplace nearby, like Barstow, we have a soda, some conversation, we see what we see. I don't want to arrest anyone, and I damned sure don't want to kick your little nest. Just want to chat."

"You don't sound completely stupid," she begrudged. "Give me your number."

Jackson was grateful it was a burner phone.

He hung up and leaned back and sighed.

"So, you're meeting him?" Ellery asked, still not looking up from whatever so absorbed him on the laptop.

"Nope. That was just the screening."

Ellery actually turned his head. "Who's screening his calls?"

"Alba. The girl who was in the clerk's office last time."

"She's what? Sixteen?"

Jackson returned his gaze levelly. "Don't fuck with smart girls," Jackson said, meaning every word.

Ellery nodded and returned glumly to his screen.

"What are you looking at?"

"An email from Arizona talking about pressing charges against Janie for obstruction of justice unless she goes on record saying who hit the woman at the crosswalk."

Jackson caught his breath. "Jesus—are you fucking kidding me?"

"Langdon forwarded it while you were asleep. I've been looking for ways to get her out of it—or at least ways to not make it worth Arizona's time."

"Wish Lacey would go after *her* for a change," Jackson grunted. He had no fondness in his heart for Arizona Brooks, the ADA Ellery dealt with on a regular basis. Ellery said she was just doing her job, but that summer her job had been to finger Kaden for a murder he didn't commit. That autumn her job had been to blow off Ellery and Jackson as they tried to get her to go after a serial killer. Apparently *now* her job was to go after an innocent girl who would rather go to jail than let the children in her care get hurt. Jackson thought the world might be a better place if Arizona wasn't so bloody good at her job.

But Ellery was staring at Jackson like he'd reinvented butter. "You know," he said, his eyes going to his right in that way that told Jackson he was about to create a really interesting strategy. "I think you're right. I think I *should* tell Arizona it was Karl Lacey. I think I should tell her *everything*."

"Except Sonny and Ace," Jackson reaffirmed.

"Oh yes. Except them. I think Arizona should make the decision to pursue this to the military. I mean, we're here. We're going to do our thing. But if suddenly the DA in Sacramento is poking around, what's the one thing Lacey isn't going to be looking into?"

"Us," Jackson said hopefully. "We're just two private citizens who made a phone call, after all. She's the DA."

Ellery smiled, all teeth. "Indeed she is."

But Jackson couldn't celebrate too soon. "Should we warn her?"

And to his credit Ellery said, "Yeah. I'll warn her. You didn't shoot the fuckin' planter that landed on your head. We've got witnesses. And you know what else I'll do while I'm warning her?"

Jackson held out his hand, inviting more.

"I'll ask her what in the fuck she did to get Lacey up to Sac in the first place. *That's* been nagging me for four days now. Why would he even have been in town to be speeding through a residential zone? The bugs in our house, the office, they've probably been there since Thanksgiving and they've got a system in place to re-up the batteries. What made him step it up so Anthony was putting a tracker on the car? We park in a public lot— why this weekend? What is going on that made the super paranoid military mind manipulator get super extra fucking paranoid right the fuck now?"

Jackson frowned. "Usually the thing that lights a fire under someone's ass is money. Think maybe Lacey has a contract that's about to get called?"

Ellery's eyes grew wide. "You know who I could ask about that?"

Jackson rolled his eyes. "Is there any pie your mother does *not* have a finger in?"

"No." He sounded proud of his mother—as he should be—but Jackson would never know how Ellery could not find her terrifying as well.

"Then by all means, call Lucy Satan and ask—whoop! There's Ace."

Jackson picked up the buzzing phone and figuratively adjusted his steel-plated underwear. "Jackson Rivers speaking."

"This is Ace Atchison, out in Victoriana, sir. You called me?"

And Jackson had to close his eyes and count to twelve. The good ol' boy dripping from Atchison's voice could be softened, mixed with garlic, and slathered on bread. Didn't mean Ace wasn't lying his ass off—just meant butter wouldn't melt in his mouth.

"Ace, I am on a secure phone, but I don't know if you are. I need to talk about someone from your and Sonny's past, and I need the information soon, and I don't want to handle it from here. I'm not a cop, I won't bring any cops to the meet, and I don't want to fucking pussyfoot around. We've got an innocent girl and the family she cares for depending on us, and somebody bugged our goddamned bedroom. Will you talk to me?"

A stunned silence echoed in Jackson's ear for a moment. When Ace spoke again, his voice was flinty hard and not sweet and not slick and not lying in the least.

"Sonny and me don't visit the past."

"This isn't the past, Ace. This is serial killers and military people who aren't doing what they fucking should. This is here and now—and don't think it can't reach out and grab you when you're not looking."

"I'll call back tonight."

The line went dead, and Jackson figured that was as good as it was going to get for a little. He looked over to where Ellery was composing an email with all the zeal of a mad maestro and stood and stretched. Ellery had packed his wallet, and he grabbed it from his duffel and swapped out the sweats for a pair of jeans.

"Where you going?" Ellery asked without even looking up.

"Walk. Got three more calls to make—might as well make them while moving."

Ellery frowned, finished a word, and turned to look at him. "Eat."

Jackson sighed, put a hand on his shoulder, and leaned over to grab a tiny hamburger from the plate stashed behind Ellery's computer. "Happy?" he asked through a full mouth.

Ellery refused to be distracted, putting his hand on top of Jackson's. "What's bothering you?"

"Say we get him. Lacey, that is. Get him how? How much do you know about military law?"

"I know the Geneva convention," Ellery said blithely. "Training people to kill outside military guidelines is illegal—"

"Cut the bullshit, Counselor." Jackson pulled away and tossed the rest of the slider in the trash. "We can't prosecute a case against him—we can only make the case and turn it over to the DA. And not the Sacramento DA, the state's district attorney, who is someone neither of us know."

Ellery took a deep breath, like he'd considered this already. "Mackenzie Jacobs, but we've only met once. And?"

"And this becomes a big state thing. And you and me, we become the prime witnesses in the state's case against a Navy commander. And you know where that gets us?"

Ellery looked away. "Dead or in protective custody."

Jackson nodded. "We gotta do it," he said after a moment. "That kid, Janie? She didn't do anything. Her boss, Evander—"

"Who just woke up from his coma and is in protective custody," Ellery supplied.

A tiny knot in Jackson's chest loosened. "That's good to know." He closed his eyes, and the face of the last guy he'd been questioning who knew more than he should flashed behind them. What was left of it after the drive-by, that is. "But he didn't do anything either. And we're the people who step up and say that's not right." Jackson tilted his head back and looked at the pristine, dustless ceiling. "I'm just… just in a new place. And I'm about to lose whatever freedom I ever had. I mean, from what I hear about protective custody, they might not even let us keep the fucking cat. I'm going for a walk."

"I'll text you when I'm done," Ellery said quietly. "I'd like to join you."

Jackson nodded, out of words about what it would mean, the two of them together under constant watch, constant threat of retribution, or the alternatives that were worse. They'd known, both of them, what this would mean.

They'd just never talked about it. They'd made love, made a home in Ellery's house, and continued to do their jobs like it wasn't all about to get ripped away because they'd stumbled into a hornet's nest in the summer and it was impossible to kill every pointy-assed bastard that was suddenly swarming around them.

"I won't go far," he said gruffly. He'd dragged Ellery into that first case, the one that cleared Kaden. He'd dragged him into it and then hadn't had the strength to refuse Ellery's insistent courtship. Somebody had wanted him, scars, nightmares, flaws, and all.

And now Ellery was as much the center as he was.

Jackson spun on his heel then, grabbed the spare key card from the TV stand, and walked out into the late-winter afternoon in San Diego.

A HALF hour later he'd walked the perimeter of the marina, through the hotel district, into the gaslight district, which featured the nice bistros and good places to eat. The temperature—midsixties—was comfortable, but the bright sunshine didn't fit his mood.

He wondered how many people wished for the fogs of June.

He'd spoken to Crystal, who assured him that Billy Bob was fine— and that no more bugs had shown up in anybody's houses and that they'd checked for traces on all the electronics and found them to be all clear.

"I don't think he's got a lot of computer resources," Jackson said thoughtfully. "I mean, we haven't seen it. He would have hacked into Ellery's computer if he did—we've got security, but we're hardly military grade."

"Yeah. I told Ellery the bugs were old—old technology. If he's government funded, they're not writing him a blank check."

"I wonder if they're thinking about stopping payment entirely," Jackson said thoughtfully, wondering again what Lacey and the crony who'd bribed Anthony had been doing in Sacramento. "That could certainly speed up their agenda."

"I'll look into it," Crystal promised, apparently reading his mind. "I mean, we don't have the greatest security—anyone who can't hack us is someone I can hack."

Jackson smiled. "Crystal, darling, you're a wonder—"

"How's AJ?" she asked quietly. Jackson had told her about the young man trying so hard to get clean.

"Ask Jade for pictures," Jackson told her, still paranoid about the phones. "He's having a good week."

"I had a bad night last night," she confessed, so openly, so easily he almost wanted to ask her what her secret was. "And the only thing that kept me from going out and scoring was remembering how hard you'd been working to help him stay clean. 'Cause you'd do the same thing for me—"

"Course!" Oh Lord—he'd had no idea she'd been on the edge. They'd been friends for years, lovers once even.

"I know you would. But I don't need to make you. Thinking about AJ made me remember how far I've come. So I needed to remember to thank you for that," she said softly. "It was just sort of floating around in my mind."

Jackson grinned. "Your mind's a lovely place, sweetheart. Don't let any of the crap flying around the world convince you different, okay?"

"I promise. Thanks, Jackson. I'll hack anything you need."

She hung up, and Jackson felt the muscles in his back, the ones locked in fight-or-flight since his discussion with Ellery, uncoil. The phone buzzing in his hand hardly made him jump.

"The Walmart in Barstow," Ace said shortly. "Just me. Tomorrow at two. Just you."

"McDonald's?" Jackson asked, because soda!

"You wish. If I'm going to Walmart, I'd better have some fucking ice cream, chips, and assorted kid food with me when I get back. No. We're going shopping, buddy boy. Bring your cart."

Ace hung up sharply, and Jackson took a few steps past a redbrick restaurant with a Lautrec-style cat on the front. He paused at the menu and saw steak, saw seafood, saw pasta, and saw wine—at thirty dollars minimum per plate.

Definitely Ellery's kind of place.

He texted Ellery the address and put his name in for a table for two in half an hour, then circled the block, grateful for the hooded sweatshirt in light of the breeze coming off the ocean. Then he called Jade briefly and got the numbers from Janie's witnesses from the private school.

"You guys okay?" she asked as his phone pinged with the info.

"Yeah. It's almost like vacation."

"Hunh."

"That's not bullshit—I swear!"

"No, no—I believe you. But you sound like you're all business, so I think you need to take better vacations."

Jackson laughed and hoped it didn't sound forced. "Maybe I like my job."

"Maybe you don't know what to do with yourself when you're not in Sacramento," she said.

Jackson grunted. "Kaden wants me to go to church and you want me to take a vacation—so much for twin telepath—"

"We want you safe," she said. "We want you happy. What do you want?"

He let out a noisy sigh. "I want Ellery not to regret knowing me. That's as far as I've gotten."

She sighed back, and before she could start again, he signed off.

"I love you, honey—text me with any new info, or with any more pictures. Oh! Ask Crystal to dinner tonight if you can?"

"Why? Is she okay?"

"No. And I don't think she'd mind me telling you that because she's frighteningly well-adjusted."

"What's that look like from afar?" Jade asked—but she sounded wistful too.

"It looks like a friend asking for help. Which is what I just did."

"You're infuriating, do you know that? No, don't answer. Just go."

Jackson hung up, trying not to gloat because he'd gotten the last word. He paused for a moment, looked around to make sure he wasn't being followed, and then clicked the number she'd sent him for one of Janie's witnesses.

Ms. Tina Paul, divorced, sounded sweet, distracted, and like she had way too many cats. She talked about Janie for five minutes, telling Jackson what a doll she was on the volunteer days and how much fun she had with the children. When Jackson asked her about Janie dropping off the kids on Friday, she actually thought hard about the question, though.

"Oh yes. Friday? That was the day Mindy Alves was killed. I remember, because about a minute after Janie pulled out, someone else had to stop short because a big sedan came speeding out of nowhere. When we heard about Miranda, I was sure that was the car that hit her. I still can't believe it was poor Janie."

Jackson stopped right there on the sidewalk and backed up against an alleyway so the brick of the building he was passing dug into the shoulders.

"Tina?" He spoke on speaker while frantically texting Jade.

"Yes, sir?"

"I need you to do me a big ol' favor. I'm going to have Carlyle Langdon, Janie's lawyer, get in touch with you. She *didn't* kill Mindy Alves—we have physical evidence to prove it, but an eyewitness who saw the other car could sure help. Do you remember who the sedan cut off?"

"Lessee…. Oh yes. Courtney Lester's dad. Would you like me to tell them that too? Oh, wait—I have another call—"

"That's them," Jackson said, relieved. "Tell them what you told me, the truth as far as you saw it, and tell them anyone else who might have seen it—"

"Principal Conrad, Eliza Jefferson—"

"Give them all the names," Jackson said fervently. "Honey, you might have just saved Janie's whole future. Answer them now, and have a nice day."

He hung up and let out a long breath. Oh thank God—Janie had a witness.

"Jackson?"

Ellery had dressed nicely, in black jeans and a black turtleneck. He'd slicked back his hair and shaved, and Jackson felt a little bit grubby, having just run out of the hotel room wearing jeans and a hoodie.

"Hey!" Jackson smiled at him sunnily, so relieved to have something good to say to him, something real that made what they were doing worth it.

"Is this the place?" Ellery looked dubiously at the brewery whose alley Jackson had co-opted, and Jackson shook his head, embarrassed.

"No—I was sneaking in a phone call before you got here—want to hear some good news?"

Ellery's face lightened as they walked, his lean mouth parted almost eagerly as he drank in the story, and he looked boyish, a young professional with nothing more serious on his mind than his next car.

Jackson walked him back around the block to the restaurant he'd picked, which possessed a little raised patio and thick glass doors between the outside tables and the inside, and showed him the menu next to the entrance.

"This looks great—seriously, though? We've got witnesses?"

"A shit-ton," Jackson confirmed, nodding at the leggy hostess with the apple cheeks, brown/bronze complexion, and sparkling sepia-colored eyes.

She smiled, showing off the adorable cheeks, and picked up two menus. "Rivers for two?"

"Yeah. That's us." Jackson let Ellery precede him through the door and put his hand on the small of Ellery's back as they walked through the restaurant. Something about the way Ellery's posture—usually ramrod straight—relaxed just a tad told Jackson he liked this maneuver, this tiny bit of public touching.

Jackson rubbed his thumb surreptitiously along Ellery's spine and wondered if they could make love again, maybe even twice, before he had to head out for a Walmart in Barstow.

He remembered what Jade had said about a vacation, what Kaden had said about letting Ellery be thankful for him.

What Crystal had done, by simply telling a friend she wasn't okay.

Maybe it was time for Jackson to set down his burdens, his worry about not being good enough, his many, many fears. Maybe he could take a vacation from his defensiveness and some of his pain.

He was out with a handsome, intelligent person who wanted to be with him—wanted, in fact, to seize his hand and run into a storm on the horizon that only the two of them could sense—just because it *was* Jackson's hand.

"What?" Ellery said after they were seated in a quiet corner. The interior was done in the same cream-colored wood as the outside front. It didn't have the intimacy of the redbrick brewery, but it did have a sense of freedom.

Jackson didn't bother to ask what Ellery was talking about. For tonight he was done with that game.

"I dream about you," he said, frowning. "I mean, I dream about everybody I love. Some nights it's Kaden and Rhonda and the kids. Some nights it's Jade and Mike. Some nights it's the damned cat. But most nights it's you. And… and the shit going on is always heinous. And it's always bloody or worse. And I'm always too late. Because I don't get nice things, right? I don't get good people in my life. But… but you look really good tonight, Ellery. You look young and happy and excited to be out. And I want to have a good night with you. I want to… to hold your hand back to the hotel and pretend the worst thing we have to worry about is some stupid homophobe that I could drop in a hot second. I want you to not have to look at me like I'll break into a thousand pieces, because I just told you my damage, and it's not hurting us tonight. Can we do that?"

Ellery's warm brown eyes had gone shiny, and his mouth parted slightly to form a little O.

"Sure," he said softly. "You just did a good thing—a thing I wanted to do and was afraid I couldn't because we came down here. My client has witnesses—not just one, but a lot of them—who back up her story. Arizona got to me before you texted. She said she's looking into the location of one Navy commander on a certain day this month. She told me that Pentagon allocations are decided upon in two weeks, so he may have had some friends in Sacramento that he wanted to go speak for him in Washington. So you and me, we're doing our job. And we did it good. And I want to take a night off, because this really hot guy with"—his face went slack—"these *amazing* green eyes has spotted a restaurant that has my favorite kind of wine."

"Does it really?" Jackson asked, taking a sip of his water.

"Does it really what?"

"Have your favorite kind of wine?"

Ellery nodded happily, and Jackson pumped his fist.

"Score!"

Ellery's chuckle warmed his soul, and together they went searching through the wine menu for fermented Kool-Aid, which was Jackson's wine of choice.

Dinner conversation revolved around work, of course, but now that they were both relaxing just a tad for Janie's safety, Jackson felt safe enough to drop in a few details about Tina Paul's many cats and the six times she'd said "Down, kitty!" as she seemed to be moving about the house.

He talked about Crystal and her naked admission that she'd had a bad night, and about how he hoped they could get AJ to admit the same thing. Ellery listened attentively, of course, and asked questions.

And was concerned in the same way Jackson was.

And laughed at Jackson's jokes.

As the waitress approached, Ellery said, "Can I order for you?" He'd been scanning the menu while Jackson talked, and Jackson shrugged.

Ellery ordered prime rib for Jackson and chicken marsala for himself, and then their wines, and as the waitress walked away, Jackson knew his mouth had twisted sardonically.

"What?" Ellery dared.

"I'm not that hungry."

Ellery let the lie bounce between them for a moment until Jackson swallowed and looked away.

"How bad's the truth?" Ellery asked softly. "As bad as watching you fight with yourself every time we sit down to eat?"

Jackson let out a breath slowly through his nose. "You stayed with me," he said quietly. "In the hospital this last time. I mean, by now it drives you batshit, but you stayed with me through my concussion. I puked up shit I haven't eaten yet, and you stayed. Why?"

Ellery regarded him warily, like this was a trick question. "You hate it there," he said. "I mean, after November, you... I'm not even sure you can walk into a morgue anymore, and you've got a friend who works down there."

Jackson let a smile slip through. "Toe-Tag," he said fondly, thinking about Toby Tagliare, the almost obscenely cheerful little hobbit of a man who was Jackson's contact at Med Center's morgue. "He'd rather see us at dinner at his place, anyway."

Ellery inclined his head, admitting this was true, but true to his nature, he didn't let go. "A dinner you don't eat."

Jackson hadn't been able to put words to this until Thanksgiving at Ellery's parents' house, when everything was about eating.

"When I get too full, it's… it's the same weight on my chest," he said, knowing that was impossible. "It's the same weight I feel in the hospital. I feel like I have to fight for every breath there now. Like I'm a million breaths overdue, and God or someone's trying to take every last breath as it's working in my chest. When I get full, or even satisfied a little… that's what I feel. Last night, when I woke up and we were on the road, I felt so… so light. I could eat and skate on the feeling. But now…."

Ellery reached across the table to cover his hand, and for an irrational moment, Jackson wanted to snatch his hand back and tuck them both under his armpits. But he'd promised. For this dinner, for this moment, he would set his burdens down and trust that Ellery could handle them.

"That's awful," Ellery said, voice still pitched low. "I can see why eating would be a burden. Maybe tonight you can pretend, just for a little, that you're free. You're so free you can eat a meal in peace. Do you want to see if you can do that?"

Jackson nodded and, feeling brave, turned his hand so it was palm up. Ellery laced their fingers together and squeezed.

They didn't say much for a few moments, until the waitress arrived with their wine and a bread plate. When they separated their hands and tasted their wine and talked about the bread, the moment faded.

It had done its job, though. Jackson's shoulders, his chest, felt a little lighter by the time dinner arrived.

He felt light enough to eat.

A GENTLE fog was crawling in off the bay as they walked back, and Jackson turned his face to the ocean and tried to see where the water ended and the sky began.

"'S pretty," Ellery said, and *whoop!* There was that innocence again.

"It's dangerous," Jackson corrected gravely, foreboding inching up his spine.

"You're both," Ellery said mildly, and Jackson rolled his eyes.

"If I was all that dangerous, don't you think I could keep my skin intact?"

And for once Ellery laughed.

Where the Desert Meets the Sky

WHEN THEY got back to the hotel room, they left the lights off. Ellery had opened the blackout curtains, and what remained was a thin layer of gauze between them and the far horizon and just enough light to see by.

Just enough light to see Jackson lick his lips nervously as Ellery shut the door and then turned to take his mouth.

Jackson responded, and Ellery's stomach fluttered like a virgin's. This was a new kind of kissing for them, delicate, dancing, as though they were learning each other all over again.

The thing Jackson had done at the dinner table that night had been huge. Tremendous. Bigger than the ocean and the sky put together.

When he'd run out of the hotel room without eating, Ellery's heart had dropped to his feet—God. Every time Jackson had a moment, in bed, eating dinner, just getting a peck on the cheek, when Ellery thought "This is it. We're going to be okay because *he's* okay," something—usually something small, like a badly timed wisecrack or leftovers gone bad because nobody was eating them—would remind Ellery that sometimes broken didn't heal.

But then… just when Ellery could see the horizon, the drop off the face of the planet for the two of them, Jackson would surprise him in the best of ways.

The nice restaurant, obviously chosen with Ellery in mind, had warmed him.

Jackson's moment of laying his burdens down had inspired him.

Oh God! His taste as Ellery took his mouth—not just food and wine, but excitement, passion, joy! Ellery drank him in, felt his sinews and bones saturate with Jackson, until Jackson was the blood in his veins and the air in his lungs.

Ellery caught Jackson's cheeks between his hands and steered him toward the bed, pulling the coverlet down with one hand while he was pushing Jackson down with the other.

"In a mood?" Jackson asked playfully. For a while—a short while— he'd insisted that he'd always topped. When they'd met, Ellery had been very content to bottom. But Ellery had never before had a relationship where the conflicts outside of the bedroom powered what went on in bed.

Now, as he knelt over Jackson and stripped off his sweatshirt and tee and then his jeans, he had to concede that was because never before had he had a man in his bed he'd loved so much that he couldn't put him in a box. Jackson had never been in a "lover" box or a "work" box—not even when all they were was just coworkers.

Jackson had always been too big, too important, too *dangerous* to cage up in a flimsy label.

As he stretched out now, naked on the white sheets, Ellery paused for a moment to spread his hand possessively at the base of Jackson's throat.

"Mine," he said softly, because truly it was the only label that mattered.

"Yours," Jackson responded, green eyes colorless in the pale light.

Ellery nodded. "Stay there," he whispered. "Just… you know. Until I'm done."

He stripped off his turtleneck and jeans, then kicked off his loafers and stood naked by Jackson's bedside. Jackson paused him with his own show of possession, splaying his hand over Ellery's abdomen because that's where he could reach.

"Mine," he said gruffly.

"Nobody else's," Ellery told him, sweetness aching in his throat. He laced their fingers together, like he had in the restaurant, and leaned forward to rejoin their kiss. Their naked bodies slid together silkenly, and the pleasant rasp of the hair on Jackson's thighs and chest prickled along his skin.

There were no words then as the kiss continued, grew greater, hungrier. The kiss was the main thing. Ellery fumbled for the lube under the pillow and slid into Jackson's ass with a smooth thrust, and Jackson, who used to fight possession until Ellery demanded he submit, simply welcomed Ellery into his body, so easy, so simply, it was like they belonged there, joined, for every breath, every moment of the day.

It was being apart that fought nature.

Orgasm started as a rumble in his belly, built to a roar in their ears, crested like a scream when Jackson spurted hotly between them, no hand on his cock to spur him on.

Ellery gasped, trembling and climaxing, welcoming Jackson's arms and legs folding him into the haven of his embrace, the warm clutches of his body.

Ellery slid off him and rolled to the side, their sex staining the sheets, although neither of them made a move to clean it off.

Their breath didn't seem to be calming down.

"Ellery?"

"Yeah?"

"Love you."

"I love you too."

"We've got the rest of the night, right?"

"To have sex? Because I think I'm done for the day."

Jackson chuckled and rolled to his side so he could kiss Ellery's shoulder. Ellery shuddered with the kiss and wondered hazily if maybe round three couldn't be arranged.

"Not sex. To be free."

Ellery had to blink hard before he understood what Jackson was saying. He'd given himself permission, just for tonight, to be free of his burdens, of his hard choices, of his pain.

Part of Ellery wanted to just scream at him, "*You are always free!*"

But Ellery had seen the moments in Jackson's life that made up the iron bars of his cage, and that wasn't fair. Nobody with Jackson's damage could be free all the time.

"As long as you can see the sky," Ellery said softly. "We'll say you're free."

"Mm...."

Jackson kissed his shoulder again and then blessedly, blessedly fell asleep.

ELLERY WOKE up in the morning, sitting up in bed with a gasp of panic, like his sister said she used to when her children slept through the night.

The shower was running and the space next to him still warm from Jackson's body, and it took him a minute to figure out what was wrong.

Nothing.

Jackson had slept through the night.

For the first time in months, he'd slept completely through the night without so much as a twitch or a whimper to indicate the horrors of his subconscious had slithered up to haunt him. Ellery took a deep breath and blinked, the freshness of his own mind telling him how hard it had been on *him* to be the calming hand and soothing voice that called Jackson back to reality.

Jackson used to sleep with any willing body when he was afraid the nightmares would come. Ellery had become the one body either of them was willing to let do the job. It was a fair trade—sleep for exclusivity—but God, it was nice to get some sleep.

Ellery flopped back into bed on a happy yawn and grabbed his phone. The first thing he saw was a text message from Arizona.

Felt out Lacey's secretary to see if he'd been in town. Call ASAP. Apparently the text had been what woke him up, so he hit Call without even getting out of bed.

"Ellery, where are you?" Arizona, fiftyish, buzz-cut iron-gray hair, sounded exactly as no-bullshit on the phone as she looked in real life wearing one of her white pantsuits. Right now Ellery had to fight the urge to get out of bed and put on a shirt.

"Out of town," he said cagily. "Why do you need to know?"

Arizona swallowed. "Stay there," she said shortly. "Your guy went back to his base on Monday, and your office dumped a fuckton of witnesses on my desk that says the girl couldn't have done it. She's off the hook completely and still in protective custody until this wraps up, but...." Arizona hissed like she was trying to keep her voice down and her profile low so somebody else didn't see her. "Seriously," she murmured. "Don't tell me where you are, but you need to know—if your guy's the bastard you think he is, he is gunning for you. I never mentioned your name, but the secretary told me—and I quote, 'Any evidence Mr. Cramer brings up in the matter can be brought into question at any time. He needs to be present to press charges—'"

"That's not true!" Ellery protested, because basic law! The DA pressed charges; the defense attorney defended the client from them.

"I know! Do you think I don't know that? It wasn't that she got it wrong, dumbass, it was the 'present' that's the problem. She was reading a message—verbatim. Somebody wanted you to know that you might not be *present* to act as a witness!"

Ellery swallowed hard. "Oh," he said, heart thundering in his chest. Oh Jesus. Jackson was actually *singing* in the shower, God help them both. Granted, it was "The Hanging Tree" from that sci-fi movie franchise that sent shivers up Ellery's spine, but still. Singing.

He had a really beautiful voice. Ellery thought wistfully of hearing Jackson sing in temple someday, and then he swallowed.

A threat to Ellery's life would stop the singing right quick.

"Does he know I'm not in Sacramento?" Ellery asked, and then, "Goddammit motherfucking son of a cocksucking whore!"

There was a stunned silence on the other end. "Uhm...."

"I didn't use the burner phone," Ellery said softly. "I, uh… fuck." He fought the temptation to clunk himself in the head with the offending cell phone. "Is there anything else?"

"Yeah. She also read—like an automaton, I'm serious—that 'Ellery's associate, Mr. Rivers, has experienced too much adversity of late to be a reliable resource in this matter.'"

Ellery almost dropped the phone. "Uhm…."

"Was he talking about November?" she asked, and Ellery wanted to laugh until he cried.

"Jesus, Arizona, do you not read anything we send to you? Did you look at the Cedric Evander transcript?"

"You know, that's weird. I got two of them—one signed by William MacPherson, who was apparently actually on scene, and one signed by Greaves, who was the guy who signed off on the Janie Isaacson incident—"

"He wasn't assigned to that one either," Ellery told her. "Another cop— Ty Spooner, I think, his name is in my notes—but call McPherson. Call him as soon as we hang up and double-check. Because McPherson was there at the Cedric Evander shooting, and he can tell you what she was talking about, and after you're done crapping a bag of ice, get back to me."

"What are you going to be doing?" she asked.

"Switching locations," Ellery said sourly. "And probably trading in my phone."

And telling Jackson. And not hearing him sing again for another four months.

"Understood." Arizona let out a sound of frustration. "Ellery, I've got a meeting with the state's attorney in an hour—is there anything I need to know?"

Ellery closed his eyes. "Five bugs, Arizona. Two in my office, one in my kitchen, one in my living room, and one in my bedroom. Our bedroom. Contact Crystal at our firm—she's got the equipment to sweep the office. All of it. Contact Carlyle Langdon and ask if she can assist you."

"Jesus," Arizona breathed. Then, proving once and for all why her and Ellery's friendship had persisted in spite of working on different sides of the bench for the last six years, "I hope you and Rivers had so much sex their ears exploded."

Ellery's chuckle was as evil as he could make it. "God, I hope so."

"Take care of yourself. Contact me when you can."

"Will do."

And she signed off.

Ellery stood and contemplated throwing the phone against the wall and then remembered he was the grown-up in this situation. He stood and stretched, his mind working furiously.

He needed a new cell phone.

They needed a new hotel.

Jackson *needed* to go to Barstow.

He needed to not freak Jackson out.

Okay, first things first.

He picked up his burner phone and texted Crystal, asking her to make reservations in another nice hotel with her credit card—or to ask someone else to do it for her.

Then he stripped down and stepped into the shower with Jackson, who was still singing at the top of his lungs. Ellery slid his hands around Jackson's hips and rested his chin on his shoulder. Jackson clasped his hands at his waist and *hmm*ed.

"What's up, Counselor?"

And Ellery couldn't do it. Not right then. Over coffee and breakfast later, perhaps. But God—he'd slept through the night. He'd laid down his burdens.

Later. I'll tell him later.

Ellery tugged on Jackson's hip so he'd turn and then kissed him, and Jackson kissed him back. They didn't actually have sex in the shower—they necked mostly, soaped their hair, made small jokes. They made love afterward, tucked under the covers to escape the chill of the water drying on their skin.

Before they went to breakfast—and before Ellery came clean about the phone and the need to change hotels and the bad things Arizona had told him—he made Jackson pose for a selfie. Ellery used the burner phone and studied the picture of the two of them, Jackson's face tucked shyly against Ellery's shoulder, hair a tousled disaster from their morning, and a small smile playing with the corner of his mouth.

Ellery emailed it to his account and texted it to Jackson and then, after a little bit of thought because it was potentially squidgy, to Jade.

For Jade, he captioned it with *Don't freak out—I just wanted you to see him happy.*

She responded *Thanks. It's just good to see.*

Before Jackson had stormed into his life that August, demanding Ellery's help for Kaden, Ellery had assumed he'd win every battle. He fought in the courtroom, and he was damned good at what he did.

But then he'd seen what happened when the battle wasn't neat, wasn't pretty, wasn't between people in suits with measured words as their weapons. He'd seen too damned much of Jackson's blood, both the figurative and the very red and real.

He knew now that every win was a big win. Any battle he fought had to mean something. And that a smile on camera from the man he loved was the one victory he absolutely could not live without.

Lone and Freaked-Out Fish

JACKSON TRIED to control his breathing. "He threatened us."

Ellery nodded slowly, sort of like Jackson was a bomb. Well, he might be. "Through two other people, yes. It was a very direct threat."

"And you called her back on your cell."

"Yes. Yes, I did that, and it was a bad move."

"And that's why we packed."

"Yes, Jackson. That's why we packed. I'm sorry. I was dumb and not thinking right, and I really should be smacked upside the head—"

"Shut up," Jackson muttered, annoyed. "It's a mistake anybody could make. Man, we're not trained to be spies. I'm surprised I wasn't the one who did it while I was walking the block last night. No, don't shit your pants about who did it, shit your pants about fucking up the meeting with Ace, because if you think I'm just driving off and leaving you in a hotel lobby, you've got another thing coming."

"The hotel lobby thing is not a problem—"

"Oh yes it is," Jackson snapped. Dammit. Jackson should have known— nothing as good as the night before came without a price. Well, his price for getting a decent night's sleep and singing in the shower was apparently dragging Ellery to Walmart in Barstow. "For one thing, you can get a new phone, preferably a different brand with a different number and a different plan, maybe under your mother's name. While you're doing that, I'll meet with Ace—"

"But what if he spots me?"

Jackson gave him a level look. "He'll know you're there before he even shows up at the meet. You don't spring surprises on a rattlesnake, Ellery. That's a good way to get bit."

Ellery sighed and ran his fingers through his hair. He'd slicked it back with product again after they got out of bed, and Jackson missed the rumpled look, and even the frizz it had in the humidity. Jackson was going to miss a lot of things about that morning and the night before until they got back home.

But somewhere in his chest was a tiny ember of hope that they would get back home. That he could have other nights when he let Ellery take his weight.

When he could let himself—let *them*—be happy.

It was almost a foreign concept, that happiness. Jackson hadn't been sure it existed, really.

Until the night before, when he'd been too tired not to believe.

"You sure he'll still show up?" Ellery asked on a sigh.

"I'm, uh… hope… uh… fifty-fifty," Jackson told him. He didn't do things any way but honest.

"I wouldn't take those odds," Ellery said glumly. "Those people in Victoriana *really* hate me."

Jackson really *didn't* do things any way but honest—which was why he didn't argue. Instead he stood and squeezed Ellery's shoulder. "You settle up with the hotel. Meet me back in the lobby with our shit. Ready?"

"Break," Ellery said with a game smile.

Jackson winked and pretended optimism, which wasn't really an out-and-out lie. "Hey—maybe we'll catch him on a good day, you think?"

HE WAS sort of half right.

"Well, shit," Ace muttered after Jackson told him. "That lawyer guy?"

"Yeah, Ace. I'm sorry. He needs a new phone, and I just don't… you know."

"Trust the fuckin' gods not to do something stupid and shitty while you're gone?" Ace snarled over the phone.

Jackson shrugged, even though Ace couldn't see him tucked in an alcove of the hotel lobby. The wallpaper above the moldings was a textured red. Jackson liked it and thought wistfully that he could have stayed there a full week.

"That exactly," he said to Ace. "In fact, I can't think of a better way to phrase it."

Ace chuckled without mirth. "Yeah—well, that's why Sonny's gonna be there. I was, like, 'Leave him safe in Victoriana with Ernie' or 'Leave him in Victoriana where he's easy to pick off without me.' Only one place I got control, you know?"

He wondered who Ernie was, but he wasn't going to break their rapport by being curious now. "You know, Ace, it's almost like we could be friends."

"That's fuckin' stretchin' it. See you at two. Maybe keep your lawyer friend in the phone section while we're buying food and Sonny won't lose his shit. And, uh, let Sonny push the cart and stay back with me. Last time he was pissed at me, he gave me a flat tire with the cart that bled for a week. Hurts like a sumbitch. I don't recommend it."

Well, maybe not friends. "See you at two," Jackson said and then hung up with a shudder. He liked Ace just fine, but Sonny.... Five sentences, maybe less, exchanged with Sonny Daye had left Jackson wondering exactly how fine the line between sanity and psychosis really was.

THE TRIP to Barstow was... well, bleak. A couple of strip-mall suburbs surrounded by desert. Of course in January the desert showed the consequences of a little rainfall, namely a thin layer of green that could be grass or algae or just land mange. But Jackson got to drive the new Infiniti, and damn. He'd finally conceded to the idea that the Honda CR-V was the shit, and now he might actually have to admit that the Infiniti was the orgasm of SUVs. He spent the first fifteen minutes of the two-hour drive having a big messy climax over the damned car, and when he'd subsided in embarrassment, he caught the utterly charmed way Ellery was looking at him and decided it was worth it to get a little excited about things.

After that they discussed the case, mostly, and Ellery spent time on his burner phone, texting Arizona and Jade and generally meddling in the case he'd claimed to have let go.

"And the state's attorney says...," Ellery muttered to himself. "Oh. Oh Lord. It's the need more evidence thing."

Jackson snorted. "It's the doesn't want to rock the boat thing. Janie is off the hook, though, right?"

"Yeah. And pending investigation she's in protective custody. Evander's out of the coma, which is nice, and apparently his family came home and *they're* in protective custody now too."

"Giving the cops lots of babysitting gigs," Jackson remarked. "They're gonna love us!"

Ellery rolled his eyes. "Because we're so well-liked already." Mm... yeah. The vote was still out about Jackson and Ellery. On the one hand, Jackson had worn a wire in an IA sting when he'd been on the force—that was bad. On the other, he'd almost been killed for wearing it, and that stung, because the cop he'd been after had been well and truly dirty. On the one hand, Ellery had defended someone suspected of killing a cop— and that was bad. On the other, the dirty cop who'd done it had brought down someone in politics, and that was actually a mark in their favor. The roster sheet of plusses and minuses went on and on, but the upshot was that they had a few staunch supporters in the system who would follow them into hell.

But the general consensus was that following them would lead you there anyway.

"Who needs the cops?" Jackson said, trying to pull Ellery out of the funk he'd been in since he'd admitted the cell phone mistake. "We've got each other."

Ellery laughed shortly and reached over to brush Jackson's hand as it rested on his knee while he drove with his left. "All true," he admitted gravely, and Jackson felt a little buzz for being the guy who gave comfort for once instead of needing it.

Jackson had always had a strange fascination with Walmart. There hadn't been one in his area until he was about fifteen, and even then, it was two buses away. As an adult who liked the odd and the eclectic, the personal, he was sort of appalled.

But then, peanut butter, jelly, and bread to last for a month for under ten dollars.

You just couldn't shit on a place that let people eat when they made diddly over squat.

"So you know the drill," he warned.

"Yes, once we get to the entrance I take off and pretend not to know you," Ellery filled in blandly. "I get it. Come get me when it's safe to talk."

Jackson smiled, and a hint of the intimacy they'd shared in the last two days returned. He grabbed Ellery's hand and leaned in to kiss his cheek, but Ellery turned his head instead and their lips met, clung for a moment, parted.

"Get the biggest, newest phone you can find," he said fondly. "It'll make you feel better."

Ellery grinned. "I'll take your permission and double down on the data plan," he said and swanned out of the car with panache.

Jackson waited a few minutes and walked up to the entrance, trying not to look like a creepy guy scoping out Walmart. He and Ellery had arrived about two minutes early. At exactly two o'clock, the roar of a souped-up racing engine in a wasp-yellow Ford SHO lit up the air with nitrous and danger. Jackson watched as Ace skidded into a seemingly unreachable parking spot like his car was the last piece of the puzzle. The quiet when the car shut off left the busy Walmart parking lot sounding deserted.

Back in Jackson's tomcatting days, he would have hit that in a hot second and then used fantasies of the encounter to fuel his spank bank for years to come.

Ace Atchison wasn't that tall—maybe about five ten—but he was built. Muscles the size of cannonballs strained at his worn sweatshirt, and his hard-eyed face was dominated by a square jaw and a lush mouth. He had a way of curling his lip when he spoke that told a potential lover it would be hard and it would be rough and it would be unmerciful. Until Ellery, Jackson had only topped. He'd changed because Ellery just demanded the intimacy of being vulnerable on both sides. Watching that hard-eyed, rough-bodied man stride toward the store entrance, Jackson was forced to admit that before Ellery he would have freely bent over and let himself be plundered by Ace Atchison.

There would be no intimacy unless Ace willed it to be, and getting his asshole destroyed by the crisp-moving, slow-talking military man would have simply been a way for Jackson to be all he could be.

But that was Ace all by his lonesome.

Watching Ace stride up to where Jackson stood with Sonny by his side was a revelation.

The hard brown eyes softened, for one, and the mouth, with that curling upper lip, relaxed thoughtfully. The posture didn't change, but there was an intimation that any violence from Ace would be aimed elsewhere. Anywhere but at the small, twitchy man at his side.

"Ace!" Jackson stepped forward with his hand extended, hoping to do things civil-like. Ace stepped forward and shook his hand briefly, nodding with firm purpose.

"Rivers, nice to see you." That was obviously a lie. "You're looking…." That lip curl came and went. "Scrawny. You're looking scrawny. You looked scrawny in September, but brother, you are looking sickly now. You get shot again?"

Jackson swallowed. That was… frank. "How'd you know I got shot the first time?" he asked, curious. Their first encounter had been short, because if Ellery had stayed in the garage any longer, Sonny might have driven a screwdriver through his eye socket.

"We got a laptop," Ace said mildly. "We looked you up. So that's a yes on the shot again."

"Mm… more like stabbed a couple times and a little bit sick. Getting better, though. Nice of you to be concerned."

"He ain't concerned," Sonny snapped. "He's sayin' you look like hell. Ace, can we go inside?"

"Nice to see you again too," Jackson said, his mouth twitching at the corners. "And let's go. I've got some stuff I need to get too." Ellery had packed fairly thoroughly, but Jackson was as incapable as the next person of getting through Walmart without buying something he hadn't planned on and had no use for.

They took a few steps in, and true to his word, Ace stepped back and let Sonny grab the cart. Sonny, five-foot-five inches of wiry, pissed-off redneck kid, shoved the cart along the tile floor fast and hopped up on the back of it and coasted along as they passed through clothes.

"Ace!" he called.

"Yeah, Sonny."

"Need T-shirts?"

"Yeah. Something fun."

"Okay. Need underwear?"

"Yup. Socks too."

"'Kay. You two talk. Right there. Stand right there and talk. I'll be back."

The clothes were situated on a carpeted area, and Sonny indicated the tile with an imperious nod of his pointed little chin. His gray eyes could have frozen chili.

But Jackson got it. *Hey, bub, that's my patch. He stays in my sight because he's mine.*

Sonny went for T-shirts, going for the XL rack and clucking over the things written on the fronts, and Jackson felt a sudden kinship.

"You can get funny ones on Amazon," he said mildly, thinking about the one he'd ordered from the hotel room and wondering if it would be home when he and Ellery returned.

"I'll keep that in mind," Ace said, smiling a little. "Our friend Ernie likes that site. Clothes shopping is still new to Sonny, you know? Two years out of the Army and he's still excited not to be wearing OD green."

Jackson breathed out through his nose. There was more to it than that—Jackson could tell—but he wasn't there to exorcise Sonny's demons any more than necessary, and Ace apparently remembered that fact at the same time.

"So what is it you need to know?"

"Master Sergeant Thomas Galway—"

Ace's face closed down like a prison gate. "Sonny—"

"No," Jackson ordered, voice low, grateful when Sonny didn't look up. "I don't care how he died." Ellery had told Jackson there was something hinky about the death report, and just looking at Atchison's grim expression told Jackson there was a whole lot there nobody asked about. "I don't give a shit—"

"Everybody cares when an officer dies," Ace hissed. "Don't feed me that bullshit—"

"I'm not the cops. I'm not the military—"

"Then why you gotta know so bad? Girl shot him, then she got killed in a mortar blast. I took shrapnel. All done."

Girl shot him? Jackson had heard that too—a nine-year-old had stolen Ace's pistol and killed the guy who was trying to kick her out of a military bunker during a shelling. Deserved? Yes. Probable that a terrified kid would steal this man's military issue?

Not bloody likely.

"Look," Jackson hissed. "Listen for thirty seconds. You say he ended up dead. Good. Because if he was anything like the guy who lost the back of his head in November, the planet is a better fucking place. But my guy was trained somewhere, do you understand? And Galway was trained somewhere. And they both ended up in the desert at the same time, but my guy went walkabout and your guy stayed wherever the hell you were to piss you off. Now my guy came back from the desert, changed his name, changed his face, and pretended to be a cop for two years while he systematically killed off young street people and got hard watching his buddy beat little girls to death."

Ace gasped, the look of revulsion on his face a clear indication of where his moral compass truly sat.

"Yeah—he was a real fuckin' charmer. But here's what I'm saying. He and Galway were *trained* together. Do you understand me? And they shipped out together, after having been part of a secret fucking unit. Now Owens served under Galway for a couple of months and vamoosed, but I want to know who trained them. Because it's one thing if you go out to war and come back crazy, or if you just started out crazy in the first place, but the last thing we need on this green earth is someone cooking up crazy in a big crazy cauldron and feeding it to us with a goddamned shiv!"

Ace's eyes got really big, and he took a few steps back. "Trained?" he said, voice cracking. His fair skin seemed perpetually sunburned most days, but as Jackson watched, the color drained right out of him. "That motherfucker was *trained*?"

"Yeah," Jackson said, keeping his voice low. "And I need to know where and how. Any light you can shed—"

"Sonny…." Ace squeezed his eyes shut, and Jackson had been shot a few times, but he'd never been to war with the man he loved. Whatever horrors were going on in Ace Atchison's head were not for the weak and not ever going to go away. "Sonny might know," Ace muttered. "Hell, Ernie and…." He stopped then and shot Jackson a hard look, like he was remembering himself. "Never mind. Galway worked in the auto bay, and Sonny worked under him. I… I was an officer, but Galway ranked me. I just… I tried to keep Sonny out of trouble, you know?" His voice pitched dangerously, and Jackson suddenly wished he could pull Ace out of Walmart and let him have this moment somewhere private.

Men like Ace and Jackson didn't like people to see this part of their hearts.

"You got him back okay," Jackson said, feeling inadequate.

"Almost didn't," Ace rasped. "You don't understand. That piece of puke…." He swallowed hard. "He was going to throw the girl out," he said after a rough moment. "He was going to throw her out into the shelling. First time I ever saw Sonny stand up to someone, trying to keep that girl alive. Then the shells hit and she was dead, and Sonny, he lost his shit. And Galway just… just advanced on him, and… and it was war, you see? Shit going sideways. And I drew on him. My superior officer. I drew on him and…."

For a moment the noise and fury of Walmart disappeared. Someone shoved past Jackson, knocking him forward, but he regained his footing and kept his eyes on the train wreck of Ace Atchison's soul.

"I shot him," Ace whispered. "I tried to tell myself the shell hit first and the gun went off, but I know what a trigger feels like under my finger. I shot him, and the shell went off, and I took shrapnel, and Sonny told that weak-assed story, and… they bought it. I kept expecting a court martial. I lived in fear for my entire month in the infirmary, but nobody ever came."

There was a brief moment of deep breaths, and then Ace's eyes focused on Jackson.

"Was that why?" he asked. "Was that why there wasn't ever a court martial? Because that motherfucker was too fucking damaged to survive and they were just as glad he was gone?"

Jackson nodded, sweat trickling down his spine. He had the irrelevant thought to buy extra deodorant and then brought his attention to where it was needed.

"That's what we think," he said quietly. "Because a Tim Owens isn't just born—he used prosthetics to change his appearance, hid a drug problem, and killed"—Jackson shuddered—"too many people." The last count had been over thirty, but Jackson and Ellery had investigated twenty of those deaths on their own.

Ace shook his head and took another deep breath. "I... I don't know how much Sonny knows," he said after a moment. "I... I protected him best I could, but I mustered recruits, gave out assignments—he...."

"This is not your fault," Jackson said softly. "Ace—these guys, they were trained and they were nurtured, and their meanness was fostered and fermented. You go into the military and you trust in the orders you're given—you don't think someone's going to be giving orders when they're not worth the shit in the crapper."

Ace visibly drew himself together. "Was that why you wore the wire?" he asked brutally, and it was Jackson's turn to gasp.

He got it—he'd hurt Ace, and Ace needed to lash back. Didn't mean it didn't sting.

"You do know your Google," he said after his own deep breath.

Ace turned away. "That was a shitty fuckin' thing to do. I'm sorry," he said woodenly. "But yeah. It was why I agreed to come, frankly. I told you, I been waiting. I ain't been a saint. I figured whatever you were here for, I wanted to know more about who you are."

Jackson filed the "whatever you were here for" part away for later. Frankly he knew too much about Ace now.

"Anything," Jackson said. "We came down here because the guy's super-secret military base or whatever is an hour away."

"It's *where*?"

Jackson looked at him sharply—it sounded like this had more relevance than just the boogeyman in his backyard. "That's drawn from the area code he keeps using to call our office," he said. "Does it mean something to you, that he's that close?"

Ace screwed up his face, and for a moment Jackson thought he was just going to blurt out Bibles full of truth. But apparently it was as hard for Ace Atchison as it would have been for Jackson himself. "It might," he hedged. "I'll let you know when I know. Were you thinking of finding it and poking around?"

Jackson shrugged. Yeah, it was the next step. "I don't have a plan yet—I'll be honest. But if we can get anything useful to go at this guy with, anything that will make him vulnerable.... God, if we even knew a project name or a program. I mean, if Galway and Owens were both parts of unit Fuck-You-Hard-Sir, we could subpoena other guys in the unit and see how they're doing. If they were in a behavioral study, we could ask for *those* records. But right now all we have is two dead assholes and a theory about how they got that way."

Ace blinked, and a little color seeped back into his face as his lips twitched. "No offense, Rivers, but I know how *my* guy got dead. And yours?"

"Clipped the back of his head on the edge of a concrete pool ledge after falling from the second floor."

Ace nodded. "And you...."

"Landed in the pool."

Ace expelled a harsh breath in what might have been a chuckle. "Your way was better."

Jackson's way had given him a literal heart attack and a permanent murmur. Still, "Can't argue that."

Ace nodded, and they both looked to where Sonny was happily picking out bags of boxer briefs.

"I used to wear the plain white kind," Ace said randomly. "Boxers, right? But he gets so excited about colors. I'm, like, whatever. Make them rainbow. As long as he smiles."

Jackson had a memory of the way Ellery swanned—neck arched, chest forward, chin out—as he got some small, silly concession from Jackson just to make him happy.

"Yeah."

They stood quietly, apparently done with emotion, until Sonny toodled up with the cart, looking pleased with himself. "They had double-X, so I got Jai something. He likes camo."

As Jackson remembered, Jai was nearly seven feet tall, for real. Becoming invisible was not bloody likely, no matter how much camo he wore.

"Sonny," Ace rasped, and Sonny's head jerked sharply.

He wheeled on Jackson, eyes spitting fire. "What did you do?" he demanded, and Jackson took a step back.

"Nothin'," Ace said, voice still in a bad way. "But.... Sonny, he's not going to hurt us, he's not going to bring us in. But he needs information."

"I'm crazy," Sonny said stubbornly. "Everybody knows that. I wouldn't have any information anyway."

Jackson regarded him impassively. "Of course you wouldn't," he said with no inflection at all.

Ace rolled his eyes. "Sonny, stop it. This is important. You remember...." Ace took a big breath and turned to Jackson. "Look, I'm going to go talk to him in the dressing rooms. It's gonna sound like we're murdering each other for a minute, but I can't do this in front of you, deal?"

Jackson nodded. "I'll be in electronics. See if I can get something obnoxious and purple for Ellery's phone."

Sonny laughed like the evil little troll he was, and Jackson sauntered off, thanking God that Walmart was big and public.

He did not want to be anywhere near the two of them when Ace said the magic word "Galway" to the guy Galway'd almost killed.

Ellery glanced at him as he walked up. "Done?" he asked, surprised.

"No. Ace needed to talk to Sonny alone a minute. There's something there—something Sonny might know—but the two of them, they've got…." He thought of the way Sonny picked out T-shirts for their friend and got excited about colored boxer briefs. Jackson hadn't seen anyone get that excited about something simple since he'd picked out his own furniture for his duplex from the discount place.

And colored sheets for his bed.

"Hunh." The thought hit him, inescapable, that as crazy as Sonny might be, they might be like two crazy birds of a feather.

"What? What was that sound? What are you thinking?" Ellery's too perceptive gaze raked his face.

"I'm thinking that Sonny and I got the same damage and that Ace is gonna have his hands full," Jackson muttered. "But I'm also wondering if you're done with the phone."

Ellery sighed and gestured to the guy in the red vest who had a line of customers behind him as he stammered his way through the presentation on the basic data plan.

"That would be no," he said drily, and Jackson grunted back. He pulled out his burner phone and looked up an actual cell phone store nearby, wincing when he heard raised voices—mostly Sonny's—coming from the changing rooms.

"Well, we might have time to get it done as it is." Jackson scanned the store restlessly. Something churned in his gut, unsatisfied. Ellery had given away his phone's position. They were in a public place, yes, but in an anonymous place. What if they *were* tracked here? How many people had bumped into Jackson while he and Ace were having their uncomfortable tête-à-tête in the middle of Walmart? Had all of those been accidental?

He was just about to call the whole thing, move it to another venue, when Ace appeared, pushing the cart, a bedraggled kitten of a man behind him. Ace looked miserable, and Sonny looked whipped, and Jackson hated himself for kicking this little nest of snakes and disturbing them. It was so damned hard to achieve peace of any sort when you had demons—of all people, Jackson knew that.

"Ace is gonna help you pick out a case," Jackson muttered. "Don't shake him and don't piss him off. I am suddenly freaking out about our location, so the two of you stay right here."

He strolled up to Ace and shook his hand firmly. "This won't take long," he promised. "I don't want to hurt nobody."

Ace nodded, and then his shoulders twitched suddenly, like Billy Bob's did when the cat had fleas.

"Keep your eyes out," Jackson said soberly. "I'm... itchy."

They both nodded, faces grim. The only thing that reassured Jackson was how accepting Ace was of a basic hunch that things were not okay.

"Sonny, Ace said you liked ice cream," Jackson said, trying for a smile.

He got a flat-eyed glare in return. "I'm not a kid."

"Neither am I, but I do like my sweets. If you're not going to get ice cream, I'll get chocolate, and we can share. How's that?"

Sonny brightened a little. "KitKats are my favorite," he said proudly. "But Ace likes the Dove chocolates. He doesn't like to admit it, though, 'cause they're expensive."

"My treat," Jackson said, nodding at Ace. Ace swallowed like he was trying to tamp down on his worry, and Jackson and Sonny headed for groceries.

"I don't want to talk about him, but Ace said I have to," Sonny said bluntly as they started off.

"Fair enough. What reasons did he give?"

"Said a girl's life was at stake because the bad guy threatened her, and the bad guy might be a really bad guy responsible for some of that shit that happened in Iraq." Sonny grunted. "I didn't get how it fit together, but Ace did." His voice dropped to tones of complete faith. "I'd trust Ace to do anything."

Well, yeah. Jackson got that—Ace did look like an extremely capable man.

"So, the guy in the desert, Galway—"

Sonny shuddered. "I hate hearing that fuckin' name."

"Understood." They approached cookies, and Jackson snagged a package of Oreos for Ellery and put one in Sonny's cart. Sonny *hmm*ed, and Jackson felt marginally better. "Here's the thing—he was in a unit with another guy we brought down. The two of them were trained, we think, how to be sadistic fuckheaded bastards. What do you think?"

Sonny grunted. "I think he wanted some of us dead. And the guys he didn't want dead—he wanted them to kill us. Like… like gave extra luxury rations to some guys if they'd bump me on the way to mess. That sort of thing."

Jackson grunted back. "Was he methodical about it? Was there bumping at mess on one day and—"

"Stealing my tools the next," Sonny confirmed. "Are those Reese's? If you're bribing me with chocolate, some of those with my KitKats, please."

Jackson smiled marginally and put them in his basket.

"Was that the limit of the torment?" he asked, pretty sure it wasn't.

Sonny shrugged. "Was constant. Petty shit, sometimes. I didn't tell Ace about it 'cause Ace already watched out for me with the big stuff. I needed to man up and deal with the fuckin' scorpion in my sheets, you know?"

Jackson shuddered. "That's special. How many times did that happen?"

Sonny looked thoughtful. "Three. Which is exactly as many pets as Galway had. Think he was making them take turns?"

Jackson grunted. "I think he was training them. Probably how he got trained."

"That's fuckin' awful. Plenty of fuckers out there that take to that shit natural—why we gotta make it a school?"

That was a fair question. "Got nothin'," Jackson apologized. "Except more questions. Did Galway report to anyone? Anyone he shouldn't have? I mean, you guys should have all reported to the same COs, right? Your base camp COs?"

"Depended on our unit, but yeah. All the officers hung together, and units reported to them. But now that you mention it, Galway got all… all squealy, like a girl on a date, for one guy when he came out once. Tall motherfucker with white hair. Galway practically creamed his shorts when the guy showed up in the auto bay. I almost felt bad for him—he goes all squealy and the big motherfucking guy in the weird uniform, like, shits all over him. Tells him he's a failure, tells him he needs to improve, his numbers were bad. Thought Galway was gonna cry. Anyway, white-hair guy leaves, Galway and his goons go after *me*, and Ace saves my life. Shortly after that, Galway gets himself killed for being an asshole. Hershey's Kisses?"

"Course." Sonny's voice was shaking, and his hands were white-knuckled on the grocery cart. Jackson had a prepaid credit card for $1000 in his pocket, and he'd use the whole damned thing on chocolate if it would make this squirrely kid feel a tiny bit better to talk about hell.

"Thanks," Sonny rasped. "I should get more noodles. Ace likes the sauce on them, and so do I. Ernie puts meat in it when he cooks for us. I always thought you could only eat noodles in butter, but sauce is real good."

Jackson took a deep breath, memories of noodles in butter with salt as a luxury food swamping his senses. He remembered the night before, and Ellery debating the risotto or new potatoes with his salmon, and swallowed.

"What's wrong?" Sonny asked. "You think noodles in butter is gross?"

"No," Jackson said, trying hard to find his footing. "I used to eat them all the time as a kid."

Sonny stopped abruptly, the stuff in the cart shifting as he did so. "Canned soup and crackers," he said suspiciously.

"You get the free crackers from the restaurants, and you can make the soup last two days."

Sonny nodded. "Jackson Rivers your real name? It sounds made up."

"Yeah. I was lucky she wasn't stoned when she named me."

"That shit came later for my mom. The guy I was...." Sonny turned his head and closed his eyes, probably so they wouldn't dart out of his head. "That name died when I joined the Army."

And Jackson got it. "That's why you didn't report your unit," he said, understanding suddenly.

"Ace was the only one who knew," Sonny said, voice low. "You can't get Ace in trouble for that—"

"Not if someone put a knife to my nads," Jackson vowed fiercely. "Sonny, me and Ellery.... Ellery and *I* just want to find out who's trying to create superkillers instead of good soldiers."

"What're you gonna do when you find him?" Sonny asked, rabbit eyes suddenly rock steady.

"Call the press, call the JAG corps, call the DOJ—Ellery's mom's got connections. I've met one of his superkillers. More than one of those guys is way worse than bad."

"I don't know who any of those people are," Sonny said dispiritedly, but then he perked up a little. "But you do. And you were like me. And people like us, we fuckin' hold grudges, right?"

Jackson smiled a little and tried to keep the churning in his stomach from getting worse. "Damned straight."

"Good. You go get 'em. Any other questions?"

Jackson paused, trying to get his brain on straight as they rounded the next corner. Instinctively he took advantage of the line of sight to check for

Ellery and Ace and was surprised to find them not in electronics where he and Sonny had left them.

"Wait. Where'd they go?"

Sonny ground to a halt too, both of them suddenly poised on the balls of their feet, scanning the store.

"Can you guys move?" said a stressed-out grandmother behind them.

"No," Sonny snapped absently. "Do you see—"

"There, by the door," Jackson shouted. "Leave the shit—go!"

Because it wasn't just Ace and Ellery heading up toward the self-checkout registers, it was two guys behind them, generically dressed in sweats and hoodies but built like tanks with hot pokers shoved up their ass all the way to connect their heads to their shoulders.

Sonny and Jackson took off at a sprint just as the guy bringing up the rear gave Ace a shove and a shout, and all of them broke into a run. Jackson could just make out the outline of the gun in the pocket of his hoodie before he and Sonny were moving too fast for the details to penetrate.

Ace and Ellery burst outside with their captors tight to their shoulders, and even as Jackson cleared the checkout area, he could see the SUV at the curb.

"No no no no no no *no*!" he shouted as they skidded outside and the SUV took off, leaving Jackson to memorize the plate while he was pulling out his phone.

"Hey! Hey! Mister! Do you know those guys?"

Jackson paused in the act of calling Crystal to run the plates. "What in the fuck—"

The kid in the Walmart vest was maybe twenty and very near tears. "Man, that guy just took off with a new phone—I just activated it and everything!"

"Who gives a—" Jackson held out his arm to block Sonny's next word. "New? Activated?"

Oh Jesus—could it be?

"Yeah—he was pulling out his credit card when those other two guys just sort of hustled them away—"

"Can you *track* that new phone that's been activated?" Jackson asked, trying to control his breathing.

"I don't know if it's legal to—"

"It's legal if I'm the guy buying the phone," Jackson told him, silently apologizing to Sonny. Who gave a shit about Oreos—that was their *lives* in that SUV, and Jackson had a way to track where they went.

"That's good," Sonny said, bouncing on his toes. "That's real fuckin' good. We gotta find out where they're going. We gotta... I gotta call Burton. Fuck, I gotta call Ernie and he'll call Burton. I gotta—"

Jackson took his life in both hands and dropped his hand onto Sonny's shoulder. "Hold it together, Sonny Daye. Hold it the fuck together. Let's get my phone hooked up to Ellery's new GPS, and then we'll call whoever the fuck you want, understood?"

Sonny nodded about sixty thousand times, but Jackson couldn't feel it because he was already vibrating at the speed of sound.

Ellery.

His Ellery.

Fussy risotto and white wine and salmon Ellery.

Ellery, the guy who had stitched Jackson back together piece by fucking piece in November. Who had promised him normal since.

He was in the hands of a guy with a really big forehead, broad enough to fit a whole other face, a guy with beige hair and military posture, a guy who had yanked the fingernails out of a liquor store clerk for not rolling over on a twelve-year-old kid just trying to earn money for candy.

Jackson had to get him back.

Fish in the Dark

"THERE A reason you put a gun in our backs and made us take off like that?" Ace drawled, and Ellery let him. Ace could sound pleasantly curious, and Ellery knew he'd sound like an uptight prick, and right now Ace's approach was less likely to get them shot.

"Shut up, Rivers," growled the guy from Anthony's police sketch.

Ace and Ellery met eyes, and Ellery shook his head. For one thing, if they thought Ace was just some random guy Ellery had met in Walmart, they might not be so eager to kidnap him and might kill him instead.

For another, if they knew Jackson was out there trying to find Ellery, they'd be ready for him. Ellery was pretty sure Jackson could surprise the hell out of them if only he and Ace kept quiet.

But that raised the question…. "What—you're mad because you missed the shot?" Ellery asked. "You killed a planter instead?"

"I didn't miss the fuckin' shot," Forehead muttered. "That was the rookie here." He gestured at the guy next to him, who looked like a ferret in a turtleneck sweater. "Told me Rivers here moves like a cat, but I ain't seen it yet."

"I save it for special occasions," Ace quipped, with a wink at Ellery.

Ellery rolled his eyes back. "Indeed you do," he said dryly, thinking about Jackson's real cat. From what Jackson said, Ace kept a little dog. Ellery wondered if he moved as fast as a Chihuahua, and then took a deep breath so he could concentrate on where he was going.

The desert, mostly, seemed to be where they were. That same mange of green on the rolling hills of what was occasionally farmstead stubble but mostly creosote bushes and juniper trees. They'd taken the main highway for a bit, but after ten minutes—which Ellery and Ace had spent staring at the rearview mirror tensely to see if Jackson was going to try to catch up with them—they'd turned off onto a little-used frontage road riddled with potholes.

The SUV had the worst suspension ever—and a slight gas leak—and Ellery wondered if throwing up on Forehead and Chinless in the middle seat of the SUV would get him shot.

The driver was the truly frightening one.

Generically dressed like Chinless and Forehead, the driver had black hair, ruthlessly buzz-cut, and a granite jaw.

And the coldest eyes—hazel, but God, fucking emotionless—that Ellery had seen since Tim Owens held a knife to his throat.

That blankness, that complete void of any feeling—that was familiar.

Hooray? They were on the right track?

"We didn't expect you to drag Rivers down here with you," Forehead was saying dismissively. "I mean, muscle is one thing, but Rivers is a dime-a-dozen punk. Unless you cake boys just get superattached to your toys, that is."

Next to him, Ace rolled his eyes as though bored.

"Wow. A gay joke. I am in fear for my life because these boys think we're gay. Aren't you, Ellery?"

Ellery tried not to glare at him. He was maintaining the façade and doing a damned good job of it. Ellery just hoped Ace wouldn't wisecrack himself into a concussion or a knife in the throat, which was Jackson's worst risk on any given day.

"Yeah. Being gay's the problem," Ellery said blandly. "That's why you get kidnapped out of Walmart by the military. My mother told me this might happen." That thought made him brighten. "Have you guys met my mother? She handles all sorts of military contracts. You guys are getting short funds these days, aren't you? That's too bad. I do hope you don't find a way to piss her off, because she does know an awful lot of military people who hold the purse strings."

"Leavins," hissed Forehead. "Did you hear that? He's got connections—this could be—"

"Shut up!" the driver snarled back. "The commander's got it covered. He wouldn't order an op on these clowns if we didn't have a plan."

Ellery and Ace met eyes again. So they knew the name of their driver, and it was a good bet Lacey was behind it.

Excellent.

Not excellent that they'd been kidnapped at gunpoint.

And definitely not excellent that Jackson and Sonny had been left frantic and alone.

But the more they knew, the more leverage they had.

Ellery took a deep breath against the next pothole and looked determinedly outside as the desert rolled by.

IT TOOK an hour and a half—and a couple of turns onto roads Ellery wouldn't have been able to spot if he hadn't been on them. The military base was small and featured some of the usual things—an airstrip with a small hangar, a handful of buildings that were obviously barracks, and an administration building. Unlike other bases Ellery had been to, this one was missing activity.

The airstrip was untended, the barracks in disrepair. The small strips of lawn in the quad had been allowed to die and then overgrow with stickers that made up most of the mange green. There were no units doing PT, no jeeps taking recruits to the shooting range, no messages being run from the barracks to the CO offices.

There were a few men by the barracks sitting in a grim huddle. They watched the SUV with narrow-eyed interest, and Ellery suppressed a shiver.

They came to a halt in the spare parking by the admin building, and Ellery saw something else that made him shiver.

"Where's the flag?" Ace asked in shock.

"Getting laundered," Forehead cracked.

"And ironed and folded," Chinless added, snickering.

Least funny joke ever.

No flag. No Stars and Stripes, no flag of Nevada or California, no flag representing the branch of the armed service that occupied the base—the base was… without standard.

Just a solid blood-colored banner made of something thick and textured.

"Oh no," Ace breathed as they were escorted across the parking lot. "Oh… this is not—" He finished off on a grunt as Chinless thrust a rifle stock against his kidneys.

"The flag is not your business," he said, voice twanging with the Deep South. "You two need to go talk to the commander, and then we'll let you know what's your business."

Oh great—something else Ellery didn't know.

He wasn't afraid necessarily—but, unbidden as they made turns through glossy corridors of broken tile, he saw Jackson as he had been the night before, unguarded, willing, just once, to hope.

If Ellery couldn't talk himself out of this with his skin intact, Jackson would never forgive him.

Like most government buildings, spare and unlovely, the CO's offices were not set apart by beauty or ceremony, and it was spooky to stride through the buildings, the boots of their captors making dull purposeful thuds in the empty space. The relief when they finally entered one of the larger rooms toward the back was acute—even Ellery was getting creeped out.

The room looked like it had been stripped—no photos on the walls, no commendations—although a minifridge in the corner and a trash can full of takeout boxes and paper plates attested to an awful lot of activity in there. A thick laptop, black and bulky, sat on the desk, and Ellery wondered if it was as outdated as the bugs that had been planted in his office and home. The desk in the middle didn't lessen the air of dated technology—made of OD green metal, it had enough peeled-back corners and bent edges to effectively skin a man if he got close enough.

And so did the man currently behind it.

When Ellery first met Commander Karl Lacey, he'd been struck by the man's ice. Well over six feet tall, Lacey had the white hair Janie had described as "like a helmet" and the square shoulders and lantern jaw that were the shiny star hallmarks of the military fetishist's favorite wet dream.

Three seconds in his presence and Ellery had sworn off military movies forever. He could hear Jackson's voice in his head saying that much ice would shrivel any boner.

Some of that ice seemed to be cracking today.

Lacey's hair—impeccable when they'd first met—was standing on end, the hair of a man who'd been tunneling his fingers through it in agitation for a long day. His steel-blue eyes were red-rimmed with dark circles, and his dress blues were missing a jacket and a good steam and iron to boot.

Apparently, for all the evils he'd perpetrated in the world, mowing down a woman in cold blood by accident was the thing that haunted him the most.

Lacey was on the phone as they entered, his voice pitching wildly as he barked orders that were apparently not being obeyed.

"I said take care of the situation—No! No wetwork! She's a stupid college kid. Can't we fake a blood test—?"

"No," Ellery said behind him, his chest swelling with anger. "Because Janie Isaacson is a good and decent human being, and my boss is in charge of her. I'm a thorn in your paw. He's a spear up your ass. You can hang up now."

"Fix it!" Lacey snarled, slamming down the phone. He whirled on Ellery and pulled up short. "Cramer? Who the fuck is this?" His eyes darted to Ace, and Ace smirked. "Gleeson? Adkins? I said bring Cramer—who is this?"

"Rivers, sir," Forehead replied sharply. "The two men were in close proximity, and we thought it prudent to bring them both." He lowered his voice. "We didn't want Rivers out there by himself—you've said he's somewhat unpredictable, and we understand they're attached."

An unmistakable look of disgust crossed Lacey's stone features. "Our surveillance team says they went after each other like rabbits." He stared at Ellery in revulsion. "How two men like *you* have managed to be such a thorough inconvenience, I'll never know."

"You know us rabbits, sir," Ace deadpanned. "It's not like we're trained to be deadly or anything, but by God we can fuck around the best-laid plans, can't we."

Ellery stared at him. Fucking Jesus—if another man had to be mistaken for Jackson, what were the odds he'd have the same inclination to talk someone else into beating him to death just like the man himself?

"You don't like livin', do you, son?" Lacey sneered. "But you're not the brains of the operation from all accounts, so you can fuck around on your own time. I wanted you, Cramer, because you're a man who can be reasoned with."

Ellery arched an eyebrow at him. "Reasonable men do not take hostages. What is it you think you're going to accomplish?"

"You're not a hostage, son." A tic jumped above Lacey's eye. "You can leave at any time—it's just a short walk across the desert. Pleasant in January—won't cook your brain like an egg like it will in a couple of months. Feel free—"

"To blow ourselves up on the land mines surrounding all but the main road?" Ace asked bluntly, folding his arms. "No thank you, sir, that would interfere with my fucking-around activities." He gave Ellery a bawdy wink. "That'd be a shame."

Ellery gave himself permission to roll his eyes—it's what he'd do if Jackson said the exact same thing—but his stomach had officially turned to ice.

Land mines. What in the actual fuck were land mines doing around a stateside base? He'd ask Ace later how he'd spotted them, but right now he was just terrified that they were out there, and Jackson was out there looking for them.

Lacey gave a predator's smile. "Good of you to spot those," he said mildly. "How'd you know?"

"Been around," Ace lied. "Teach you more'n you think in the academy."

"You *do* have an education," Lacey said smoothly. "I'd forgotten that was in your jacket. Weren't you wounded early on in your career?"

Ace's eyes crinkled at the corners. "You want to see my scars? For all your bitching about us homosexuals, you want to get awfully close to my body."

"I've seen pictures of Rivers from far off," Lacey confessed, eyes narrowed. "There is something off—"

Ace lifted his sweatshirt up and over his head in one quick motion, and his chest—well, Ellery wasn't that surprised. Unlike Lacey, he and Jackson had done homework on Ace, and they knew he'd taken shrapnel and had been involved in at least one major car accident. His chest looked as bad as Jackson's did, minus the big scar right below Jackson's left nipple where the bullet had missed his heart. But Lacey wouldn't have seen that scar—he wouldn't know the difference here, and Ellery appreciated the hell out of Ace standing shirtless in the confines of the office, meeting Lacey's eyes without blinking.

Lacey blinked first, and Ace pulled up a corner of his mouth and put his shirt back on.

And Ellery knew, right then, that whether Lacey knew it or not, he was a dead man.

"So it's Rivers!" Gleeson said abruptly. "We knew that! What do you want—"

"What will it take?" Lacey asked, voice flinty. "Son, you are interfering with a US Navy operation here, and I need to know what it will take for you to back off and stop trying to finger me for Janie Isaacson's mistake."

Ellery's body grew very still, and his mind flew about a thousand miles an hour.

So many things wrong here—things Ellery was not supposed to know.

He wasn't supposed to know that the base was not operating under the auspices of the military—but Crystal had been right. There was no money coming in here. Whatever funding Lacey was getting had been siphoned off from other sources.

He wasn't supposed to know what the lack of flag—or the presence of that heavy piece of corduroy on the flagpole—might mean, but he *had* grown up with a military fetish, and he *had* watched *Top Gun* about a thousand times. Enough times to know what the pieces of bling on Tom Cruise's shirt had meant, and enough times to know that a base never operated without its flag. Whatever the unofficial square of fabric meant, Lacey was not serving the US government, and Ellery was afraid of the master in its place.

And Ellery was supposed to think Janie Isaacson was guilty—or at least that there was no way to prove her innocent.

Which meant that somebody was feeding *Lacey* bad information.

Lacey didn't know what Jackson looked like, for one. Didn't realize the extent of their connection—knew that they had sex, and lots of it, but didn't know they had a *relationship*.

Knew that Ellery and Jackson were down here but didn't know the extent of their knowledge.

Oh, this was going to be a very tight game, and Ellery had to win or he and Ace—and probably Jackson and Sonny—were not going to live very long at all.

He was going to start with the truth.

"Janie Isaacson's case is out of my hands," he said guilelessly. "Rivers and I came down here because Jackson is still recovering from events this last fall, and he wasn't ready to be thrown back in the game. I insisted. My boss, Carlyle Langdon, is responsible for keeping Ms. Isaacson out of jail. You're going to have to talk to him."

Lacey scowled. "Don't try to bullshit me—"

"You need to talk to my firm," Ellery said, his snake-oil-salesman smile firmly in place. "I'd call them myself, but your men know I'd just turned in my phone as they approached me." He'd tucked his new phone into his pocket as they'd been hustled out, hoping if nothing else that security would stop them, but no such luck. As it was, he was pretty sure Jackson would find a way to track it—which, given the land mine thing, scared the holy crap out of him.

"I'll do that," Lacey said, giving him the same smile in return—minus the oil-salesman part.

"You might want to talk to my mother while you're at it," Ellery said, not sure what prompted this bit of recklessness, except he was worried and angry and tired of being worried and angry. "I understand you have a great deal of interest in her military contracts. You've really been useful—she's given her protégés a lot of your work."

A muscle clenched in Lacey's jaw. "Not my work," he growled.

"Well, no. But the work that you pressured to use other firms. She's mentored half the Fortune 500 contract lawyers in the country—she's pretty good at turning a downfall into a windfall, you know? And she knows *everybody* in Washington." An exaggeration. A very slight exaggeration.

"So, consider you a contact," Lacey said, a bland smile on his face.

"Consider me plutonium," Ellery returned flatly, pleased to see him taken off-balance. "I'm a pebble in your shoe? My mother is a missile up your ass. You need to find something to offer her—something good—that would make her overlook this little... meeting. Think about it. Think hard. A... nd Jackson and I can wait."

Oops—almost slipped up there. Ellery kept his eyes level and his breathing even, though, as he smiled into a killer's eyes. He'd played a game like this before—logic, threats, and leverage—to get a man to turn himself in and not to turn Ellery over to his henchman. That guy, a congressman's aide, had been a cakewalk compared to Lacey, but Ellery's goal was much simpler here.

Keep himself and Ace alive long enough for the cavalry to come—and hope the cavalry didn't blow itself up in the rescue.

Lacey's face flushed practically purple. "Waiting is a good idea," he ground out. "Adkins, take these two someplace secure, and send Leavins in. I need some recon."

Recon. Like this was a military *op*, not a base. Oh, this was bad. Bad bad bad bad.... Ellery did not know the many flavors of bad here, but each one made his gut churn worse than the last.

"Sir!" The two henchmen—no uniform, rank unknown—saluted, and Ellery smiled blandly.

"A place with a restroom if you can manage it," Ace said cheerfully. "So much coffee—you have no idea."

Gleeson grabbed Ace's arm and slammed him into the adjoining wall. "You'll piss in your buddy's mouth and like it—"

"The brig is fine," Lacey barked. "And they need to be intact. Not the jail itself," Lacey said, holding up his hands to stave off Ellery's protest. "Just the supervision room. The whole section locks from the outside, just in case you're tempted to wander—there *are* land mines, you know."

"I do now," Ellery said sweetly. His heart pounded in his ears from the sudden violence to Ace, but unless he saw blood, he knew enough not to let his expression crack.

Trial Lawyering 101: Never let 'em see you sweat.

Going After Bad Guys Section A: Make sure they sweat first.

THE BRIG was about as cheery as the rest of the building—and even though they weren't sitting in one of the two ten-by-twelve cells that made up half the space, the sound of the door slamming shut behind them was oppressive as fuck. Ellery met Ace's eyes tensely until they both heard the bolt slide home, and then Ellery found a desk chair and slumped into it in relief.

Ace caught his eye again and touched his ear cautiously. Were they bugged?

Ellery shrugged and tilted his hand. Maybe? Lacey hadn't had much time to prepare for them, even if he'd tracked Ellery's phone from his fuck up that morning—and their tech seemed truly spotty. But then, who wanted to find out the hard way?

"I guess I love your mother," Ace said, and Ellery half laughed.

"She probably still terrifies you," he said. "You call her Lucy Satan."

Ace laughed tensely, and together they looked around. The office was pretty bare—even the desks were empty—not a pencil or paper clip to be seen. Dust had accumulated in the corners of the tile, and the last drawer Ellery checked might possibly have had a dead cockroach in the bottom. Ellery slammed it shut too fast to be sure.

Ace shut his own drawer on the other side of the room, and they convened in the center of the room again, sinking into the squeaky office chairs that remained. Ellery pulled his phone from the front pocket of his sweats and was unsurprised to see one of his apps flashing. He pointed to it and nodded, and Ace nodded back. He understood.

For a moment he considered just *calling* Jackson—or at least texting him—but (a) if they were miked, that would mean Jackson could be walking into a trap, and (b) if there was any sort of monitoring whatsoever, it would give away the advantage of the phone entirely.

"How'd you know about the land mines?" Ellery asked, figuring it was a neutral question.

"There were piles of disturbed dirt—grass growing on top but still red. Probably a few months old." He sighed. "Hard to get grass to grow out here. Need to import potting soil and sod and shit. Fucking desert."

This seemed to be a cause dear to his heart, and Ellery's own heart ached a little. Jackson had called Ace and Sonny rattlesnakes—deadly to outside forces but actually fairly sweet to each other. Trying to grow a lawn was such a domestic thing to do.

"I'm sorry you got hauled into this," he said softly. "That was not... not the plan."

Ace's mouth twisted. "Bad guys. They will frequently fuck up your plans."

And Ellery was forgiven—like that. Jackson had been right, really. Yeah, Ace had probably killed his fellow officer, but if the guy had been anything like Tim Owens, and had been after Sonny, Ellery couldn't say he wouldn't have done the same. He used to think he had a moral edge over the people he defended, but that fall he'd been forced to prioritize Jackson's life, his mental health, over the life of a police officer, and he'd suddenly realized what kinds of compromises people had to make to just live in this fucked-up world.

Ellery didn't know Ace and Sonny's story, but he knew Jackson's. He knew enough about people being born into the fucked-up and trying to claw their way out to think that maybe killing Master Sergeant Galway had been one of the most moral murders he'd ever investigated. He almost wanted to defend it in court.

The thought was interrupted by a rattle of the door handle, and both of them shot up, determined not to be caught unawares.

The handle continued to rattle, like the lock was being picked. Ace pressed himself flat against the wall where the door would crack, and Ellery pressed himself on the opposite wall, far enough from the door that it wouldn't rebound in his face, close enough to the corner of the room to hide behind it if he had to.

Slowly it creaked open, and they both held their breath. There was a pause, and Ellery saw the flash of a phone being used like a periscope, and then, in a rush, a man strode in and shut the door behind him.

About Ace's height, with a shaved head and skin tone an earthy bronze umber, the man had a broad face with a square jaw and a turned-up, almost precious nose. He was undeniably appealing to look at, and that was before Ellery noticed the biceps straining his khaki T-shirt that would bust a tape measure. His OD green cargo pants were tight around his thighs and loose around his hips, and good God, the guy was built.

The effect he had on Ace was electric.

"*Burton?*" Ace breathed, and their new friend's tense, wild-eyed expression melted in pure relief.

"Ace? What the hell—"

In a heartbeat the two were embracing tightly—that muscular, violent kind of hug Ellery had seen Jackson give to Kaden or Mike—men he considered his brothers.

Ace pulled back, mind obviously in a whirl. "Holy fucking God, Burton—is this where the fuck you've been all this time?"

Burton shook his head and nodded briefly at Ellery. "Ace? Mr. Cramer?"

"Yes?" Ellery's curiosity was going to burn a hole through his chest. "Can we help you?"

Burton rolled his eyes. "I'm the one who needs to get you the fuck out of here—and I need to do it quick, because your guys are on their way, and there's not a goddamned thing I could say to stop them."

But Ace wasn't buying the urgency. His own eyes narrowed, and he pinned Burton with a no-bullshit glare that had his friend avoiding his gaze restlessly.

"Sure there was," Ace said, his voice taking on the flinty tones of an older brother. "You could have talked to Ernie and calmed him down and told him what you were doing here, but that's not what you did, was it?"

Burton scrubbed at his face with his hand. "Now is not the time—"

"When is the time? When they get here and start setting off land mines?"

"I warned them about those," Burton said, and Ellery's bladder relaxed with such startling immediacy he almost wet himself with relief.

"Yeah, whatever. Tell us what you're doing here, and *then* tell yourself more lies about your love life."

Burton swallowed like he'd seen the lecture coming. "Fair enough. Lacey's crazier than a shithouse rat. That thing I got Ernie out of?"

Ace nodded, and Ellery hoped he'd have time to get the entire story.

"Well, I came back to see what was doing—and I stumbled across this bullshit."

"I thought Ernie was being targeted by the military—these guys ain't—"

"They were," Burton said, voice laced with disgust. "They *were* military, and Lacey was apparently building a better monster, if you know what I mean."

"We killed one of those," Ellery told him. "How many of them are there out there?" It was the question that had been plaguing him and Jackson since Owens had escaped custody in August.

"You so don't want to know." Burton shivered. "But what you *have* to know is that Lacey lost most of his funding about a year ago. He's still on the military payroll, but they think he's operating from San Diego, like a good little drone. Fact is, most of the time he's AWOL with a couple of flunkies covering for him—and when you called him up last year, Mr. Cramer, you poked a hornet's nest with a cattle prod, if you feel me."

Ellery nodded. "We got that impression when he started pressuring my mother's firm. We were not impressed."

Burton's face split with a delighted smile. "Son, I've been monitoring this asshole's coms since October, and I've got to tell you, your mother is a delight." A new expression crossed Burton's face. "And you and Mr. Rivers need to fuckin' slow down—nobody should have that much sex, that's all I'm saying. I mean, it worked for you—nobody else wanted to take surveillance on you two, but dude. *Dude.*"

Ellery refused to blush. "It *should* have been in the privacy of my own home, thank you very much! And how long before they figure that this isn't Jackson?"

"Well, it'll sure tip them off when he gets here, won't it?" Burton snapped. He took a deep breath and obviously remembered himself. "All I'm saying is you two have to get out of here, and I think I can help you. How's that?"

"Sounds awesome," Ellery said. "Do you have time to break down a plan, or are we just going to have to trust you? Oh!" Because he could never be too careful, and he'd just dropped a big piece of info. "Are we being bugged?"

"Yes," Burton told him, "but since I'm the one in charge of monitoring, you're safe for the moment. I don't have a plan just yet, but give me an hour—"

"What happens in an hour?" Ace asked, but he sounded like he knew.

"Dark falls, our guys get here, and all hell breaks loose," Burton said grimly.

Ace *hmm*ed. "You know, if they brought Jai, there's almost more of us than them. We could probably take this unit—you know that, right?"

"With *Ernie*?" Burton's voice squeaked, and he caught Ellery's eyes as he tried to get himself back together. "And civilians. No civilians—we need to avoid that. No, you two sit tight." He pulled out a small transmitter, a green light flickering fitfully in the center. "Here—when this is green, you're free to talk. When it flashes red, it means someone besides me is listening. If it starts going back and forth, remember your Morse code." He paused. "You *do* know Morse code, right, Ace?"

Ace looked disgusted. "No, Burton, they only teach you jarheads that because us Army boys are too fuckin' stupid to know our dots from our dashes."

Burton had the grace to look embarrassed. "Sorry, Ace. Red's a dot, green's a dash, hear me?"

Ellery and Ace nodded, and Burton checked the door. "I've got to get back—they'll be missing me. Watch the damned transmitter, and be ready!"

And with that Burton slid back through the door, leaving Ellery and Ace alone and baffled. Help was coming—but at what cost?

A Gang of Fish

JACKSON WAS two deep breaths from banging Sonny Daye on the back of the head, throwing him over his shoulder, and *forcing* him to follow the little flashing light that represented Ellery on the map on his phone.

But Sonny had other ideas.

"We gotta talk to Ernie," he muttered, climbing in next to Jackson in the SUV. He didn't even make a move toward the SHO, which told Jackson all he needed to know about who drove the car and who kept the car running. Sonny might keep that thing purring like a kitten, but that kitten didn't take a dump without Ace.

"I don't know who Ernie is," Jackson muttered, starting up the SUV. "Seat belt."

"Ernie's fuckin' Ernie, but he can get Burton on the phone, and that's who we need. Fuckin' Burton—that's his job, right? He bails us out of the shit, right? He fuckin' backed me up with Galway, he told Ace how to do that other thing—"

"What other thing?"

"*None of your fuckin' business!*" Sonny yelled so shrilly Jackson jammed the brakes as he was backing out. They both thumped against their seat belts, and Jackson turned to him slowly, with his first deep breath.

"Scream in my ear one more time and I'll push you out of my moving vehicle," he said, meaning every word. "Now I'm going to back out and start for the freeway. You have until the on-ramp to tell me why we need to worry about the two gay guys on *Sesame Street*, okay?"

He'd managed to get the car in drive before Sonny pulled himself together enough to talk again.

"I thought of *Sesame Street* too," he said, voice shaking. "When Burton brought Ernie home. You reckon everybody thinks that?"

"Burt and Ernie are really popular," Jackson said neutrally. Ellery was traveling southeast—a little toward Vegas, a little toward someplace Jackson didn't know. He figured he could find the roads, as long as he had a direction, and the one thing—the *only* thing that kept him from losing his mind, losing it completely, was that they could have killed Ellery but they hadn't, and they'd apparently taken Ace with them. "Why do we need to talk to them?"

Very carefully, because his first instinct was to *stand* on the gas pedal, he turned right out of the parking lot and merged into traffic.

"Burton's a superhero," Sonny said, so simply and with such faith Jackson wondered if he'd taken his meds today.

"He can fly?" Right lane, pass the guy in front of him, left lane, pass the guy on the other side… his mouth was engaged, but his brain was threading the needle, not too fast, not too fast, smooth like butter until they hit the freeway.

"No, asshole! Not like that! Like he was a Marine, but he sort of went off-road, like black ops and shit! Can he fly—Jesus, how stupid you gotta be to drive a car like this?"

"Stupid enough to let you in here with me!" Jackson snarled. He jerked his finger at his phone, which he'd set up on the dash. "See that? They're heading toward Victoriana, but the minute they turn off, I'm following them unless you stop talking about how stupid I am, got it? What do you mean, black ops?"

"Like black ops!" Sonny snapped back. "He fuckin' kills people for a living—and if he doesn't kill them, he covers it up."

Whoa. "How do you know that?" Jackson demanded. "He sounds like a great guy to have on our team, but how in the hell—" Suddenly the name hit him—it had been in the jacket Ellery had shown him on Sonny Daye. "Lee Burton," he said, feeling stupid. "He testified in the Galway shooting."

Sonny nodded, like it would just be natural that Jackson would know that. "Ace knew him. Then, when we got out, Burton… well, he was going off the grid, and he wanted a place. A safe house. People who knew his name. So he gave Ace some money he won betting on Ace in a street race, and Ace built an addition on the house. And it just sat there. Two years. Every now and then, Christmas and such, Burton shows up, looking like hell, and stays in his room for a week or two. Just normal. A roommate. Ace even built him a shower. He'd get his shit together and go back out in the field. Anyway, come November, he shows up with Ernie."

"Boyfriend?" Jackson asked.

"Vote's out. Ernie seems to think so. Burton gets this look on his face like he's suddenly stupid whenever Ernie talks, but as soon as he's out of the room, it's like he's wondering what he drank the night before. Anyway, Ernie's got a phone. He and Burton text and shit, and Ace has another phone, and they don't say squat 'cause Ace says that's not his place. But Ernie can get hold of Burton, and Burton—"

"Knows what to do," Jackson said. Sonny's on-ramp appeared and he took it.

"This looks like the way to our house," Sonny said, hope a fragile thread in his voice.

"Can you call Ernie?" Jackson asked shortly. "Does he need to come with us?"

"He's got the witching," Sonny said, just like someone would say "He's got fallen arches," and for a minute Jackson was going to kick him out of the car and tell him to take his witchy friend and go to hell.

But… but Crystal.

His friend. The one who'd asked for help just as simply and just as sweetly as a little girl asking for a kitten.

She frequently read his aura—and she was always right.

"How strong?" Jackson asked instead. "Useful if we're going in after two guys surrounded by guns?"

"He can tell if you're good," Sonny told him seriously. "And he can tell if there's good people or bad people somewhere. Like, last month, Ernie wakes up early, 'cause he sleeps in the day, and tells Alba she didn't work that day. She takes off and this SUV pulls up, right? Ernie says, 'They're bad guys,' so Ernie and I hide in the house, and Ace and Jai go out and deal with the bad guys. Jai's a badass, and he was packing, and Ace brought his service pistol and they fixed the car together, but with one of 'em under the car and one of 'em watchin' the other guy's back. Ernie and I stayed outta sight until the SUV was gone. Like, Ace got paid and shit, but he and Jai had to power hose the bathroom 'cause there was drugs all over the toilet and he didn't want no one touching 'em. We waited until Ernie said they were in San Diego and then called the cops. Ace seen guns and shit in the back, and drugs and shit taped to the quarter panels. They got pulled over at a stoplight and there was a shootout and shit—we saw it on the news. They never knew it was us."

Jackson swallowed hard, feeling the near miss in his bones. "Ace and Jai were pretty smart," he said, feeling Sonny's need to hear it.

"He takes care of me," Sonny said forlornly. "We gotta get him back. Like when he was in a car wreck couple years ago, I damned near lost my mind. Like Burton had to hold me down 'cause I was gonna storm the operating room and shit, and I'm… I mean, you ain't had to hold me down, Rivers, but I ain't doin' real good without Ace."

Jackson nodded and took a breath and realized the bulk of calming Sonny down was on him. "Okay. Okay. I get it. You need him. I need Ellery—"

"You do okay," Sonny said nastily. "Boss me around sure enough!"

"Yeah, well, we all got our baggage, Sonny. I can't take another hospital. I was in there for a year once, while they put me back together. Went back three times in the last six months, and every time feels like I can't breathe. Like I'm going to lose it—they're going to have to drug me and knock me out until it's time to go home. And the only thing that keeps me from just screaming until they do that is that Ellery's been there. He's bitching and nagging and making sure I was doing everything I could to stay out of the fucking hospital, and if he wasn't doing that, I'd never get out, you hear me? They'd have to lock me up in one. So we've got to keep calm, think clear. You were thinking clear when you told me we should call Burton. I put up a fuss at the beginning, but I was thinking clear enough to listen. So we're going to keep our heads on our shoulders and talk to your witchy friend and call your superhero guy, and we're going to get them back, understand?"

Sonny nodded tensely, and for a moment the only sound was the wheels on the road. "Why you hate the hospital so bad?" he asked after a minute.

"I'm okay with dying," Jackson said, because it was the truth and he didn't think it would freak Sonny out like it would Ellery. "But hospitals— on the street you can duck, you fight, you can run. In a hospital all you can do is hope. Lay there and hope. And since Ellery, it's like that's it. That's as good as my life is going to get. Hoping feels wrong somehow, like asking for too much. But you're lying there and your head or your body hurts or whatever, and this person who drags you out of hell every goddamned night is there, and all you want to do is hope you get one more minute with him. Just a little bit of peace. But you *know* just having him there is violating something in the world, right? And it piles up on your chest, all the reasons you don't deserve to get out of there, until hope is just one more thing that's crushing your lungs in your body."

"I never thought of it like that," Sonny said, voice low and reverent.

"Like what?"

"Like I don't deserve Ace. He's the only thing I ever wanted. As long as I have him, I'm not gonna stop wanting him. How you go and think that much? It would make me crazy."

Jackson laughed shortly and looked at his phone. They were heading for the part where they had to get off the freeway and take a frontage road if they wanted to hug Ellery's heels, or where they took another half an hour and drove toward Victoriana to talk to the mysterious witchy Ernie and his superhero not-quite-boyfriend.

In the end, what did it was the look on Sonny's face. Jackson looked at the phone, then looked at the off-ramp and looked at the phone.

"I'm sure you're good at your job," Sonny whispered, tears shining in his wide gray eyes. "But Burton.... Burton's who I trust."

Hell. Jackson wasn't thinking square himself. "Man, I expect a guy in tights who can fucking fly," he muttered, blowing past the off-ramp.

"Burton won't let you down," Sonny said, voice catching. "God, please, don't fuckin' let us down." He pulled out his phone and started texting. "I gotta wake Ernie up, though. His brain is wired to sleep in the hot part of the day. He does our books and stocks the shelves at night when it's cool and keeps an eye on things, but if we gotta wake him up early, it helps to give him a warning."

Jackson nodded. "Okay. Fine. I gotta make a phone call of my own before we get there."

"Not the police?" Sonny asked, and Jackson snorted.

"As if. No. Ellery's mother. She's... well, she's fucking terrifying, but if I go after Ellery without her blessing, I'll regret it to the pit of my balls."

Sonny grunted. "I don't get women. You do that. I'll talk to Ernie. He makes sense."

If Jackson hadn't been doing ninety, he would have done a spit take at that. As it was, he hit the button on the phone. "Siri, call Lucy Satan."

The phone went to speaker, and Jackson took a deep breath. "Taylor Cramer, attorney at law. May I ask who's calling—"

"Taylor?" Jackson hated himself because his voice shook.

"Jackson, is he okay?"

God love Ellery's mother for knowing nothing on the planet could make Jackson call her that wasn't dire.

"Lacey's got him. Couple of minions snagged him in the middle of Walmart. I'm sorry, Mrs. Cramer—"

"Do you have backup?" she asked sharply.

"Getting some now," he said. "Guy who got taken with him has a friend in special ops. Going to contact him, make a plan—"

"Not alone," she snapped. "You are not to go in alone—"

"Mrs. Cramer...." And to his horror, in front of Sonny, his voice broke. "I gotta get him back. You know that—"

"Not alone, Jackson. Is that understood?"

"We'll get him back, ma'am," he rasped. "I promise."

"Jackson?"

"Yes, ma'am?"

"Unless my son is dead, you are to call me Lucy fucking Satan, do you understand? And even then, calling me Mrs. Cramer is right out. Now you wait for backup, and I'll be down in as few hours as possible. I'll be making phone calls before then, so be prepared for more backup than you can handle. Are we clear?"

"Yes, ma'am."

"Keep your head, boy," she said crisply. "Did they gag him?"

Jackson had to smile. "No, ma'am."

"Then all should be well, my boy. My son's mouth is better than an assault rifle. I'm hanging up now—you treat his property right."

"Yes, ma'am," he said quietly, and the call ended.

The car was silent for a moment, and next to him Sonny breathed, "Jeeeeeeeesus! That was his mother?"

"Yup." The tightness in Jackson's chest had eased somewhat. He thought he might be a human being long enough to get his shit together before he and Sonny and Burt and Ernie went out to get the boys back.

"Does she eat sharks for breakfast or what?"

In spite of the situation, the terrible fear, the rubber band constricting Jackson's heart, he managed a rusty chuckle.

"And bear for dessert," he confirmed.

"Well, good thing she's coming down here. Bear eaters are mighty useful when you're going after bad guys," Sonny said sagely. "Only reason Ace and me stayed alive."

Jackson nodded. Ace was Sonny's bear eater.

Ellery was Jackson's.

Maybe the world wouldn't end before Sonny and Jackson got them back.

He ignored the little voice whispering maybe it would.

THE GAS station at Victoriana was much as he remembered it.

The town itself was hardly more than a Carl's Jr. and a Chevron station on one side of the road and Sonny and Ace's garage on the other. Jackson had looked Victoriana up on the map after their visit in September and had been surprised to see a little stretch of suburb if you turned off what looked like a farm track on the east side of the Chevron station. There was a grade school, a middle school, a high school, a couple of blocks of tract homes and apartment buildings, and one—*one*—strip mall that featured a mom-and-pop grocery store that was more like the liquor store Anthony's friend had been killed in than anything remotely having to do with groceries.

But none of that took away from the bare and vulnerable look of the garage on one side of the highway and the gas station on the other.

These two structures might have been the only two signs of civilization at the last outpost before hell.

Jackson turned into the garage's driveway and pulled around the shop to park in front of the house, right before the mossy, algae-spore lawn started.

For some reason it felt like that lawn was cared for, nurtured, and loved.

"Wait!" Sonny cried as Jackson put his hand on the handle.

"What?"

"Ernie—he's… he's not like other people. You… I mean, I'm a fuckin' mess, but Ernie knows me. You… you gotta be gentle with him. Like he's a wild creature, like an owl or something, wounded."

Jackson nodded, unsurprised, and took a deep breath. "My friend Crystal is like that," he said. Once upon a time Jackson wouldn't have told this rabbity psychopathic kid a damned thing that was personal, but if the last two hours had taught Jackson *anything*, it was that Sonny Daye didn't do squat for you unless he saw you as a person. "Crystal is… sensitive. She needs protection sometimes from how awful the world can be."

Sonny nodded, his face flooding with relief. "Ernie too. He likes it out here in the desert—he told me so. 'Cause there's not so many people. He says it's like silence in his head for the first time in his life."

Jackson nodded. "Crystal needs the hum of the city, because otherwise loud noises scare her. It's like their brains are so special, they've spent their whole lives learning to live with them so they don't lose themselves."

"You're…." Sonny's throat worked. "You're nice. I… I can see why Ace trusted you. I just don't know if I can forgive you if he gets hurt 'cause he did."

Fair enough. "I won't be great at forgiving myself," Jackson told him. "Now let's go talk to Ernie."

The door opened as they walked over the spongy moss-lawn, and a tall, thin young man stood in the doorway, holding a tiny tan dog.

"Duke!" Sonny cried, and the young man put the dog down, where it gave a single little yip and ran into Sonny's arms, whining and shivering and begging for reassurance.

Jackson was reminded of Billy Bob, and he had a sudden notion that maybe when your lives were broken in the same places you had some of the same patches over the damage. Then Ernie stepped forward and took his hand.

Jackson stared at the boy's earnest, delicate features and fell immediately into the infinity pool of his brown eyes.

And fell.

And fell.

He was in a peaceful darkness with the *whoosh* of the ocean in his ears, and his breath, heartbeat, frantic worry, all of it stopped.

Ernie stepped back and broke contact, and Jackson filled his lungs with oxygen like he'd been underwater.

This boy made Crystal look like a brain-deaf state worker.

"Sonny?" Ernie said softly, never looking away from Jackson's face.

"Yeah—did you talk to Burton?"

"I told him you were going, whether he said yes or not. He said to take Jai, and so I called him."

Sonny nodded, shaking like the dog in his arms. "Fair enough. You're coming, right?"

Ernie stared at Jackson for a moment, considering—but what he said was "Of course."

"Burton know that?"

Ernie's jaw hardened. "He's not making that call."

Jackson wondered what it was about his face that made this boy decide to walk into hell, but Sonny was already on the move. "I'll go get the guns from the drawer—that gonna freak you out any?"

Ernie glanced at him and shook his head. "No. Burton left some under the bed. I'll bring those—"

"You can't come," Jackson blurted. No. Not this kid. Sonny, yes. Sonny knew how to handle a gun. This kid—

"Burton will need me," the kid said calmly, then bit his lip. "You... you are not okay. You are good—so good—but you... how have you not bled out yet?"

"Because the guy we're going to go get holds me together," Jackson said harshly. "Look—I can't... I can't talk about feelings like I have them right now. Tell me what else Burton said, okay?"

Ernie nodded. "Here. He sent me a link—let's go look at the map."

IT HAD taken them an hour to get from Walmart to Victoriana, and Ernie had used the time damned well.

He beckoned them into the house, which was just as square and utilitarian on the inside as it had been on the outside—but cared for, in a way.

The carpet was newish, and judging by the boots and shoes in the entryway, everybody did their best to keep it like that. Jackson kicked off his sneakers as they walked in, using the same instinct that kept him from parking on the sad little lawn.

The house opened directly into a kitchen, where everybody's shoes sat back behind the door, and as he walked in he could pretty much see everything else. There was a bathroom to the left and a doorway just past the kitchen that opened into a bedroom, but the bulk of the house was a living room, with a futon and what looked like dressers on either side of it. On the far side of the living room, what appeared to be the addition to the house sat—a plain wooden door, painted white like the wall that apparently divided one side of the world from the other.

There were posters of race cars on the walls, and a cheery throw on the futon, and even a couple of beanbag chairs between the futon and the television.

The smell of motor oil and fresh wood pervaded the place, and Jackson felt the wrongness of invading it in the pit of his balls.

"Don't worry so much," Ernie chimed, moving past Jackson. A small Formica dinner table sat by the counter that separated the kitchen from the rest of the house, and he sat down in front of the laptop set up on it. "You fit here just fine. You're as damaged as the rest of us—it's like this could be your home."

Jackson thought of their real home, Ellery's luxurious bed, the closet filled with suits Ellery practically lived in, and oh God, Billy Bob, who was probably lost and alone at Crystal's house.

"I'd miss my cat," he said faintly. "Tell me what the map says."

"Okay, both of you come here and look—it's super important. Burton says there's bombs in the ground all around the place, and you can't see all of them by looking at the piles of dirt."

"Land mines?" Jackson squeaked, watching as Ernie traced a path around the dot on the map. "Oh dear God—why?"

Ernie blinked slowly at him, probably masking the infinity of his soul as he did so. "Because these are bad men who like to hurt people," he explained patiently. "I know you're thinking they're soldiers, like Burton, but not anymore."

"Not anymore?" Jackson tried hard to swim in the reality pool and forget that breathless moment of tranquility that had happened when Ernie shook his hand.

"No. See, back in early November, Burton was given this contract to kill me—"

"I'm sorry?" Jackson's brain almost cracked.

"Kill. Me. He's a government assassin, and I was his target. But he usually only kills bad guys, and so he just watched me and tried to figure out what to do."

Behind them Sonny snorted inelegantly, and Jackson looked at him.

"Burton's totally in love with him and not talking about it," Sonny said, with the same air of someone talking about a favorite soap opera. "It's weird. It's like the guy is made of solid one-hundred-percent no-bullshit, but he looks at Ernie and turns into an ice cream sundae."

Ernie shrugged and smiled, but his infinity-pool eyes grew shadowed and sad.

"I was a surprise," he said softly. "And I was really a surprise when he realized I had no business being a target."

"Why *were* you a target?" Jackson would probably like to know more about the Burton and Ernie show—sometime when Ellery hadn't been hustled out of Walmart at gunpoint.

"I was a special project," Ernie said without self-consciousness.

"Of Burton's? Do assassins have special projects?"

"No!" Ernie rolled his eyes. "No. Have you ever heard of Project Stargate?"

"Like the TV show?" Sonny asked—apparently he hadn't heard this part either. "Because those two guys totally belong together, and you can't tell me they don't."

"No," Jackson said thoughtfully, looking at Ernie with speculation. "Like the CIA project where they tried to use psychics to get an edge in the cold war."

"You lie!" Sonny burst out, eyes huge.

"No, it was a true thing," Ernie confirmed. "I… I wasn't on the books, you understand. But Commander Karl Lacey—"

"Fucking scumbag," Jackson clarified.

"Yeah. Him. He… my parents were killed in a car accident, and when I went into the foster system, I… I wasn't too coherent, but I was an open nerve, you know? So I was reading people left and right, and it actually made it into my foster care records. I'm not sure how Lacey got hold of it, but right before I turned eighteen, I got to be a ward of the state. I got to be a ward of *his* state. He kept me for a year and…." Ernie shivered. "I saw…

I saw what he was doing to the new recruits. He… he kept trying to use me, as like a meter."

Jackson swallowed. "Like when you said I was good." Oh. Oh no. God. Ernie. Jackson thought *his* damage was bad—

"Your damage *is* bad," Ernie said, like Jackson had said it out loud. "I wasn't mistreated. I wasn't starved. I didn't see horrific things. What he did to the soldiers was… well, awful. But no worse than I'd seen in high school, sometimes. Just more… organized, more—"

"Systematic," Jackson filled in.

"Exactly. And my job—my only job—was to tell him if the person I touched was, in his words, 'good' or 'bad.'"

"That's so dangerous," Sonny breathed.

"That's so *stupid*!" Jackson argued, appalled.

"Why's it stupid to know if someone's good or bad? Good or bad saved me and Ernie's life when those bad guys came by!"

"Well, yeah—but that's because they were bad because they meant harm!" Jackson blurted.

"Don't most bad guys mean harm?"

"The guy we chased in November didn't think about it like that," Jackson said, stomach a cold stone, bowels a frozen river. "That guy we chased in November didn't see his victims as people—they were dirty pretty—they were like him. So he wasn't ever thinking 'I'm a bad guy, I'm going to do harm—'"

"He was thinking dirty-pretty people have to be stopped," Ernie supplied with a shiver. "I think I met that guy. I knew what he was becoming. I tried to tell Lacey too, but he just wanted to know if he was good or bad. And he never defined that, you know? But I finally realized that to him, 'good' meant a good soldier, and 'bad' meant someone who would question orders—but by then, so many of my 'good guys' had washed out of his super-special behavior modification unit that Lacey let me go." He shivered again. "Had his guys drive me to Albuquerque and leave me there with ten thousand dollars in the bank and enrollment in the local junior college. Like he was doing me a favor, right?"

"And that was how long ago?" Jackson asked, the timeline in his head coming together.

"That was about four years ago," Ernie said, looking at him curiously.

"So when Galway and Owens were being trained—"

"And they got shipped out not long after that," Sonny said. "'Cause Owens was a legend and Galway was an asshole four years ago. Ace and I got stateside two years after that."

Jackson nodded. "Okay. It makes sense. I… I'm pretty sure they're not the only two serial killers he created with his little behavior-mod schtick—"

"They weren't," Ernie said with grim confidence. "I… there were a lot of bad guys I tried to warn him about, but they were perfect soldiers, you know?"

"Yeah." Jackson couldn't sit at the table anymore. "But Owens was the one who got caught—or at least put in the spotlight, when Scott Bridger got arrested. We realized Bridger was just muscle for a corrupt politician, but his buddy Owens was a scary piece of work—"

"When was that?" Ernie asked, like it mattered.

"August." Jackson laced his fingers behind his head. "Why?"

"Because the hit on me was issued in early November."

Jackson had heard the time mentioned before, and his stomach suddenly clenched. "So we think Lacey is looking for funding—all the tech he's using is out-of-date, and he has a small group of men working for him but not unlimited resources."

"Wait!" Ernie stood up excitedly. "I got it! See, that's the thing. Lacey used the military to put the hit out on *me*, but he also hired a mercenary group called Corduroy to finish the job. So he loses his funding—people hear the name Tim Owens—"

"We tried to make a stink about it," Jackson said softly. "We thought nobody was listening."

"Well, Lacey heard, and then in November—"

"In November Owens killed the wrong person and we got close," Jackson said tightly. God, no—this kid was traumatized enough. Jackson wasn't going there. "We got Owens, and Ellery made the connection between Lacey and Galway and Sonny and Ace—"

"Why'd it take you so long to call us up, then?" Sonny asked curiously.

"I got hurt," Jackson said tersely. God, they were so off track here. He wanted nothing more than to go charging after Ellery. For Christ's sake, Jackson *knew where he was*. But the more they knew about their enemy, the more they knew who they were facing, the better chance they'd have to get him back alive. "I just went back to work last week and…." He let out a weak little laugh. "The first thing I did was get concussed and end up in the hospital again."

"Stop it," Ernie begged softly. "You're doing this thing in your head where your heart is screaming and your mouth is saying these really simple things. I hate it. I hate that. Just tell us what your heart is saying—"

"*We don't have time!*" Jackson snarled, and Ernie made a hurt sound. Oh fuck—Jackson had promised to be gentle. "I'm sorry," he whispered. "So sorry. Look, Ernie—maybe I should just go alone. I'm sorry—you and Sonny and Jai—you know each other. You're a family. Let me go, do some recon, see where Ace and Ellery are being held. I can scope things out, make a plan—"

"And get killed," Ernie said softly. "Please, Jackson. Wait. Let's reason this out together. I won't make you tell any more about yourself than you need to."

"I'm sorry," Jackson muttered again. "I didn't mean to—"

"You were making a long story short," Ernie said perceptively. "I forget sometimes, because I can see it, because I can *feel* it, that doesn't mean people are ready for the rest of the world to know."

"Exactly." Jackson's ears hurt, his throat was so tight. "So November, the shit hits the fan, Owens gets taken down, and Lacey—who has no funding at this point—starts using what he's still getting to hire mercenary groups to clean up his loose ends."

"That's you, Ernie," Sonny said in all earnestness. "You're a loose end."

"Literally the story of my life," Ernie said winsomely, and Jackson thought of AJ and Anthony and the lost boys in AJ's flophouse. Gagh! This kid—no wonder a superhero didn't know what to do with him. He gave Ernie his kindest smile and kept thinking.

"So, Ernie—what's Burton been doing since November—besides ditching out on a relationship, that is?"

"He sort of joined Corduroy," Ernie said, like that wasn't a bomb. "I mean, not really. He wanted to see what Lacey was doing, so he pretended to be a bad guy and, you know—"

"Infiltrated the enemy camp," Jackson said in wonder. "So he's actually *where they're being kept* right now?"

"Yes." Ernie smiled a little. "He worked their coms. He says he got to listen to you and Ellery have sex a lot. Said you fucked like rabbits. I think it made him sort of horny, so thank you for that."

Jackson's brain exploded.

"Ouch!" Ernie held his palms to his eyes. "Jackson! It wasn't bad, I swear! He didn't hate you! He didn't want to do it! He took the job because he didn't want anybody else to hear because they were mean! I swear—it wasn't dirty. It wasn't."

"It was ours," Jackson said, voice low and violent. "I... I get that might be why we're still alive, even, because I don't know if Lacey knows how close we are. But it was *ours*."

"Yeah." Sonny nodded at Ernie, like confirming Jackson had a right to be upset. "I'd get sort of upset too. I don't got a lot that's mine, but my time with Ace—that's fuckin' mine."

Ernie nodded sadly. "I'm sorry," he said, his heart in his eyes. "And I think Burton is too. But don't you see? He knows how they work, and he knows how to get Ace and Mr. Cramer out."

"How's that going to happen?" Jackson asked, and his head ached fiercely. "And do you have any painkillers? My brain is going to blow out my eyeballs."

"You wish," Ernie said with an almost familiar bitterness. "Then you wouldn't have to feel anymore."

"Right here." Sonny showed him the cupboard and got him a glass of water. "My head would hurt too if I found out people listened to me and Ace have sex. That's no good—"

"They're louder than alley cats," Ernie informed Jackson bluntly. "But he means without your permission."

"I figured that," Jackson said, washing down the ibuprofen. "Now tell me what you know about where they're being kept. We know we're not dealing with normal military, so driving up and asking for our guys isn't going to work—"

"You were just going to do that?" Sonny asked, wide-eyed.

"Fuck no. But see, this means Ellery's mom isn't going to have the leverage she'd need to pop Lacey's cork and get him to let them go. It's going to have to be us, or they'll be moved—"

"Burton says it's an old military base—it's got a small airstrip."

"Moved to fuck-all knows where," Jackson said sourly. "Especially if it's a paramilitary group. One gassed plane and they could be in South America for the rest of their short lives. Okay. That's not good. So what else do we know?"

Ernie pointed to his little diagram. "See—here's the base. These're the barracks right here, and Burton says there's thirty men here. Says they come in, train together, and then take the contracts they get offered through the actual leader of Corduroy, who works there with Lacey too."

"Why does he work with Lacey, you think?" Sonny asked, sounding pensive. "He sounds like sort of a tool."

"That's exactly what he is." Jackson looked at the diagram and saw things like a shooting range and a PT area and a gym and a com room. The base wasn't full, but there were places a small paramilitary group would definitely need to gather. "He's feeding them intel, probably intercepting legitimate contracts, and very definitely finding military personnel that fit the mercenary profile. He's literally training the perfect killers there—the killers who won't betray their CO."

Ernie made a sound of revelation. "Ohhhhhh…."

"What?" Jackson asked.

"That's why Burton had to be the one," Ernie said softly. "He couldn't explain it—and Sonny's right, some of it does have to do with me. But he said he had to be the one to go undercover. It's because he *does* question orders. He did. If he hadn't, I wouldn't be here. So he knew he could go undercover and not… not change. Not—"

"Lose himself," Jackson said softly.

"Yeah. His CO cut him loose so the government doesn't have to admit what's happening here—"

"He'd stay true to his code," Jackson said, knowing that if Burton had been a Marine once, that code was something he lived and died by.

"Yeah." Ernie took a cleansing breath. "I feel better," he told them benignly. "I was starting to worry that I read him wrong."

"If you read him any way but stupid dumbassed in love and fighting it, I'm not gonna think you're a witch anymore," Sonny said in complete seriousness. "I don't know people, and I really don't give much of a fuck most times, but that shit I know."

Ernie's smile made all the world better, and Jackson smiled back weakly.

"Okay, so Burton's expecting us—you said that."

Ernie nodded. "Yes, and I told him I'd be there and he said he didn't want me and I said he'd need me and he made that sound he makes when he doesn't know what to do with me, and I said okay. So I'm pretty sure that's a no, but it really doesn't matter 'cause I'm going anyway."

Jackson had the sudden notion that Ace, living here in this little house with Sonny as his lover and Ernie as his charge, must be finding captivity someplace quiet and sane like a paramilitary assassin's camp to be a bit of a vacation.

"Okay—so that's four of us counting your friend Jai"—they all heard the sound of a perfectly running Toyota pulling up in front of the mossy yard—"and he's here. I've got an idea for how to get everybody's attention so we can run in and get our guys. It'll keep Ernie out of the line of fire, give me and Sonny a chance to arm our bear eaters and sneak out, and use your friend Jai as backup."

The front door opened and closed, and Jackson looked up in time to see Jai stomp into the kitchen. He paused to unlace his boots and crowd behind Jackson and Ernie as they studied the computer. Jackson took in the craggy face under black eyebrows and a gleaming dome of a head and realized his memories hadn't exaggerated: this man was well and truly close to seven feet tall.

"You're going to have someone drive a car over the land mines near the airfield," Jai said, his Russian accent thick and disdainful.

"Yes," Jackson said, unsurprised that a guy who was probably former mob saw the plan immediately. "But, you know—use a brick on the gas pedal or cruise control or something and be long gone before the land mine goes off."

"Da," Jai muttered. "So the best place for the other team to come in is the airfield—where are they being held?"

"Burton says the admin building," Ernie told him. "The airfield runs behind it, and he says there are planes and hangars and stuff to hide behind."

"Da. So, who is doing what, yellow-haired man?"

Jackson smiled in relief. "I'm Jackson Rivers, Jai. I remember you from September."

Jai shrugged. "Remember you, yes. Give a shit, no. But you have a man in there, and you're not a complete imbecile, so I assume you will work to get Ace out without harm." Jai looked at Sonny, and his granite features softened. "Sonny is no good without Ace."

Sonny nodded disconsolately, and Jackson looked at the diagram again.

"Okay, guys—here's the plan."

At the Mercy of the Fisherman

ELLERY LEANED back in the office chair, toed off his loafers, and tucked one foot under his thigh. If death was going to come bursting through the door at any minute, he wanted to be comfortable.

"How's the light?" he asked, more for something to do than anything else.

"Green," Ace said, from the floor. Apparently comfort for Ace was up against the corner, legs crossed so he could lean forward, stare at Burton's little light, and brood.

To each his own.

"Your guy ain't gonna get Sonny killed, is he?"

Ellery glanced at him and smiled briefly. "Himself, yes. Anybody else on his watch, no."

"Well. Sucks to be you."

Deep breath. Another. "It has its moments."

"He's skinnier than he was in September. And he was right puny in September."

Ellery glanced up at him and saw nothing but friendly interest. Not judgment. Jackson's assessment of this man rang truer with every moment they spent together.

"He almost died in November. His heart stopped. I had to give him mouth-to-mouth. Hard coming back from that."

Ace nodded, shivering. "Sonny got stabbed once. Surgery. Took him a week before he could walk again."

Ellery shuddered for him. "Sucks to be you."

"Yeah."

"Who stabbed him?"

Ace's face closed down. "A dead man."

Ah. "You do know what kind of lawyer I am, don't you?"

"There's kinds?" Ace looked up in surprise, and Ellery suppressed a laugh. Ah, lawyer jokes—except Ace wasn't joking. Like Jackson, there were things in his life he had to know and things he didn't. Jackson had joined law enforcement—he knew cops and robbers and defense and prosecution. Ace had joined the Army—he knew rank and file, and he knew cars.

"I'm a defense lawyer. Which means I spend my life defending people who've committed crimes and keeping them out of jail. So if you ever need someone to keep you out of jail for something you felt you absolutely positively had to do, remember we were kidnapped together, 'kay?"

Ace grunted, and his eyes went shadowed. Haunted.

"Thank you, sir. I'll keep that in mind."

"So. Did you?" Ellery was bored, and his defense attorney sense was tingling, and he didn't want to think about Jackson losing his shit.

"Did I what?" But Ace's breathing had quickened. He knew this question, same as Jackson knew what Ellery was asking when he snapped *What?*

"Did you absolutely positively have to kill somebody?"

Ace swallowed. "You'll be my lawyer if this ever comes out?"

"You have my word."

"Yeah. I absolutely had to kill someone. You know my only regret?"

"What?"

"I didn't kill him before he broke my boy."

Ellery nodded. "Jackson's mother," he said softly, "was a junkie. And a prostitute. And I don't even want to know the parts of his childhood he won't tell me about."

Ace grunted. "Sonny had one of those too."

"And you think, 'If this person we love survived all that, and is still someone we can love, what would he have been like if he'd had the shit I'd had?'"

Ace rested his cheek against his knees. "Yeah."

"But there's no time machine yet, so we just have to be grateful there's still enough of them to love." Ellery's heart, nervous and frustrated after all the shaky months of healing, smoothed a little. These were good words. Suddenly that far horizon, the one where he and Jackson dropped off the map, disappeared. The earth was round, and they were sailing together as long as they could survive the trip.

"Every day," Ace said, not surprising Ellery at all. He'd been living with this secret for a while. "Every day together is a good day."

Ellery closed his eyes and nodded. "Then let's make it through today for a good day tomorrow," he murmured.

A moment later Ace's gasp surprised him. "It's flashing. You got something to write with?"

Ellery scrambled for the piece of chalk he'd seen in his initial search. He crouched down by the dark green baseboard, prepared to write. "Shoot."

"T-H-E-Y…." Haltingly, letter by letter, Ace called the message out while Ellery scrawled it on the vinyl baseboard.

Finally the light switched to green permanently, and Ellery stared at the string of text.

THEYRECOMINGWAITFORBOOMHEADFOREASTWINGHANGAR

"D'ja get it?" Ace asked, eyes glued to the little green light.

"Wait a sec…. *They're coming. Wait for boom. Head for east wing hangar.*"

In Ace's hand, the little light switched on and off again, just once. "I think that means yes," Ace murmured, and it did it again.

"Wait for boom?" Ellery muttered. "Oh dear God."

"Why—what do you think that means?"

Ellery groaned. "I think it means my mother's going to need to pull strings to get me car insurance, that's what I think it means."

Ace stared at him impassively for a minute. "Why would he use your car? Isn't it brand-new?"

"Why use his car? I don't know. Maybe yours wouldn't have the right kind of spring in it. Maybe it doesn't have cruise control. Maybe there's a kitten in a tree or a kid in the middle of the road that Jackson can only rescue by sacrificing a perfectly good car that doesn't even have plates yet. I got no idea—but I would give you *money* that it's his car."

Ace let out a rusty chuckle. "I'll tell you what. That boy turns his car into toast to get us the fuck out of here and me and Sonny will *make* him a car. Tell us what he wants, tell us what he needs, and we'll get our hands on something unmarked and fucking invincible—"

"Air-conditioning?" Ellery asked, because as far as he knew, only an idiot wouldn't want air-conditioning in a California summer.

Ace shrugged. "If that's what floats your boat. We sacrificed AC for the SHO so it could have nitrous and really fuckin' pop, you know? But it's not the most comfy vehicle in the world, and it smells like steel and armpit, so if you want something with less zoom, AC is fine."

Ellery stared at him. He was dead serious. All of it. Building Jackson a car to order. The car smelling like steel and armpit. Giving up air-conditioning when he lived in the middle of the fucking desert.

"How fast is your damned car?" he asked, voice rusty.

"Hits sixty in two and a half," Ace said, like that wasn't the fastest car in the world right there. "Does the quarter in ten."

"You *wrecked* in that car?" Ellery was horrified. He'd seen the yellow car pull up as he was walking into Walmart, and he'd rolled his eyes to himself about boys and their toys.

This wasn't a toy. This was a life's fucking work is what it was.

"A kid's dog got loose at the race. Kid followed it." Ace shrugged. "Had to swerve in front of the other car—wasn't fast enough, I guess, 'cause he clipped me."

"Holy God."

"Yeah. So don't worry if you come up short a car. I mean, Sonny won't give up the SHO, 'cause that car's—"

"A miracle," Ellery said, feeling numb.

"Yeah. Sorta is. Can't get one like it nowhere else. But we won't leave you hanging."

Ellery took a deep breath and tried not to cry. It was about the sweetest fucking offer he'd ever had from someone not Jackson. "I won't either," he said softly. "If I don't get out of this, Ace, my mother's name is Taylor Cramer. If shit comes back to haunt you, you tell her one of the last things I said to you was to trust her, okay?"

Ace's lower lip wobbled. "That's real kind. I'm sorry I was an asshole to you back in September."

"Yeah, well, I deserved it then."

"Don't now?"

"God, I hope not. I'm going to be pissing my pants until we see what's going boom."

"I hope it's okay that I want you to be right that it's the SUV and not the SHO."

"Not at all. I'd love to see your car go zoom."

They were quiet then, each in his own thoughts, but then they'd said quite a bit in the last couple of hours.

About an hour after the message, they heard a tampering with their lock again. The door didn't open, but as they stared at the handle wiggling, they both heard the distinct pop and click of the latch.

"Wait for it," Burton whispered from the other side, and then he disappeared.

Ellery and Ace were left just staring at the door, wondering if it was really unlocked and who was on the other side.

"Wait," Ellery said, his throat gummy. "Which way's east?" Because who just knew that, right? A soldier might. A woodsman might. If Ellery was outside and could see the ocean to the west and the sun rising in the east he might, but here in this dingy little room, he had no idea.

"Know how we drove for a while past the property, turned left onto a small road, and then turned in to here?"

"Yeah."

"We were heading east before we turned left, then we were heading north, then we turned left again, so we were heading west. So the airplane hangar is toward the east anyway—you just gotta keep running that way."

Ellery nodded, and then something caught his eye. "Oh shit," he whispered, and Ace looked at the switch in his hand.

"Oh shit! You don't suppose—"

And that's when shit went boom.

Fish in the Army

JAI DROVE his Toyota, and Sonny and Ernie rode toward the base in the Infiniti, Jackson at the wheel.

"You're a good driver," Sonny said, almost clinically. "You tell the car what to do and the car listens. Ace is a good driver too, I mean he's a better driver, but, you know, that's cause he's got the SHO but you're not bad, I mean, it'd be okay if you wanted to do a quarter in a decent car, you'd come in second, I think you would, don't you, Ernie?"

Ernie was right behind them, buckled in by his middle but with the seat belt stretched way out so he was practically in Jackson's lap. He reached forward and touched Sonny's elbow.

"I think Jackson's a good man to have behind the wheel," Ernie said softly, and to Jackson's relief, Sonny nodded and sort of melted back into his seat. Jackson didn't think he could have taken that manic chatter for the next forty-five minutes to their destination.

"Thank you," he said quietly. Sonny was staring out the window, biting his lip, but he wasn't quivering like the little dog they'd put in a crate back at the house.

"Someone'll... 'll come get him out, right?" Sonny had asked plaintively before they left. "I mean, he's got food and water and...."

"Da," Jai said gently. "Alba called me after Ernie sent her home. She'll check."

Sonny nodded and looked relieved, but the tension hadn't left him— until now. Until Ernie's touch.

"You do that a lot?" Jackson asked, to keep out of his own head. Right now his inner home entertainment center was fixed on the moment Ellery and Ace had been hustled out of the store, and he didn't think he could see that panicked look Ellery had cast behind him one more time.

"No." Ernie yawned. "Takes it out of me. But mostly Sonny doesn't need it with Ace. Ace got him people, all around him, so he doesn't have to worry about that death spiral in his head."

"Ace did really good," Jackson said with feeling. "Can't be easy, living with someone with damage." Poor Ellery. God, he deserved so much better.

"It's not," Ernie said softly. "But it must be worth it because it keeps happening, right?"

Jackson smiled weakly. "Yeah. So we know the plan?"

"Course. I blow a car up in the west end of the base, you and Sonny sweep in from behind the base—the east—and Jai uses the gun stash to pick off everyone who comes out to see what happens when the car goes boom. We've only got a few people. It's not that hard."

"What are you doing after you set the car to go?" Jackson asked, because they'd managed to get a lock on the farthest point west that wasn't mined. They'd seen an outbuilding there, and Jackson would check it out before they set the plan in motion, but the biggest takeaway was to keep Ernie safe.

Ernie didn't belong in a firefight, and Jackson didn't want to know what his superhero not-boyfriend would do to Jackson if that's where he ended up.

"My job is to get the hell out of there and leave the rest of the op to the gun-wielding psychopaths who think they're the grown-ups," Ernie said pertly. "How's that?"

"As a gun-wielding psychopath, I'm fine with that," Jackson told him, not particularly insulted. "The world's better with you in it, Ernie—it would be a shame if that changed."

Ernie growled. "Jackson, do you know how long I knew Burton before I knew I would love him forever?"

"I got no id—"

"I hadn't even seen him yet. He walked into my bakery and asked for crullers. He was scoping me out, but I could feel him, all of him, this terrible heat and fury and rock solidness just walking around Albuquerque, setting its sights on little ol' me. When I saw him for real I was stoned stupid, but just hearing his voice again woke me up. Because the thing with the gift is you can either know somebody instantly or you can never know them at all. It makes me very selective who I care about. Burton, Sonny, Ace—I know them. I'd die for them."

"That's…." Jackson took a deep breath. "It takes the rest of us a while longer," he said truthfully.

"Bullshit." Ernie shrugged like that level of clairvoyance was no big deal.

"You had enough ESP to become your own Naval Intelligence experiment," Jackson muttered as that damned mange-green desert flowed by him. "How can you call—"

"How long have you known him? Not slept with him or dated him—known him?"

He didn't even have to think about it. "Six years, three months, four days. He took one look at me and…." Jackson paused. His assumption about what Ellery had done and Ellery's own confession of that moment were two very different things.

"What?" Ernie asked breathlessly, like a kid at the movies.

"I thought he dismissed me. He looked at me and blew me off and hated me. But… but he told me later that I… he was attracted to me. And he thought I was out of his league. So he got that pissy sound in his voice and looked down his long nose at me, and we sniped at each other for the next five and a half years."

"And the whole time…," Ernie prompted.

"We thought about it. When we were with someone else, we'd know this wasn't the person we wanted. But as soon as we got together, we knew…." How embarrassing. Seriously. Hearts and flowers and chocolates and romance had nothing on this.

"You knew what?"

"There wasn't anyone else we wanted to be with," Jackson finished.

"Hmm." Ernie didn't sound like he was gloating. He was just pleased. "See? You knew. In that first thirty seconds, you knew. But you both had shit to do in your heads first, right?"

And then, because the kid deserved the truth. "My head's an awful place, kid. Wasn't as easy as it sounds."

"Yeah, it is. I been there. I thought Sonny was the worst I'd seen, but you two, you could swap stories."

Oreos, KitKats, soup with more crackers than soup. A knowledge of *Sesame Street* because it was public broadcasting, and Jackson didn't get to see other TV until he met Kaden in the fifth grade, and Sonny probably didn't get to until he'd joined the Army.

A pathological fear of losing the one person they trusted to care for them, based on the empirical evidence that suggested they weren't worth enough to be cared for.

"We swapped the stuff that mattered," Jackson said. "Everything else is just one-upmanship."

Ernie grunted. "I am so not impressed by your stoic 'I can deal with this' thing. I'm sure Ellery isn't either."

"It's mine. Where are you going after we blow up the SUV?"

"Nowhere," Sonny said unexpectedly, like he'd been with them in the car all along. "We're blowing up Jai's Toyota."

"Why in the hell—"

"Because this is a brand-new fuckin' car, and you may not give a shit about it, but to my people that's sacrilege. Jai's driving a POS, and I may have made it function, but it's not a goddamned Infiniti QX30. Besides, we're gonna need this car for the getaway—it's big, it'll fit everyone including Burton, and when you stand on it, it'll fly." Sonny's sound of disgust was clear. "*Their* SUV needed a tune-up and its belts are goin', and it's got maybe thirty miles before the brakes go."

Jackson did a slow blink, but when his eyes opened the road was still the road, Ellery was still gone, and he was still stunned.

"How in the *hell* did you know that?"

"'Cause I heard it pull away. What did you hear when it pulled away?"

Ellery's voice in the dark, saying, "Mine."

"Nothing useful—ouch! Ernie!"

"You heard what you needed to hear," Ernie said, voice thick—but Jackson's head hurt from the smack to the back of it, and his low-level headache indicated he wasn't doing too hot as it was. "Now after we blow up the Toyota and I get to the outbuilding—"

"Shit," Jackson muttered. "Okay, we need to rethink this. Sonny's right. This *is* the getaway car—how do you get away if we're on the other side of the goddamned compound? We need you to drop us off at the airplane hangar and then you and Jai to circle back around after the Toyota is blown—"

"But then Jai can't give you cover!" Ernie protested.

"Maybe not—but he can get you to safety if this whole thing goes south."

Sonny grunted. "Yeah. Like that plan. You and me, we don't get our guys out, might as well go up like the car."

Sonny got it. They were good.

Behind them Ernie said, "I don't fuckin' *believe* this!"

But Jackson couldn't think anymore. He had to find his happy place and center himself or he wouldn't be able to move when he got there.

JACKSON KNEW where the main entrance to the base was, but having looked at the overhead map—and then really zeroed in—he'd seen a series of smaller service paths. Dirt tracks, really; they were for jeeps schlepping recruits out to the rifle range and hauling back any soldier unlucky enough to get winded on long runs. Coming up from the east, Jackson turned off on one of those immediately after the main road and swung back behind the airstrip, behind the airplane hangars—one more of a sunbreak than anything else but with three small and one larger complete hangar which stood, bay doors open, like it was ready to send a flight out or take one in. Two copters sat, one a rather vast Black Hawk and one a smaller, spryer Jayhawk, on the helipad behind the airstrip, and Sonny grunted.

"What?"

"The UH-60A Black Hawks ain't been common use for a couple'a years. Most units updated to the Ls or the Ns. This guy shopping Army surplus?"

"Fits, doesn't it?" Jackson said. "He's sort of squatting on this base as it is. He's got limited funds coming in, and he's seriously losing his grip on whatever legitimacy he ever had. He starts training guys for this Corduroy group, and they're giving him money to keep doing his behavioral modification or what the fuck ever, but in the meantime he's getting no love from the military. He may have been US Navy, but military surplus has been his MO."

"I do not get people coming in and starting shit like this. Like what? Killing people's like a job skill? Like, oh, hey, I'm gonna start up a camp for people to go kill people?"

"Uh, Sonny?" Ernie sounded hesitant, as well he should. "What was boot camp in the Army like?"

"But this ain't for a country! This is like… like a special class! Like Alba planning to go to junior college to learn how to do algebra, but this is killing people instead. Murder 101—today we learn about poison and tiny little piano wires so you don't make no fuckin' noise!"

"Garrotes," Jackson supplied, liking Sonny more every time he went off.

"What in the fuck is a garrote?"

"That's what you call it when you strangle someone with a tiny little piano wire. It's a garrote."

Sonny's mouth fell open, but he didn't look at Jackson because the three of them were too busy scanning the base as they jounced over the godforsaken road. Not even the Infiniti's suspension could make up for a shitty dirt track that had probably not been tended for a couple of years or so.

"How in the fuck did you know that?"

Jackson let out a mean and dirty chuckle. "Police academy, Sonny. They taught us all about killing there."

Sonny's chuckle sounded unhinged and mean and delirious and a lot like Jackson's own voice in his ears. "That there is fun shit."

"Amen. Is Jai behind us?"

Ernie checked quickly. "Roger that—do you think he figured out the hole in our plan?" Ernie's phone buzzed, and he shifted to answer it. Jai's thickly accented voice thudded through the phone's speaker, and although Jackson couldn't make out words, he could make out tone. Ernie soothed his feathers, though, and they continued to circle around the airstrip, sticking to the track.

The hangar was at an angle from the actual base, out of the line of sight and hidden from the road by the rise at the fence line. The entire base, in fact, was surrounded by a ten-foot fence topped with razor wire, tucked into a wide shallow valley and hidden by the rise that appeared to circle the entire thing.

If you were hiding a secret military base in the expanse of the desert, this was a way to do it. From looking at satellite maps, Jackson would hazard that the shooting range was situated such that a stray bullet would have spent itself, died, and oxidized before it even hit the fence line rise.

On the one hand, civilians didn't have to worry about what was about to go down, because they would never know.

On the other, if anybody in their little band got hurt, it was a long goddamned way to help.

They came to a stop and Jackson motioned to Sonny to get out. Sonny ran around to the back to grab the two assault rifles Jai had apparently just had lying around under his bed. Jackson pulled his pistol out of the glove compartment, checked the cartridge, checked the chamber, and grabbed the two spare clips he kept as well. He double-checked the safety and tried to tuck the gun in the back of his jeans and then grimaced.

"What?" Ernie asked, and unlike Ellery, Jackson couldn't play the "what" game with Ernie.

"Fucking jeans are sliding off my fucking ass," Jackson muttered. He set the gun down on the island between seats and pulled his belt tighter, then forced a hole through the leather and tried again. Yeah, this time the gun felt tighter, like it might not end up a load in his shorts, and he hoped the clips in his pockets wouldn't cause his death by pulling his pants down in the middle of the op.

"You get tired of being told to eat?" Ernie asked mildly.

"God, kid—you ever get tired of knowing everything?"

"Not yet." Ernie slid out of the car and opened Jackson's door while Sonny talked to Jai. "You and Sonny be careful, you understand? I know you're both going in thinking you need to save your one person, but they're worried about you as well." Ernie's serenity slipped then, and he bit his lip in a show of uncharacteristic fear. "And I'm worried about my person, and you guys need to be careful not to hurt him."

Jackson nodded gravely and had a sudden thought. "Hey—what's he look like? Any distinguishing characteristics?"

To his surprise Ernie smirked. "Yeah—he says he's the darkest thing this base has seen since the last eclipse. He slid in as a member of Corduroy, and I guess Lacey's sort of a fucking racist."

Jackson's lip curled scornfully. "Is there any other kind?"

Ernie gave another short bark of angry laughter. "He's made Burton's life miserable these last few months. If we don't get shot, he'll probably be glad to blow this place."

For a moment Jackson's urgency stilled. "You don't know for sure?"

Ernie's full mouth twisted. "We text. There's a lot you can say in text, but there's a lot you don't know either. For all I know, my name comes up as 'Piece of ass' in his phone, in case it gets discovered. Not far from the truth, you know, but not flattering either."

Suddenly Jackson wanted Burton and Ernie's Happy Ever After as much as he wanted his own.

"Stay safe, Ernie. I'll make it a point not to shoot your boyfriend."

"Thanks, Jackson. Don't throw your life away—it's worth something."

Jackson nodded. For once he thought he had to listen to this advice. If he was the one getting Ellery out of captivity, he had to be very careful indeed.

Jackson double-checked his gun, double-checked his ammo, and said, "Take care of the car, okay? It really is our only way out of here."

"That we know of," Ernie said, but then he slammed the door and put the SUV into gear. Jackson strode to the passenger side of the little Toyota, where Sonny and Jai were apparently having a discussion in a redneck/Russian hybrid language Jackson could hardly follow.

"Sonny?"

"He's gonna get himself killed."

"He's not going to be in the car when it hits the bank of land mines," Jackson soothed. They'd even found a brick and a broom handle to rig the gas with a little help from some rope and duct tape.

"It won't matter if he ain't," Sonny snapped. "Jai filled the damned car with C-fucking-4 and fuses—"

"No fuse," Jai said. "Will figure it out."

"Well, that's just perfect!" Sonny was shaking with rage. "So the car'll hit a land mine, there'll be a boom, and then there'll be a *big* fuckin' boom that nobody on the planet can ignore, and then all that shrapnel's gonna come down on these two dumbasses' heads."

Jackson blinked. Part of him liked this plan. Part of him was a little appalled. "You think you and Ernie can get the fuck out of there in time?"

Jai nodded. "Will make a big boom. Will not make a bigger hole. C-4 leaves behind nothing. Car will have already exploded."

Jackson grunted. He knew very little about explosives. "Ernie," he said helplessly. "You can't—"

Jai nodded soberly, like a substitute teacher told not to let the children hang on the cupboards. "I like Ernie. I don't want to see him dead."

Jackson looked at Sonny. "You trust him?"

Sonny nodded, unhappy but seeing the truth. You had to trust him all the way, especially here. "Please—all of us need—"

"I will not let the scrawny little chicken die. No worries."

Jai was looking at them both with incredible sincerity, and Jackson took a deep breath and hoped. Not for himself, but for this small group of people he'd inadvertently drawn into his and Ellery's drama.

"Good luck." He held out his hand, and Jai took it. "If shit looks bad or it looks too dangerous, dump the C-4, grab Ernie, and get the fuck out of there."

"That is a deal." Jai's paw pumped Jackson's smaller hand once, hard. "And if you do not get your man back, I will keep you." His craggy face erupted into a winsome smile. "You have a strong stomach, and that and the yellow hair...." He shook his head wistfully, as though Jackson and Sonny were just too precious for words, before rolling up the window and driving away. Ernie let him go first, and together they moved out and it was just Jackson and Sonny, running the perimeter of the hangar.

"You should feel special," Sonny muttered as they pressed into the shade, backs to the corrugated aluminum. "He's been crushing on me for two years. You're the first other person he's gotten soft on."

Jackson grunted and peered around the corner, jerking back when he saw three guys dressed in jeans and boots, hair in various stages of give-a-fuck, scruff and beards aplenty, walking toward the hangar entrance. They wore backpacks, and one of them was wheeling a duffel bag behind him.

"Military my ass," he muttered.

"No, it ain't the military that makes him crush," Sonny rambled, like they weren't in danger with every breath. "He says it's the hair."

"It's not the hair," Jackson told him, hoping this wouldn't hurt Sonny's feelings. "It's the damage. We're both broken. He thinks it's sexy."

Sonny grunted. "I'm not broken enough to throw Ace over for Jai, if that's what you're thinking."

"Nope, never crossed my mind. Hush."

Together they listened, trying to differentiate the inside sounds from the outside sounds. For a moment it was a lost cause, and then Jackson heard a murmuring at the same time he spotted a small vent about twenty feet away. He trotted over, fingers on his lips, and hit the deck, pressing his ear to the vent.

"The Cessna, not the Jayhawk—you're sure?"

"Sure I'm sure. They're taking the lawyer and his butt-buddy with them. Jayhawk won't take four people plus luggage."

"Great—Lacey's bailing, Hamblin's going with him—leaving just us nuts, twisting in the wind?" It was the first time he'd heard the name Hamblin—but the guy who ran Corduroy had to have a name, right?

"We got orders to move out, overland. They've got a base down south. Don't stress, Perkins, company's never done better. We just gotta get these guys outta sight before big dicks start twitching."

"Hear you. Go inside and do the check. I'll do the landing gear and flaps."

Jackson scooted away from the vent and stood up, thinking furiously. "Shit. Shit shit shit...."

"What?" Sonny hissed. "Can we kill them? They're bad guys—can we fuckin' kill them?"

Jackson reached out and closed his hands over Sonny's restless fingers as they twitched on the Beretta. "No," he said shortly. "We're not here to kill mercenaries, Sonny. If we kill assassins, assassins will be all over our ass with lead diapers until we die in a puddle of blood. We're here to get our guys."

Sonny closed his eyes and nodded, then put the gun in the back of his pants like Jackson had.

"Then if we're not gonna kill them, what's wrong?"

"What's wrong is that when the shit goes boom, everybody including the bad guys are going to be going in the direction we're gonna be. We gotta—"

"See that big helicopter?" Sonny said, like "Oh hey, look, there's a flower!"

"I noticed it."

"That there is a cargo helicopter. Why do you suppose they're not flying *it* down south? They can certainly take more shit if they do."

"I got no idea."

"'Cause see that prop? It's bent. That thing won't go up—just loop-de-loop all over the fucking ground if someone turns it on. Think I could figure out how to turn it on?"

"Think you could get the fuck out of the helicopter before it started to loop-de-loop all over the fuckin' landing pad?"

Sonny grinned. "If I don't, it'll be a hell of a ride. You head for the buildings. I'll create a distraction. They'll be so busy figuring out how to not let that thing kill them before it destroys all the other planes and shit, they'll never see us run behind the hangar when Ernie's there to pick us up."

Jackson took a deep breath and put his hand on Sonny's shoulder. "Sonny, don't kill anybody who's not trying to kill you first. I got awful shit in my head, but that is one thing I don't got, you understand me?"

Sonny paused. "They hurt Ace, I'm gonna—"

"There won't be any remains, I get it. But otherwise, think beyond this moment, you hear?"

Sonny nodded, and Jackson looked around the corner again. He could see nobody in front of the main hangar, and nobody out in the open before the campus itself started.

"Wish me luck," he murmured and jogged away.

As soon as he hit the strip hangar, he moved to the back and kept to the wall, but once he cleared that structure, it was just him, Jackson Leroy Rivers, all on his lonesome in a paramilitary base full of hostile assholes.

He would have felt less conspicuous naked at the office. At least there nobody would shoot his dick off.

After the hangar, it was a good hundred yards to the next-closest outbuilding, and he figured it only took him five, six years tops to get there. Once he hit the shade, he looked around the corner again and jerked back. This was apparently a barracks.

And these guys were obviously off duty.

They were pretty innocuous—playing cards, reading. Jackson had heard that a lot of military time was spent waiting around for orders, and he guessed mercenaries would be no different. These guys were just doing what soldiers do when they waited.

But they were in Jackson's way.

He felt the time prickle on the outside of his skin. He had to get to the admin building—or at least close to it—before Ernie and Sonny sprang their little surprises.

With a burst of clarity, he remembered his words to Janie. Bad guys were not omniscient—and this place was run by two leaders, neither of whom was completely trusted by their men.

That gave some wiggle room, and wiggle room meant he could breed some confusion in these jackoffs, no problem.

He pulled his sunglasses off the vee of his sweatshirt and looped them over his ears. Then he set his sights on the big, square admin building with the three-story rise in the middle like a squat penis.

"Hey—who are you?"

Jackson paused and took off his glasses, because that's what you did when you had no qualms about somebody seeing your face. "New recruit from down south—Hamblin called me to escort the prisoners."

"I didn't hear about this. I'm the damned master sergeant. I should know if there's new people coming in!" He wore fatigues, with insignia well placed and a name tag that said Cooper.

So they still maintained vestigial bits of military hierarchy—good to know.

"Hey, it's not my fault Hamblin and Lacey can't get their shit together. I was getting laid when I got the call to come out—how do you think I feel?"

"You know, I didn't see no fucking car—"

"Infiniti QX30, asshole. It's gorgeous. You can't see the parking lot from here—what's your deal?"

"The deal is, I'm escorting you to Lacey's office. You don't fuckin' smell right."

"I'll take deodorant if you've got any," he said, sounding bored. "It's a long fuckin' drive."

"C'mon—" The guy reached for Jackson's arm, intent on hauling Jackson away like a truant kid, and Jackson reacted. He kicked out sideways, quick as a snake, and kneecapped the guy, who fell to the ground screaming.

He didn't hear the men around him drawing their weapons, but he did hear the click of their safeties.

He held his hands up sourly, heart pounding in his chest. He'd done this sort of thing before, right down to being in the sights of unsafetied guns, but never with Ellery's life in the balance. A part of him wanted to cringe, cower. *I'm sorry! I'm sorry! I'm sorry!* Beg for forgiveness, beg for Ellery's life.

But nobody touched him like that—*nobody*—and the small part of his brain that was still rational kicked in. "You assholes let him drag you around like punks? Jesus, what kind of mercenaries are you?"

For a breathless pause he thought he'd gone too far, and then, holy God thank you so very much, the gun right behind his head clicked, safety engaged, and all the others in the group of ten or so guys did the same.

"We're mercenaries fucking tired of being in this military camp being given orders," the guy behind him said in disgust. He walked around to the man squealing on the ground and kicked him in the ribs. "Shut up! I don't give a shit what your rank is—that's not your fucking flag overhead, is it?"

Jackson's eyes went automatically up to the flagpole outside the administration building, and his stomach cramped.

Corduroy.

Like Ernie had said.

An assassin's guild. Lacey had surrendered his castle, and he was no longer in charge.

"Do you have, like, a medic or something?" Jackson asked, jerking his eyes away from that incriminating flagpole. "The screaming. I mean… dear God."

The guy who'd spoken was fucking huge. Shoulders like a linebacker, six foot five if he stood an inch. Brown hair, brown eyes, tanned skin—pretty in a squashed-nose, average-white-boy kind of way, but apparently he gave zero fucks.

He put his size fourteen steel-toed boot up against the guy's neck.

"Cooper!" he snarled, and Master Sergeant Cooper clamped his lips together and whimpered.

"My knee!"

"I don't give a shit. Your knee, your balls—he could have ripped your spleen out, and you know what? I don't care. Drag your sorry fucking carcass to the medic and get some morphine or some heroin or some goddamned crack in a cat food bag and stop—oh dear God."

Average Refrigerator White Boy jumped back in disgust as Master Sergeant Cooper lost control of his bladder.

"I will give a hundred dollars to anybody who wants to drag this bozo to the fucking medic. You assholes have until the count of five before I shoot him."

Jackson looked around and had the sick realization that he was about to make a hundred dollars.

Two minutes later he was half dragging the man two buildings over to the hospital barracks.

"That'll teach ya," he muttered.

"I'm a soldier!" Cooper almost wept. "I… I don't understand. I was loyal to my CO, I did what he ordered—I did my goddamned job!"

"Did he order you to be a bastard to people to see if you could make them meaner?" Jackson asked, trying really hard not to let any of the wet spots on Cooper's uniform touch him.

"I followed orders," Cooper said weakly.

Jackson grunted and urged him to the ramp that led up to the medical building. "You bailed on your own free will," he said, not particularly sympathetic.

"You follow orders or there's chaos." Poor man sounded lost, and Jackson actually felt his sympathies stir. He wondered how many men had been twisted like this one, into bullies, into killers. They'd probably signed up looking for a set of rules to help them navigate the human race—they'd been vulnerable to the type of manipulation Lacey had been offering.

Such a fine line, that boundary between rules orchestrated so tightly you had to ask to break wind and the sort of miserable mean-assed chaos Jackson had just seen.

"You use your freewill to make good decisions or the order is an illusion," Jackson shot back. Cooper moaned, and Jackson figured him for a lost cause. He got up to the top of the ramp and knocked hard on the door.

A gangly kid, twenty maybe, stoop-shouldered, freckled, opened the door and grimaced.

"Who'd he finally piss off?" the kid asked. Then he smirked. "Before he pissed on himself."

"Me," Jackson said shortly. "I actually have business with Lacey and Hamblin, so if I could maybe…." He jiggled Cooper, and the kid put his own shoulder under Cooper's other side.

"Who're you?" the kid asked.

"Whatzitooya?" Jackson asked back, remembering the old kid's joke and wondering if he could maybe get the fuck out of here before shit went boom.

The kid sighed. "I just keep hoping we'll get orders to go back to San Diego. God, I don't know who I pissed off to get assigned to this hellhole, but this place is fuckin' weird."

Oh hell.

Jackson helped the kid through what looked like a legit reception room to a regular clinic. The desk where a private or ensign would sit taking information was empty, and the rest of what had been a full-functioning clinic echoed with disuse.

"Here—let's get him on the table," Jackson murmured.

Cooper moaned a little, and the kid unlocked a small refrigerator and pulled out an ampoule of what Jackson figured was morphine and some bandages.

"He'll want the painkillers," Jackson told him, "but not the bandages. He dislocated his knee—you'll have to push it back."

The kid grimaced. "And guess who's never done that before."

Cooper let out a terrified little whine, and Jackson tried to wrap his mind around the rabbit hole he'd fallen into.

"Kid, are you even an actual—"

"Medic? No. I'd taken three EMT courses and then I signed up. Boot camp, training, six months out at sea, where I worked in the medical bay to assist. We get back to port, I get a week stateside, get laid, and suddenly I'm here."

Jackson grunted. "Did you lay somebody you shouldn't have?"

Kid's lips twisted, and he cast a contemptuous look at Cooper. "Admiral's son," he said conspiratorially. "I seriously had no idea—and neither did the admiral."

Oh Jesus.

"Kid, this place is a punishment. But worse than that—it's not part of the US Navy anymore. It's become a mercenaries' guild, do you understand?"

The boy—seriously, twenty was a stretch—clapped his hands over his eyes. "This explains so much."

Jackson leaned over. "Kid?"

"Yeah?"

"If you get a chance, get the fuck out of here. But don't forget about the land mines surrounding the place, you feel me?"

"But… desertion!"

"Hitch a ride to the base in San Diego and tell them about this place. Seriously—fix Cooper's knee and find your way out."

Jackson could read this one's name tag—it said Saunders.

"But… but how can I not be with the US military anymore?" Saunders wailed.

"Don't ask. Just… just get out, and don't get shot."

And that was it. Jackson turned on his heel and made his way out of the care center, broke into an active jog, and crossed the pavement. The administration building loomed large, and he felt like he was in one of those dreams where he really needed to be somewhere and shit kept popping up to get in his way.

He managed to make it through the administration building, his tennis shoes ringing spookily in the empty tile hallways. He didn't go straight back to where the offices were. Instead, going by the schematics Burton had sent Ernie, he went to the right, to the com rooms. He passed two empty hallways cutting through the building and then, jackpot.

He could hear the low hum of computers and the clack of keyboards, accompanied by subvocalized comments into coms.

He didn't walk into the room and look around—that would be obvious. Instead he walked past it, taking in the organized chaos of a com center with incurious eyes.

Burton was easy to spot. He was sitting in the near corner of the room, facing the door itself. He was supposed to be studying a keyboard, but he was awake enough to catch any action outside. Jackson made eye contact with him as he passed the doorway, caught Burton's nearly imperceptible nod, and kept walking.

He'd spent most of his life as an irrepressible tomcat, and enough of that was left in his system to think Ernie was a lucky boy before the tread of boots in the corridor alerted him to someone else in proximity.

Without breaking stride he took the first right, almost groaning as he ended up at the restrooms. Quickly, he walked in and started checking the stalls to make sure they were empty.

"Please tell me you took your morning dump," said the man behind him, "because this could be a real inopportune moment to get caught with your pants down."

Jackson cocked his head and flashed Burton a grin. "I'm expecting to be really busy in about…." He checked his phone. "Shit. Eight minutes. If it's not done now, I'm going to have to wait until tomorrow."

He turned and gave the decked Marine-bodied man behind him a cocky smile. Burton's eyes were big and black and fathomless. When he smiled, he popped a dimple in the corner of his cheek, and Jackson wondered how long it had taken poor Ernie to fall hard *after* he'd seen Burton. One minute? Two? A whole half hour?

"Eight minutes?" Burton asked soberly, keeping his voice too low to echo. "That's not a lot of time."

"Less than you think. Did you know they were gassing a plane for wherever in South America? We've got to get them out of here."

Burton scowled. "Oh, for fuck's sake. There's people at the hangar?"

Jackson shrugged. "Sonny's got a surprise going. I got no idea when it's going to pop, but we've got—" He checked his phone again. "—six minutes until chaos ensues."

"Sonny? Where's Ernie?"

Jackson grimaced. "Dumping a Toyota full of C-4 in a minefield?"

Burton's face went hard. "I'm doing you a solid and this is how you repay me?"

"Hey—you let that kid know he's got you when he's got you and I don't think he'll be so eager to prove himself. But Jai's with him—I think that guy would rather blow himself up than let Ernie get hurt, so he's safe."

Burton scrubbed at his eyes with one hand while he pounded a tattoo on the sink with his other palm. "Goddammit—you couldn't have stayed in Sacramento for a couple more days?"

"While these assholes listened to us have sex? God no—"

"*I* listened to you having sex, and I've got one word for you. Soundproofing. But you don't get it—have you seen many soldiers here?"

Jackson shook his head. "No. And the ones who are don't realize the place isn't US military yet. They're just following orders and hoping to get sent home."

"That's right. Do you know why that is?"

"Because Lacey sent the other guys overseas to go kill in someone else's pond?"

Burton let out a growl. "You wish. See, I'm working black ops, right? My *job* is to kill people in our own country too dangerous to let loose. When I went under, my handler was supposed to let me go, cut me off, pretend he didn't know me for shit. Then he gets word—his guys, off doing their thing? Are getting preempted. And *then* they're getting killed. And so are the people around them at any given op. So no. This guy trained himself some psychopaths, put them in the hands of the guy running Corduroy—"

"Hamblin—"

"That's the asshole. And then he turned his monsters loose on the world at large."

Jackson shuddered, his stomach churning. Oh God. Even if he got Ellery out of here, he might never eat again.

"How many?" he asked, mouth dry. "We faced one of these guys. How many are there?"

"Between seven and twelve," Burton told him, voice rusty. "And I met a few of 'em. Did Sonny Daye freak you out?"

Jackson thought about it. "He's okay," he said honestly. "Let's just say we speak the same language."

"Psychopath?"

"No—we flunked out of psychopath school. What's left is just wildly codependent loose cannons."

Burton grunted, and his sculpted mouth twisted into an almost-smile. "Someday, Rivers, you and me gotta get a drink together. I don't want to pick out curtains, but God, I miss talking to a smartass. My point here is that you're right. Sonny's scary. Don't hurt Ace or you're toast, and he's got a gradually increasing circle of friends that he'd die for too. But he's not evil. He doesn't want to hurt people—"

Jackson wrinkled his nose. "If you hear shots, that's him not wanting to hurt people, but go on—"

"These guys are evil. They make Sonny Daye look like a kitten. And they're loose. Whatever happens here today, these psychopaths are out in the world, and we're about to take out the one place they call home."

Jackson closed his eyes. "Shit." He opened them and dealt with reality. "You got files?"

Burton shook his head. "Not on me—"

"We get out of this, send them. Me and Ellery, this is sort of our mission from God."

"Well, fuck you both for being my fucking assignment these last months, because now it's mine too. Deal."

Jackson checked his phone. "Two minutes."

"I'm going to take a left, a right, and two lefts and unlock the door that says Detainment. The minute shit goes boom, you go get your guys and get out of here."

"Ernie wants you home," Jackson said bluntly, because Ernie had been damned human to him, and Jackson felt like he owed the boy.

"I'll...." Burton looked away, and his almost perpetually stoic expression deserted him, leaving him hurt and alone. "I miss him," he said apologetically. "I'll... I'll find a way to make that boy my home."

"Good. Now move."

Jackson left first and listened for the bathroom door behind him before he checked his phone.

One minute left.

No minutes left.

Two more minutes passed, and Jackson could have pissed fire, he was so nervous.

Then his phone buzzed with Ernie's number.

Wait for it….

Jackson was down the three hallways, Ellery's door in sight, when an explosion shook the administration building, breaking windows and shaking tiles loose from the ceiling.

Jackson ignored all that and broke into a run.

Rescue Fish and Going Boom

THE EXPLOSION rocked the detention room, throwing Ellery to his knees and sending the office chairs spinning across the floor.

"Jesus fucking Christ!" Ace snarled, pulling himself up against the wall. "That was a land mine?"

"Oh, like I'd know?" Ellery retorted. "Do you know anyone with a shit-ton of explosives?"

Ace grimaced. "Goddammit—I told Jai to set that shit off in the desert. I don't even know where he got that."

Ellery stared at him. "I'll take that as a yes."

Then the door opened, and Ellery forgot that they'd almost been blown all the way back to the fucking ocean.

"Jackson?"

Jackson took two steps and crushed him to his chest, hard and without mercy. For a sweet moment, Ellery went boneless in his arms, as close to being a damsel in distress as he ever hoped to be.

Then Jackson stepped back, and that moment never happened, and they were trying to get out of the base alive.

"Okay, guys—we're winging it through the building and then getting behind the hangar, where Jai and Ernie will pick us up."

"What about Sonny?" Ace asked, and Jackson grimaced, compassion in full evidence.

"He's setting up a surprise in the hangar. They were planning to fly you guys out, so we had to do something to distract everybody there. C'mon, let's git—Ace, keep your eye out, Ellery, with me!"

Ellery allowed himself to be dragged by the hand through the building, surprised when it didn't sound deserted anymore.

"Where you going?" Ace asked after they'd jogged through several corridors. "The entrance is—"

"Where everybody's going," Jackson said shortly. "We saw a schematic—there's a back exit down here."

Ellery would have missed it—he was damned glad Jackson knew where he was going. In a sudden turn that looked like they were going to a bathroom or a copy room, they were outside, the sun lowering in the thin sunset of January.

God. Was it still the same day?

They could see men running past the front of the admin building, heading west toward where the explosion had occurred, and Jackson kept his eyes on the soldiers while dodging them behind a small building marked with a red cross on the front.

"Medic," Jackson whispered harshly. From the front of the building, they could hear a clatter of feet coming down the ramp and an absurdly young voice muttering, "Fuck fuck fuck bugger goddammit—"

"Hey! Saunders! Where do you think you're going?" A refrigerator of a man turned from the running mercenaries and disappeared around the front of the building. The sound of their raised voices snapped through the thin wood of the portable surgery like rubber bands.

Jackson grimaced and looked apologetically at Ellery. "Uh... do you mind?"

"I'm sorry?"

"I... I sort of... you know...."

"You made friends with the enemy?" Ellery should have known—holy God. This fucking man.

"No!" Jackson snapped. "I just... you know. Gotta go do a thing." He turned and glared at Ellery. "Look for the SUV coming up behind the hangar. If you see it, you guys run—I'll be there."

"Jackson!" Ellery begged, and Jackson gave him a sort of winsome smile before reaching out to graze his cheek with a knuckle and shoving the gun he'd held in front of him into the back of his jeans.

"Stay safe, Counselor," he said softly. "Back in a sec."

Ace grunted as Jackson disappeared. "He do that a lot?"

"I'd say it's a hero complex," Ellery told him sourly, "but he'd deny it completely."

"Isn't that what makes him a hero?" Ace reached around the back of his jeans and grunted. "He had a gun. Goddammit, why does he get a fuckin' gun and I got nothin' to hold but my dick? I left my fuckin' knife in the car at fuckin' Walmart, even."

From the front of the building, they heard the sound of bodies hitting wood and the grunts of men hitting each other.

Ellery kept scanning the far horizon restlessly, irritated that they were stuck here in the shade of the medical bay in what felt like plain sight. A gangly figure with reddish hair and blood pouring from his nose distracted them both as he stumbled behind the bay, and then—even from the other side of the building, the snapping sound of a bone and a man's pained scream.

Jackson came hauling ass back at that point, holding a small semiauto in his hands and looking considerably worse for the wear.

"You're bleeding," Ellery said, horrified.

Jackson gave him a fierce smile, ignoring the cut on his cheek and another one on his forehead. "He's bleeding more. Ace!" He shoved the semiauto into Ace's hands, and Ace actually grinned.

"You're a good friend," he said happily, and Jackson grunted.

"C'mon—Saunders, you're with us or you're back there doctoring that asshole's arm. Can you deal with that?"

"Yeah, sure." The boy smiled cheerfully, and Ellery had a sudden image of one of those cats tapping a computer screen fitfully with his paw. Yeah. Okay. Jackson had good instincts for whom to rescue and whom to break like a matchstick—Ellery would give him that.

They turned and trotted as a group, sticking to the shadows behind the buildings, coming up behind the smaller hangar while Jackson and Ace scanned the space behind the campus.

"How far did they go out?" Ace asked.

"Couple of miles," Jackson said. "At least around the perimeter. They had to swing back around to get to us."

They kept going, passing across the space between the big hangar and the smaller linear hangar, more like a carport, with their hearts in their mouths. When they got back behind the big hangar, Jackson tried to peek around.

"Fuck," he swore. "Sonny, goddammit—"

"Lemme see."

Ace pretty much shoved Ellery out of his way and took a look out front. "What in the fuck is he doing?"

"Rigging the big helicopter to flop around like a fish—I hope," Jackson told him. "But he wasn't looking—fuck—"

Jackson started like he was going to run out to save Sonny too, but Ace grabbed him by the back of the collar and yanked him into Ellery's arms.

"Goddammit, Sonny!" Ace hollered, heading for the copter. "Would you watch your fucking back?"

"Ace?" Sonny's joyful cry was loud enough to be heard all the way to Victoriana. "Ace—oh fuck, Ace, get that fucker!"

The gunfire from this distance didn't sound as loud as it should have, but Jackson had gotten back into position to watch, and he jerked away, grimacing, until it stopped.

"One, two, three—okay. We're short a guy. C'mon, Sonny, tell him… tell him to watch his back…."

Ellery turned his head then, alerted by a vehicle moving toward them from the fence line. "Jackson—is that your car?"

Jackson looked up, squinting. "Two guys in there, right?"

"Yeah—yeah. I can see someone in the passenger's seat. Why?"

"Ernie's okay," Jackson said on a breath. "Burton was fucking worried. But yeah—and hey. It's intact!"

"It's missing all the windows," Ellery told him, appalled.

"Is it blown up, Ellery? Seriously. If it's not blown up, we're okay."

Ellery scrubbed his face with his hands. "Jackson, we've really got to work on your definition of okay—"

And in the middle of the shooting, the windup of what sounded to be a helicopter on its last gasp, and the sound of what was once a new automobile but could now be heard from two hundred yards away, Jackson turned to him with his green eyes wide and shiny.

"If we get out of here with your skin intact, that's all I need," he said gruffly. "I will *kill* anyone who lays hands on you again."

He turned away then, dashing the back of his hand against his eyes, and stiffened. "Ace! Behind you!"

Ellery was standing just a step behind him—close enough for Jackson to back up into him when he took a pace back as gunfire started to rip into the corner of the hanger that had been their shelter.

"Shit!" Jackson muttered. "Shit—that's not a flunky. I thought it would be, but goddammit!" He looked beyond Ellery for a moment. "Saunders!"

"Yessir?" Saunders spoke around Ellery's shoulder.

"Give me your pistol and get to the car! Ellery, go with him!"

"Yessir!" Saunders removed his service revolver from the holster at his waist and thrust it into Jackson's hand before he began a gangly lope toward the oncoming SUV.

"Who is it?" Ellery asked, frustrated to realize that Jackson was standing in front of him, shielding him.

"That's fuckin' Lacey himself," Jackson told him, handing him Saunders' Sig Sauer. "Go get in the car!" With a deft move, he dumped the empty clip from his Berretta and shoved another one from his pocket in its place. Not for the first time, Ellery was reminded that Jackson Rivers had been born in violence—that he believed it was where he fit in best.

"No!" Ellery snapped. "I'm not getting in the fucking SUV—"

"Jai and Ernie will get you to safety," Jackson muttered. "We need you out of here—that thing is only so big!"

"I'll go when you go." Madness. He and Jackson had spent a couple of days at target practice in January. He understood how to handle a gun, but the Sig didn't feel any lighter in his palm now than the Berretta Jackson had bought for him then. "What are you going to do?" Ellery asked. God forbid Jackson just hop in the SUV and leave the fighting to the soldiers.

"Talk to him," Jackson said tersely.

"Wait—what?"

"If we get out of here, we need to know what he was planning. The leader of the mercenary group may get away too, and there's maybe a dozen trained killers that were given missions and sent into the general population. This ain't over when it's over."

"Oh dear God...." The numb horror of what they'd gotten themselves into threatened to overwhelm him, but Jackson had more immediate concerns.

"Lacey!" Jackson called into the open space. "Lacey, give it the fuck up! Just give it up and let us go! That boom shook up every town from here to Barstow—they got it on satellite. You're already rogue—own it and get the fuck out of here!"

"You think that's gonna happen?" Ellery recognized Lacey's voice from their two meetings, but now—now the man didn't sound icy or in control. He sounded unhinged. "You think the military doesn't have crews just like this one? Ready to take me out?"

"Man, you let serial killers out into the public—don't you think they're going to have enough to do?" Jackson risked a look around the corner, dodged back, and swore.

"What?" Ellery whispered.

"I can't fuckin' see him," Jackson said. "Where's his voice coming from?"

"Uh—"

"There's a vent to your left, along our edge. Go back to back with me. Gun at ready."

"What are you doing?" Ellery asked, pulling the gun into the safety position Jackson had taught him. Some people spent New Year's Day nursing hangovers. They'd spent theirs teaching Ellery gun safety—go figure.

"Still using my mouth as a weapon! Now watch my back."

Cautiously Jackson advanced around the corner, going just far enough to keep Ellery still behind the hangar.

"Lacey!" he called. "Wherever the hell you are—you think I haven't called Taylor Cramer?"

"Who *are* you?" Lacey demanded, but it sounded like his voice was coming from inside the hangar. Jackson advanced a few more paces.

"Who does he think I am?" he asked Ellery.

"He has no idea. I think Burton's been feeding him shitty intel. He assumed Ace was you."

"Awesome." Jackson advanced a few more paces, and Ellery followed him, keeping his gun down but his arms in front of him. What was left of Jackson's Infiniti had gotten close enough for Ellery to see two men with decidedly singed clothing in the front, and that the once silver paintjob had now been scorched beyond repair. Saunders was racing up to them, hands up in classic surrender position, and both men looked to Ellery like they knew him. Ellery held out his hand to stop them, and they came to a halt. They were behind the long hangar right now and out of sight for any of the active players in this little op. Ellery thought they would be more useful unshot—and Saunders could take the opportunity to get in the car and out of something he never should have been part of in the first place.

"I was a victim of your little behavior experiment!" Jackson called to Lacey. "Those basket cases you sent to war—what do you think they did? Just kill the enemy? They didn't know the enemy. They weren't trained to fuck with the enemy. You trained them to fuck with their *brothers*, asshole. How many soldiers didn't return because you manufactured sadistic psychopaths to be their COs? How many of our boys are raining blood on your conscience? You ever ask yourself that?"

Ellery took a deep breath. This was personal. Jackson knew someone affected by this man's actions in this way. Jackson was talking about Sonny and Ace, and Ellery suddenly wanted Lacey's blood.

Sonny and Ace were Jackson's brothers now. They were Ellery's. And this man had hurt them.

Ellery should have been prepared for the red wash in his vision, but he wasn't.

"Weak!" Lacey called from inside the hangar. "Weak men shouldn't go to war—they'll never come back. It's not my fault those men weren't strong enough to deal with a killing machine!"

Oh God. Right by them. Lacey's voice came from *right by them*. Jackson stopped abruptly, and he and Ellery looked at each other long enough for Ellery to catch the jerk of Jackson's chin.

Lacey was in there.

They couldn't see his exact location. They didn't know who was with him.

But odds were good he was armed, and he was maybe twenty feet away.

"Run!" Jackson hissed. "Take the gun and run for the car. Fucking now!"

But Ellery was too angry. "Weak?" he screamed, voice breaking in his own ears. "You sit back here and bully men to death and you call men in the field *weak*? Why aren't you in the action, asshole! What are you doing back here by the—"

Three shots, precisely spaced, blew out one at a time in front of Ellery.

And that day of training, the last few months of fear, snapped into Ellery's sinews and bones, and he turned and fired back.

In slow motion, he saw Jackson turn to push him to the ground.

Just when he heard the shot that ripped through his body and stopped his breath.

Fish Down

JACKSON CRASHED on top of Ellery, but he'd seen the shot hit, couldn't unsee the shot hit, knew when he looked Ellery's mouth would be open and blood would be on his lips.

He stayed on top of him for a breath, a heartbeat, until the shots stopped. Then he rolled off Ellery, gun in hand, and screamed, firing his clip into the hangar, opening up the thin aluminum wall, shooting until his gun clicked and clicked again.

Secure the suspect.

Old training—good training—pulled him to his feet, and he peered tentatively into the hangar through the grapefruit-sized hole he'd opened up while emptying his gun.

He saw the body—silver-white hair, wide-open eyes, the same sized mass of spreading blood on his chest that Jackson had opened up in the siding of the hangar. Oh Jesus—he'd been standing maybe ten feet away. *Bullet through the siding, slowing down—did it bounce off his ribs? Did it hit his heart? Oh Jesus....*

He turned his back on Commander Karl Lacey, traitor to the US Navy and his country, father of killers, without another thought.

Ellery hadn't moved, was lying on the ground twitching, and Jackson fell to his knees beside him because *Ellery, because please, oh God, please.... Ellery... please....*

Ellery moaned, eyes closed, blood trickling from his lips, spreading across his abdomen. *Ribs, lungs, kidneys, spleen, liver, intestines, not heart not heart not heart....*

Jackson hauled in a breath he'd forgotten he was holding and stopped trying to categorize Ellery's injuries.

"Fuck," he muttered, brain numb. "Fuck fuck fuck fuck—"

"You're Rivers."

Jackson whirled, empty gun out, the small rational voice in the back of his mind telling him he should have grabbed Ellery's Sig, which still had a full clip.

"Who are you and why shouldn't I kill you?" The hands holding the empty gun were covered in blood.

He was covered in blood.

Ellery's blood.

The man in front of him wasn't tall—was, in fact, about Sonny's size, small, compact, and wearing, of all things, an impeccable pinstriped suit. He had trimmed salt-and-pepper hair with a goatee, tanned skin, and a sort of sleek otter look that indicated he was moisturized, manicured perfection, right down to his pubes in fancy cotton boxers.

"I'm Lacey's business partner—to my shame. Rufus Hamblin—I run—"

"Corduroy," Jackson said numbly. "Why are you even fucking here?"

"Because Lacey's dead—well done, by the way. But my plane is intact, and I'd like you to let me and my men leave."

Jackson gaped at him. "My gun is empty," he said, because that should be obvious. "What in the fuck—"

"Your friends—they will back off." With the word "friends" Jackson could suddenly hear chaos again—Ace was still shooting, the broken helicopter was still flopping, and a fierce firefight had opened up from the other hangar. The world was still burning, and Ellery was lying injured in it. "They can fix the rogue helicopter—as entertaining as it's been. You order them down and I'll take the Cessna and my six decent men and leave."

"Why should I do that?" Ellery was still breathing. Jackson could hear his breath, rattling through his punctured lungs. God, Saunders was a medic—he could help. They could put Ellery in the SUV and drive like fucking bats out of hell and call an ambulance and—

"Because if you know someone who can fly, I can let you have the Jayhawk," Hamblin said, unmoved by the man bleeding at Jackson's back. "Provided your men haven't sabotaged it, of course. And I can send you files of Lacey's… assets."

Jackson's breath caught. "The psychopaths—"

"Yes—and their intended targets. This is your call, Mr. Rivers. Lacey was not a good soldier—he was easy to kill and foolish to shoot blind. I *am* a good soldier—and my men *are* well trained."

The man Jackson had fought—the refrigerator-white-boy who'd been going to kill Saunders, the one who'd been going to shoot the guy Jackson kneecapped—he'd been amazing in combat. Jackson hadn't wanted to tell Ellery, but he would fall asleep to the thudding of their flesh, the flexing, dancing muscles, the sheer poetry of the man's violence, and wake up screaming for many years to come.

"They are," Jackson said through a dry throat. "Give me the keys. I'll call to my men."

Hamblin half laughed. "Oh dear God. Who *are* you?"

"I'm nobody. What's your fucking problem?"

"Helicopters don't have keys. All you need is a pilot—and *not* to get shot when you're trying to get in it. Now what's it going to be, young man?"

"Sonny!" Jackson screamed at the top of his lungs. "Ace! Stand down!"

Hamblin held a walkie-talkie to his mouth. "*Corduroy!*" he barked. "Stand down!"

Abruptly the shots, the shouting, the chaos that had filled the air around them ceased. The only thing still going was Sonny's sabotaged helicopter, but Jackson wasn't sure how they'd fix that without blowing it up.

"Rivers? Status!"

That was Burton's voice—from the long hangar.

"Ellery's down!" Jackson shouted back. "He's injured but still breathing. Lacey's dead. I've got an offer of a helicopter and jackets on Lacey's trained killers if we just let Hamblin the fuck out of here. I'm taking it!"

"Fucking Jesus," Burton swore. "Hamblin's the goddamned leader!"

"Oscar, is that you?" There was a certain disappointment in Hamblin's voice. "Oh dear. You were one of my six."

"I'd say choose your men better," Burton snapped. "But—"

"But you're the best of them. And now I know why. Your friend here is right. Standing down is your best option. I like you, Oscar, but I won't hesitate to kill him as he sits. You know that."

"Fuck."

As Burton swore, Jackson knew the guy's innards must be twisted in a knot. "Sonny's friend is here!" he called, knowing what would move Ernie's lover more than any other plea. "He's safe now!"

Burton's next words sounded defeated. "But not for long. I hear you. Go, Hamblin—but don't count on the US military to just let this go. This is a mercenary flag on American soil. It might not be me, but—"

"But we will all live to fight another day!" Hamblin called back. "I understand. I was offered assets—that was all. The rest of this—the flag, the base, all of it—delusions, you understand? A dead man who wanted to make the world in his image. All petty demagogues are like that." He gave Jackson a razor-thin smile that chilled Jackson to his groin. "I should know. I've killed plenty. Good luck with your man there, Nobody. You should be proud. You toppled a minor king."

Hamblin turned then and walked unhurriedly toward the front of the hangar, and Burton rushed to Jackson's side.

"Ellery?" Jackson said quietly, turning to see him. "Ellery, you with us?"

"Fucking. Ouch," Ellery mumbled, lips thick with blood. "What in the hell?"

"Sucks, right?" Jackson took a breath and realized he couldn't see. His vision was black, everything in his body shutting down. "Keep breathing," he whispered. "You gotta promise me, okay? We got a ride to the hospital, but you gotta promise me you'll keep breathing—"

"It hurts…," Ellery whispered, eyes rolling in confusion.

"I don't fucking care!" Jackson shouted. "*This* hurts. I've got your blood on my hands and it fucking hurts, and I'm not stopping! C'mon, asshole—I'm like made of promises! 'Talk to me, Jackson, tell me things! Open up your heart, Jackson, open up a vein! Promise to be faithful, Jackson, trust me!' Well, I did! And I do! And look at you! You're bleeding! So you'd better promise me to keep breathing and keep that fucking promise or I'll never fucking forgive you for it, you hear! I'll curse your name until the day I die—which'll be fucking tomorrow if you don't *keep breathing*!"

"Rivers!" Burton snapped, his voice like a slap to the face. "Move! Ace and me got a backboard—we're gonna get him to the Jayhawk, you understand!"

Jackson nodded dumbly, not surprised to see Ace or Burton. The shooting had stopped. Even the Blackhawk had stopped.

All Jackson could hear was the roar of the small plane in the hangar and… oh God. "Is that the Jayhawk warming up?" he asked. An hour from Barstow—by car. Ten minutes, maybe, by helicopter.

"I can fly it," Burton said, kneeling by Ellery's head while he belted Ellery to the board. "Just pull your shit together and follow us."

"Saunders is a medic," Jackson said, his brain seizing on that one thing.

"So I fly, you and Saunders come with, everyone else meets us there. Let's hurry—your guy's breathing like he promised, but he's gonna need a little help. Jackson, you and Ace get the board to the copter—it'll be a squeeze, but you can make it fit. I'll go get the medic. We got shit to do."

It wasn't until Jackson was on the copter that he realized Burton had used the excuse to go to the SUV to talk to Ernie. He hadn't seen them, but privately he hoped Burton had kissed him. Held him. Yelled at him. Told him to never fucking do that again.

Let Ernie know he cared. That what they had was real. That it would have ripped a hole in the world if his other half had been injured or killed.

But Jackson couldn't say that, not even with Burton calmly behind the controls, because Ellery was next to him, struggling for breath. Because Jackson and Saunders had to keep their hands on the backboard, which was awkwardly placed on the two seats between them, and watching Saunders work with gauze and tape and a tube he'd shoved into Ellery's chest with an alcohol chaser was taking all his attention.

Because he couldn't think about Burton's pain for more than a minute, couldn't think about how much it might have scared him to have his gentle lover drive up to a land mine and shove a load of C-4 on it.

Because it hurt too much.

If someone had tried to rip him from Ellery's side at that moment, he would have snapped their neck.

BURTON SPENT the trip on coms with someone—Jackson couldn't hear who. Whoever it was, they knew how to make stuff happen, because there was a response team waiting for them on top of the hospital in Barstow.

Jackson clutched Ellery's hand tight as the building came into view.

"How you doing?" he asked, making himself look. Still breathing. Blood spattering up with every breath. "Keeping that promise, right?"

Ellery focused on him, shaking under the trauma blanket Saunders had produced from apparently out of his ass. "You keep yours, I'll keep mine."

"You'd fucking better," Jackson said, but without heat. "Because you know what this means, right?"

"You're not the one getting flowers?" Ellery rasped.

"I have to call your mother, dickhead. I have to call her *Taylor*. You fucking owe me."

"I expect you to collect." He could barely whisper it, and his eyes closed just as the helicopter touched down.

After that it was mostly staying out of the way as the team took the backboard and transferred him to the gurney, calling out stats, taking vitals even as the medic team ducked their head to avoid the blades and wheeled toward the building, taking Ellery away.

Jackson stood, shell-shocked, and watched him disappear into the emergency roof entrance, Saunders forgotten at his side. Saunders bumped his shoulder, and he realized Burton was calling to him.

"Go inside!" he ordered as Jackson leaned into the copter. "Go inside and follow him—he'll go straight to surgery prep, so that way. I'm taking this guy to my CO to get debriefed. Saunders? Hop in."

"Shit," Saunders muttered. "I was really hoping this was my get-out-of-the-Navy-free card."

Jackson held on to his sanity with both hands. "Debrief and beg for mercy," he told the guy. "I'm Jackson Rivers, PI—look me up in Sacramento when you're done." He almost said *Ellery too*, but he couldn't. Just couldn't.

"Thanks." Saunders shook his hand and hopped into the copilot's seat.

"Rivers!" Burton called, stopping him from running for Ellery just in time. He turned. "Tell Ernie I'll be back. I... I need to make sure nobody knows about him and Ace and Sonny, you understand?"

"I'll back anything you say. Keep them out of it. Nobody needs to know."

Burton's smile was a little bit wicked. "Knew you got it. See you before he gets out of surgery—promise."

Burton gave a two-fingered salute, and Jackson ran toward the entrance.

Once in the hospital, he managed to find the waiting room for surgery without a problem. It wasn't until he approached the gimlet-eyed, retirement-aged nurse, who assessed him with a cool top-to-bottom scythe, that he remembered how much of Ellery's blood he was wearing.

He swallowed and opened his mouth.

"The trauma victim that just came in," she said, reading his mind. Well, Barstow was a little town. He wasn't sure how many gunshot victims they got helicoptered in, but he'd wager it was less per year than he had fingers.

"Yes, ma'am."

"Doctors are scrubbing in now, and he's being prepped. You're his partner?"

It took him a minute to realize she meant, like, "police partner."

"Yeah," he graveled. "We work together." Work together, fight together, live together, sleep together.

"Do you need us to call his family? His injuries were fairly serious—"

"I'll call his mother," Jackson said, starting to shake. Blood was crusting on his hands, in his nail beds, in the ridges of his knuckles. It was sticking his sweatshirt and shirt to his skin. "She'll need to... she's on her way... she needs to...."

"Here," the nurse said, more kindness than he'd expected given her no-bullshit gaze. "Scrubs. Have you been in a hospital like this before?"

"I'm usually the one in surgery," he told her as he took the scrubs out of her hands.

Her eyebrows went up. "One of those. How's the view from out here?"

"It's fucking awful. I'd give my right nut to be gutted like a trout right now."

"I'm not the one who makes those deals, sweetheart. The bathroom is down the hall and to the right. The chapel is the hallway past that, to the left, follow the corridor down to the end. I suggest you use them both."

Jackson nodded, proud of how still he kept his face, how his lower lip didn't crumple. He could smell the hospital all around him, feel it pressing down against his chest. But he couldn't leave, couldn't run, couldn't go anywhere without Ellery, because dammit, that's just the way it fucking worked.

"I'll clean up and make the call," he said, and she got one of those looks that sometimes crossed Ellery's mother's face. It hadn't been until recently that he'd identified it as compassion.

"Visit the chapel too," she said softly. "Doesn't always help, son, but it really can't hurt."

He nodded in spite of himself and made his way to the bathroom in silence, the scrubs swinging in their little plastic bag.

Ten minutes later he'd changed and washed his hands and chest in the bathroom sink again and again until the water ran clear. He looked at himself in the mirror and grabbed paper towels for his face, schooling his expression to blankness. Who wanted to see him cry? Seriously. Ellery was the only one remotely interested in that, and Ellery had his own shit to do.

He could finally put the scrubs on, and he checked his phone as he pulled it out of his pocket.

Me, Ace, and Ernie are at Walmart. We'll bring you clothes.

He stared at the text for fully a minute before he realized it was Sonny, telling him they were coming to the hospital. He almost asked why but realized that would make him sound like a dick.

Burton says he'll meet you here. He's reporting to his CO and keeping your names out of it.

He's a good guy. See you there. We'll bring food.

Jackson just gazed at the text string for at least a minute. There was no reason for them to do that. He and Ellery had brought them nothing but fucking trouble. Clothes? Food? Why would they even want to know if he was dead or alive?

But apparently they did. Jackson swallowed against that knowledge and pulled up Ellery's mother's number.

Hospital in Barstow. He looked at the plastic bag which had the name and address on it, which he relayed. *He's in surgery. I'm so sorry—it's bad.*

Awesome. He had to text the woman that her son had been shot? Fucking Jesus. Motherfucking Jesus H. Christ—

He screamed and hit the mirror with his fist before he even knew what he'd planned. For a moment, he just stared at the glass embedded in his knuckles, at the blood trickling down them, at his shattered reflection in the mirror, at the disaster he'd made of the antiseptic beige bathroom like he'd made of the one good thing in his life.

And then the hospital started to close around him, pressing against his chest until he couldn't breathe.

Oh God. He couldn't breathe. He couldn't breathe. He was going to die here, shaking like a coward, because he didn't have the courage to take his next breath.

For a terrifying second, his bladder threatened to void, and he pulled himself together just enough to slide down the wall next to the sink, in front of the trash can, arms wrapped around his knees.

It was where Ernie found him twenty minutes later, Ace hard on his heels.

Ernie sank to a crouch in front of him and took his hand. "You've got glass in it."

"I'm fine," Jackson lied. "Pulling myself together. I'll wash it off. Sorry. Just—"

"Oh Jesus," Ernie muttered. "Shut up. You're more honest when you're not talking."

"How's he doing?" Ace asked, matter-of-fact like. "How was he when they took him in?"

"Breathing. Like he promised." God, Ellery. Keep that damned promise.

"Great. Now stand up." Ace's voice rang with authority—probably used to ordering terrified recruits around.

"Fuck you," Jackson replied without heat. "I like it here. It's awesome. Great view of the hospital."

Ace crouched in front of him, looking totally serious. "I been where you been," he said, voice quiet. "Now see, you're lucky. You got to kill the guy right off. I had to plan that murder after Sonny got out of surgery, and I'm lucky I'm not in jail. But I know this part sucks. I know what it's like when the one thing holding you together might just not be around that long. But he's breathing for now. You gotta just keep acting like that's not gonna stop, you hear me?"

Jackson glared at him. "I can't breathe. I hate hospitals," he confessed, and it hurt. It hurt worse than his hand, where Ernie was picking out glass. With Sonny it had felt detached, like he was talking about someone else, but this was the pain, the fear, up close and personal, and it was terrifying.

"I can't... I can't breathe. Months of my life in these fuckin' places. Months. But I'm not gonna leave. You get that? Not gonna leave until he does. But I gotta remember how to breathe."

Something in Ace's face softened. "Oh," he said.

"Look at me," Ernie told him. "Just... look me in the eyes—"

Jackson closed his eyes. "Don't wanna fall." God, he could barely talk. How was he going to be there for Ellery when his courage, his mind, his words were all deserting him?

"You won't fall," Ernie murmured. "Just... just trust me, okay?"

"I trust one person on this planet," Jackson told him, eyes still closed. "You're not him."

"God, he's stubborn," Ernie muttered under his breath. "You've got to let us help you!"

Jackson took a breath, mindful that the first surgery lasted two hours, maybe, and he had to be in the waiting room in what? Half an hour? To get news. He got his feet under him and shoved up, keeping his face turned from the broken mirror.

"I'm going to the waiting room," he said, running water over his knuckles. He grabbed the last piece of glass with his thumb and forefinger and ripped it out, not even flinching as a new gush of blood spilled. "I'll... I'll check in there. You guys can come. You can eat there." He wrapped paper towels around his hand like a bandage and wondered if he asked nicely, if he could just get a regular towel from the nurse without any hassle about the mirror or the blood or the cuts on his hands.

He couldn't look at them. Couldn't look at them, couldn't look at himself. He walked like an automaton into the surgery waiting room, knowing Ace and Ernie were hot on his heels.

Sonny was in the waiting room, sitting next to bags of takeout and looking restlessly at his phone. He glanced up and smiled at Ace tiredly, but still, something about his joy and relief at seeing Ace, especially after what they'd just done together, hit Jackson in the stomach.

Sonny probably thanked God every day for Ace. Ace—who'd just admitted to murdering a guy who'd hurt his man—probably did the same thing for Sonny.

Who was Jackson fucking Rivers that he couldn't get on his knees and beg a little in the hopes that God might, just this once, not fuck him over?

He walked up to the nurse, who scowled at the paper towel around his knuckles. "Stay right there," she muttered, coming out around the partition and gesturing imperiously for his hand. "What happened?"

"I slipped," he said, voice wooden.

"Yeah, I can see that. Let me call a nurse to take you down to get that—"

"Not going anywhere," Jackson said.

"Son, this is going to heal badly and then it'll be infected and—"

He had trouble focusing on her face. He had the impression of wide cheekbones, comfortable and soft. "Do you think I haven't been in a hospital before?"

"I think I'd like to take you to the psych ward *now*," she snapped. "Don't lose hope for your friend—not at this stage in the game. Your faith means everything—don't you know that?"

Jackson swallowed, and something he'd managed to keep firm and strong in his chest broke. Tears spilled, one and then the other.

"How long do they have?" he asked, his sense of time stretched and skewed.

"They just sent for more blood—I'm guessing another hour," she said gently.

He swallowed, his chin wobbling, his throat too tight to talk. "I… I'll be around the corner," he said.

"The bathroom? Because that worked out so well for you last time!"

"Not the bathroom," he said, his voice cracking. "I'll… I'll be back before then."

He turned around and fled.

THE CHAPEL had paneling—not too dark—with a window that opened up to a scenic night view of… well, Barstow. But beyond the town he could see the desert, and from three floors up in the dark, the green didn't look like mange, it looked… green. Hopeful. Like water and life. There was farmland out there—he knew that. Sure, it was in drought, but look! Rain! Rain was hope too!

Hope, right?

"I don't know how to hope," he said out loud. "If you'd wanted somebody who could hope, you maybe shouldn't have burned it out of him, you know? I was a baby the last time I hoped. I hoped my mom would pay attention to me, and she snorted lines instead. So now we're in this fucking place again, this fucking death machine, where live people come in and dead people come out."

There was a small line of pews on either side of the room, a walkway between them, and an altar up front. Different symbols—a Star of David, a cross, a star and crescent, even a triskele—had been embroidered into the altar cloth.

He stared at it and swallowed. "Yeah," he said, lips twisting. "But do you have a three-legged cat? Because seriously, that's, like, the only thing I have faith in. I have faith in Ellery, and I've got faith in my cat. And you fucking shot Ellery."

That's not fair. Lacey shot Ellery.

"I don't *give a shit* if it's fair!" he shouted. "Everybody fucking telling me I should talk to God, give thanks to God—as far as I know, you've done shit for me! But Ellery? He's fucking *been there*. Were you in the goddamned room when I was throwing up with a goddamned concussion? Were you by that fucking pool when he called me back from the dead? What about this summer? I didn't see a whole lotta God then, but I sure did see Ellery! What about eight years ago? What about then? I died on the table, remember? And sure. I saw the fucking light. I've seen it twice now. I know there's something on the other side. *Who gives a fuck?* It's not that I don't believe in you, asshole. *I'm pissed off at you!*"

He shoved at the pew in front of him, and it toppled. "Yeah! How's that feel! I'm fucking pissed! Where the fuck you been, God? Toni Cameron died—did you even fucking notice? Ten years ago she fucking died. Nicest woman on the planet, right? Closest thing to a mother I'm ever gonna fucking get—and you kill her off? I'm supposed to think that's okay? I don't remember an entire year of my life, God—you just took that, 'cause, you know, twenty-one, twenty-two—that's no big deal, right? Wearing a wire, getting ripped from the inside out in the name of… fucking law and fucking order—that was just my fucking dues? So I'm pissed. Jesus fucking Christ, I'm *pissed*!"

He kicked at the pew brutally, vaguely surprised when it held firm and didn't crunch under his tennis shoe. He turned his body and kicked harder.

"You're a fucker, God! All this pretty shit! The fucking pews and the walls and the stained glass—yeah, I seen it. You think I'm gonna just… what? Throw myself on the fucking ground for you?"

He fell to his knees in the empty room and held his hands out in supplication. "Yeah, here I am, oh mighty ass-reaming sky-daddy! Here I am! Fucking offering my goddamned penance! Prostrating myself before you, and you know the fun thing? The laugh-riot thing? The goddammit all, God's gonna laugh until he pisses on us thing?"

His voice broke, his hands fell limply into his lap, and he dropped his head, humble before God as he'd never been humble before anything in his life.

"I'm here," he whispered, shoulders shaking. "I'm begging. I know you don't care. I know you don't listen. I know you just gaze down from the sky and watch us walk into the hospital young men and come out fucking corpses. But I'm still begging. I'm still bargaining. I'll give you my life—I swear I will. Not worth much—I mean, you've gone out of your way to show me that, God. But you can have it. Just...."

He jerked in a breath, trying to keep his dignity, his personhood, here in the face of the ultimate humility, but he couldn't.

"Just let him live. Please. Just... just let him live. Please." Another deep breath, but it didn't work. Not all the deep breaths in the world could hold back the flood when the dam had broken.

"Please, God. Let him live."

He slumped to the ground then, elbows holding his weight as he buried his face in his arms and cried.

HE WASN'T sure when he became aware of the hand in his hair. He turned his head, too tired to even wonder who would have found him here.

And then he saw the legs, sensibly attired in support hose, crossed daintily at the ankles. He didn't even raise his gaze up—his entire body stiffened, and he buried his face in his hands again.

"Taylor?"

"He's not out of surgery yet, but you may still call me Lucy Satan," she said, her voice weary. Her hand in his hair moved to his elbow, and oh hell, he was still bleeding.

He rocked back onto his heels and tried to yank his arm away.

And was stunned when she grabbed his elbow and reached for his hand, making a startled exclamation when she saw the damage. "Oh. Jackson. Son...."

Jackson scowled, compelled to look her in the eyes, and something in his chest twisted at her appearance. He'd seen Ellery's mother out of uniform during Thanksgiving vacation—she'd worn comfortable leggings, soft house shoes, and drapey sweaters, all in neutral colors—but her hair and her makeup had been perfect.

She was wearing a business suit, support hose, and pumps, but her hair had been hauled back into a no-bullshit ponytail, so severe he could see the gray roots at the base of the dyed rich chestnut, the same color as Ellery's. Her eyes, usually impeccably circled by kohl, were smudged, and her mouth was bare and naked of lipstick.

For the first time ever, she looked like somebody's mother, tired and worried and sad.

"I'm sorry." Dumbest, most inadequate thing he'd ever said.

"Did you kill the man who shot him?" she asked, her voice measured and dispassionate.

For a moment Lacey's corpse flashed—white hair over a blood-spattered face, eyes wide and surprised. "Many times over," he said, shuddering.

"Good," she said softly, rubbing her thumb gently over the back of his wrist. "But not, I think, easy on your soul."

"First guy I actually killed," he told her truthfully. "Wasn't as fashionable ten years ago as it seems to be now."

"Maybe we just need more men like you on the force." Her lips quirked up, although her eyes were still fixated on his damaged hand. "How'd this happen?"

"Doesn't matter." He used his free hand to drag through his hair as he surveyed the damage in the chapel. Mostly it came down to the one upended pew.

"Oh, it does," she said softly. "Ellery will be most displeased. I'm sure he'll think you were trying to steal his thunder."

Jackson let out a choked laugh. "He's going to start to hate hospitals as much as I do."

"I have no doubts. Tell me, am I going to have to hire lawyers to buy you another car?"

Another half laugh. "Possibly. Maybe we can give Sonny a commission and see what he and Ace can do."

She cocked her head. "Were those the two men who greeted me when I went into the surgery waiting room? The poor blond one was terrified—hid behind the bigger one with the amazing chest. Does he do that often?"

Jackson couldn't help it. This laugh was all one piece, if not hearty. "I think you might scare him a little. He… he doesn't have much experience with mothers."

Taylor Cramer's mouth threatened to wobble for a moment. "And you don't have much experience with prayers," she said, eyes taking in the pew. She moved her legs under her, and Jackson made to stand up.

"No, son. I'm going to show you how. Knees underneath you, eyes cast down in humility before God."

Jackson followed her example and went to put his hands together, but she clasped his fingers lightly, unmindful of the blood.

"Don't you have to speak Hebrew or Latin or something?" he asked. He'd been hauled into a few Catholic missions in his time as well.

"If you know the words, but it's not necessary. Now hold my hand and listen."

"Yes, ma'am."

"God, my son was wounded as he fought forces beyond his control. He's a good boy, and he works hard to do what's right, and we love him very much. We ask that you care for him, and heal his wounds if it is your will, and care for his soul if it is not. May the one who blessed our ancestors, Abraham, Isaac, and Jacob, Sarah, Rebecca, Rachel, and Leah, bless and heal Ellery Joseph Cramer. May the Blessed Holy One be filled with compassion for his health to be restored and his strength to be revived. May God swiftly send him a complete renewal of body and spirit, and let us say, Amen."

"Amen," Jackson repeated. Some of those words sounded old—the ones with all the biblical names. But some of those words were pure Taylor Cramer, and he felt some relief at that. He just trusted Ellery's mother more than he trusted a holy book or God.

She let go of his hand then, and he stood up and offered her his undamaged hand to assist.

"Now let's right the pew," she said, stretching a bit. His own legs were cramping from his time on the floor—he imagined hers were too. "You set it straight and I'll get the books in the back."

He did so, testing the wood at the end and grimacing when it wobbled.

"Well, I'll have them send me a bill," she said mildly, hand going automatically to check her hair after she picked her handbag off the ground. "I understand we owe them for a mirror in the bathroom as well."

"I'm sorry," he said, looking at his hand. "It was... uhm...."

"A reaction to stress," she said simply. "When I went to find you, the nurse in the waiting room told me she'd had a portable stitching station brought up. I think now would be a good time to put that to use, before those cuts heal open."

Jackson nodded meekly and followed her out of the chapel. He paused and looked behind him as they left and realized the serenity had been restored. The storm of Jackson Rivers was hardly a drop on the face of a lake, compared to the turmoil such a place had seen.

"How did you know where I was?" he asked, holding his arm out to her as they walked. She took it without question—people observed the niceties with Ellery's mother, under all circumstances.

"The young man with the curly hair—"

"Ernie."

"Is that his name? How appropriate. I walked in, and the blond young man hid behind his friend, and Ernie stepped forward and told me you'd gone to the chapel. The small one peered out from behind his friend and said, 'How do you know that?' and Ernie said, and I quote, 'My damned ears popped. All that pressure he was under finally gave.'" Mrs. Cramer *hmm*ed in her throat. "I didn't really know what he meant until I saw you on the floor, Jackson. Did you and God come to an agreement?"

Jackson grunted. "Yes. We both agreed he needs to put three-legged tomcats on the altar cloth, because I'm not talking to anybody who doesn't worship cats."

This time she was the one who let out a strained laugh.

"I'm sure the Almighty is reconsidering his choice of symbols as we speak." They came to the waiting room, and Jackson had to take a deep breath against the weight that fell back on his chest. "Courage. Both of us must have it. Now come, let's get your hand stitched."

Jackson escorted her in, and they surprised the guys—Burton included—as they were digging into the bag of takeout Sonny had brought.

"Guys?" Jackson said, getting their attention, "This is Ellery's mother, Mrs. Taylor Cramer. Is there any news?"

Ace set his hamburger down on the bag on the waiting room table, wiped his hand on his jeans, and turned around to shake Taylor's hand. "Mrs. Cramer? Your son thinks you're God. You need to know that, like, right here and now. I mean, I got a mom and everything, but the most I ever expected from her was that she'd know how to cook. I damned near expected you to shoot fire out your eyes when you walked in."

"Well, there is a reason Jackson calls me Lucy Satan," she said regally. "And you are…."

"Jasper Atchison, ma'am. People call me Ace. This here's my partner, Sonny. We own a garage in Victoriana. Your son and Rivers there, they done us some solids. We're grateful."

"We got you kidnapped," Jackson said sourly.

Ace rolled his eyes. "That was totally an accident. The solid favors, though, those were on purpose. We'll count those."

Jackson nodded, humbled. "Well, I'm obliged."

"Ace," Sonny mumbled, literally from behind Ace's body. "Ask 'em if they want a hamburger. It ain't nice to eat without them."

The thought of food made Jackson's stomach churn, so he was truly grateful when Taylor said, "Food—how thoughtful! I'll probably eat in a moment, if you don't mind. Jackson, go see the nurse about getting your hand stitched. I'll see to your friends."

"Yes, ma'am."

The nurse had already pushed the stainless steel cart prepped with sterilized needles and silk, as well as an irrigation bowl and several tubes of saline and some prefilled syringes with lidocaine, around the back partition. "Come back here," she commanded. "We have a chair and an armrest for you."

Jackson moved behind the partition, and she reset the station.

"You look like one more word is going to make your head explode," the nurse said quietly. "But since you got civilized for her, I figured I'd save you the small talk."

"Thank you," he said, feeling cosseted. "I take it there's—"

"No news. Did you think we'd hide it from you?"

"No," he said, scanning the waiting room, where Ellery's mother ruled like the monarch she was. As he watched, Burton broke away and came around the partition, looking directly at the nurse, who shrugged and let him.

"How you doing, Rivers?"

"Peachy."

Burton inclined his head, rubbing a hand over the back, probably just to feel the rasp of his super-short-cut hair. "I can tell. I get that there's no news yet, but I need to tell you something important."

Jackson grimaced as the nurse stuck a syringe into the widest cut across his knuckles. "This might take a bit," he said.

Burton nodded and sank down into the patient chair next to Jackson's.

"So, you were losing your shit, but I counted the guys who got into the Cessna and the guys left on the base—and there's a lot of guys left on the base, you feel me?"

Jackson grunted. "So there's the seven to twelve out on assignment—"

"And doing extra credit, if you know what that means—"

"Horribly enough, I do."

"Good. I'd hate to have to lay that out. But here's the thing—I was assigned to listen to you guys—and I fucked up as much intel as I could to keep them off your tail or this bullshit would have gone down a lot closer to Christmas, you understand?"

"I could barely run," Jackson said numbly. Five miles—that had been his minimum for going back to work, imposed by Ellery and fiercely upheld.

"Yeah, I know. You pushed yourself hard to come back, don't think I don't appreciate that. But the thing is, while I caught most of what you were saying, I didn't catch all of it, and somebody else was monitoring your computer activity. So the three guys who grabbed Ellery and Ace—they were Lacey's favorite team, and they were just back from *not* killing you, do you remember?"

"I wasn't the target," Jackson reminded him.

"No—they were just there to be Lacey's lapdogs and maybe plant a few more bugs. But Lacey hit that woman because apparently he's an idiot—"

"We figured it for an accident," Jackson said. Arrogant prick driving like an arrogant prick. Go figure.

"Yeah—and after that I think the guys took 'getting rid of witnesses' literally. Not that he didn't deserve to die, but I think Lacey really just wanted them bribed and intimidated. Trying to shoot the girl's employer was a mistake."

"And my concussion was a bonus," Jackson said numbly. His head ached dully—yes, he'd thrown himself around a lot today. He wasn't sure whether to hope his brain exploded before or after the doctor came out with news.

"Yeah—and that was some nice detective work, by the way. Anyway, Adkins, Gleeson, and Leavins were Lacey's favorite pets, and they picked up Adkins's police sketch on the police website—and they were not pleased. Before everything went boom, they were planning on taking care of any witnesses to back that sketch up—is there anybody you know who might be in danger?"

Jackson made a whimpering noise in the back of his throat.

"Everybody," he said softly. "Fucking... Mike, Jade—"

"Your tenant and his girlfriend—"

"She's like my sister, man. And our brother, Kaden, and his wife and kids and...." He swallowed. "I sent a friend up to them—they live in the hills. He brought the witness to their house, because the police wouldn't spring for protection and it was the safest place I could think of."

Burton let out a low whistle. "I've got men on standby," he said quietly. "Do you want to go with them?"

Jackson's brain melted into slag. "Ellery...." His family. God, he had to take care of his family. But *Ellery*. He couldn't move, couldn't fix it, couldn't save a soul if he didn't know how Ellery was.

Burton nodded and leaned back in his chair, scrubbing at his face with his hand. "I... I used to think this decision would be a no-brainer," he said after a moment. "Signed on to do my job. Go do my job." He looked out into the waiting room, yearning written clearly on his face. "But there's some things...."

"They're my family," Jackson said, heart roaring in his ears. "God—let me text them. Let me call them. They're... they're my family!"

Burton looked at him, obviously thinking about something. "You stopped using your phone in the last few days—which was awesome, because Lacey pulled strings for actual military-grade surveillance, which will look good on the report when my boss explains this mess. But we couldn't find you until Ellery used his once."

"He shut it off immediately," Jackson said, defending him irrationally.

"Yeah—but once we had his location, we tracked you by satellite. Anyway—he used his phone but, but yours stayed dark."

Jackson looked at him sourly. "We got burners the minute we found the kid trying to put a bug on our car."

Burton chuckled. "They don't know you found the bugs, by the way. Some shit just never made it past my desk. But you've been talking on burner phones—good. That's smart. We didn't pick up on those yet. Your family is monitored on and off, though. I'm not sure how much of the com equipment the rogue team grabbed on the way out. I heard the boom and went back to trash as much as I could, but some of it was gone. After that it was chaos and...." He swallowed. "I just really needed to see what went boom, you know?"

Jackson let out half a laugh. "Jesus. I'm dumb. I mean, I am—I'm dumber than a box of diapers. But you... tell him you love him. Make plans around loving him. Put your stuff in his drawers. Leave a toothbrush. Get a...." God, he missed Billy Bob. "Get a cat together. Don't just look at him and plan how to leave him. That's a horrible idea."

Burton cocked his head and nodded. "That's some excellent advice. But back to your family—"

"Ouch!"

"Sorry, son," the nurse said. "Forgot to inject that one with lidocaine. You just sound really wise for someone who lost a fight with a bathroom mirror."

"Is there a name for being afraid of hospitals?" Jackson asked rather desperately.

"Nosocomephobia," the nurse replied, so smart her voice cracked. "Do you have it?"

"I've had one decent meal since November," Jackson said baldly. "Because hospitals make me feel like I can't breathe. And now the one guy who could make me eat is *in the fucking hospital*. I'm sorry I lost my shit."

The nurse, who had been somewhat brusque, looked up at him and melted. "Oh, hon. He's not your work partner, is he?"

It took a few deep breaths to beat back hysteria. "We *do* work together," he said, screwing his eyes up because he didn't feel like doing that here. "Because he's a hell of a lot of fun to work with. Burton, my family. Do you need me to go keep them safe?" He took a deep breath. "I will. Jesus help me, I will, but…."

"But it would be like ripping your soul in half. Got it. Can you call them up for me? And do you have some pictures? You're a civilian— honestly, if you could give me the info I need and give me a way to talk to them that Lacey's men can't track, you are better off here."

Jackson had dropped the plastic bag with his clothes in it on the floor before he'd gone to the chapel, but Ace had it. He produced the phones— and Burton produced a charger—and before the nurse was done with his hand, he was texting Anthony.

Hey, kid—how's it going?

Great! Today we stayed in and watched movies. AJ bought me a big tub of Legos—we've been making spaceships.

Jackson smiled fondly and thought of the pictures on his regular phone. This kid deserved lots of days like this.

I'm glad, kid. Give the phone to Kaden for me, okay?

Okay. Do I have to come home soon?

Jackson blinked. *I have no idea—but you guys may have to go somewhere else for a night, okay?*

Okay. Not just me?

Let me talk to Kaden—he'll fill you in.

Not unexpectedly, the phone rang in his hand. "Jackson, you made the kid cry—you're not sending him back already, are you?"

"He doesn't have to go until you're ready to send him," Jackson told Kaden honestly. "But this is serious, so you need to listen."

"Uh-oh."

"Yeah. It's bad, but there's some backup heading your way and it'll probably beat the bad guys up there, but in the meantime, here's my friend Lee who's going to talk you through some shit, okay?"

"You coming up?"

Jackson's breath shook his chest. "That's... that's under discussion," he said. God, to have a gun in his hand, to be tracking a perp, to have his mind and his heart empty and clean of all distractions.

To not care, to not worry, to not wish he was dead.

"What's going on?"

"Ellery was injured... shot. He was shot. He's in surgery. It was bad. It was so bad, Kaden. I'm... my clothes have his blood on them. It soaked through to my skin. We... we don't know... we don't... but we think they're coming up there. We think they're on their way and—"

Burton took the phone from him, and he gulped in air and tried to calm himself down.

For something to do, he called up a picture on the other phone—that soul-sustaining picture of Kaden and Rhonda and the kids—and pointed to Kaden while he caught Burton's eyes.

Burton's eyebrows went up, and he took a quick look at Jackson, but the nurse took that moment to pull extra-specially hard on the silk sliding through his skin. He focused on that. Focused on the pain of it, the simplicity of acute discomfort, so he didn't have to think about leaving Ellery, leaving his mother. About how running into danger didn't feel like he was helping anybody right now so much as it felt like he'd be running away.

The nurse had just finished snipping off the last of the silk and wrapping a bandage around his hand when the doors to the OR burst open. Jackson pushed past Burton—who was still on the phone—and the stitching station to stand by Ellery's mother when the doctor spoke.

"Are you two Mr. Cramer's family?"

Taylor's hand found Jackson's, and she squeezed his fingers. They both nodded.

"He was a bit of a mess, honestly—we had to do a lot of stitching, and he needed three units of blood. But he's all put back together now—he'll be in recovery for a while, and you may go talk to him when he comes out of the anesthesia. When we move him to ICU, you can go sit with him. We're going to have to watch him closely, you understand. He may have wounds we didn't catch the first time around. We had to stitch together things that can spell infection if we didn't get it all out. Trauma surgery has to be done fast—the body isn't ready to be shut down so long after a traumatic event. We do our best, but we'll need to be vigilant to catch any unwelcome surprises, you understand?"

Jackson did. He'd been on the other end of that scrutiny, had felt his body burn with fever, his insides ache with leaking blood.

"It's gonna suck," he said softly. "It's going to hurt for a while. We'll be there. It's okay."

The doctor nodded, his middle-aged face showing concern and interest as to whether Ellery would have friends smart enough to watch over him tonight. Jackson liked him for that alone. "Excellent. Give us another hour to situate him, and we'll call you in."

With that he backed up and let the nurse buzz the door open for him, and Jackson tried to remember how to breathe.

A sharp pain in his hand made him gasp, and he glanced at Taylor—who was not looking well. Her face was so pale she was almost green, and she sagged so quickly he barely caught her.

"Lucy Satan, the fuck?"

She took another shaky breath, and Jackson looked over at Ace. "Help me sit her down," he commanded, and together they backed her into a seat, where she dragged in great gulps of air and shook.

"Let me get you some water," Jackson told her, stroking the back of her hand.

"No—don't go just yet." Her voice sounded normal, modulated, commanding, but her grip on his hand was icy and fearsome.

"Sonny, could you—"

"Water, soda, coffee," Sonny said smartly. "Back in five."

A reluctant smile twitched at Taylor Cramer's mouth. "Such a sweet boy," she said, but she didn't open her eyes.

Jackson asked himself what he'd do if she was anybody else—Janie Isaacson, Crystal, Jade—and then manned up and wrapped his arms around her shoulders awkwardly and pulled her face against his chest.

And Lucy Satan, the woman he was most afraid of in the world, burst into quiet sobs of relief.

SONNY WAS back by the time she recovered, and she smiled almost shyly, in a way that reminded Jackson sharply of Ellery when he was at his most vulnerable, as she thanked him.

"This was kindly done," she said after a few sips and with a regal incline of her head. "Now, if you'll excuse me, I'll go powder my nose. Jackson, if you'd like me to feel better, I'd love to see you eating when I return."

She stood shakily but on her own power, secured her handbag, and exited the room. As soon as she was gone, Ace grabbed the food bag and handed Jackson a cold cheeseburger.

"Get that any closer to my face and I'll eat your hand," Jackson told him, meaning it. "She knows I only listen half the time."

Ace didn't move. "You look like shit. Eat the cheeseburger and we'll let you change into jeans instead of scrubs."

Jackson shook his head. "Ace, if you knew—"

Ace sank to a crouch and nailed him in place with a flat brown-eyed glare. "Eat the fuckin' cold cheeseburger, Jackson. You do nobody any good if you keel over. It's fuckin' fuel. Sometimes the fuel tastes great, sometimes it tastes like ass, but what matters is it helps you run. She needs you to run. Now fuckin' eat."

"Jesus fuckin' Christ—"

"*Eat!*"

"Bossy fuckin' asshole—"

"Master Sergeant Bossy Asshole to you, fucker. Now eat."

Jackson snatched the burger out of his hand and shoved a bite in his mouth before getting up to see what Burton was doing. He'd moved from the nurse's station when the surgeon had come out, and Jackson found him around the corner outside the waiting room, saying a very private goodbye to Ernie.

Burton disengaged reluctantly, but he didn't let Ernie move from his arms. "I got info from Kaden—the roads are pretty blocked up there, so I'm having him stay put. My guys'll be downstairs in ten," he said. "We're taking a chopper up to your brother's place—we should beat them by a good hour. I called local law enforcement to look after your sister—they, uh, don't seem to like you very much."

"I wore a wire before my career ended," Jackson muttered. "Not enough blood to pay for that."

Burton gazed at him levelly. "Was the guy dirty?"

Jackson looked around the hospital. "Would you believe this is part of that same goddamned pig wallow?"

"Then worth it, and fuck 'em. I'm sending another chopper of guys to your sister. They don't got your back and I don't trust 'em."

"He's… he's going to be okay." Jackson's heart twisted in his chest. "I could still go—"

"Don't you dare," Taylor snapped, emerging from the hallway with the restrooms like some sort of phantom. "And eat."

"It's my family, Lucy Satan—you know that, right? They're going after—"

"Will his presence make the difference?" she asked Burton, unflinching. "Will his presence in your party be the difference between his family living or dying?" She'd fixed her hair in the bathroom and put her makeup back on like armor, but her eyes were still red-rimmed, and she still looked vulnerable. But she didn't back down from Lee Burton and his scary-looking weapons belt and his no-bullshit demeanor.

"No, ma'am," Burton told her like an equal. "We're special forces. Living and dying is our business."

"Jackson," she said softly. "I know Ellery left you to go finish up the Bridger case. But he was the only one who could. You're the only one who can be here, do you understand?"

Jackson nodded and kept his voice steady. "Yes, ma'am." And then he begged Burton with his eyes. "I… I don't trust easy. I'm trusting you with my family. They took care of me when there was nobody, you understand, right? This is a shitty way to pay them back." He thought of Ace and grimaced. And Ellery. "Seems like that's my specialty."

Burton had the audacity to look bored. "*You* need to accept that you can't save the whole fuckin' world. Fuckin' Jesus, Rivers—I've been listening to you and Cramer for three months. You do your fuckin' best. It's all I got, it's all you got. Accept that." He nuzzled Ernie's temple for a moment and then took a measured step back. "You watch after my family until I'm home. I'll go take care of yours."

And with that he thrust Jackson's phone into his hand, turned on his heel, and left.

Ernie looked after him with pure radiance on his face. "We're going to have our own house in the desert," he said randomly. "And cats. And it'll be walking distance to the garage. And I can look after Ace and Sonny, and they can keep me when he's gone. Did I mention we'll have cats?"

"Cats are necessary," Jackson said, pulled out of his own misery by Ernie's natural-as-breathing charm.

Ernie's smile faded. "It's good you're staying. Burton's super scary— he won't let anybody hurt your people. I know you just met him, but he told me he felt like you and Ellery were old friends. He's worried too. He won't let you down."

Jackson nodded, and Taylor tugged at his elbow. "Let's sit down," she said softly. "I need to call my husband and…." She swallowed, her face taking on a mask of pride he knew well. "I am not at my best."

"Of course," he said, offering his elbow. The other hand held the half-eaten cheeseburger, and as they passed the trash, he made to throw it away.

"All of it, Jackson," she said imperturbably.

"You totally lied to that man about needing me, didn't you?" He scowled at her, but he took a bite of cheeseburger.

"I'm a lawyer. I don't lie, I prevaricate. You need to be here. Ellery needed to avenge you, but you took care of that already. You need to stay here and see with your own eyes that he's going to be all right."

"It was a shitty choice," he muttered. "Who has to make that fucking choice, ever?"

She patted his arm as they entered the room and sat down. "You do, sweetheart. You're one of the few men who could."

He narrowed his eyes. "Don't call me sweetheart. Now I think *I'm* the one who got shot."

Her mouth quirked the tiniest bit. "I call *you* a stubborn asshole when you've been shot. When you're really hurt, I call you sweetheart."

He let his mouth relax and looked around as she extricated her cell phone from her bag. Sonny and Ace were leaning on each other, and Ernie was standing in the doorway, looking beat. Jackson wondered suddenly at the toll being in such a crowded place would take on someone like Ernie.

"Guys?" he said tentatively. "Guys? I'll call you. I promise. I won't blow town without calling and stopping by to say thank you. You've got a drive, and it's been a day."

Ace nodded and stood, and Jackson met him to shake hands.

"Sorry I, uh... got you kidnapped." He grimaced. "And thanks for everything. Thank you."

Ace shrugged and handed Jackson the new clothes. "You helped us put a lot of shit in our rearview. We're obliged. Text us if something changes. And definitely come by."

"He's gotta come by, Ace—we got his car." Sonny was nodding urgently.

Oh God. "What's left of it."

Sonny shrugged. "The SHO was worse. Don't worry. By the time you're ready to take him home, we'll have it drivable."

"We'll pay for parts," Taylor said, and Sonny blushed and ducked.

"Tell her she don't need to pay for anything, Ace. We'll do it free on 'count of them keepin' their word and all, 'kay?"

Ace looked at Taylor and inclined his head. "That's not a problem, ma'am."

Jackson reached for Sonny's hand, not surprised when Sonny shook too hard and popped a stitch, but getting good at not letting it show. "Thanks, Sonny. We're indebted to you."

Ace and Sonny turned to leave the room, and Ernie came running back. Without slowing down he threw himself into Jackson's arms for a hug.

Jackson hugged him back, and he whispered, "Give the money to Burton. He'll hide it in their finances—he does that a lot 'cause they're keeping me there."

"Thanks, kid," Jackson whispered back, and then Ernie hugged him tighter.

"Have faith," he said. "Heal."

And then he was gone.

Jackson and Taylor sat back down again, and Taylor texted her husband quietly. The phone rang in her hands, and she picked it up, answering with a calm and a self-possession Jackson didn't have on his best day.

"He was shot, dear. Yes—Jackson killed the man who did it."

She reached out and grabbed his good hand, which was nearer, and squeezed.

Maybe he was needed after all.

With a sigh he leaned back in the hospital chair and let his mind go blank. Ellery was alive; he was resting. Jackson could stop panicking now.

Forty-five minutes later the doctor came out and told them they could see Ellery in recovery.

It wasn't until Jackson was throwing away the wrapper that he realized that, sometime between squeezing Taylor's hand and going to the restroom to change, he'd managed to eat the goddamned cheeseburger.

Intravenous Fish

GAH! "EVERYTHING fucking hurts," Ellery breathed. His brain thought it in hyperspeed, a thousand hundred times. His mouth and lungs managed to make it an entire speech.

"You think?" Jackson said from right next to his bed. "You kept acting like being on this side of the bed is fun. Where's your circus tent, sparky?"

"Fuck—" Breath. "—you."

"Your mother's here," Jackson said, voice strained. "So ask yourself, 'How do I think Jackson will answer that?' before it comes out of your mouth."

"Hello... Mother." Oh Jesus. His mother was there. "I'm dying?"

"No." She stood at Jackson's side. "But you did your best. I'd appreciate it if you picked another hobby if you can't master this one in one go. It's hard on my heart, Ellery."

They were worried about him. Ellery studied them, his vision blurry but not so weak that he couldn't see his mother looked sad, and Jackson.... Jackson looked like a man who'd seen hell.

"How's... that... side... of bed?"

Jackson closed his eyes. "Sucks so hard. Almost ripped my balls out my eye sockets. I hate it here."

"How about... a nice B and E... next... time."

Jackson smiled tiredly. "We could do a breaking and entering in our sleep. I'm all for it."

Ellery smiled a little and reached toward him. Jackson took his hand, his own wrapped in a disintegrating bandage.

"How?"

Jackson looked at their hands together. "Don't remember. Too worried about you."

He was lying, but Ellery hurt and, frankly, was just so warmed that the two of them were standing by his bed, together.

"Ace?" By Ace he meant everybody—he figured Jackson would know.

"They're all fine." Jackson's eyes darted sideways, and Taylor nodded. "Burton's... afraid some of the guys who got away will go after the kid, go after my family. He called in... well, the Marines, I guess, but the Marines who aren't affiliated with the Marines. Whatever. I can't keep that shit straight, you know that. They left about two hours ago—he texted they landed, but....” He shrugged.

“Waiting?”

“Yeah.”

“Hard.”

Jackson shrugged again. “Well, you know. Rest of the day was a cakewalk, right? Until somebody decided to shoot blind at the asshole shooting at us.”

Ellery grimaced. Yeah, he’d done that. He didn’t have words now for why.

“He needed to die.”

“I won’t argue. Can’t, really, since I killed him—a lot. I killed that fucker a lot.”

He’d said it to make Ellery smile—and it worked. “Thank-you note is in the mail.”

“Skip the note,” Jackson said, voice thick. “Get better. Just... heal.”

“Yeah.” Ellery couldn’t keep his eyes open. “Deal.”

HE WAS in and out for the next few hours, but someone—Jackson or his mother—was always there when he woke. Jackson wouldn’t move from his bedside, and even when he slept, head on the bed next to Ellery, he looked tense.

In the early part of the night, Ellery managed to stroke his head.

“You really scared him, son.”

Mother—she hadn’t been a dream. “He’s okay.”

“He’s a box full of broken dishes, and you just rattled him pretty hard. He’ll be sorting himself for a few days before we know.”

“Mm.” The night before—oh my God, really? Just the night before? Jackson, laying down his pain. Having faith. Having hope. “Stronger than you think.”

“Stronger than *he* thinks—and that’s really the point, isn’t it?”

“Mm.”

He felt his mother’s kiss on his brow. “I’m going to beg a cot from the nurse, sweetheart. If I try to sleep like Jackson, I’ll break my neck.”

Ellery closed his eyes again.

HE WASN’T sure what woke him again. His mother, true to her word, was asleep on her back, hands crossed over her middle like a painting, on a nearby cot. Jackson was... well, twitching, head still on the mattress next to Ellery.

Was that what had awakened him?

Wait. There was a doctor in the doorway. Familiar? Dark buzz-cut hair, cold hazel eyes, the face of an automaton, he moved toward Ellery's IV with a hypodermic in his hand.

But Ellery had morphine, right?

Wait. Wait. Ellery *knew* this man. Knew him. He hadn't spoken much but had driven the car… oh God.

He clenched his fingers in Jackson's hair and croaked, "Leavins!" just as Lacey's driver thrust the needle into the intravenous tube. Ellery kicked out, his core and chest screaming from the sudden exertion.

He tagged Leavins in the thigh just as Jackson jerked upright.

"Wha—"

"Bad guy!" Ellery rasped.

Anybody else—*anybody* else, even his mother, would have questioned that. Would have said "Isn't he a doctor!" Any other person on the planet would have given Leavins the chance to depress the plunger of that deadly little hypodermic needle into the tube of the IV.

Would have signed Ellery's death warrant with a breath of hesitation.

Jackson damned near levitated across the bed, screaming "*Stop, asshole!*" as he used his foot to push off from his chair so he could grand-fucking-jeté over Ellery's prone body.

He and Leavins crashed to the floor, leaving the needle in the tube.

"*Lucy!*" Jackson screamed, struggling hard with his opponent. "Lucy! Get the needle!"

Leavins leveled an elbow at Jackson's temple, and Jackson went down hard. Leavins took a step toward the IV stand in the tiny room and then just… disappeared, yelping as his chin hit the floor. Jackson stood from where he'd apparently grabbed his opponent's feet and aimed a kick at Leavins's ribs.

And then Jackson disappeared because Lacey's men *were* trained in the martial arts, and Leavins had grabbed his foot and yanked.

Ellery's mother crept around the bed, avoiding the grappling men—but not avoiding Leavins's notice. With a lunge he was on top of her, pushing her back onto Ellery's legs while she struggled. Jackson wrapped his arm around Leavins's throat just as Ellery's mother lifted a violent knee.

She didn't get him in the groin—Ellery was pretty sure that would have incapacitated him, given his mother—but she must have come close, because he moved protectively to the side. Jackson managed to pull him off her and back into the corner of the room by the lavatory. He held Leavins there while Leavins threw his elbow back again and again and again, straight into Jackson's core, his ribs, until Ellery could swear he heard a crack. Once more, and Jackson's grip slackened enough for Leavins to throw him off.

Leavins advanced to the IV rack again just as Taylor yanked the hypodermic out of the tube, and Jackson threw himself over Leavins's back. This time, instead of pinning him to the wall, Leavins scrambled for the pocket of the lab coat he was wearing and produced a slim, glittering object that terrified Ellery as much as the hypodermic.

"Knife!" he croaked just as Leavins brought it down against the outside of Jackson's arm, slicing cleanly through his sweatshirt and his flesh.

Jackson didn't let go.

He kept hauling backward, away from the bed, away from Ellery's mother, who was calling for help at the top of her lungs, away from where Leavins could do any harm.

Leavins shifted the scalpel in his hand, turned it downward, and threw his fist back, right under Jackson's ribs.

And Jackson didn't let go.

Again. Again.

Jackson whimpered—and then roared.

He spun them around and threw Leavins at the lavatory door, kicking him in the thigh for good measure. Leavins went to his knees with a grunt, and Jackson kicked him in the back of the head. Leavins's forehead rebounded off the door, and he struggled groggily, trying to get to his feet.

Jackson paused for a moment, bringing his hand to his midriff, and that gave Leavins the moment he needed to whirl and rush Jackson, scalpel slashing.

Ellery saw it sparkle in the light and swoop downward. He saw Jackson reach forward, grabbing for Leavins's wrist, and then propel himself toward Leavins, thrusting with his legs. Then Jackson was sitting, one knee pushing into Leavins's middle as he used the leverage to drive the scalpel between Leavins's ribs.

Straight into his heart.

For a moment Leavins caught his hands, clutching to stop him.

Then his bloody hands flailed, then slowed, then fell limply to the ground. The blood pooling across his ribs spread to the floor. And spread and spread and spread.

Security crashed through the door just as his last breath sputtered wetly through his lips.

Jackson raised his hands in the air as the door rebounded back, and let out a sound that Ellery knew by now.

"Mom," Ellery whispered. "Mom—he's hurt."

Taylor let out her own sound, and Ellery looked up at her as she held the hypodermic needle between her thumb and forefinger. Her hair flew wildly around her head, and she massaged her throat gingerly with her free hand.

"You're hurt," he said, his heart in his throat. "Oh God."

"I'm fine, Ellery." He recognized her tone, even though her voice was roughened by, oh my God, *that man's fingers around her throat.* "Jackson—Jackson, are you okay?"

"Peachy," he rasped, and she let out a little moan.

"Stop trying to handcuff him and escort him to the ER," she snapped. "I know that word—that's the word he uses when he's half-dead."

"No ER," he muttered.

"You know this man?" asked the security guard, a fresh-faced young man, heavier than he should have been but struggling valiantly to assist Jackson up in spite of the appalling amount of blood on the floor.

"He's with us," Ellery breathed. The adrenaline was fading from his system, and he hurt all over. God, he needed morphine, and he needed to sleep, and he knew his body would suck him under in a moment, but first....

"Can I see his front? Please? God, Jackson—he got you. I saw it...."

Jackson grunted, face turned away. "Maybe the ER isn't such a bad idea," he said, like this had just occurred to him. "Lucy Satan, you want to maybe dose him the fuck up with morphine? Lots and lots of morphine?"

"I'd like to make sure whatever our friend there was trying to inject him with didn't hit home," she said, her voice strained. "It's okay, son. We just want to see your face."

Jackson turned, and Ellery and his mother gasped. His sweatshirt and T-shirt—new, it looked like—hung open from his collarbone to his armpit, and they could see the flesh underneath, and the half-inch-deep slice that followed the line of his sweatshirt.

And the holes and blood below that, in his oblique muscle, a network of wounds that would need more than just a little stitch.

"You asshole," Ellery said weakly. "You just couldn't let me have the circus and the ponies all to myself, could you?"

Jackson shuddered, his first indication that it hurt as bad as it looked. "Lucy Satan, you'd better make sure we share a fucking room." He paused then, grimacing, and reached painfully into his back pocket, where his phone was buzzing.

"Rivers."

He listened for a moment, and then, horribly enough, started to laugh a little hysterically. "Missing one?" he said. "You got Adkins and Gleeson, but you're missing one. You're *missing* a bad guy. Missing. Heh heh. Missing one.

Uh-huh. Like, a shoe. Sorry, y'all, got all the bad guys, but we're missing a homicidal shoe. Why, yes. Yes, we found your homicidal shoe, why the fuck do you ask? Can you talk to him? No, Burton, you can't talk to him. Because he's dead. Yes, that's what I said. Dead. Your missing shoe is *bleeding out* on the hospital floor. Yup. You heard me. Bleeding out. No—everybody's fine."

Taylor grabbed the phone from him.

"Jackson's being admitted momentarily. You can debrief him when you return. I take it the Cameron families are both in good shape? Yes? Yes, I will. I'll tell him that just as soon as he *goes to the ER*!"

In his entire life, Ellery had never heard his mother scream like a fishwife. The chaos in the room—the people who'd spilled in to work on Leavins, the security men who couldn't decide whether to cuff Jackson or escort him by the elbow, and the nurse currently changing out Ellery's IV—all stopped.

Taylor Cramer didn't bat an eyelash. "Please do have them all text him. He needs to be reassured. But we have a body to take care of, and Jackson—"

Jackson was still laughing, bitterly and damned near insanely.

"The first thing we're going to do is sedate him. Yes, young man, we will see you when you return."

She hit End Call and glared about the room. "Could somebody get Mr. Rivers a sedative and a gurney? For Christ's sake, you'd think this wasn't a fucking hospital!"

"Ellery," Jackson chortled. "Ellery, we broke your mother."

Oh Jesus. "Get stitched up, asshole. We'll fix her when you're sane."

And that was pretty much all he could manage. He saw Jackson being hustled into a wheelchair, and another nurse picking up the hypodermic and a doctor checking his pupils, and he checked out after that.

Goddammit, they'd been *kidding* about the fucking circus.

THREE DAYS later, Jackson, at least, would have welcomed the fucking circus.

He'd needed surgery, and his sentence had been a week for recovery. Ellery was still more damaged—hooray?—and he was awarded a two-week sentence.

It had taken Ellery two days before he realized they were talking about the hospital the way criminals talked about prison.

The only good news was that Ellery's mother had come through and gotten them the private room together, complete with a home entertainment center rental. While their enforced time together wasn't under the best of circumstances, Jackson was at least not climbing the walls.

Much.

"You'd think we could at least go outside," he grumbled on day five. "I mean, it's nice outside, right? Sixty-five, not raining. Damned near springlike. Don't you want to see blue sky?"

Ellery looked fondly at him, noting that a nick in the liver let a guy roll over to his side, while Ellery's intestines of mushy goo kept him pretty much on his back for another four days.

"Of course," he said simply. "I… I want to go swimming with you." He smiled slightly. "I've always loved to see you swim."

Jackson rolled his eyes. "I have no idea wh—"

"Because you're graceful." Ellery had been sort of loopy on morphine since he'd come out of surgery. He found he rather liked being able to just toss compliments out like dog treats. "You're graceful in the water." He smiled dreamily. "You're just so damned pretty."

Jackson chuckled, the sound nearly too robust for their shared hospital room. "You're fun like this. You're like a one-man ego-stroking show."

"I'm the only man who should be stroking your ego," Ellery said, but even under the morphine, this was only meant playfully. Nobody who'd watched a man fight to save his life the way Jackson had fought for Ellery would be in doubt.

"Well, lucky you, you're the only person I want stroking it," Jackson placated. Then he sighed. "But, you know. Not anytime soon."

"The irony is incredibly cruel," Ellery agreed. Enforced bed rest. No sex. There oughtta be a law.

"By the time we get sprung out of here, I'll be lucky if you can stand me."

Ellery scowled. "No. Not playing the hating-on-Jackson game. It's boring. Let's play something else."

Jackson grunted. "How about the 'What happened to the twelve serial killers' game. That should be a hoot!"

Ellery groaned. "God—the firm will love that!" Technically they were still on vacation. Ellery's mother had left that morning to fly up to Sacramento and reassure Jade and look after their house. She'd been planning to stop by his firm and debrief on the Karl Lacey situation as well.

"No rule says they've got to be ours," Jackson said, surprising him. "I mean, we tracked Owens in our spare time. This could be that too."

"Doesn't that violate the Jackson Rivers hero code?" Ellery asked curiously. He'd be honestly fine with just doing his own goddamned job for a little while.

"Janie Isaacson thinks we're heroes," Jackson said humbly. "Anthony thinks we walk on water."

"*You* walk on water." Ellery smiled softly to himself. Anthony had been put on speakerphone when Jackson got out of surgery the first day. He'd been excited and scared—apparently Gleeson and Adkins had gotten quite close to Kaden's house that night—but mostly?

He'd been happy.

Kaden and Rhonda had applied to be his foster parents.

He was in a place with a room, and a dresser, and people who cared about him.

And toys. And kids to play with him.

And—in Jackson's words—he seemed to blame all this on Jackson and a little bit on Ellery.

"I spent less than two hours with him," Jackson grumbled. "I think he should blame some of that on Kaden and Rhonda."

"I'm sure there will be plenty of blame to go around," Ellery soothed.

Jackson let out a sigh. "I miss my cat."

And that complaint Ellery was on board with 100 percent. "I miss your cat too."

"AJ's moving in with Crystal, you know. What if Billy Bob likes them better?"

Once the threat to the Camerons was over, AJ took reluctant leave. But apparently Jade had put him and Crystal in touch with each other—two people with the same baggage, she'd thought. Maybe they could help each other.

Two days after the introduction, Crystal had made the offer. She'd told Jackson in her own dreamy way that AJ was very grounded, and she liked his aura in her home. AJ had told him that she was easy to talk to and affectionate, and bright and funny and educated. All the things his current roommates were not. Crystal would sit on the couch with him in her jammies and watch a romantic movie on television.

She was a sister.

Two people who needed each other, together.

"We bribe him with love and affection," Ellery said. The probability of Billy Bob forsaking Jackson was miniscule, but telling Jackson that wouldn't register. Telling him they had a plan—*that* would calm him down.

Jackson grunted. "If we ever do this again, I want to be home," he said plaintively.

Ellery fought hysterical laughter. "If we ever do this again? Are you high?"

"A little. Morphine."

Ellery giggled some more. "Jackson, I love you. I love you so much my heart aches with it sometimes. I imagine you when you're old, and your hair's gone salt-and-pepper, and you still don't have an ass to fill out your jeans. Could you... maybe, just for me, imagine a different challenge for the two of us? You know, besides side-by-side recovery beds?"

"Keeping a car longer than a minute and a half?"

"Ace says the new one will stick," Ellery told him practically. Ellery, of course, would wait and see, but Jackson seemed to have a lot of faith, based on the car he'd watched Sonny and Ace drive up in that fateful day.

"That would be pretty neat," Jackson said, and he must have been high, because he sounded like a schoolkid from the fifties. "A car. For a while. But what sort of challenge do you mean?"

"I don't know. Maybe us. Living in peace. Maybe that's a challenge. What do you think?"

"Mm." Jackson's eyes were closing, because he was still in recovery too. "Someday we'll have to plan a wedding." And then he fell asleep.

Ellery was stuck, eyes wide as he stared at the ceiling, wishing either one of them could get out of bed. He wanted to grab Jackson's hand and hold him to that half-stoned promise, dammit, but they didn't have any witnesses!

But hey. Just having him say the words... that was an improvement, wasn't it? That was.... Ellery's eyes closed of their own volition. That was a miracle right there.

A miracle.

But not a challenge.

Funny how life had a way of throwing challenges at them all on its own.

Different Bowl, Same Fish

THE HOSPITAL was pressing down on him. Dark, antiseptic, cold. Ellery was in that echoing dim hellhole somewhere, and Jackson had to get him. Someone was after him—the square, blank, unempathetic evil of Karl Lacey, or Grant Leavins was chasing Ellery Cramer with weapons flashing dully in the light, and Ellery, earnest, hard-working, doing things by the book, was sitting with his nose in his laptop, filling out paperwork.

And Jackson was lost, lost in the labyrinth of the hospital, and every move was harder, moving through molasses, moving through hardening concrete, and Ellery wouldn't look up.

The bad guys were coming, and Ellery…. Ellery was hurt, and he could bleed, and Ellery wouldn't look up!

Look up!

"Baby, I'm here."

Jackson gasped and flailed, groaning when his wrist hit the rail of the hospital bed. Shit. He had a bruise there already from the night before.

With a concerted effort, he pulled his shit together, taking in Ellery's hand on his chest, his other hand in his hair.

Then common sense seeped in.

"You're not supposed to be out of bed." Jackson was allowed up now— he'd even been able to relieve himself so he could go home tomorrow. But they'd cut off his morphine drip the day before, which meant the nightmares were back.

"Some asshole kept yelling my name in his sleep. Had to do something."

Jackson grimaced, sweat wringing from his stupid hospital gown. He wanted a shower. He wanted his cat. He wanted home.

"I'm sorry," he whispered.

"I'm sorrier." Ellery dropped the side of the bed so he could lean his head sleepily next to Jackson's. "You… I can never make them stop."

"I… I'm so afraid you'll get them." Oh God. That was his worst fear. Ellery had always had this curious innocence to the horrors around him. Jackson had known them intimately. His dreams were always that he couldn't protect the people he loved from the things that had touched him with slimy fingers.

Ellery's shrug was just as pure as Jackson feared. "I have faith. Say a little prayer before I close my eyes. Superstition. It's surprisingly effective."

Oh! Jeez. "I think I have to go to temple with you," Jackson mumbled. "Does the year start again when we go back home?"

Ellery let out a short laugh. "Sure. Why do *you* have to go?"

Jackson raised a hand and feathered a touch down Ellery's cheekbone. "Do you think…." He swallowed. So much had happened, so much of it violent. "Do you think I didn't ask God for you to be all right?"

Ellery's smile held a sort of boyish delight. "Really? How'd that go?"

Jackson remembered the upended pew. Before Lucy Satan had flown back home yesterday, she'd told Jackson quietly that the pew had been paid for, and so had the hospital mirror. There were some things Ellery didn't need to know.

"Not so great the first time. Your mom got there and helped me out, and it got better."

Ellery's eyebrows went up. "There's a story behind that," he said, running his finger along the tape on Jackson's hand.

"I don't… let's not… I just wanted to tell you I'm grateful for you," Jackson said at last. "Can we just leave it there? I'm grateful. This whole stupid mess—our house being bugged, assassins—I mean, *assassins*. Rogue military leaders. It's all so out of our league, you know? You and me… we belong back in your house in Sacramento, defending the innocent and the not-so-much, right? We don't belong here. But here we are—and all I want out of it is you. I'm grateful for you. I… I wouldn't be much good if you weren't here."

"I beg to differ. But you asked God, and here we are. So, you'll go to temple with me."

Jackson sighed. "The rabbi was okay. I don't think he'll kick me out, right?"

"Only if he's a fool." Ellery's eyes were focused intently on his face, and Jackson couldn't even pace to get away from it.

"So your dad gets here tomorrow," Jackson said, an attempt to change the subject.

Ellery nodded, but his eyes didn't dim. "You okay with that?"

"I like your father."

Ellery smiled fondly. "Pretty much everybody does. I mean, are you okay with the plan? Leaving the hospital, flying home, checking on everybody." Jackson had texted his family a lot in the past week, itching with frustration that he couldn't *touch* them and *see* that they were okay. Ellery's mom had been the one to suggest he go make sure everything really was good when he got back home.

Unspoken was the knowledge that the hospital was wearing on him. That he'd needed to be sedated in those first few days to stall out the panic attacks that would hinder his healing. Jackson would stay by Ellery's side no matter what—but he was pretty sure Taylor and Ellery had planned the trip home so he didn't have to.

He couldn't decide if going home to see his cat and make sure his family was okay made him a coward or not—another thing to obsess about while he fought not to lose it in recovery.

"I cannot tell you how happy I am that you're going to the firm to check on things," Ellery said now into the dark of the wee hours. "The texts I'm getting from them—they're starting to set my teeth on edge."

Jackson had seen those texts—they'd been frustratingly vague. Lots of stuff about *Just heal, we'll talk when you're better.*

Jackson had heard that shit before he'd left the police department. *We'll talk when you're better* had been code for *You don't really have a job right now, but we don't want to break it to you while you're in the hospital because that will make us feel bad.*

"Think they're getting pressure from the government?" Jackson asked, wondering. Burton had visited the day before, looking like sautéed death. He'd been on his way to Ace and Sonny's—or to see Ernie, more likely, but he wouldn't say that, not even now. Before he left he told them that Lacey still had friends in high places, people who did *not* buy the story that Lacey had been killed by mercenaries because of his involvement in the behavior modification project that had brought him disfavor in the first place.

He'd reluctantly admitted that he and his handler hadn't been able to keep Jackson and Ellery's names entirely out of it.

"It was either talk about your investigation after Lacey hit the woman in Sacramento or talk about Ace and Sonny. You guys, I'm sorry, but—"

"Thump-thump," Jackson had said cheerfully, miming the bus they'd been thrown under. "Yeah. We get it. No worries."

Burton had grimaced. "They can make things uncomfortable," he said with a sigh. "Which is a shitty way to pay you guys back. You did a huge thing, do you realize that? I was undercover for months, and you two—"

"Mostly Jackson," Ellery had said, rolling his eyes. "You may recall, Ace and I were locked up."

"Mostly the two of you," Burton said. "If I'd blown up a car and come in guns blazing for nothing but my own enjoyment, they'd be shipping what's left of me back to my parents in a box. But you guys caught them by surprise. Not military. Not law enforcement. They weren't expecting to take you and have consequences—and whatever your mother has been saying to people, Ellery, those are some fucking huge consequences—and they certainly weren't expecting a military assault from a scruffy PI."

Jackson had chuckled then. "Did you hear that? I'm scruffy."

"You work hard at scruffy," Ellery had returned. "The last set of new clothes you got was scalpeled in half."

"Heh heh heh…."

Well, it had seemed funny when he'd been on morphine. Now that he had a bandage across his forearm and one from right clavicle to left armpit, with stitches underneath and *no morphine*, it wasn't quite so amusing.

Not now, when Ellery was looking at him with worried brown eyes.

"I don't know what they can do," he said quietly. "But… you know. I like my job."

Jackson nodded thoughtfully. "Not the only place you can do it," he said, hoping to reassure.

He wasn't sure if it worked or not, but Ellery got a speculative look in his eyes that meant he was thinking about something important.

Good.

"You should go back to bed, Counselor," Jackson said gently. God, he yearned for the two of them together, in the same bed again. At home, Billy Bob by his ear. He swallowed hard against the fierce, painful cramp in his stomach, but Ellery looked up anyway.

"Baby…," he whispered, reaching up to brush Jackson's cheek.

His fingers came away wet.

"I want to go home," Jackson whispered. "I want to go home with you."

Angry, painful cleansing tears pushed behind his eyes, pushed at his throat.

"I want that more than anything," Ellery said gruffly. "Even my job."

Jackson nodded and stopped fighting them. He was just so tired of fighting.

Ellery stayed there by his side, stroking his hand, his forehead, his arm, while Jackson purged the fear, the terrible soul-crushing anxiety that had stopped his breath since before they'd left Sacramento.

It wasn't until Ellery held Jackson's hand to his cheek that he realized Ellery was crying too.

HE'D CALLED Ace and offered to come visit, but Ace, in his own laconic way, had told him to wait another three days, and then he could come visit and pick up the car in the same trip. Then, before Jackson could get his feelings hurt, he added that Burton had arrived right after he'd visited Jackson, after being gone since they'd taken out Lacey and company. He'd knocked on the door, shaken Ace's hand, clapped Sonny on the back, and pretty much walked into Ernie's room, and that had been that. Ace assumed they were eating while he and Sonny were sleeping and said the shower went on at four in the morning, but other than that, the two of them had dropped off the map.

"I think he might be sleeping some," Ace confessed. "He looked like fuckin' death warmed over."

"I remember. But that's a lot of people for such a small space—I'll come see you the day Ellery gets out. How's that?"

"More'n fair," Ace proclaimed, and they hung up.

But Jackson didn't leave until Ellery's father showed up.

Sid Cramer was a sweet-faced man with a curly halo of graying hair and such a gentle way about him that Jackson suspected him of magic. He was possibly the one person Jackson had ever met that Jackson would nap in front of. No nightmares with Ellery's dad in the room. It was like a rule.

"You've got all your clothes?" Sid asked him, kicking back in khakis and a dad sweater in the corner of the hospital room with his own laptop. Ellery told Jackson he was a lawyer as well—family law. It seemed fitting that such a sweet man would make his living seeing to adoptions and making sure that orphaned children were taken care of, but a corporate shark, Sid was not.

"Ace brought them by when we were both laid up," Jackson confirmed. He'd also brought their laptops, but—according to Ace—things had happened, and now they were both radioactive paperweights. One of Jackson's jobs after he flew back to Sacramento was to secure them both new laptops and set them up. Ellery was starting to twitch without work from the firm to finish up.

"Don't forget to tell everybody hi for me," Ellery said. Jackson searched his face carefully for signs of fever, of fatigue. It had been a lot more fun when he'd been on morphine too—there'd been no worry then. But Jackson was never going to forget that moment, Ellery bleeding underneath him, realizing that there were some things Jackson's counselor couldn't talk away.

"I will," he said soberly. "I'll even tell the cat."

"You're not visiting the cat and leaving him there, are you?" Ellery asked, horrified.

"No—I'm taking him to our house, spending three nights there, and then leaving him for twelve hours to come get your sorry ass. Is that okay?"

Ellery smiled faintly. "That's more than fine. I just…." He looked embarrassed. "You know. Didn't want to taunt him about things going back to normal when they weren't quite."

"No, Ellery, that's me you're taunting. 'Cause I'm going to be home without you, and it's gonna sorta suck."

Ellery grimaced. "Well, you'd drive us both crazy here," he said, looking troubled. "I... just call me, okay? Middle of the night, call me."

Jackson looked away. The night before lay heavily between them, but they both knew this was the only option. "Yeah, sure—"

"Dad," Ellery said calmly, "go grab his phone."

Sid stood stiffly up, stretching, and held out his hand. Jackson squinted at him and handed it over.

"Now drop it on the floor and smash—"

"What in the hell!" Jackson flailed, snatching the phone back while Ellery's father looked bemusedly at his son. "What are you doin—"

"So help me, Jackson, I'll report the phone stolen right now if you don't promise me you'll call. I'll be sleeping next to my phone, do you understand me?" Ellery's voice cracked, and Jackson felt like shit. "Remember when you slept with anybody that breathed so you didn't have to be alone?"

Jackson looked at Sid Cramer apologetically. "Yes, fuckwad, and I so appreciate you bringing that up in front of your father."

"Dad forgives you—and so do I. But I took that away from you, and now I'm sending you back home without me, and I want your word of honor that you won't try to do it alone."

Oh God. With another apologetic grimace at Ellery's father, Jackson moved closer to the bed so he could lean down and kiss Ellery's forehead soberly. "Okay, Ellery. I promise. You'll regret it, but I promise."

"Thanks, Jackson."

Jackson pulled in a deep breath and remembered what it felt like to set down some of his burdens. "Do you... I mean, I could invite Jade over to sleep in the guest room," he said after a moment. "Maybe if the first night doesn't go well."

Ellery smiled, his eyes red-rimmed and shiny. "That would be fine," he said. "Crystal, AJ—you have friends who'll do that for you. Let them."

"Sure."

Jackson kissed him on the lips this time, tasting the faint brine of tears. "Three days. You won't even miss me. Get some sleep, okay, Counselor?"

"Sure, Jackson. I love you."

"Love you too."

And then he shook Sid Cramer's hand, grabbed his duffel bag, and left.

JADE PICKED him up at the airport with Billy Bob in a carrier in the back of the car, meowing piteously.

Jackson hugged Jade, put his seat belt on, and let his cat out of the box in spite of Jade's vociferous objections.

"Jackson, he's a cat! He fucking hates the car—goddammit, he's been screaming in my ear for a solid fucking hour, you think he'll just—"

Billy Bob leapt into Jackson's arms and shut up, rubbing Jackson's nose and smoothing his whisker's back against Jackson's cheeks.

"Hey, buddy! Did you miss me?"

"Meow." Billy Bob's snaggletoothed face searched Jackson's features unhappily.

"I'm sorry, man. We hated leaving you—you can't even get laid anymore. I mean, I know it was solid at Crystal's place. I think she was feeding you raw hamburger, the choice stuff, you know?"

"Meow." With a wiggle the cat curled up his remaining back leg so it fit in the crook of Jackson's elbow and rubbed whiskers again.

"Yeah, you're sort of a street cat. We got basic Meow Mix at home. I bet you miss that, right?"

"Purrrrrrrr...." Billy Bob rubbed his face against Jackson's bandaged chest, and Jackson just held him closer.

"Yeah, buddy. Missed you too, you no-thumbs-having motherfucker."

Jade had yet to pull out from the side of the arrival pickup curb. She just stared at him like she'd never seen a man make out with his cat before.

"What?" he asked defensively.

"Doesn't Ellery get jealous?"

"Naw—Billy Bob gives him whisker rubs too." Jackson let out a sigh and rubbed noses with his first, best roommate again.

"That's disturbing," Jade said with a sigh, pulling her boyfriend's SUV away from the curb. "How you doing today? You look like shit. I think you need to go home and sleep and catch up with your email and shit, what do you think?"

"I think I need to buy another laptop," Jackson told her. "And one for Ellery too. Our laptops were... uh... damaged...."

"Doing what?" she demanded, and Jackson had to wince.

"You wouldn't believe me if I told you." When Ace had dropped off their luggage, he'd muttered something about exploding lithium batteries as detonators and using a screwdriver to open up the two MacBooks and how it left a scar. At that point Jackson didn't want to hear any more—he was just glad his favorite T-shirts were still intact.

"Really? That's what you've got?"

Jackson grunted. "Uh, what did Ellery's mother tell you?"

"That Ellery was kidnapped from Walmart, which is about the funniest goddamned thing I've ever heard. And then she said you went to get him—which I can believe. And that he got shot—which I can believe too. And then me and Mike and the kids next door had cops and military guys knocking on our doors and telling us to stay inside under the bed." She snorted. "Mike and I kept watch, him in front with the shotgun, me in back with the pistol. It's a good thing those military guys move fast, because I almost shot them going for the bad guy sneaking over the fence."

Jackson smiled, the comfort of his cat seeping into his bones as Jade dodged in and out of the giant trucks that hung out on I-5 as she headed for the J Street turnoff.

"Well done," he said, scratching Billy Bob in the secret place at the base of his tail. The cat's tail kept pointing… up, up, up! Yes! Catgasm achieved! "Kaden still won't tell me what happened."

Jade grunted. "What happened was *their* bad guy got in through the guest room window and grabbed Anthony. AJ offered himself in exchange, and the badass who called you—"

"Burton?"

"Yeah. He took the guy out with one shot from under my brother's legs as he was negotiating for Anthony's safety."

Jackson grunted. "Oh my God—"

"Yeah. AJ left the next day, and Kaden was pretty sure he was heading to score. We let him drop the car off at the duplex, and then Crystal and I took him out for ice cream. You know the rest."

The roommate situation. "I think it's a good thing," he said softly. "I think it's a really good thing. You did good there, Jade. You should be proud."

"Yeah, well, you started the rescue process. Me and Kaden are just following your lead. Now, Burton couldn't tell Kaden how you got hurt. You got any stories to tell?"

Billy Bob started to knead his chest, right where the bandages sat, and Jackson gently disengaged his claws.

"Not so's you—"

"Finish that sentence, asshole. I fucking dare you."

Jackson leaned back and closed his eyes, exhaustion in every pore of his body.

And then he let go.

Jade, Kaden—they'd faced down the bad guys, and they'd done damned well. Jackson hadn't grown up alone in a shitty part of town. He and the Camerons—even Rhonda, Kaden's wife—they'd all grown up together, and they'd fought hard and fought plenty. When Jade had come to school with her hair under a hoodie to keep it out of the fight, girls all over campus had gone ducking into the bathrooms, hoping Jade wasn't after them.

So Jackson trusted her. Like he'd trusted her with AJ—and she'd come through.

"Well, it's sort of long," he said. "You want to stop for coffee and a snack on the way?"

She hit a Starbucks in Natomas. He almost fell asleep while she ran in, since they didn't have a drive-thru, and when she came back, he sipped his coffee appreciatively.

Then he quit stalling and told Jade the story of two lost fish on a road trip to the desert.

And Jade stopped bossing him around enough to listen.

He wrapped it up as she pulled into Ellery's driveway.

"Take your cat inside and I'll get the luggage," she instructed quietly.

"I can help—"

"You're going in, putting on some pajamas, and getting into bed."

Jackson yawned, his whole body hurting, and thought of the basic painkillers he'd put off taking. "Yeah, sure," he said through another yawn. "Why am I doing this?"

"So I can hang next to you and do work and have Mike bring us dinner. Baby, we came way too close to losing you again. Remember when we were dating, and we used to sit and watch TV in our pajamas?"

Just like AJ and Crystal would. Jackson smiled faintly, unexpectedly tearful. "Yeah."

"We'll do that. Mike'll let me stay in the guest room. You're not sleeping alone for a while, okay?"

"Ellery will be relieved," he rasped. He wanted to open his door, but instead he hugged Billy Bob closer.

"I hope so," she muttered. "It could be the best news he gets for a while."

Jackson heard her, and his heart sank. But he wasn't going to borrow trouble. He had a meeting with Ellery's boss the next day. He figured the least he could do was not make Jade tell him Ellery had been fired.

HE GOT inside and barely made it to the bed to nap, cursing recovery and the limits it placed on his body. When he woke up, his phone was buzzing with an unfamiliar number.

"Rivers," he mumbled.

"Oh, Jackson! Ellery told me I'd probably find you at home. I hope I didn't wake you!"

"No. Who're you?"

He heard a deep breath, the kind praying for patience. "This is Rabbi Watson. I called Ellery because I was worried—he seemed so excited about attending, but he disappeared for the next two weeks. He said you both planned to come back soon but that I might want to stop by and talk to you. I was in the neighborhood, and I was wondering if I could knock on your door."

Jackson sat bolt upright in bed so fast his middle hurt. He gave a little groan and scrubbed his face with his hand. "Define 'in the neighborhood,'" he said suspiciously, and in response, he heard a knock on the door.

"Jackson! Do you know who that is?"

"It's Ellery's rabbi! Tell him I'm dead!"

Over the phone Rabbi Watson said, "Jackson, I can still hear you."

"That's playing dirty!" Jackson accused.

Through the phone he could hear Jade trilling, "Rabbi! Come in! I'm so happy to meet you! Jackson has been telling us all about his visit to your temple."

Jackson hung up, muttering, "Suck-up." Then he grabbed his jeans off the end of the bed and hauled them on, and a sweatshirt over his T-shirt as well. He padded out to the kitchen barefoot and hoped God or whoever would forgive him.

"Jackson!" Rabbi Watson hadn't changed one bit over the last two and a half weeks. Salt-and-pepper beard, kind brown eyes, narrow face. It was almost comforting.

"Rabbi." Jackson extended his hand and shook and then indicated the table. "This is my sister, Jade Cameron. Here, I'll get us some coffee. What can I do for you?"

"I'll get you hot chocolate," Jade corrected, going through their cupboards and shooing him back to sit. "And look! Ellery has cookies— your favorite kind!"

"Where'd you get those?" Jackson asked. Ellery had a habit of producing them when Jackson was at his most depressed. Like magic.

"I'm not telling," she said. "I have the feeling they're supposed to be hidden. Now sit and talk to the man."

Jackson smiled gamely. "I'm, uh, sorry I said I was dead."

"You look like you came close to it," the rabbi said. "I hope Ellery had a better vacation than you did."

Jackson knew his face closed down, but he couldn't do anything about it. "Ellery's still in the hospital. I got out early."

Rabbi Watson looked instantly concerned, and Jackson girded himself for questions. If he'd realized he'd have to debrief twice, he would have made Jade wait.

"He didn't tell me that when he called. That must be hard," the rabbi said. "Coming home without him."

Jackson swallowed. "It's his house. I, uh, sort of moved in when my duplex got shot up, and he just… never made me leave."

"He's a good man," the rabbi said softly. "I'm sure the arrangement was to his benefit as well."

Jackson grunted. "I don't see how. He has to keep buying me cars. My cat's shredded his couch and his rug. He's in the goddamned hospital. And I freeload off him. I'm pretty sure I'm getting the best of the deal. Jade, how's that hot chocolate?"

"Still cold. Ellery loves you. Tell the nice rabbi that!"

"Ellery loves me," Jackson said with a shrug. "There's no accounting for taste."

Rabbi Watson had that familiar look about him—the one where his forehead was bunched up and his eyes were closed, and he was massaging the tight part of his forehead right between his eyebrows and his hairline.

"He said you killed two men to keep him safe."

Jackson's eyes got so wide his head started to hurt—although he'd been assured his concussion had healed completely. "Can he tell you that? Jade, can he tell the rabbi that? I thought we weren't supposed to tell people that shit!"

"I think the rabbi is one of the people you *can* tell," Jade said, coming out of the kitchen with two glasses of milk and the box of cookies. "The hot chocolate was taking too long. You're going to need some sugar for this conversation."

"I'm not hungry," he said, because why would that have gotten any better?

"Eat!" She punctuated it with a flick to the ear.

Unbidden, Jackson was hit with a memory of Jade's mother and a very different kitchen.

"Jackson, why aren't you graduating the eighth grade? Kaden says he got the paperwork, Jade got the paperwork, but you got nothing."

"I... you know." Jackson hadn't wanted to talk about this. "I can't do my homework." His mother had burned up his math book the year before when she'd been cooking her spoon, and he hadn't taken another one home. But for a moment pride reared its ugly head, and he didn't want to admit that to Jade and Kaden's mom. "Besides, Kaden knows I'm too stupid to do it anyway."

Toni Cameron had never raised a hand to him—until that moment, when she'd flicked his ear. "That right there is the only stupid thing I've heard you say. Go get Kaden's math book. And his English book. And his history book. You and me have some work to do this week, because I'm not going back to that school next year to watch you walk across the stage."

"Why aren't you hungry?" the rabbi asked, jerking Jackson's eyes from Jade, who was looking hurt and stern at the same time. Rabbi Watson took a cookie and dipped it into the milk with glee. "I mean, cookies. Why do you have such a thing against cookies?"

Jackson smiled faintly, charmed. "Cookies are the best," he said with a sigh. He took one of the cookies and dipped it into milk too. "I don't mind cookies at all. So why are you here again?"

"Eat the cookie, Jackson. Then tell me why you think Ellery might have called."

The cookie turned to ashes and sugar in his mouth. "He probably thinks I need someone to talk to," he said. "Ellery's big on being well-adjusted."

"Mm." Rabbi Watson took another cookie. "What does he think you should talk about?"

"The two dead guys, probably. And Ellery getting hurt. And...." Jackson took a deep breath. "And how much I hate hospitals. And why I can't eat. And fucking—uh, damned nightmares every night."

"They're getting worse?" Jade asked quietly from the kitchen.

"Since November," Jackson said. God—he and Ellery had traveled seven hundred miles away and tangled with forces so far beyond their control they might as well have been on Pluto. But somehow his entire life came back here, to the moment he'd seen his mother on a slab in the morgue and realized his shitty childhood could never be redeemed.

"Do you think you're going to sleep any better now?" Jade asked, leaning over the counter into the dining room. "You saw him get shot. You love this guy more than anything in the world, including your damned cat, and you saw him get shot! And more shit that's worse! Do you really want all that hanging over your head when he comes back home? Don't you think that man will have enough to deal with besides being the only goddamned pair of shoulders you are willing to lay your burdens down on?"

Jackson looked dispiritedly at the cookie currently disintegrating in his milk.

"Yeah," he said. "I think Ellery could maybe stand to haul less of my dead weight."

"So," Rabbi Watson said thoughtfully. "You are tired, and your heart is probably sore. I promise I won't overstay my welcome. Let's talk about one thing, and one thing only—for a half an hour, and then I'll take my leave, I promise. Your choice. A burden, maybe, that you could tell to me, so I can lay it at God's feet and you can live without it for a while. What do you say? One thing—and if this conversation tells me anything, it tells me you've got so very many burdens you could stand to put down. What's one thing you're willing to give up and let God take care of today, so you can heal?"

Jackson shoved the rest of the sopping cookie in his mouth and swallowed. "Hospitals," he said after a choked moment. Hell, he'd told the entire world this one, so why not do it again? "I... I freak out inside hospitals. I can't breathe there. Ellery sent me home so I could feel useful, but also to get me the hell out of the hospital so I can calm the fuck down and maybe get some sleep. So let's start with hospitals."

"Sure," said the rabbi. "One more cookie, Jackson, then tell me all about hospitals."

The first bite of the cookie helped.

By the time the half hour was up, he'd talked about being in the hospital eight years ago and eaten two more cookies, then drank a mug of Jade's hot chocolate.

The rabbi sat there and listened kindly, pretending not to see how hard every word was. Pretending not to see Jackson's eyes grow red and shiny.

Just when Jackson was about to pretend he heard a burglar outside so he could run the fuck away, the rabbi said, "Oh my—you're a good storyteller, Jackson. Thank you so much for talking to me."

"Yeah, sure," Jackson mumbled.

"Would you like to stay for dinner?" Jade asked excitedly. "My boyfriend is bringing stew, and he's a pretty good cook."

"That's a kind offer," the rabbi said. "But my wife is waiting at home. Perhaps next time I stop by—next week, at this time?"

"I might have work," Jackson told him reluctantly. It seemed rude, somehow, to refuse. He might feel gutted right now, and like he could go back to sleep for a week, but the man had been damned human to sit and listen to Jackson—and Jade, who interjected with facts and her own worries and clarifications like "Your entire fucking insides were on the operating table, Jackson. You're a damned lucky jigsaw puzzle is what you are!" Jackson didn't feel like he could tell him no.

"Well then, how about after dinner. We'll make it a plan, and then, after you and Ellery come to temple again, we can revisit when I come by."

"Uh… sure. Uh, I, uh, told Ellery I'd come in this time."

"So I heard." Rabbi Watson smiled slightly under his beard. "What changed your mind?"

"I asked God to save Ellery's life, and Ellery's still breathing."

To his surprise Rabbi Watson sighed. "You know, sometimes that's luck and science and not God."

Jackson shrugged. "Luck and science don't do me any favors. I'm going to call this one a miracle and take the win."

The rabbi smiled then, wide and beautiful, as pure as a child. "That sounds reasonable." He shook Jackson's hand. "You're a good man, Jackson Rivers. Don't worry about picking up the burden we talked about today. God can keep it for as long as you trust him to have it."

And then he gave Jackson a hug, a long, warm, human hug, and took his leave. When he was gone, Jackson sank into the kitchen chair like a deflated balloon.

"Jade?"

"Yeah?"

"Can I go watch cartoons or something?"

"Yeah, baby. I'll join you. I'd be beat too if I had to do what you just did. Do you want to call Ellery?"

"No. That involves words."

"Gotcha. Go."

But as Jackson stared blankly at the television, his cat in his lap, he realized that he felt lighter. For the first time in over a week, he could breathe.

Well, damn. That laying down your burdens thing really worked. Unbidden he felt a couple of tears fall, and he wiped them away.

Healing apparently came with a price.

But he was so ready to pony up. Anything to be able to sit in this house with Ellery again and not be Ellery's burden to bear.

HE FELL asleep on Jade, and she fell asleep on Mike as they watched *This is Us* on television. He woke up because Mike was sniffling, and for a moment Jackson wondered who died.

"Mike… are you crying? Over the TV?"

Mike had white hair and an ageless face. He shot Jackson an annoyed look through sky-blue Virginia farm-boy eyes. "You know, I didn't think a girl's soap opera would ever get to me—used to make fun of Jade for watching *Grey's Anatomy*, you know? But… but this one does." He looked down at Jade, soft and vulnerable in sleep against his side like she never was awake. "I think it's because I've got my own family now. The kind that doesn't look like it should go together but it does."

Jackson smiled a little. Jade and Mike had fought for years before they'd gotten together. Mike was too backwoods, Jade was too militant. He wondered which one of them had laid down *their* burden first.

But that was a personal thing—it was an interaction that belonged only to the two of them.

"That's good," he said, wiggling to sit up. He hurt. He needed to take his ibuprofen and go stretch out in his own bed. "I appreciated the stew tonight. Leave the dishes in the sink and—"

"And the love of my life will cut off my balls in the morning," Mike replied matter-of-factly. "No. I'll clean up and go home. I'd stay here, but Albert's more high-strung than ever. He'll drive the neighbors batshit."

"Does he still hate the boys next door?" Jackson's little halfway house was a place of redemption for Jackson's boys, but a bunch of strange men to Albert's sensitive German shepherd nose.

"They started bribing him with hamburger. I think he's taking a shine."

Jackson laughed quietly. "Tell him Billy Bob says hi." Billy Bob and Albert had been bosom fuck-buddies and beloved antagonists when they'd been neighbors. Jackson missed Mike's companionship. He didn't always say the right thing, but his heart was almost always in the right place.

"I'll do that, kid." Mike let out a sigh and looked at him over Jade's sleeping form. "Kid, I'll tell you something. You want to know why I watch things that make me cry? You *really* want to know?"

Jackson swallowed. "Sure."

"Because sometimes, when I'm worried about something that's really important, the TV makes me cry so I don't have to cry over somebody or something that would laugh at me for crying."

Jackson took a moment to parse that, and Mike just rumbled straight on.

"I'm watching this show because I keep asking myself how awful it would have been if you hadn't come back from wherever the hell you went, and that makes me want to fucking cry. So I watch the show so I can get rid of all the fucking tears and be glad you made it back."

Jackson swallowed. "I'm... I don't know what to do with that," he admitted. "I was terrified when I thought people might come hurt you and Jade."

"Yeah. I know it. But me and Jade can take care of ourselves. Every time you go out on one of these adventures, you come back looking worse."

Jackson let out a sigh. "I'm trying to fix myself," he admitted. "I...." He looked around Ellery's house. "I'd really like to not break Ellery in the process."

Mike nodded. "Good. That's a place to start. Get some sleep, kid—you look like shit."

"Thanks for dinner and coming over tonight."

Mike waved him off. "Your boyfriend has the biggest fucking TV of anybody I know. It's like getting your pain in stereo. Glorious way to watch this fuckin' show."

Jackson chuckled and stumbled off to bed, making sure to hook the phone to the charger before he fell asleep.

HE FELT the dream coming, but he was too tired to wake up and too raw to wait it out. Real and visceral, he sat in a tiny black box, watching his family move farther and farther away from him through the walls, calling his name while they searched.

And the box he was in just got smaller and smaller and smaller, and nobody could hear him scream.

"Jackson? Honey? Wake up! You're okay!"

Jade's hand on his shoulder grounded him, and he fought to get his breathing under control.

"Yeah," he gasped. "Okay. I'm fine." Was Ellery having bad dreams? Ellery had been in this one, freaking the fuck out because he couldn't see Jackson. Jackson reached for the phone before he even knew who he was calling.

"Calling him?" Jade asked softly.

"Promised," Jackson mumbled. "Stay here a minute."

"Yeah. Sure."

He felt the other side of the bed depress, but he kept his back turned. He didn't want to look over there and see someone who wasn't Ellery.

You up? he texted.

His phone rang. "Bad?" Ellery sounded loopy, and Jackson wondered if he'd just turned his phone volume up to maximum so he'd hear the ping.

"Not great. You sicced the rabbi on me."

"And yet you're still talking to me."

Jackson grunted. "You made me promise."

"You didn't call earlier—mad?"

Oh. No. "No fucking words left," Jackson muttered. "I don't know what to tell you. He came, he talked, I was wiped out."

"I'm sorry." Ellery didn't say that usually. Not when he was being a Machiavellian asshole. "Not that I did it. Just that it was hard."

Here, in the dark of the night, Jade settling in under the covers at his back, Jackson felt like he should tell the truth. "I want to be less of a pain in the ass for you."

And Ellery's filthy chuckle—of *all* things—reassured him. "God willing, you'll always be a pain in my ass."

Jackson's laugh was raw and soft—but it was still a laugh. "I'll do my best—since you like it and all. Pervert."

"There's my grown-up middle-schooler. What're you doing tomorrow?"

"Laptops and talking to bosses."

"Sounds like fun. Don't overdo it—you're still recovering."

Jackson let out a soft groan. "You are telling *me*. God, when did this shit get so hard? I came home and slept and then woke up and talked to the rabbi and slept and then got up and went to bed and slept some more. I'm about to become the most boring person in history, I swear."

"You ever think this is the sleep you should have gotten over the last two months but you couldn't?" Ellery asked soberly. "Take advantage of it. You'll be pushing to be back at full speed soon enough."

Jackson grunted. "Gotta admit—I feel like the gods owe us a little. I want a week when we both feel great and we can go on a real vacation and fuck like lemmings."

"That's it," Jade muttered. "You don't need me here. I'm going to my own bed."

Jackson turned gingerly. "Thanks, sweetheart. I appreciate it."

Jade stood, looking absurdly old-fashioned in a winter-weight white flannel gown, glowing like the moon against her skin. "Tell him I'll stay here until he gets back. They really have gotten worse, Jackson. It's going to take a lot more talks with the rabbi and a lot more vacations to fix it."

She left, and Billy Bob jumped back onto the pillow she'd vacated.

"Did you hear that?" Jackson asked soberly.

"I did. That's okay. You let the rabbi in, you talked to him—lots of good for one day, you think?"

"Yeah, sure. Any of the nurses there hot?"

"Nice change of subject, and no. You met them all when you were here. They have not substituted any young hot nurses of either gender just because you've flown the coop."

"That's a disappointment. I was hoping to live vicariously through you."

Ellery laughed softly, and they bantered a little bit more. No big revelations, nothing heavy. But Jackson had called and Ellery had been there, and this time when Jackson fell asleep, he was pretty sure he'd stay that way until his bladder woke him up in the morning.

THE NEXT morning, standing in the tasteful, cream-painted, blond-paneled offices of Pfeist, Harrelson, Langdon, and Cooper, Jackson actually had a moment when he wondered if he'd woken up at all.

"I'm sorry," he said, blinking hard. "You're going to need to repeat that."

Carlyle Langdon, Ellery's immediate superior, smiled genially. He was usually a good guy—tall, elegant, silver-haired, blue-eyed. He looked and acted the part of the seasoned professional, good at glad-handing, so competent at his job he made it look effortless.

Right now he was sweating, tiny glistening drops of perspiration on his high forehead that rode his tanned, moisturized perfect skin like little marble tiles.

"I was just saying that while I know you and Mr. Cramer are, uh, close, I hope there's no hard feelings here. Mr. Cramer's activities in pursuit of the real criminal in the Janie Isaacson case made our government very uncomfortable, and he's become a liability. I can't authorize another laptop for him—"

"I bought him a laptop. I just need the pass codes." Jackson knew what Langdon was saying—had even anticipated it. But hearing it out loud was a slap in the face.

Ellery was so very, very proud of his job.

"I can't authorize those either." Langdon swallowed uncomfortably. "It's… it's my understanding that there's a majority—the other three partners will be asking Mr. Cramer to resign."

"Resign."

"With two years' salary, full benefits package, and glowing letters of reference, of course."

"Resign."

"As soon as he's back after a fully paid medical leave."

"Hunh."

"We've taken on all the rest of his cases. Ms. Isaacson's case has been dropped, and she's been hired back by the family, if that's any consolation."

It wasn't, really. "He's given his heart and soul to this firm," Jackson said, shaking. So had Jackson, for that matter. Jackson had gotten this job right after he'd gotten his PI's license. Carlyle Langdon and Murray Pfeist had been the first people to believe in him after the force turned its back.

But Jackson would fucking cut them all for doing this to Ellery.

"I've gone on record with my objections," Langdon said, sinking dispiritedly into his office chair. "But you've done some very fine work here, Jackson. There's no reason for you to leave the firm. You and Ms. Cameron are valued employees, and Mr. Cramer will land on his feet."

Jackson had to swallow hard against the ball of rage in his chest. "So you're firing Ellery, but you want me to stay."

Langdon smiled weakly, like he expected Jackson to explode or kick something or act violently. "We were hoping so, yes. I know you're still recovering from a concussion—"

Jackson lifted his shirt, viciously grateful that his stitches hadn't been removed yet. "And a stabbing, sir. Ellery's mother told you he was in the hospital. Did she tell you why?"

"A shooting—"

"The person we were investigating for the vehicular murder that was pinned on Janie Isaacson shot him. I was there. I shot him back. The pressure—the people Ellery has offended—are defending the guy who shot Ellery, and that guy is also, coincidentally, the scumbag who trained the scumbag that tried to kill us both."

Carlyle Langdon closed his eyes. "Jackson—you've got almost seven years here—"

"And this job was my life. I know—"

"Just think about it," Langdon said quietly, resting his head on his hands. He looked defeated, and Jackson couldn't blame him.

Jackson knew how he felt. "If you'll excuse me," he said, "I've got some things to do in my office."

Langdon nodded and gestured weakly. "Please. Just—"

"Thinking," Jackson said sweetly. Because this wasn't the man he wanted to offend.

JADE LOOKED up from her desk as he walked down the hall. "So?" she asked tentatively.

"Do you have a Sharpie?"

"What color?"

"Black, but maybe some neon ones too, for effect."

Her eyebrows went up. "Because…."

"I'll show you in our office."

He kept walking, and she caught up to him in the hallway, a bouquet of permanent markers in her hand.

"Jackson, what are you going to—" He closed the door and started to take off his pants. "Do? We don't do that anymore, right?"

"No, we're not doing that anymore," he muttered, bending over his desk. "I want you to write, 'I quit, you cowardly fuckwads' across my ass and take a picture of it."

She paused for a moment, and he looked over his shoulder to see her assessing his backside skeptically.

"You can't talk me out of it," he told her. "They're firing Ellery—"

"I figured," she said, not sounding surprised or even like she was going to talk him out of it. "I just don't think it will fit across your scrawny ass. I mean, you might get 'I' on one cheek and 'quit' on the other, but you need more room for the whole message. Pull up your pants and wait here."

He stood and watched her go before buttoning his jeans. He took the moment she was gone to grab a file carton and start throwing his few possessions into the box. Unhappily, he looked at Ellery's side of the room and fought against the tightness in his throat.

Ellery's desk chair, his desk—technically those all belonged to the firm. But he had law books—well thumbed—and awards and certificates on the wall. Jackson started there instead, because being kind to Ellery's things kept him from trashing the place.

His hands were still shaking with rage.

He'd gotten most of the plaques from the walls before Jade walked in with Crystal behind her.

"Good idea," Crystal said. "Let's get his stuff first so you can carry the boxes on your way out. I'll call AJ."

"Uh—"

But Crystal was already helping Jackson pack. Between the three of them, it took about fifteen minutes, and by the time they were done, there was a knock on the door.

"Come in, AJ," Crystal said, hushed excitement in her voice. "They're about to take off their clothes."

Jackson stared at her. "We are not shooting porn in Ellery's office."

"As. If." Jade rolled her eyes. "But just like I told you, right?" she asked Crystal. "Here's the Sharpies. AJ, embellish. If my ass is going on film, it had better be tight, hot, and flashy."

Jackson looked at her. "You are not—"

"Yes I am."

"You love this job."

She paused with a look of tenderness in her eyes. "I do. But I can do it somewhere else. Besides—you know Ellery is going to start his own firm, and I want to be on the ground floor of that shit. Imagine what I can do in an office with a little bit of power."

Jackson tried to talk her out of it. There was no guarantee Ellery would start his own firm. There was no guarantee she could get another job. God, there was no guarantee *Jackson* could get his own job.

But in the end it boiled down to the two of them, bent over Ellery's desk while AJ and Crystal decorated their backsides and commented on how good their body wash smelled. After the tickle of the Sharpies, Crystal backed up. "Okay, guys—turn your heads so we know who 'we' is. That's it—there, what do you think?"

Jackson pulled up his pants and did his belt while Jade wrestled with her pantyhose. Then they both looked at the picture on Crystal's phone.

"Not bad," he assessed. "The gold and silver foil looks really good on Jade's skin. Especially the lightning bolts around 'fuckwads.'"

"And your ass isn't that furry," Jade said, "so the neon really pops. Well done, guys." She smiled at AJ and Crystal. "I like it. In fact, I like it so much, I think we should make copies. What do you think, Jackson?"

He stared back. "What are we going to do with copies?"

"Well, Mike will want one for sure—and I think you and Ellery will want one framed for the new office. Don't worry—I'll take care of it. Kaden gets a framed one too. Birthdays, Christmases, it's the gift that keeps on giving."

"Righteous," AJ said proudly. "I can have them on all the walls of the office before you guys hit the street with your stuff."

Jackson had to smile. "Crystal, you keep your nose clean, okay? I mean, I sort of need you here."

She kissed his cheek. "Just until Ellery can afford me," she said, sounding certain.

Jackson wondered how he was going to tell Ellery that people seemed to expect them to start a business, but he couldn't squash on his friends with his worry after what they'd just helped him do.

"Go make the copies," he said. "Jade and I can sign the one we give to Pfeist, Harrelson, and Cooper."

"I'm gonna deliver those by hand," Jade said with a snort. "Best day of my professional life."

Sure.

AN HOUR later Jade was at the wheel, and all Ellery's stuff was shoved in the back of the SUV. Jackson's body hurt, bad enough that his hands shook as he fished his painkillers out of his pocket and washed them down with the soda he'd made Jade get as they rounded Howe.

"You look like shit," she said quietly. "You okay?"

"I can't believe we did that," he said, smiling for her benefit.

"I think Langdon thought you were going to go ballistic. He was lucky you're still recovering or there might have been property damage."

That got a laugh. "I really am pissed," he said, pondering. "I... I mean, you and me, we grew up knowing life wasn't fair. Ellery's just always... you know...."

"Believed the system worked?"

"Yeah."

"Hunh." Jade chewed her lip, absentmindedly getting a bit of mayo leftover from her hastily eaten sandwich. "You say that, but, you know, he could have picked corporate law, right?"

Jackson thought about it. "Well, yeah—"

"Those corporate law guys make a fuckton. And they don't get called in for pro bono at the prison once a month. I mean, yeah. A lot of criminal defense is wading in the slime bucket, but remember our system, Jackson. A lot of rich people made that slime bucket and are afraid of getting their toes dirty. I think Ellery knows exactly what's wrong with the system."

"I just didn't want my own slime to touch him."

Jade let out a breath. "You ever think that Ellery sees the goodness under the guy with the scrawny ass?"

"Well, it's certainly not my stunning technique in bed," Jackson said bitterly. "Not after the last two weeks."

She laughed then, like he'd meant her to, and then his phone buzzed, effectively ending the conversation.

"Hey, Ellery, what's up?"

"...."

"Ellery? Are you there?"

He distinctly recognized the sound of Ellery's indrawn breath when he was trying to hold on to his temper.

"Is there something you maybe wanted to tell me?" Ellery asked sweetly. "About work?"

"Uhm… I'm sorry, man. They're going to let you go. Two years severance, benefits—Langdon said he was waiting for after you got released from the hospital."

"Oh." The syllable carried a weight of surprised hurt in it. "I assume they were going to ask me to resign?"

"Yeah. Bullshit, but—"

"No, no. The severance package is more than generous. The benefits too. And two years salary is more than I would have asked for myself. They were getting pressure from someone?"

"The government?" Jackson was guessing at this point. "I guess Lacey still had friends."

He could hear Ellery's swallow. "Oh. Well, then—"

And Jackson felt awful. "I'm sorry, man. I was going to tell you when I came to pick you up. I didn't want to do it over the phone. I just… wait a minute. You didn't know. If you didn't know about getting fired, what were you calling about?"

"I was calling about you quitting!"

Jackson looked at Jade. "How did he know?"

She shrugged. "We were trying to get out of there before they opened the letter. I got no idea."

"Ellery, who told you? Crystal? AJ? Who? Mike doesn't even know! I mean, we haven't even gotten home with your stuff."

Ellery started to chuckle, and while the sound was strained, it was also whole and unbroken. "The internet, asshole. Pictures of your resignation letter blew up the fucking internet. That intern of Harrelson's who's always ogling your ass posted it on her feed, and she's got, like, two hundred likes by now. It's going viral."

Jackson tried not to boggle. "Jade, our asses are on the internet."

Her laugh was downright evil. "That is *tremendous*. Think we'll go viral?"

"Jade wants us to go viral," Jackson told him.

"Well, you're well on your way." Ellery's laughter had faded, and Jackson could feel his hurt from seven hundred miles away.

"I'm sorry," he said quietly. "I… you're so proud of your job. I just… I couldn't work for them anymore if they were going to do that to you."

"I get that," Ellery said, holding his voice together with an obvious effort. "Why did Jade quit?"

"We couldn't fit the whole message on my ass. I've lost too much weight."

Ellery's laugh bordered on hysteria now. "Well, you could have left off the term 'fuckwads,' but they might have had to write 'cowards' on your balls, and that just wouldn't do. Seriously. Why'd she quit too?"

Jackson looked at her, driving confidently, loyal as a pit bull, beautiful like a goddess. They couldn't let her down.

"She seems to think we're starting our own firm," he said, hoping for the best.

"Hunh."

"That's my word."

"I can use it."

"That's fine." Jackson was getting irritated. "What does it mean when you use it?"

"It means I was thinking about it already, but, you know, we were in the middle of things. I mean, Mother's been looking at properties, and I probably would have drawn up a business plan by next year."

"Hunh." Jackson's brain went kablooey.

"You didn't think about it? I mean, all those times you ran down an alibi and came back and said, 'Yeah, our guy totally did it, but the alibi will hold up if that's the way you want to go.' I knew what you were thinking."

"The criminals were less scummy than we were?" Because yeah, that's what he'd been thinking.

"That you wanted a choice. You wanted to say, 'Yes, we'll represent this person,' or 'Let's represent the guy who got pulled in on a pocket full of X and is about to get sentenced to life instead.'"

"You do what the man tells you," Jackson said numbly.

"Well, now we're the man. How's that feel?"

"Terrifying. How are you even imagining this from a hospital bed?"

Ellery chuckled weakly. "It's exhausting, frankly. We can hammer out details later."

Jackson felt the moment his painkillers kicked in, and he yawned, about in the same place. "I'm all for that. Text me when you wake up."

"Sure. Call me tonight."

"Sure."

"And I want one of those pictures. It'll go up in the new office."

Jackson guffawed. He couldn't help it. "Dude, Jade nailed that one. She stopped for a frame on our way out of town."

"Excellent," Ellery said grandly. "Put it up in the living room. And have one made for my mother. I think she'll put it up with the grandkids."

"Now I know you're stoned. Go to sleep, Counselor."

"I love you, Jackson. Good job on not torching the place and pissing on the ashes."

And Jackson was vulnerable enough to be honest. "That shit takes energy. God, I hurt."

"Saying that takes courage. Way better than the flashy exit. And the resignation letter is so much classier and more photogenic. Call me tonight if things get hairy."

"I promise."

"And I'm not talking about your ass—it's scary how smooth it is, you know that, right?"

"I've been told. Get some sleep." Jackson hung up just as Jade pulled into the driveway.

"Go inside," she ordered. "I'll have Mike unload. God, those boxes of books were heavy."

"Sure." Jackson wasn't going to argue. Not after what they'd just done together. "Jade?"

"Yeah?"

"I love you. Like, without reservation. I'd die for you. Ellery knows it too. Just… you know. If I never come back from one of these little adventures, I just thought I should say it out loud."

Her eyes welled up. "I love you too. But you know, you've got to be more responsible now. You've got a business to run."

Jackson smiled and dragged his sorry ass off to bed. He had one more day to sleep before he flew down to get Ellery, and for once, being told to rest didn't sound like a death sentence.

It was like he had something to look forward to if he got better.

Planning the New Pond

ELLERY'S FATHER left for his flight about an hour before Jackson arrived at the hospital.

"You'll be okay?" he asked, his eyes crinkling in the corners like they did when he was concerned.

"Yeah, Papa." Ellery swallowed—it was what he'd called his father as a child, because the endearment, classic and a little old-fashioned, just seemed to fit his father so well. "Yeah, Dad. Thanks for coming out. It would have been a shitty week without you."

Sid kissed his cheek and hugged him. "Wasn't going to be a walk in the park either way," he said before taking a step back. "It's good that Jackson left. You got to rest up, and he got to remember he could do it alone—but it wasn't so much fun."

Ellery grinned. "We do have fun," he said, although he'd never tell Jackson that all their bickering was fun. Jackson was just perverse enough to stop if he knew.

"He'll be okay," Sid Cramer said softly. "He loves you—it's like nothing I've seen before, how that boy looks at you. He'll find a way to make it work."

Ellery nodded and smiled, biting his lip. "Mother will be very disappointed if I end up with somebody else."

His father chuckled. "Indeed she will. I don't know if she's ever met her match in stubbornness before. She almost loves him more than she loves you." He winked. "Almost."

Ellery was pretty sure he and Jackson were neck and neck in his mother's affections. God knows, Jackson had exasperated them both to the point of fury on more than one occasion, and that only happened to somebody you really cared about.

His father hugged him one more time and went downstairs to catch his cab, leaving Ellery alone in the hospital room with his paperwork and the suitcase Ace had brought from the Infiniti, looking more the worse for the wear.

He had no emails to catch up on, no briefs, no cases.

For a moment he felt sheer, unadulterated panic, but when he hauled in a gasp of air, his body reminded him that he was barely ready to go out into the big wide world.

He settled back into the bed, since it was there, and pulled up a mystery suspense novel on his phone. There would be worrying and planning and frantic activity later, he was sure of it.

Right now he had peace, and the man he loved was coming to get him, and he was going to relax.

Jackson woke him up gently, shaking his shoulder and kissing his temple. "C'mon, sleeping beauty, you're going to turn into a pumpkin if you keep snoring like that."

Ellery scowled at him. "I don't snore."

"You were just now. I leave you for a few days and you pick up bad habits."

Ellery swung his legs around stiffly and let Jackson help him stand. "Then don't leave," he said shortly. "I mean, it was great that you got a chance to moon our former company without me to intervene, but seriously, it's like you can't be left unsuper—"

Jackson kissed him firmly, cupping the back of his head and holding him still, and Ellery simply melted into his touch.

"Mm...."

"Yeah." Jackson wrapped his arms around Ellery's shoulders and pulled him in—again, not too rough but firmly, like he was letting Ellery know he wasn't going anywhere.

"I missed this," Ellery sighed.

"Like water and sunshine," Jackson agreed. "God, Counselor, there really oughtta be a law that we can't split up, even for a few days."

"I'll write one up," Ellery mumbled against his chest. "We'll sign it, it'll be unbreakable. God, I want to go home."

Jackson's chest rumbled against his. "Well, good—wait until you see our ride!"

Ellery squinted as they drew near the SUV. "This is the Infiniti?"

Sonny had gone all out. He'd reinforced the frame like it was a race car, added bulletproof tinted glass on the sides and back, added a roll bar over the front of the vehicle, adjusted the suspension, and added big off-road-certified tires.

"Yup."

He'd also painted it oyster gray, with just a tint of blue in the mix.

"It looks like a tank."

Jackson grinned. "I knew you'd like it!"

"Everybody in town will notice this car!" Ellery said, a little horrified. He'd gotten Jackson's first CR-V in the hopes that *nobody* would notice the car because *everybody* had one. Jackson was a private detective, for sweet Christ's sake!

Jackson shrugged. "Yup. And it'll drink gas like it's water. I'm thinking I should probably use some of my savings to buy a used Honda as a second vehicle. But you gotta admit, this thing's safe."

He threw the luggage in the back, and Ellery used the handy new running board to heave himself up into the seat. The interior had been redone—not leather, but that stain-resistant fabric most cars had these days. As much as Ellery had appreciated the leather, he had to admit Jackson was probably more comfortable this way.

The rest of the interior looked… stripped down, somehow. Like it was missing panels here and there that weren't necessary but made car interiors look less like the inside of rolling tin cans.

But there were still cup holders, an island in the middle, and interior lights, so Ellery figured it was probably streetworthy.

Sonny and Ace would know.

Oh! And the seat belts were extra special race-webbing across the chest with three buckles on the side.

"This is… inconvenient," Ellery muttered.

"There's suicide lap belts for short trips," Jackson told him in complete seriousness. "But our next stop is in two hours to pee, so it's best to buckle up the whole enchilada."

Ellery chuckled and did as requested and then sighed. "The seats seem way more comfortable. How is that possible?"

Jackson chuckled too. "I got no idea, but right? And oh my God— purrs like a kitten. I mean, it's a little louder inside because they removed some of the insulation, but seriously, this is as quiet as I've ever heard an engine. I don't know what this thing's destiny is, but I'm thinking it's not going to be just another Jackson Rivers vehicle casualty, you know what I'm saying?"

Ellery grinned at him, because he was as excited as a child. "I do," he said quietly. "Can't wait to see what it does on the open road."

Jackson's laugh was as free as he'd heard it, even before the Kaden Cameron case, when Jackson was cool and detached and out of Ellery Cramer's league.

For a moment driving felt like an adventure, and everything was in their grasp.

Three hours later, just on the other side of Bakersfield, Ellery wasn't sure he could even get out of the car if he had to.

"Jackson?" he said weakly, calling uncle.

"You hurt too?" Jackson swung the car into the nearest off-ramp, where a circle of moderately priced hotels stood like beacons to the lonely.

"God, yes! Why didn't you say anything?" Ellery dug out his painkillers and grabbed the mineral water Jackson had brought for him to wash it down.

"If you could do it, I wanted to get home, but Jesus, between the flight and the drive—even when I was a passenger after Ace picked me up. God, either we're getting old or—"

"Or we almost died," Ellery said sourly. "The Holiday Inn Express looks like the best one. Can Jade take care of the cat?"

"I'll text her. She might even bring Albert over so those two lovebirds can reunite."

Ellery grunted. The last time Jade had done that, Billy Bob had broken every vase on his mantel. "Terrific." He sighed as Jackson pulled up in front of the lobby. Wasn't home, not yet, but it was sanctuary for a little while.

Twenty minutes later Jackson had him propped up on the pillows in the bed, watching something mindless with lots of explosions on television. Jackson ran around, situating their clothes, their toiletries—things Ellery would do but he'd never seen Jackson do, not once, when they'd been in a hotel room together.

"Stop fussing," Ellery muttered. "Bring me my water and your soda and come sit next to me. God, Jackson, I just want to touch you."

Jackson stuck his head around from the bathroom. "Pervert," he said. "I mean, seriously—all the super-hard shit we've done, and it all comes down to a grope in a cheap hotel."

"You're hysterical. Get over here. Now!"

He did, stretching out so his head was near Ellery's chest and his arm was thrown over Ellery's hips, far away from any of the surgery stitches or the soreness.

"Did you take your own pain meds?" Ellery asked through a yawn.

"Yep." Jackson yawned too. "God, you feel good."

"Then why aren't you touching me?" Ellery had scars now. Bad ones. He'd stared at his pale abdomen for ten minutes in the mirror that morning, wondering if Jackson would see the damage and not the man.

"I'm afraid of hurting you," Jackson told him. "It's still tender. I mean, mine's still tender, and yours is worse. Don't worry. I still want you—did you think that was going to change?"

Ellery half laughed. "You think I don't worry sometimes too?"

Jackson lowered his head and kissed the bare strip of skin between Ellery's sweatshirt and the waistband of his sweats. "Please don't," he murmured, placing another kiss right below Ellery's navel. Ellery moaned a little at the extravagance of kisses on his body. "My damage is my damage, but you... you're still... well, bossy and persnickety and sort of prissy and...." He punctuated the list with little kisses, delicate and tender, as he pulled Ellery's sweats down inch by inch.

"Do I still have a stick up my ass?" Ellery asked dreamily, reminding them both of Jackson's assessment when they'd first began to explore their attraction.

"Nope." Jackson's wicked, wicked tongue darted under the waistband of Ellery's boxers, almost grazing the head of Ellery's cock. "Not enough room in your tight ass after I fucked it."

"Nungh...." Maybe it was the dirty word, or Jackson's breath on Ellery's head—or even the painkillers that had just kicked in, which was sort of a buzz right there—but Ellery was suddenly swelling softly, tingling and heavy with arousal.

"You want I should suck your cock?" Jackson breathed. "I mean, I'm pretty sure fucking's out, but this, I think I can do."

"Oh God, yes." Ellery parted his legs and arched his hips just a tiny bit so Jackson could slide his sweats and boxers down. He was left erect, cock pale in its thatch of dark hair, while Jackson teased the holy hell out of him. Breath, lips, tongue, the barest edge of teeth—all of Jackson's seduction and expertise were in full force as he brought Ellery up, up, up with a minimum of pressure or jostling—with a minimum of pain.

Ellery was moaning quietly, so grateful for the attention, for Jackson's touch, for his mouth, that when Jackson engulfed him completely, hot, wet, and hard, he spilled without thought in a climax so gentle and easy, it was almost like physical therapy for his abused muscles rather than sex.

"Mm...."

Jackson pulled up his shorts and sweats, then inched up the bed. He reached around his back and pulled out a quilt that usually lived on their couch at home that he used to cover both of them.

"This is nice," Ellery murmured, settling down into the snuggle with Jackson's head next to his on the pillows. "What made you think to bring this?"

"Just... you know. Same reason I brought a change of clothes and my shaving kit. In case we couldn't make it back today. I wanted home with us."

Tears prickled behind Ellery's eyes. "I'm going to say the cornball thing here. You ready for it?"

"Shoot," Jackson told him and then giggled, obviously teetering on the edge of his own exhausted nap. "I mean, go ahead. I'm fucking done with shooting for a while."

"You are my home. Do you need to throw up?"

Jackson giggled some more. "If I did, at least I'd know you wouldn't run away screaming."

"I can hardly move to call for takeout," Ellery muttered, "but no, I'm pretty sure I proved that."

"I ordered takeout on my phone while you were whining at me to come snuggle," Jackson said with a yawn. "It'll be here in two hours, because I was pretty sure there'd be sleep first."

"Oh God." Ellery yawned too. "You're turning into me."

Jackson kissed his cheek. "Now you're being mean."

They both settled into their recovery naps, but Ellery had a moment between sleeping and waking when he saw the near future.

Tomorrow they'd drive home and talk this time, planning where they wanted their office, what they wanted their mission statement to say, how they would advertise, how to apply for their business license. Ellery would look into partners, sending out feelers, seeing if he could get a line on anyone else he'd care to practice law with or, at the very least, someone who would want to open a law practice in the same building. They would plan for the future, looking at budgets and time and the things they wanted to do versus the things they swore they'd never do.

They'd get the jackets on the dangerous men let into the world—they'd spend their free time looking for clues to help Burton get them out.

In the meantime they'd set about making the world a better place for the Janie Isaacsons of the world, the Ace Atchisons and Sonny Dayes.

The Kaden Camerons or Anthony Coopers or Jacksons.

They'd be grateful for each other and their family every day.

They'd have new adventures, hopefully ones not quite as scary or as painful as this one had been.

They'd grow. Together.

"Jackson?"

"Mm?"

"You ready for us to have our own business?"

"Sure. But only because you're the man."

Ellery laughed a little and slid under.

They had so much more to do.

Cooking Filet of Soul

This is a short ficlet from my blog that covers the Thanksgiving before the events in this book.

JACKSON STARTED out Thanksgiving morning curled up on the corner of the gigantic white couch in Ellery's mother's sitting room. Ellery had woken him up in time for a brisk walk around the block; then they'd gotten back to the absurdly large house in the prestigious Boston neighborhood and showered.

Not together. Because Ellery's entire family was sleeping somewhere in this giant old rabbit warren of a house, and Jackson wasn't sure if his dick would ever work again. Instead, Jackson had sent Ellery ahead and told him to start breakfast, but Jackson wasn't feeling hungry.

He hadn't felt hungry, in fact, since he'd gotten out of the hospital, really. Food—one of his most favorite things in the world—had lost its appeal in the last two weeks, and given that he'd gotten out right before Thanksgiving, his life had turned into a long boring game of pushing food around the plate and trying to convince people he was stuffed.

He wasn't stuffed. He didn't want to be stuffed. He was afraid. There was a feeling in the hospital, of the entire concrete building pressing against his chest, of being trapped underneath it and not being able to breathe. He was afraid if he ate too much, he'd feel like that.

He'd eaten while he was there and enjoyed it. But food or no food, that oppression would squash him against the bed, so he might as well eat.

But out of the hospital….

It was irrational.

Jackson knew it.

He didn't want to tell anybody.

Ellery and his entire family were rational as fuck. It was almost creepy. Ellery's sister Rebekah was there, along with her husband Ira and their two adorable, terrifyingly well-behaved children. They sat at the breakfast table and weighed the pros and cons of going out to play in the cold, or staying inside and getting a beneficial amount of exercise from the video game their grandmother provided, or, possibly, having an obliging adult drive them to the mall so they could trot down all the corridors of the mall, which, they'd estimated, were a full mile if walked front to back, twice.

And those were the children.

Ellery's mother and father actually discussed the sodium content of turkey and the amount of water that was necessary to preclude any bloating in the extremities after that much salt.

Jackson couldn't face them. He told Ellery he'd meet him downstairs, put on his sweats, and made his way to the sitting room, which was sort of out of the way. Jackson snagged the remote and would have clicked for a game, figuring nobody in this household would actually watch football, but it was too early. He found the parade instead, mildly surprised that he was watching it in real time. He was there, ducking his head below the back of the couch, when Ellery's father found him.

Mr. Cramer (Jackson wasn't sure what his first name was. Everybody but Jackson called him "Dad" or "Daddy") was a lanky man with curly gray hair around his head like a halo. He had a knife-blade nose much like his son's, and lower cheekbones, with a firm chin and sort of an average jawline. He didn't look like a Marine or a scientist or someone who led armies.

He looked like a children's book writer, or maybe a lawyer—which he was—and a father. The father thing seemed to be his favorite.

"Oh! The parade! How wonderful!"

Jackson gave him a sideways look and nodded. "I enjoy it," he said quietly. He and Jade and Kaden used to wake up early on Thanksgiving to see it. Jackson kept memories like that to himself, though. He wasn't sure how much Ellery's parents and family knew about him. He was used to wearing his past on his sleeve, proudly, almost offensively so.

But these were Ellery's parents. He couldn't offend them. He was terrified of that happening.

"Well, excellent. I'll be right back, then."

Mr. Cramer disappeared, and Jackson let himself be absorbed back into the couch.

"WELL?" ELLERY demanded when his father came into the kitchen.

"Let me bring out some food," Sid Cramer said patiently. "We'll just sit and eat together. No pressure."

"Can the kids come and watch the parade?" Rebekah asked, looking at her perfect children to make sure that was all right. Both kids nodded back soberly, and Ellery grimaced at his dad.

Jackson had put on a good face about the kids, but Ellery could tell—sometimes he'd open his mouth to be real, to finally say something not excruciatingly nice and terrifyingly polite in front of Ellery's family, and one of the kids would come in. Jackson's eyes would get big and he'd clamp his mouth shut.

It was silly—Jackson had a niece and nephew back home. Diamond and River, Kaden and Rhonda's children, bless them. Ellery had seen him—not a week ago!—playing, razzing, wrestling with River, telling Diamond firmly that nobody had better try to kiss her without her permission. He was great with kids.

But Rebekah's kids seemed to scare him shitless.

Sid looked at them assessingly. "Hm… one at a time, I think. Sarah, you come in about five minutes after I set up. Simon, wait here for another five minutes. Come in, sit quietly at my feet, don't say anything. We're going to let him pretend we're alone."

"Can we eat?" Simon asked practically. "I know dinner is at four, but I'm starving!"

"Of course we can eat!" Sid ruffled Simon's curls—much like Ellery's, before Ellery had learned the trick of straightening his hair and gelling it back.

"But he never eats!" Simon hissed. "It's rude to eat in front of a guest who's not eating!"

Ellery sighed. "Well, we won't get him to eat if we don't eat, so I need you to be rude while he's here, is that okay?"

"What's wrong with him?" Sarah asked bluntly, grabbing a pita square from the basket Sid was making. "He looks like he's afraid we're going to bite."

Ellery grunted. "He's had sort of a bad"—month, year, lifetime—"time. He's was sick in the hospital, and it wasn't easy on him."

"Should we bring him flowers?" Rebekah's daughter had wide, limpid brown eyes, and Ellery had a hard time looking at her and telling her no to anything. But Jackson, hardened PI and tomcat, was not really the flower loving—

"I think that would be a lovely idea!" Sid said happily. "You think of the best ways to cheer people up!"

Ellery did a slow pan. "Dad?"

"So how is this for a plan? I take the snacks out for the table, Simon comes out five minutes later, and Sarah goes out to the side of the house and cuts the last few mums to put in water for Jackson. Is that a deal!"

"But wait!" Simon wailed. "What can I give Jackson? I want him to like me too!"

Ellery sighed. "He likes you very much," he said, pretty sure it was true. Jackson was usually great with kids. Kids, small animals, women with a pulse, gay men with eyes—Jackson was sweet to those people. Cops, doctors, bosses, bullies, authority figures of any kind, and lawyers with sticks up their asses—not so much.

Ellery fit into a strange gray area—he should have been Jackson's least favorite life-form, but somehow he'd become one of the few creatures Jackson cared about unequivocally. Which possibly explained why poor Jackson was so freaked-out about Ellery's family.

"You will sit on his lap," Sid decided. "You will give him a reason to stay in the same room. How's that?"

"That's a good job, *zayde*," Simon approved, and Ellery's father took the tray of pita bread, hummus, and vegetables that he'd been saving for hors d'oeuvres that afternoon into the living room at nine thirty in the morning.

Ellery watched him go and fought the urge to call after him, "What do I do, Dad? C'mon, I want a job!" He hadn't realized that taming his feral boyfriend had become a family enterprise.

Sarah said, "I'm going to go get flowers. Make sure Simon doesn't go early," and then she disappeared out the back entrance to behind the house before Ellery could so much as remind her to wear her scarf and gloves.

"Is it time yet?" Simon asked, like he was a spy about to run the op.

"No," Ellery said, trying not to be short with his nephew. "Just wait a minute, okay?"

"What are we waiting for?" Ellery's mother asked, walking into the kitchen cradling an empty coffee mug. "And where did the tray of appetizers go?" Unlike the other times when Jackson had seen her, Taylor Cramer's holiday attire consisted of soft cream-colored leggings and long cream-colored tunic sweaters that hung gracefully past her hips. For Jackson, seeing her in her casual clothes must have been like seeing his cat shave itself while dancing to pop hits. Ellery totally understood why the poor man had been dodging out of rooms the minute she'd entered for the past two days.

"Isn't it exciting, Nonni?" Simon asked, looking at his grandmother with wide eyes. "We're trying to get Ellery's boyfriend to stay in the room and eat!"

Ellery grimaced and Simon tugged his sleeve. "Now?"

"Yeah. Sure. Go ahead."

His mother cocked her head while venturing to the coffee maker. "Is this what we're doing?" Taylor asked, pouring her generously sized mug and adding sugar.

Rebekah looked over the windowsill to outside. "Well, it's why Sarah is on the side of the house, butchering the last of the mums."

Crap. "It was all Dad's idea," Ellery mumbled, cheerfully consigning his father to the bus. "Now hush, or he'll think we're talking about him."

"Ellery!" Sarah called breathlessly, running back into the kitchen. She had a passable handful of bright purple mums in her hand that she shoved into his grasp. "You have to prepare them. I can't just give them to him—they need rinsing and wrapping and—"

"Yeah, yeah," Ellery mumbled, his heart beating every second of Jackson's exile in the TV room as slow as it could. He rinsed of the flowers, recut the stems, and put them in one of his mother's plainer ceramic vases. "Here, Sarah. Go in, set this on the end table by Jackson, and then sit between him and Grandpa."

"This is more thoroughly planned than my dinner," Taylor mused. "Is Jackson just sitting there, waiting to be smothered in your relatives, or did you drug him and he'll wake up later?"

"He's watching the parade," Ellery told her shortly. "And after that, I'm pretty sure there's a football game. We're anesthetizing him with pop culture and children. Do you mind?"

Taylor lifted an elegant eyebrow. "I don't mind in the least. It sounds very much like your father."

"Well, Dad!" Ellery mumbled, and Rebekah—who looked most like their father, with a sweet round face and little point chin—laughed quietly.

"Dad can charm anybody. Are the flowers done yet, Ellery? We need Sarah to go play her part before Jackson skitters off like a stray cat."

Ellery put the vase firmly in Sarah's hands and shooed her off. "You say that like it's not a possibility, Bek."

Rebekah snorted. "That man is devoted to you. I saw the way he looked at you last night at dinner. You were talking about some case he'd solved with a couple of good questions somewhere and he just… his mouth dropped open. It was like you were standing at the portal of heaven and gesturing him in."

Ellery shuddered. "Sure," he mumbled. His mother knew the story, but he wasn't sure how much she'd told the rest of the family. "He was probably wishing for death."

Bek laughed, and Taylor said kindly, "Or he could just love you and be feeling vulnerable right now, Ellery. Don't be dramatic."

Ellery grunted and looked at the clock. "So, how long do we have before I go in?" he murmured.

"Now is good," Rebekah said softly. "You shouldn't be timed, Ellery."

"Go," Taylor told him. "Rebekah and I will bring more food in a little while."

"But won't he spoil his dinner?" Bek asked, and it was all Ellery could do not to hiss "Suck-up!" in her general direction.

"Mmm…." Taylor shook her head. "Let us see. We may have to… change our idea of what dinner should be," she said. "Let's just see how things feel, shall we?"

Ellery raised his eyebrows. "See how things feel?"

"Mm-hm."

His mother, the woman who had planned his and Bek's every last moment as children, had just announced that during a major holiday—one, for which, he knew for a fact, his father had been cooking for two days— would now be served according to how "things feel."

He was almost afraid to go take his place next to Jackson.

But only almost. His palms actually itched with the need to go sit at his feet, wrap his hand around Jackson's calf reassuringly.

He cast a look over his shoulder at his mother and grimly hoped she knew what they were doing.

ELLERY CAME in and sat on the ground in front of the couch, leaning his head against Jackson's knee, and Jackson was so comfortable he managed to bury his hands in Ellery's nonmoussed hair and stroke his head once or twice before just resting it on Ellery's shoulder. The little boy, Simon, sat on his lap, head back against his shoulder, snoring softly. He'd just clambered up there before Jackson could complain, and Jackson wondered if the late-night card games he'd hear the boy having with his sister had finally caught up with him.

The girl had walked in on the other side of the couch.

"Here, Jackson. I brought you flowers. Is that okay?"

And seriously—what kind of asshole scared a little girl about bringing in flowers, right?

She'd set the flowers down on the end table and then scooted to the middle of the couch, between Jackson and Ellery's father. Sid Cramer had wrapped an arm around her shoulders and was pointing out the giant Snoopy balloon going down 5th Avenue.

So there Jackson was, surrounded by the sweetest people with big brown eyes, just like Ellery, and nothing to do but watch the parade—what was he supposed to do?

"Here, Jackson—I'll take him."

The parade was almost over, and Ellery's sister—who looked spookily like their old man—pulled the little boy off his lap and then sat down in the space between Jackson and her daughter, Simon curled up on her arms.

He tapped Ellery on the shoulder. "It's a good thing I don't have to pee," he mumbled.

"Do you?" Ellery asked, all solicitousness.

"No. But I'm sort of all squished in if I did."

Ellery shrugged. "I could move and let you out."

"I'll let you know."

So peaceful, there in the press of bodies, the quiet conversation between the adults and the children. The parade ended, Jackson got up to go to the bathroom, and when he got back, there was a cup of coffee and a tray of food by the flowers on the end table. Rebekah had laid Simon in the adjoining love seat, and he was awake now, playing quietly on a tablet, while his father drank coffee next to him. Somebody—Ellery's father?—had pulled up the pregame coverage for the Niners game.

Lucy Satan, Ellery's mother, was nowhere to be seen.

Ellery had pulled up to the coffee table and was munching on his own plate of appetizers. He looked at Jackson incuriously as Jackson sat down.

"The game's going to start," he said softly. "Want some rolls or oatmeal or something?"

Jackson shook his head and grabbed the plate next to him. "Won't I wreck my appetite?" he asked.

"Frittata and fruit, Jackson. It's hardly a chocolate-covered lead pipe."

Jackson grunted and started eating, lulled into submission by the peace in the room.

ELLERY VERY carefully didn't watch him eat. When Ellery himself was done with pita bread and hummus in front of him, he crawled into Simon's vacant position on the couch and leaned his head against Jackson's arm, pretending to watch the game, and he stayed there until Jackson closed his eyes in sleep.

His father got up quietly, holding his fingers to his lips, and his mother sat down the same way.

"Asleep?" she asked, voice low.

"Yes."

"He ate," she said.

"Yes."

"Should we bring Thanksgiving in here for him?"

Ellery looked at her, curious and aghast. "You'd do that for him?"

She looked back, biting her lip in an uncharacteristic display of vulnerability. "That young man would die for you."

Ellery shuddered. He almost had. Twice. "Yeah."

"Small rituals are a small price to pay," she concluded. "Your father started the preparations already. Let us know."

She got up, leaving Ellery leaning on his sleeping boyfriend.

Jackson didn't eat enough. He hardly slept. Ellery thought it would take a miracle to get him to do either thing without an excess of nagging.

Not a miracle. Just the combined force of his incredibly reasonable family.

Ellery listened to Jackson's breathing and wondered if his father's Thanksgiving dinner tasted more or less wonderful when it was eaten on the couch, next to Jackson. He just might have to find out.

Death of a Pilot Fish

JACKSON REMEMBERED hating that time between Thanksgiving and Christmas when he was a kid. It seemed to serve no purpose—you went to school, but everybody was too wound up to do much learning, and that was when finals and papers were due anyway.

It just always seemed to be the time of waiting—waiting for Christmas, waiting for vacation, waiting for the promise of the New Year.

Even if he knew these things weren't going to be awesome—they never had been in the past—he could recognize the painful optimism, even as a child.

As an adult, recovering from his injuries in Ellery's house while Ellery went back to work, the time was even worse.

It didn't help that Ellery was doing his best to do all the paperwork that putting an end to Tim Owens's reign of terror demanded, keeping the bulk of it from Jackson's shoulders. All that meant was that Ellery got home from work later than he usually did, and Jackson had spent the whole day knocking around the house fretting, not physically up to do more than wash the dishes, and not mentally up to keep the monsters at bay.

And the monsters were incessant.

What was he doing here, in this stellar house with the matching dishes and the soft leather couches? What was he doing taking advantage of some poor lawyer who seemed to think it was okay that Jackson just leech off him and not pay food or rent or for his own goddamned wrecked vehicles?

Both of them.

Wandering the house alone, Jackson had lots of time to tell himself the things he wasn't.

He wasn't smart.

He wasn't rich.

He wasn't polished.

He wasn't that good-looking (particularly now when he was looking thin and haggard, thank you very much to the fever and infection and just not wanting to fucking eat).

He was pretty much a useless has-been, his best function was cannon fodder, he was a human shield for better people than himself, and it was just too goddamned bad Owens hadn't shot at him, because everybody knew that shot would have found its mark—finally.

When Ellery got home, exhausted and distracted, Jackson was a mess—he knew it. But he was damned if he'd tell Ellery.

For one thing, Ellery was working so hard for their future. For another, there just wasn't any time between Ellery getting home, changing clothes, eating some reheated dinner, and then falling asleep on the couch, his laptop precariously balanced as he worked in front of the television.

And Jackson, dammit, couldn't stay up much longer.

But sleep didn't come either—even if he'd gone running, dragging his sorry body out in the foggy cold to make himself tired wasn't helping at all.

This night, about five days before the firm cut everyone lose for winter holiday, was possibly the worst day of them all. Jackson had tried to run five miles and failed miserably, and Ellery had come home in a snit because the neighbor had called him at work to ask him pointedly who that man was lurching into his house.

They'd bickered when Ellery had gotten home—but at least he'd gotten home early, and bickering was how they communicated. That part had been fun.

But then Jackson had fallen asleep early in front of some science show, and Ellery had shooed him to bed while he stayed up and worked.

Jackson had been sort of hoping for sex—it's what the bickering often led to, and he'd gotten himself all ramped up, really.

So his nightmare started in a sexual haze of black.

There was a light here—there had to be. There was always a light—sometimes it lied, sometimes it led to monsters.

But there was always a light.

He breathed, he kept the fear away. He knew his dreams by now.

The light appeared. Dangling, bobbing, leading him away from the warm haze of want, the whirling place where the eels of despair kept stripping the flesh from his bones.

He followed it anyway. He needed to see. Needed to know there was an end.

Come away, come away, leave the blackness, come to the hope....

There was never hope. Nobody knew this like Jackson.

But he followed it anyway, because the whirl of his own doubts was a terrible place to be.

The light grew brighter, and he saw the silhouette of the light bearer. His heart clenched.

No. Oh no. Don't do this.

But the dreams were merciless.

And now he kept following the light, not because the light gave him hope, but because the light bearer was his only hope and he had no choice.

The straight posture, the narrow waist, the stiff, uptight walk. Even the chestnut-colored hair precision-cut, shaved on the sides and the back, a little long on the front, and ruthlessly scraped back with product.

In the dream Jackson could even make out the individual comb marks from behind.

He kept going.

"Ellery?" he asked tentatively. Oh Lord, how he longed for Ellery to be the one, in real life, who led him from the dark to the light. "Ellery, is that you?"

He was almost relieved when Ellery turned around with a horribly distended lower jaw, man-sized teeth, and protuberant fishy eyes.

But that didn't mean he wasn't terrified, didn't scream, when the pilot fish that looked like Ellery tried to devour his soul....

"Jackson!" Ellery's voice echoed in his head, and then cold hands held him down by the shoulders and shook him. "Jackson! C'mon, asshole, snap out of it!"

Jackson squeezed his eyes closed and started to shake. "Did I wake you up?"

"Baby, you were screaming."

"Sorry."

"No—"

"So sorry...."

"Don't be."

Ellery's surprisingly strong body engulfed him, tucked Jackson's head against his chest in a gesture of protection Jackson normally hated—anytime but this time, exactly, when he was at his most vulnerable.

"It's okay," Ellery whispered while Jackson continued to shake.

"Sure."

"What was it tonight?"

When they'd met, it had been once a week, maybe. Now it was almost nightly.

"Pilot fish. Looked like you from behind."

Ellery shuddered. "Those things are so fucking icky!"

Jackson chuckled against his chest. "You are telling me."

"Jesus... it tried to eat you?"

"Yeah."

"Gross."

"I'm saying." Jackson took a breath. "Looking like you was the worst part."

"Yeah." Jackson felt a kiss on the top of his head. "I'm sorry about that."

Jackson half laughed. "Wasn't your fault."

Ellery kissed him again. "Oh no. This one was all me. Sorry."

"I don't understand how," Jackson mumbled. Ellery's voice in the darkness, his touch, his heat, all of it chased the dream away, leaving Jackson free to make himself comfortable in the tatters of his earlier sleep.

"I'll show you in the morning."

"Okay. Fine. Want waffles."

"Will you eat them?" Ellery sounded sufficiently dubious, but Jackson, warm and comforted and oddly optimistic, couldn't imagine not wanting anything different.

"Yes. Bacon too."

"I will get up early to make them. And we'll kill the pilot fish dream over breakfast, promise."

"You're good to me."

"Love you, Jackson."

Jackson sighed, melting into the words, the comfort, in a way he wouldn't have the year before.

"Yeah. You too."

And he fell asleep, dreaming of Ellery's hair standing straight out all over his head.

That morning he was eating his waffles, as promised, and trying not to let on what a struggle it was to just eat, when Ellery came in from the living room with a DVD and dropped it on the table.

"What's this?" Jackson asked, confused.

"This is why I turned into a pilot fish."

Jackson picked up the case. "*Mysteries of the Deep.*" He gasped. "You were watching this?"

Ellery grimaced. "Just as you fell asleep."

On the front was a picture of a giant glowing pilot fish, so real and close-up Jackson got the willies just looking at it.

"Oh my God! Can we... I don't know...."

Ellery reached over his shoulder, smelling like shower and cologne, and cracked the DVD out of its box. "Break it. Destroy it. Pound it with a sledgehammer. I don't care. Make it your mission in life."

"But wait!" Jackson saved it from Ellery's hands. "I want to watch it!"

"But your nightmare!"

"Yeah—but now that I know what it was about, I want to see it!"

"But... but your dream!"

Jackson shrugged, looking at the back of the DVD case. "Yeah, but when I know what something looks like, I'm not afraid of it."

Ellery sighed. "That's bullshit. You know what I look like and you're obviously afraid of me."

Jackson sighed back and stood, wrapping his arms carefully around Ellery, being careful not to ruin his new suit.

"I just...." So hard to say. "It's hard to trust. You love me. You know? How do I trust that?"

"So I'm leading you to the light, but I'm going to eat you instead," Ellery said, sounding a little crushed.

"Well, maybe if I see a real fish eating a real fish, it won't be you anymore."

Ellery grimaced. "Jackson, you ever think... maybe...."

"Nope."

"Of course not. Why would you possibly need a shrink. Never mind."

Ellery struggled out of his arms and Jackson let him go. "Hey, Ellery?"

"Yeah?"

"I love you."

"Yeah, but you still think I'm going to eat you."

"Just let me watch the movie!"

"Fine."

Ellery flounced off to work, leaving Jackson to finish his waffles in front of the TV and learning about mysteries of the deep.

WHEN ELLERY came home, Jackson was watching the whole rest of the series on Netflix. His heart fell.

"Oh dear God, what's that?"

Jackson looked at him happily. "It's a moray eel—isn't it awful?"

Oh, it really was. "So, are we trying to give ourselves nightmare fodder?"

"Nope! This is one more thing I won't dream about tonight!"

Ellery was about to argue with him, but it was fruitless—because it made sense. If Jackson didn't know about something, it scared him.

The one thing Jackson didn't know about was love. Power. Hope for the future.

"You might still dream about me," he said gently, because Ellery was all of those things for Jackson.

Jackson shook his head and looked away shyly. "Naw. Usually I dream about you in danger. I don't think you're going to eat me again anytime soon."

Well, it was a start. "So, we really did kill the boogeyman this time?"

Jackson grinned. "Yes! And there were some amazing shots of things being eaten. Want to see the rest of the series with me?"

Well, why not. "I'll order takeout."

They made love that night, Jackson taking him playfully, Ellery on his hands and knees to give Jackson more control. As they fell asleep, naked, covered in spend, still breathing harshly, Ellery panted, "So, no bad dreams."

"I didn't say that," Jackson said, wrapping his arm tighter around Ellery's waist as they spooned. "Just you won't be a mystery of the deep anymore."

Okay, well, it was a start. If they had to fight Jackson's dream one nature special at a time, Ellery was going to see that he had a decent night's sleep or die trying.

All things considered, it was easier for them both to kill the pilot fish—at least figuratively—using a nature documentary, though.

Choose your Lane to love!

Orange

Amy's Dark Contemporary Romance

Guess who's swimming in the same pond...

FISH
OUT OF
WATER
Amy Lane

Fish Out of Water: Book One

PI Jackson Rivers grew up on the mean streets of Del Paso Heights—and he doesn't trust cops, even though he was one. When the man he thinks of as his brother is accused of killing a police officer in an obviously doctored crime, Jackson will move heaven and earth to keep Kaden and his family safe.

Defense attorney Ellery Cramer grew up with the proverbial silver spoon in his mouth, but that hasn't stopped him from crushing on street-smart, swaggering Jackson Rivers for the past six years. But when Jackson asks for his help defending Kaden Cameron, Ellery is out of his depth—and not just with guarded, prickly Jackson. Kaden wasn't just framed, he was framed by crooked cops, and the conspiracy goes higher than Ellery dares reach—and deep into Jackson's troubled past.

Both men are soon enmeshed in the mystery of who killed the cop in the minimart, and engaged in a race against time to clear Kaden's name. But when the mystery is solved and the bullets stop flying, they'll have to deal with their personal complications… and an attraction that's spiraled out of control.

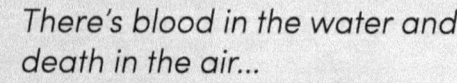

There's blood in the water and death in the air...

RED FISH,
DEAD
FISH

Amy Lane

"Deliciously tense . . .
a satisfying mix of sweet
angst and steamy suspense."
KAREN ROSE,
NYT Bestselling Author

Fish Out of Water: Book Two

They must work together to stop a psychopath—and save each other.

Two months ago Jackson Rivers got shot while trying to save Ellery Cramer's life. Not only is Jackson still suffering from his wounds, the triggerman remains at large—and the body count is mounting.

Jackson and Ellery have been trying to track down Tim Owens since Jackson got out of the hospital, but Owens's time as a member of the department makes the DA reluctant to turn over any stones. When Owens starts going after people Jackson knows, Ellery's instincts hit red alert. Hurt in a scuffle with drug-dealing squatters and trying damned hard not to grieve for a childhood spent in hell, Jackson is weak and vulnerable when Owens strikes.

Jackson gets away, but the fallout from the encounter might kill him. It's not doing Ellery any favors either. When a police detective is abducted—and Jackson and Ellery hold the key to finding her—Ellery finds out exactly what he's made of. He's not the corporate shark who believes in winning at all costs; he's the frightened lover trying to keep the man he cares for from self-destructing in his own valor.

www.dreamspinnerpress.com

If you enjoyed
A Few Good Fish,
check out
Burton and Ernie's story, *Hiding the Moon*
and
Ace and Sonny's story, *Racing for the Sun.*

Hiding the Moon

Can a hitman and a psychic negotiate a relationship while all hell breaks loose?

The world might not know who Lee Burton is, but it needs his black ops division and the work they do to keep it safe. Lee's spent his life following orders—until he sees a kill jacket on Ernie Caulfield. Ernie isn't a typical target, and something is very wrong with Burton's chain of command.

Ernie's life may seem adrift, but his every action helps to shelter his mind from the psychic storm raging within. When Lee Burton shows up to save him from assassins and club bunnies, Ernie seizes his hand and doesn't look back. Burton is Ernie's best bet in a tumultuous world, and after one day together, he's pretty sure Lee knows Ernie is his destiny as well.

But when Burton refused Ernie's contract, he kicked an entire piranha tank of bad guys, and Burton can't rest until he takes down the rogue military unit that would try to kill a spacey psychic. Ernie's in love with Burton and Burton's confused as hell by Ernie—but Ernie's not changing his mind and Burton can't stay away. Psychics, assassins, and bad guys—throw them into the desert with a forbidden love affair and what could possibly go wrong?

Coming in October 2018
www.dreamspinnerpress.com

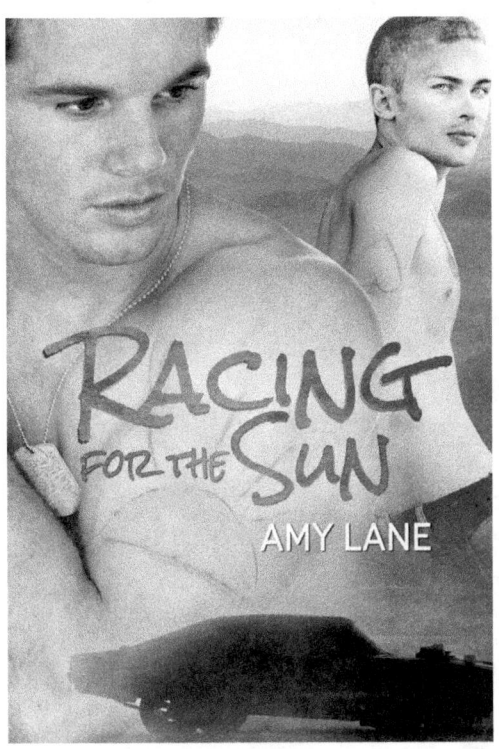

"I'll do anything."

Staff Sergeant Jasper "Ace" Atchison takes one look at Private Sonny Daye and knows that every word on paper about him is pure, unadulterated bullshit. But Sonny is desperate, and although Ace isn't going to take him up on his offer of "anything," that doesn't mean he isn't tempted.

Instead, Ace takes Sonny under his wing, protecting him when they're in the service and making plans with him when they get out. Together, they're going to own a garage and build race cars and make their fortune hurtling faster than light across the desert. Together, they're going to rewrite the past, make Sonny Daye a whole and happy person, and put the ghosts in Ace's heart to rest.

But not even Sonny can build a car fast enough to escape the ghosts of the past. When Sonny's ghosts drive them down and run their plans off the road, Ace finds out exactly what he's made of. Maybe Sonny was the one to promise Ace anything, but there is nothing under the sun Ace won't do to keep Sonny safe from harm.

www.dreamspinnerpress.com

AMY LANE is a mother of two grown kids, two half-grown kids, two small dogs, and half-a-clowder of cats. A compulsive knitter who writes because she can't silence the voices in her head, she adores fur-babies, knitting socks, and hawt menz, and she dislikes moths, cat boxes, and knuckleheaded macspazzmatrons. She is rarely found cooking, cleaning, or doing domestic chores, but she has been known to knit up an emergency hat/blanket/pair of socks for any occasion whatsoever or sometimes for no reason at all. Her award-winning writing has three flavors: twisty-purple alternative universe, angsty-orange contemporary, and sunshine-yellow happy. By necessity, she has learned to type like the wind. She's been married for twenty-five-plus years to her beloved Mate and still believes in Twu Wuv, with a capital Twu and a capital Wuv, and she doesn't see any reason at all for that to change.

Website: www.greenshill.com
Blog: www.writerslane.blogspot.com
Email: amylane@greenshill.com
Facebook: www.facebook.com/amy.lane.167
Twitter: @amymaclane

www.ingramcontent.com/pod-product-compliance
Lightning Source LLC
Chambersburg PA
CBHW051530260626
47170CB00003B/874